The Thirteen Relics of Doom

The Thirteen Relics of Doom

The Rise of Skreal

Marquinhos Martins

Cover Designed by Jen Vermette

AuthorHouse™ LLC
1663 Liberty Drive
Bloomington, IN 47403
www.authorhouse.com
Phone: 1-800-839-8640

© 2014 Marquinhos Martins. All rights reserved.

No part of this book may be reproduced, stored in a retrieval system, or transmitted by any means without the written permission of the author.

Published by AuthorHouse 01/11/2014

ISBN: 978-1-4918-4801-2 (sc)
ISBN: 978-1-4918-4800-5 (hc)
ISBN: 978-1-4918-4802-9 (e)

Library of Congress Control Number: 2013923742

Any people depicted in stock imagery provided by Thinkstock are models, and such images are being used for illustrative purposes only. Certain stock imagery © Thinkstock.

This book is printed on acid-free paper.

Because of the dynamic nature of the Internet, any web addresses or links contained in this book may have changed since publication and may no longer be valid. The views expressed in this work are solely those of the author and do not necessarily reflect the views of the publisher, and the publisher hereby disclaims any responsibility for them.

This is for my Father who always believed in me, and for my family who helped me get it done, and for Jen's son Apollo.

Contents

Chapter 1	The Final Visit	1
Chapter 2	Troubling Message	13
Chapter 3	Escape	17
Chapter 4	Shepard	31
Chapter 5	Cestator	51
Chapter 6	Training Begins	61
Chapter 7	The Dance	79
Chapter 8	Shepard's Farm	105
Chapter 9	Trouble on the Horizon	125
Chapter 10	The Hunt	139
Chapter 11	The Village	159
Chapter 12	Sheminal	167
Chapter 13	Leaving Home	183
Chapter 14	Master and Student	193
Chapter 15	Plans Coming Together	205
Chapter 16	The Proposal	225
Chapter 17	The Undead Bane	241
Chapter 18	Nightmares Among Them	255
Chapter 19	The Light Falls	273
Chapter 20	The Labyrinth	293
Chapter 21	Attacked	325
Chapter 22	Finding help	345
Chapter 23	New Beginnings	369

Chapter 24 Being Followed 393
Chapter 25 The Wizard 407
Chapter 26 Mother 421
Chapter 27 A Challenge Answered 431

Prologue

In a day when the dead walk in an army and the seas roil with danger, the people of the grandest place will find nightmares among them. Then in the time of greatest need the people's shining light will fall. A thunderous roar will erupt, and a mighty fire will rage. All that dare to stand against it will be consumed in its fury. Then in the calmness after the blaze the world will stand still, the past will bow their heads in sorrow for their loss, and the stones will weep. Yet in this darkest hour the phoenix will rise up from the ashes and be reborn. The day will be won but an evil unlike anything ever seen will rise to destroy all life. Many will come together to battle this terrible evil, but it is yet to be seen who is to prevail. They will each have to battle their own evils before they can become strong enough to battle that which has chosen to destroy them. The phoenix itself may not be strong enough to defeat this evil. Innocence will be lost, and love will flare then turn to hatred. The only hope for all will be to take the ancient text to the place where even the mighty dragons fear to go.

Chapter 1
The Final Visit

Slanoth walked down the cool and musty corridor. The sound of rushing water could be heard behind the walls. It was dark and dingy, with a foreboding feel in the air. Torches were set in scones upon the walls, but they did little to cut the darkness. He could have easily taken one down to light his way, but the gloom reflected his mood so he decided he would not.

Slanoth had walked this corridor many times before, and it had never affected him this way. This time however, it was hitting him on a personal level. Slanoth was going to see his dear friend Randor. They had been friends since they were apprentices at the temple. He thought back to all the time they had spent together, and sighed at the memories. With his youth long behind him his memory was fading, but his memories of Randor were very clear.

Randor was the closest thing he had to family. The two of them had spent nearly a lifetime together, and were nearly inseparable. They had been on many adventures together in their youth, and had faced many dangers at each other's side. Yet on this night he had a sinking feeling in the pit of his stomach that he was going to see his friend for the last time.

Randor had been sick for the last three months. He would slip in and out of delirium while speaking in strange tongues, which no one could understand. Randor's illness puzzled all of the clerics. No one had ever seen, nor heard of anything like it in recorded history. It seemed to destroy his mind as well as his body. It came upon him suddenly with no warning, first attacking his ability to walk then it spread like wildfire throughout his body.

As Slanoth drew near the room he could hear yelling coming from inside. He smiled in spite of his mood. Randor was never one to allow people to do things for him, and it sounded as though he was feeling well enough to make that fact clear to the apprentices charged with his care. In fact from the sound of things Slanoth was slightly surprised that they were not fleeing the room.

Slanoth paused a moment when he touched the door handle, and memories flooded his mind. A sense of urgency pushed them aside however, for Slanoth knew there was no time to waste. He pushed the door open, and the hinges let out a loud screech of protest interrupting Randor's yelling. Slanoth found this odd for he knew the hinges were oiled often enough to prevent that from happening. It felt in some strange way that he was being announced.

The room was well kept, and had a warm and calming feel about it. There was a single bed in the center with a soft mattress instead of the typical vermin ridden mat found in most healing chambers. The clerics of Cargon had found that a clean environment more than doubled a person's chance for survival. The space around the bed was well open and clear of clutter. In fact there was little in the way of other furniture in the room. What little there was included a small metal bound chest to store the person's personal items. In a corner there was a small table where medicines and incenses were placed. By the head of the bed there was a well-worn wooden chair with no padding, which did not do much in the way comfort. Over the years Slanoth had seen many people sleep in it while they waited for the person they visited to recover. He himself had spent many hours in that chair recently. The dim light in the room came from a single oil lamp hanging from a rung on the wall. Slanoth could smell a faint aroma of herbs, and burning incense in the air.

As Slanoth walked into the room he heard Randor yell something about inconsiderate people opening doors, and making all kinds of noise. Slanoth could not help but to smile at this. The three apprentices paid no attention to Slanoth's intrusion which was not surprising, for many people entered and exited healing rooms on any given day. They simply went about their duties not even realizing who had entered.

When Randor saw that it was Slanoth who had come in he smiled. "Ah Slanoth my friend, it is good to see you. Would you do me a service and tell these bumbling idiots that I do not need their help, and to leave me be."

At hearing Slanoth's name the apprentices turned towards the door and fell to their knees in awe. "Lord Slanoth, I beg your pardon. I did not realize it was you there." They each said nearly in unison.

Slanoth smiled warmly and waved off their continuing apologies. "Worry not my sons. I have not the temper that Randor has, and as it were just ignore his ramblings he has grown quite irritable in his old age. His bark has grown to be far worse than his bite." He finished with a small chuckle.

"Oh is that so?" Randor interjected, "well I will show you that my bite still has a bit of a sting left to it. As for my age you are not much younger than me, and the only reason I am in this bed is because of what these three did to me."

The three men looked up at Slanoth shaking their heads vigorously. "No lord we have only done what we were . . ."

Slanoth waved the three off. "Worry not my sons, Randor only jests. I know you have done nothing wrong. But please leave us Randor, and I have matters to discuss. I will summon you if I require assistance later."

The three men bowed as they backed up out of the door, thanking and praising Slanoth all the while. Randor found this quite amusing, and he laughed loudly all the while. "New aren't they?" He asked when they were gone.

"Yes they joined us only a few weeks ago. They have not quite gotten adjusted to the way things work around here. But If I recall correctly we were much like them when we first came here."

Randor chuckled at the memories of their first days. "Yes well I remember you being quite the troublemaker when you arrived. You had us in Lord Denerobe's office many times over the years."

Slanoth smiled at the memories. "Yes well you did not have to follow along. You after all are the older one. I never meant to find any trouble you know that."

"Well someone had to watch out for you. You may have never gone looking for trouble, but trouble had a knack for finding us." Randor said with a twinkle in his eyes. That twinkle was quickly replaced with a twinge of pain, and Randor closed his eyes.

Slanoth was impelled to help his friend, and try to take the pain from him. But before he could, Randor opened his eyes and waved him off. "Save you strength Slanoth. The wave has passed. There is something I need to tell you, and there is not much time."

"Randor if you are in pain let me help you. I may not be able to cure you, but let me take the pain from you my friend."

Randor shook his head sadly. "No my friend, I will soon be free of the pains of this body. Our lord beckons me as we speak, but he has a message for you that I must convey to you before I die."

"No I will not accept that. I have the knowledge to cure any wound and I will find the strength to do it. If Cargon has a message for me let him come and tell me himself."

Suddenly as though called up by Slanoth's words a Blinding light filled the room. It seemed to come from everywhere, and did not leave a shadow anywhere in the room. It was as though the air itself was alive with it. The light radiated no heat yet it felt replenishing, then just as quickly as it appeared it was gone.

When Slanoth could finally clear his vision once more he noticed that Randor's eyes were closed and he was not breathing. Slanoth hurried over to try and revive his friend. Just as he was reaching down to lay his hands on Randor's chest, his eyes flew open. Slanoth jumped back in shock, surprised by this sudden change. Then Randor called out to him, but the voice was different. It was other worldly, one that commanded power. The voice was that of Cargon the Lord of Justice.

Slanoth dropped to one knee in respect for his deity, and averted his eyes so not to offend. He then heard Cargon say, "Raise my friend. You need not kneel before me. We have known each other a long time. I have much to tell you, and having you there staring at the floor makes it difficult to speak with you."

With an elated heart Slanoth rose to his feet. He was delighted that his lord would call him friend, and speak so openly to him. "I am here Lord with open ears and mind, but I also have a question. Why would you take Randor, and why now like this?"

"Ah Slanoth your faith is like a breath of fresh air. It is not just in your words, I can see it in your heart and soul. Yet you still have the strength to ask questions. To answer you, it was simply his time and he has accepted it. I cannot control any man's destiny or his will to do anything."

Slanoth bowed his head sighing deeply. "I understand, and I thank you for your answer it puts to rest many of my concerns."

Cargon smiled warmly. "You continually please me Slanoth. That is why I have chosen you for this very important task. I need one who is strong in his faith and who can handle himself. I could not think of a better man than you my friend. I will not lead you wrong in this however. It is no simple task that I ask of you. This surely will test your faith as well as your strength."

Cargon paused a moment to be sure that Slanoth had no further questions. When he was sure none were forthcoming he went on. "The light you saw moments ago has replenished your strength and made you whole again. You shall not feel the pains that have come upon you in the last few years."

Slanoth's eyes went wide with surprise. "This must be a great task to warrant such a gift as this. I had just grown accustomed to the pains, and now you have taken them away. I thank you Lord for blessing me like this."

Cargon shook his head. "It is not so great, as it is difficult, and likely to try your patience. Listen carefully and try not to interrupt for I have much to say and little time."

"I will do my best Lord, but I cannot promise I will not have any questions."

"Good," Cargon replied. "It will make this much easier, for what I have to tell will not be easy to hear." Cargon took a deep breath then continued. "A time of great darkness approaches and threatens to consume this world. Valclon is amassing an army of creatures, and he has called up his greatest warlocks to lead them. He intends to conquer this world."

Slanoth shook his head in confusion. "Lord, Valclon has tried many times to destroy this world, but always he has been defeated. Surely there are others more suited for the trial of war than I. This could not be why you need my help?"

"No my friend if that was my only concern I would have left you in peace. The war is trivial opposed to the other news I have for you. I have reason to believe that Valclon may be close to learning the location of The Tome of Islangardious, if he does not already have the information."

"What? How is that possible? It has been locked away in the vault since Randor and I put it there, and only one other person knows of its existence. We made it well known to all key people that it was somehow destroyed in the accident. Unless of course Malketh let the truth be known."

"No, Malketh has not spoken to anyone in all these years. But Valclon is not one that can be fooled in such a way. He has been searching for it since it disappeared, and I fear he is very close to finding it."

Slanoth shook his head in disbelief. "So it is only a matter of time before his army is at our doorstep. Well then, I must find somewhere else to conceal it."

"I am afraid that will not work my friend. No matter how careful you are there will always be signs, and a trail it leaves behind for those who know what to look for. But I fear that is not the worst of it yet. It would appear that Valclon is trying to free The Dark Knights. He has somehow damaged the seal to their prison, and sadly it will not hold them for long. We have tried to mend it, but it is beyond all repairs. We will do all we can to hold them back, but it will be only a matter of time before they are free."

Slanoth fell back into the chair in mute shock. The Tome was one matter but this was beyond comprehension. The Dark Knights had ruled the world with an iron fist in their long reign. Thousands had died by their hands for little more than saying a cross word against them, but what was far worse was that they once had control of The Thirteen Artifacts.

When Slanoth was able to speak again he looked up at Cargon and with a shaky voice he went on. "That is dire news indeed Lord, if The Dark Knights are freed there will be no stopping them, and they will surely be searching for the Tome. We will be doomed unless of course yourself, and any other gods are going to join in the fight against them."

Cargon shook his head sadly. "I fear that our hands are tied in this matter. We can do nothing to change the course of these events that are unfolding. All that we are able to do is choose who it will be that is going to fight for us. But again I am sorry to say that is still not the worst news that I have to share with you."

Cargon paused a moment to let Slanoth absorb the tidings before he released the final bit of news. "Somehow unknown to all of us there has been a greater evil than The Dark Knights themselves released upon the world. Even Valclon himself seems to have no power over this thing. We do not know what or even where it is. It is somehow able to conceal itself from our sight. All that we find are the remnants of its rampages, so there is no doubt it is here. A new age is quickly approaching and I fear there may be no sanctuaries from the evil until this is all over."

Slanoth nearly fell over at this news. Once again he found that he could not say a word. He sat there in mute shock pondering the implications of what Cargon had just said. If there was something worse than the lords of destruction there was little hope without help.

Cargon noticed Slanoth's reaction and understood completely. "I know things look dire, yet there's a glimmer of hope. Valclon's own son has betrayed him. He now serves the light under my guidance, and at this very moment he is battling his way out of Valclon's domain. He will be going by his ancient name, Cestator so he will not be recognized by any, but those who know him."

Cargon looked down at Slanoth and saw the doubt and fear he knew would be there. He laughed and placed a hand on Slanoth's shoulder. "I see you are having trouble accepting this, and I understand, but fear not my friend all will be well with him."

Slanoth shook his head doubtful of what Cargon had just said. He wanted to believe, but it was not easy. "I am sorry to question you on this Lord, but are you sure he can be trusted. He was born evil he did not turn to it. I have seen some of the atrocities he has committed. They were of one who was purely evil. Though, if you are sure of his intent he will make a welcome ally."

"Slanoth, I must say that is the very reason I knew you were the one for this. You do not hesitate to ask questions when you are unsure of something. Yet you show compassion to a sworn enemy.

It is a pleasant change most people just follow blindly not truly knowing what they are getting into. I must admit at times it is quite amusing, But in most cases I would rather they ask more questions."

Slanoth smiled, "yes well if you remember I was once one of those people. It was only after a few experiences that I learned it is best to get as much information as possible."

Cargon laughed heartily. "Yes I remember quite well. You have always been one of my favorite disciples. No matter what happened you have always come through." His smile then faded as he continued. "Well enough of the past, we must continue with what is to come. As for Cestator he has changed. There is something about him that is noticeably different to any who have ever faced him. He also has some personal reasons for the change of heart. He now strives to become one of my paladins. He has watched some of the greatest over the years, and he has taken great interest in Randor and yourself. One day he came to me explaining his situation, and asked if I could help him serve such a grand purpose, and accomplish such wondrous deeds. I of course told him I would be more than happy to help. He had only one request that he could learn under your guidance. I agreed knowing you would be perfect for the task."

Slanoth sat there in shock for a moment then nodded. "Lord I would be honored to do this service for you, and Cestator if as you say he has turned to the light. You know well that I have always done what is needed of me." Slanoth said with a tear rolling down his face. "But lord there is one problem in this. I am an old man now, and am unable to train him in the way that is needed for this task."

"Yes Slanoth I know this. That is why I have another surprise for you. Go over there and look into that mirror." Cargon said as he pointed to a corner behind Slanoth.

Slanoth began to say there was no mirror in the room, but when he turned to look where Cargon had pointed he found there was. He laughed to himself, and shook his head. *"I should have known better, and remembered who I was speaking to."* Slanoth stood and started towards the mirror. As he did he noticed something strange he felt stronger than he had in a long time. Not only were his pains gone but he felt as though the vitality of his youth had returned.

The Final Visit

When Slanoth finally stood before the mirror he stared in silence. He saw something he had not seen in many years. He saw a young man staring back at him. He managed to stutter a few incoherent words before he fell to his knees crying with joy.

Suddenly Slanoth felt something slender, and heavy resting on his shoulder. When looked to see what it was, it took his breath away. He saw the blade of a sword the center was covered in runes all the way up to the hilt. They were runes that he knew well for he had seen them countless times. This was the sword Cargon had bestowed upon him many years ago, when he was named a paladin. This was the sword Justice.

"Here my friend I think that you might need this once again. It has been awaiting your revival," he heard Cargon say.

Slanoth stood and took the sword. The mighty blade measured four feet in length, yet felt as if it were a sword half that size. Its weight allowed it to be wielded in one or two hands. The hilt and crosspiece were made of red platinum formed in the shape of the great phoenix. The blade coming from its mouth like fire the great bird was said to breathe and in a time of great need the wielder could call upon the sword to do just that. The blade would be engulfed in red flames so hot it could cut through steel with ease while being cool to the touch of the wielder. Slanoth had used the power many times in the years he had wielded the sword.

It was also said that the sword could summon up the great phoenix to fight for the wielder. Slanoth was not quite sure if this were true, because the only mention that the creature even existed was shrouded in myth. He searched every library for any mention of its existence, but nowhere in recorded history was there any mention of such a creature. He even researched the history of the sword, and all who had ever been known to wield it and found nothing.

When Slanoth could finally clear the tears from his eyes he turned to Cargon. "Lord these are the kind of gifts that all men strive for. Surely there are others more deserving than I."

Cargon shook his head and chuckled. "Slanoth my friend you are far too modest. There is no one who could deserve it more. You have served me well all these years. I think that you have earned it, and the fact you are willing to give it to others makes you all the more deserving."

Slanoth smiled and looked into the mirror again. "Lord you must have given up much to bestow this upon me. I know that there must be a balance in the order of life. I must have cost you much to do this so sorrowfully I will have to decline the offer."

Cargon looked upon him with sad eyes and a frown touched is lips. "Slanoth my friend, worry not of it. This is well within what I can do. You will need the strength of your youth to train Cestator. I do believe he will be a strong if trying student."

Slanoth turned and looked at Cargon and was puzzled by his sad face. "Lord why do you look so sad? If as you say, this is within your power to do it is a wondrous thing."

"It is nothing that need concern you at this time my friend." Cargon said with a very forced smile.

Slanoth decided to let the matter go for the time being, and made a mental note to question Cargon again later.

"Well enough of that, you are quite welcome. It was my great pleasure to gift you with your youth." Cargon then walked to the window and looked out at the water. He turned back and sighed. "Now back to the matter at hand. Cestator will arrive here in a few days now. He has been traveling for some time now, and will require healing for he will be severely wounded. He will arrive at the west gate so as to not frighten anyone by traveling through the city. He will ask for you specifically. Bring him here heal him, and let him rest."

Slanoth spoke up in shock interrupting Cargon. "But Lord is Cestator not immortal, how could he be hurt? Any wound he received would heal itself instantly, would it not?"

"Yes it would were he still immortal, but he gave up his immortality to join us. He heals faster than any average person, but he is very much a mortal. Oh yes and he has no knowledge as to what I have planned for him. If you would not mind I would rather keep it that way."

"I see, so now he is a mortal." Slanoth said thinking out loud. "The price he paid for his betrayal I would gather?" Slanoth looked to Cargon for conformation to his question, and Cargon nodded. "So it is now Cestator and I in this battle. That does help some, but there certainly will be more dangers than even the two of us can handle if there is going to be a war. We certainly will need much more help especially if Valclon does free The Dark Knights."

Cargon chuckled, "fear not my friend. I always make sure I am prepared. Others shall join the battle later. I have chosen each of them for their abilities. They will be good companions in the times yet to come."

"Do these companions know that they have been chosen for this, or are they completely ignorant of it?" Slanoth asked with a smirk, knowing well Cargon's sense of humor. He had been on the receiving end of it many times in the past.

Cargon laughed heartily. "You do know me too well. No they do not know anything about it. It is best that they do not, so they act normally, and do not worry if what they are doing is right."

Slanoth was not surprised, but he knew Cargon was right. If they knew it could affect their judgment, which in turn could prove to be dangerous if not deadly. Yet even knowing this he could not help laughing a bit. He knew they were in for quite a surprise.

Cargon looked at Slanoth and frowned. "I know what you are thinking, and you are wrong. I decided to be kind to them. Most of them will be slightly compelled to join the battle. In their eyes it will be their own decision to go along. They will never know I had anything to do with it."

Slanoth laughed inwardly knowing well that this would likely change their entire lives. He had seen it happen to many people, himself included. Slanoth cracked a smile then began to laugh outwardly from some of the memories. "I am sorry for laughing Lord, but I find it hard to believe you would let them off too easily."

Cargon chuckled. "Yes . . . well, I will say they will be strongly impelled to go along. They will also find it to their benefit to do so. Yet even then I do not have complete control over what happens to them. Well then I do not have much more time here, so is there anything else that you need or any questions that cannot wait for another time?"

"Yes Lord there is one thing. Take Randor to your side and let him have peace. Tell him that I love him as a brother, and I will miss him dearly."

"I love you as well my friend. I will be waiting for you in the heavens." Randor said in a strong youthful voice. He walked up to Slanoth who had a dumbfounded look on his face and hugged him. "Until next time my brother," he whispered. "Now I must go, so goodbye old friend."

A tear rolled down Slanoth's cheek in the memory of his friend. "Good bye for now my dear friend, and until we meet again have peace."

A bright light appeared behind Randor. It was warm and comforting, and had an inviting feel about it. Randor let go of Slanoth, and walked towards the light. Just before he stepped through he turned and waved goodbye to Slanoth. The light suddenly flashed brightly and he was gone.

Slanoth sat down on the bed to ponder what had happened this evening. He was deep in thought when he fell asleep for the first time in days. On this night he also was not troubled by the nightmares that had been plaguing him of late, and he got more restful sleep than he had in many years.

Chapter 2
Troubling Message

Walking up to the large metal bound doors was always an unsettling and gruesome experience. Drean knew, as soon as he saw the runes scribed on the doors, his spirit would grow cold and it would begin to wither as it had so many times before, for the power emanating beyond the doors radiated a feeling of darkness and evil. He raised a trembling hand up to knock, but he found himself hesitant. The runes were there to keep out any unwanted guests. There was no known force that could get through those doors. Not that anyone ever wanted to enter the room on the other side anyway. Most people avoided it like it was riddled with plague.

Drean sighed, he decided there was no way he could avoid the wrath of his master. There was only one thing for him to do and that was to face his consequences. Valclon had a tendency to kill the bearer of bad news, and Drean had some very bad news to tell. *"I do hope he is not in a foul mood. I would like to walk out of here alive, and in one piece."*

Drean took a deep breath and raised his hand once again. He was about to knock when he heard a voice from inside that sent a chill up his spine. "Come in Drean I have been expecting you."

The doors opened outwardly and Drean jumped back. The open doors revealed a massive chamber. Pillars as wide as he was tall ran up both sides, disappearing into the darkness above. The walls were lined with thousands of books containing centuries of knowledge and power. The stone floor was stained blood red, as a reminder of all those that had vexed Valclon, or any poor fools who simply became a victim to his whims. The air was cool and dry, the odor of many herbs mixed with the pungent smell of dried blood made his stomach turn. All of this gave the room an ominous feel.

"Tell me, what news you have of that traitor Cestator," Drean heard the same dark and ominous voice say.

As Drean walked forward he noticed that his master was sitting at his desk watching the door. The desk itself was in the exact center of the room and was raised upon a dais. It was made of a pitch black stone that seemed to absorb the light, which only added to the intimidating feel to the room. Yet it was not the room that made Drean tremble with fear. His gut wrenching fear was focused solely on the man behind that black desk. The Lord of Destruction exuded power and his black cowl made it impossible to see his face, but Drean could feel those eyes boring their way into his soul.

Drean stepped up to the dais and knelt down placing his forehead on the floor in a bow. He hoped that his hooded cloak kept his master from seeing the fear in his eyes. After a moment he got up onto one knee, but did not dare look up at his master. With all the strength he could find within himself, he began to speak. "Please forgive me master, for your plans were not executed in the manner you had hoped for. I must take full responsibility for this failure." Drean paused a moment to gather his thoughts, for he knew what he was about to say could surely bring him death. "I bring you news that I heard just moments ago . . . and it is not going to be to your liking."

Drean did not have to look up to know Valclon was not happy. He could feel his master's glare burning into his back. He began to quiver in fear. His insides were screaming at him to flee before it was too late, yet he knew that if he did he would surely meet his end.

Drean then heard Valclon telling him to rise and look up. He could hear the anger and frustration in that voice, and it frightened him. He began shaking, as he stood with beads of sweat dotting his brow. He lost all of his composure, when he saw a ball of flame dancing across Valclon's knuckles.

Drean swallowed hard before going on. "It would appear that Cestator is heading towards the portal of Trecerda, and he is nearly out of our grasp. He killed the bogera earlier this afternoon, and has foiled every other attempt to capture him. I fear he may escape through the portal and we will certainly loose him there."

Drean looked down, so at the very least he would not see his death coming. He stood there in silence for a few moments, and to his surprise nothing happened. Puzzled he looked up and was shocked to see that Valclon was laughing insidiously, as though he was mocking him. He was unsure what to make of this. "Lord Valclon, are you well? Cestator is nearly out of our reach, and you are laughing?" Drean asked confused and relieved that he was still alive.

"You fool, do you truly believe that this is not part of my strategy. I foresee all things and had already planned ahead for what is to happen next. Let me explain it to you, since you cannot see through your own stupidity," Valclon laughed wickedly.

"It is obvious now, that Cestator has sided with Cargon, and there is only one place Cargon would send him. Send out a few hounds and two greal. The hounds will easily overtake him and give the greal the chance to catch up. He has become far too much of a nuisance, and the fact that he has sided with my brother, makes him too dangerous to keep alive. Order the greal to kill him and bring me his traitorous head. Even if by some odd chance of luck he does survive he is heading for Trecerda. I am amassing my armies there, and we know where he will go, so I will have the time to kill him at my leisure."

Drean smiled at the thought. "Yes Master I can see where you are going with this. The greal will be more than enough to overtake him. I know just the two to send as well. It would take a great miracle for him to defeat them."

He paused a moment to see if Valclon had anything more to say, but his master seemed to have forgotten his presence. "If that is all, I shall send them after him immediately."

"Leave me now. Report back when you have more information of that traitor." Valclon said waving Drean off without looking up.

Drean bowed, and silently crept out the door. He sighed deeply, relieved that he was still alive.

Chapter 3

Escape

Cestator stopped abruptly; his senses were suddenly awakened do to a strange stillness to the air, as though the world was holding its breath in anticipation of something. He knew there was something wrong, yet he could not place it. He was instantly alert, listening and scanning the horizon for what could have caused this strange sensation. At first he saw nothing but sand, and the wavy illusion from the sweltering heat. Suddenly, he heard a bone chilling sound. It was a sound he knew well and would never forget. It was a sound that could instill panic in the hearts of the bravest of men.

"Hell hounds," he swore under his breath. "Now he is sending the hounds after me. This is an unexpected turn of events."

Cestator knew then that all attempts were over to try and capture him. His father was out to kill him now. The fiery beasts could track anything over any type of terrain, and there was no way to escape their fury. Yet it was not the hounds that worried Cestator, he knew how to deal with them.

His reason for concern was what would be following them. He knew that not far behind the hounds there would be a greal. Most people who ever faced one of these hulking beasts never lived to tell the tale. They usually underestimated the greal's speed, which was a grave mistake. Even if the person was lucky enough to strike a blow on one, their weapon would usually bounce off of their thick skin, as though they were throwing a small pebble instead of a sharp spear.

Yet that knowledge still did not settle the foreboding feeling he had in the pit of his stomach. He knew there was something he was missing. He knew his father too well to assume that everything was in plain sight. Valclon would know by now where he was going, what he was doing, and so would stop at nothing to prevent him from escaping. Cestator knew there had to be something more than a few hounds and a greal.

He looked over at the horizon and all he could see at this time was a giant dust cloud. "Well if I am going to face these things I am going to do it on my own terms," he sneered. "If it is a fight he wants, then it is a fight he is going to get."

Cestator looked around for some kind of an advantage. He quickly spotted something that could serve his purpose. There in the distance he saw a large shape that looked like a large rock formation. He smirked wickedly and let a small chuckle escape his lips. *"Well what do you know, it is even in the direction I am headed. This is a little too convenient,"* he thought to himself.

Cestator looked to the sky with a slight frown on his face. "Cargon, I do hope this is your doing, this is almost too good to be true." Even as he said the words Cestator realized Cargon had nothing to do with this turn of events. He knew well that Cargon had almost no power in Valclon's dimension. Even though he knew it was a ridiculous thought, it never hurt to have a little faith.

He moved swiftly towards the distant shape. As he drew closer to it, he noticed that it was indeed a rock formation with what appeared to be a large tree resting upon it. There was something odd about the tree, however from his vantage point it appeared to be dead. This did not surprise him in the least, especially in this desolate land. Here where the air was dry and hot, and never a drop of rain fell. All life here had long since been wiped out. This was a testament to the destruction Valclon laid upon this dimension. He did this when he arrived to put the fear of himself in the hearts of all men.

It seemed to him that it took nearly half a day, but Cestator finally reached his destination. It was a little over thirty five feet high with a single sloping side, and a sharp drop on all of the other sides. The sound of the hounds was getting dangerously close at this point, and he could feel it wearing at the edge of his sanity. Thoughts of fleeing raced through his mind. Yet he knew that if he did, it would mean certain death. He looked back again to see if he could tell what he faced, but all he could see was the cloud of dust the creatures stirred up as they ran. Being cautious he knew he needed to take a few moments to rest, as he settled himself on the shady side of the rock formation he took a long draw from his water skin.

Cestator then climbed to the top to get a better vantage point so he might see what followed. When he reached the top he noticed he was wrong about the tree, it was indeed alive, the most dreaded kind of life. The thing looked diseased and decrepit. It oozed out a bad smelling green slime, and had long vine like branches that looked like hundreds of snakes slithering over the ground. The massive trunk was twice as wide as he was tall, and seemed twisted and appeared to be breathing. The branches all encircled the top of the trunk seeming to leave it bare. Cestator knew however that at the top of that trunk was the mouth of the carnivorous tree.

"A hangman's tree, I should have known." He cursed under his breath. "Well it will be just one more thing to watch for. It is far too late for me to find anything better. I will just have to make this work."

Avoiding the tree's reaching branches Cestator looked out to where the hounds followed. "Damn," he shouted. "I really do hate it when I am right. I have got to learn to keep my mouth shut."

What he saw was indeed hellhounds, three, but that was not what bothered him. Behind the hounds was not one greal but two. "Well this should be interesting. It would seem Valclon truly does want me dead." Cestator looked up to the sky for a moment. "Ok Cargon if you are ever going to help me get out of here, now would be a good time to do it."

Suddenly he heard Cargon's voice in the back of his mind. "You know that I have little strength there in your father's land, but I will do what I can for you. I will give you the knowledge of a freezing fire spell. It is a very simple spell, but it should work well against those beasts. For it to work you will have to speak the words that I have placed in your mind then physically touch whatever it is you want to freeze. The spell is very limited however, and it can only be used once so be sure you use it wisely. I am afraid that I cannot do more for you, but it should serve your purpose well."

Cestator nodded, "Yeah that ought to do me a lot of good," he mumbled under his breath. Putting the conversation to the back of his mind, he concentrated on preparing for the battle ahead. He looked out, and noticed that he didn't have much time before the creatures arrived.

The hounds reached the rock formation first, they howled in a frenzied anticipation of the kill. As they howled, their hunger for blood could clearly be heard. Their fiery mouths and nostrils flared brightly making them look like some kind of demonic wolf. They appeared to have just come out of a roaring fire, for their entire bodies were scorched, and appeared to still be burning.

What little skin was left on their blackened bodies seemed stretched taunt over their charred bones, and their muscle sinew could clearly be seen through their almost transparent skin, making them a hideous sight to behold. The stench of burned and rotting flesh nearly made him gag. His eyes began to water and burn from the sulfuric smoke that emanated from their mouths.

One of the fiery beasts hungrily raced out ahead of the other two. It ran up the slope and leaped at Cestator, as it reached the top. Cestator spun to the side to avoid the attack, and in one fluid motion he pulled his sword from its scabbard. The dark steel of his blade glinted in the bright light of the land. He swung the sword as he came back around, and the blade caught the hound in its open maw. With the force of the hound's leap and his swing Cestator cleaved the vile beast in two. The hound's acidic blood spattered the tree, and poured out over the stone plateau causing an acrid smoke to billow up from anywhere it landed.

Cestator did not waste time thinking about it however, for the second hound was charging up the path way created by the first. This one proved to be no smarter, for when it reached the top, it leaped at him as well. This time Cestator jumped out of the way. It hit the tree with such force that it shook causing the stone at the base of tree to crumble.

The hound fell to the ground hard, but it stood quickly and shook its head as if it were shaking off a fog. When it finally cleared its head it began to growl deeply. It was about to attack, when suddenly one of the tree's branches wrapped itself around the hound's neck. The branch then jerked it up into the air so violently its neck snapped instantly.

The hound went limp, and dangled there for a moment. The tree lifted its victim up over the center of the trunk, where it dropped it. The hound fell and disappeared into the mouth of the tree. Cestator could hear the sound of bone being crushed as the tree devoured its meal.

"Two down one to go," he snickered. The last hound proved to be smarter than the others. It held its' head low to the ground watching every move Cestator made. It slowly stalked him matching him move for move. The opponents' eyes were locked in an epic battle, neither one willing to give ground, and admit defeat. As it drew closer he noticed this hound was much larger and stronger than the rest. It stood four feet tall at the shoulder, and had a huge barrel chest. The creature's paws were as large as both of Cestator's fists put together. All around this was a massive beast. When the creature reached the top it began to growl loudly, and it sounded like a low rolling thunderclap. Fiery drool dripped from its open mouth and singed the ground beneath it. "Come on you big bastard, let us dance," Cestator sneered at it, and began waving it on with his fingers.

The hound did not hesitate it came charging straight at him. Cestator waited until the last moment possible then leapt out of the way. The hound stopped quickly, just short of going off the edge of the stone. A small bit of gravel gave under its paw falling to the ground far below. The hound's growl grew even louder as it turned back towards Cestator.

It howled loudly, and Cestator could hear the anger and bloodlust in the creature's call. He smirked, as if he wanted to play a bit longer, and again waved the hound on. Not wasting any time, it charged at him full force. Avoiding the reaching branches Cestator poised for the attack. As the hound came at him, Cestator turned away swinging his sword around. The hound quickly twisted its body avoiding the brunt of the blow. Yet the tip of Cestator's dark sword caught the hound in the side.

Seeming to not have noticed the wound, the hound turned and charged again. Becoming weary of this game Cestator waited until the last moment then he jumped out of the way. Before it could turn around and charge again he leapt onto the creatures back. The hound hardly seemed to notice the additional weight for it instantly went berserk. It jumped, and twisted its' body in unimaginable ways, and did everything it could to try and dislodge its rider. For the first few moments all Cestator could do was hold on, but soon he found a way to lock his feet in place giving him the chance to free his hands. He gripped the hilt of his sword in both hands, and raised it above his head. With all his might he drove the blade down into the creature's neck, just at the base of the skull severing its spine. The hound dropped to the ground, but much to Cestator's surprise the head was still snarling and snapping at him. He quickly dismounted the creature, and walked around it to face the beast. "Well now we know who is the better of the two of us," he said in a matter of fact way. Looking down he found a nearby probing branch, then using the tip of his sword Cestator tapped the limb, and jumped back. The branch shot forward, found the hound, and wrapped itself around the creature's neck. The beast then shared its companion's fate.

Meanwhile back in Valclon's study, Drean stepped back from the looking pool knowing his master would be upset. "How is this possible Master? I thought they would have been more effective, yet it seems that hounds have failed to even harm him. I should have sent more."

He then heard Valclon chuckling wickedly. "Ah Drean, I knew there was a reason I kept you around. Your fear of my wrath is quite amusing. I expected nothing less than this from Cestator. Now come here look into the pool, and see what I have found in this."

Trying not to appear to give into his fear, Drean cautiously moved closer to Valclon. He looked into the pool and saw a replay of Cestator's fight with the hounds. He frowned not understanding what his master was doing.

"Look here Drean, do you see how he handled the hounds with such skill. Remember now that he is a blade master, and the hounds were only to find him and act as a diversion to the greal. I knew well they would not be able to kill him. Also look how he uses the tree to do the work for him, shear brilliance. I commend you for adding it. It was a good touch, it adds to the excitement of this battle."

"Thank you Master. I thought it would be more of a distraction to him, giving him something else to worry about and perhaps to make him slip up a bit. I am sorry it did not work out that way."

Valclon shook his head knowingly. "Hardly, Drean you should know better. He is nearly unmatched in the dance. Very few could ever come near to his skills. Even I would be no match for him at the dance, but then again swordplay never was my suit. That is why he was entrusted with the sword of shadows."

Valclon then looked back down at the pool and smiled at the scene. "Enough of that let us get back to the action at hand. I am quite curious how he will handle the greal." Valclon waved his hand and the pool showed the scene of Cestator awaiting the greal.

Cestator looked out over the edge of the cliff to see where the greal were at this point. When he could not see them he looked around, but they were nowhere to be found. *"Strange, they must be here somewhere they could not have just disappeared."*

Suddenly, as if conjured up by his thoughts they appeared. They were climbing up the sloping side towards him. Instantly he realized he was in the wrong place to face these big brutes, but the only way down was through them. With each of them being over eight feet tall and pushing six hundred pounds of raw muscle, that was not an option.

The greal cackled wickedly knowing they had Cestator cornered. If the situation were different he might have found this amusing. They sounded like some kind of mad children. As it was however, he was far too concerned with how he was going to win this round to find it amusing.

He took a good look at them to size up his situation; he then realized he was in serious trouble. The first thing he noticed about them was what they were wielding. The first greal carried a massive two headed battle axe. The weapon which a normal man likely could not even lift, the greal held in one hand. It had to of been at least five feet long with blades two feet across on each side. The second carried a massive spike covered club that that weighed nearly two hundred pounds. Yet the creature carried it on its shoulder like it was a child's toy.

Cestator looked into their eyes and flinched at the images he saw. They had the joy of the kill written all over them. Their hate for Cestator was deeply rooted and he knew these greal were out for revenge. He had punished many severely in the past. With their limited intelligence they hardly ever understood why they were being beaten, and often took it personally. For this was the only way to keep the chaotic beasts in order.

Cestator backed up as far as he possibly could without touching the tree. Quickly he thought of and discarded a dozen courses of action, but before he could come up with a solid plan the greal reached the top, and it was too late.

Seeing that they had him trapped, the greal sneered showing their broken and rotting teeth. They charged at him swinging their massive weapons. Without a thought Cestator dove to the ground away from their swings. He hit the ground hard, and grunted from the impact of a jagged stone in his side.

An instant later a branch from the tree came straight at him. He tried to avoid it, but was just seconds too late. The limb wrapped itself tightly around his waist and began to squeeze. He held his breath knowing if he released it he would not get another. The branch was wrapping itself tighter every moment, and it was working its way up to his chest. The branch then jerked him up into the air violently and began roughly shaking him.

The greal below him cackled in glee. They seemed to be thoroughly enjoying the show. The two ran around taking a swing at him whenever he came near. After a few minutes Cestator's lungs began burning for air, and the greal were his last concern.

The branch began to work its way up his chest squeezing tighter as it went. The breath was then squeezed from his lungs, and as he feared he could not get another. He could feel his ribs beginning to give, and he knew he had to act fast or he was dead.

Just as the tree was about to lift him over its waiting mouth, Cestator worked his sword free and severed the limb. The moment he hit the ground the branch loosened its grip on him. He coughed hard, took a few gasping breaths, and then unraveled himself from the limb.

Nearly too late Cestator remembered the two greal were still out to kill him. When they realized that he was still alive, they cackled their insane laughter and charged at him, swinging as they came.

Acting out of shear instinct Cestator used the branch like a whip and swung it at what could be a solid jutting rock. The end of the branch wrapped itself around the stone, and he tested it to be sure it would hold. When he was sure it would not give way under his weight, Cestator held on tight to the other end and dove off the edge of the cliff. He fell for what seemed like a split second, then his makeshift whip went taut and it nearly slipped out of his hands.

"Now what am I going to do, this was not the best idea I've had." He said as he looked down, and saw that he was still a good fifteen feet above the ground.

Cestator looked around for some sort of handholds or cracks in the cliff below. He found a small place that he could get his hands into, deciding to risk the climb over jumping, he let go of his makeshift rope. Suddenly, he heard the greal at the top yelling and fighting amongst themselves. He looked up and saw they were standing at the edge picking up big chunks of rock, then began hurling them at Cestator trying to knock him off his precarious position.

Cestator chuckled to himself for the creatures' aim was terrible they could get nowhere near him. Not worrying too much about the greal actually being able to hit him, Cestator began his climb down. Then somehow out of sheer luck one of the greal struck the cliff face just a few feet from where Cestator was climbing. The boulder was so large and thrown with such force that the vibrations caused him to lose his footing and he fell to the ground below. He hit the ground hard with a loud thud, and a swell of dust rose up around him. He screamed in pain as two ribs cracked, and knocked the breath out of him. He felt blood pouring down into his face, and eyes. Never in his life had he ever been in such agony.

The two greal seeing that Cestator had escaped roared in frustration. They then took their anger out on the tree. First the one wielding the axe split the tree in half with one massive swing. A strange green liquid poured out from the remnants and began hissing and spitting as it hit the stone. The acid like liquid singed his leg, this was just enough to throw the greal into a berserker rage. The second greal smashed what was left of the stump, and half of the cliff face with its own mighty swing.

At that exact moment in time, suddenly, Cestator heard a loud crack like the splitting of a large log, and seconds later he heard a thunderous explosion from above. He wiped the blood, and dust from his face and looked up. He rolled away as quickly as he could to avoid being crushed by the two halves of the tree and a large portion of the rock face. It all came crashing down missing him by inches.

Having nothing more to take their frustration out on, the two greal turned to run down the other side of the huge rock, but the large rage filled brutes got in each other's way. This only infuriated them more, and they began taking it out on one another. They pushed each other out of the way trying to reach the bottom first and nearly knocked each other off the side of the slope.

Cestator scrambled to his feet trying to avoid the gushing green ooze pouring out of what was left of the tree. With adrenalin rushing through his broken body, and all of his pain forgotten for he knew he could not dwell on it. He decided his only chance was to face these two brutes one at a time. He knew well he had no chance facing both of them even if he was in pique condition.

Somehow he was going to have to outsmart these two. He quickly looked around for some advantage, and noticed a small crevice in the rock face. He scurried into the fissure before the greal reached the bottom. Once inside he leaned against the back wall trying to slow his breathing, and for a faint moment he stood there hoping that they would pass him by. Though he knew the chance of that was slim.

The crevice was tight, but he had a little room to maneuver and with lack of anything better he accepted it. "Well this certainly is not much better than up there on top," Cestator snickered. "But at least they will be forced to come at me one at a time."

When the greal reached the bottom of the cliff where Cestator had fallen, they could not find him. Already frustrated with one another they began fighting amongst themselves. This gave Cestator a few extra moments to collect himself. When he could finally catch his breath he stepped forward to see how his situation fared.

When he reached the edge his boot slipped on a loose stone, and he cursed under his breath as he lost his footing. This caught the attention of the greal, and they instantly forgot their fight with each other. Their quarry was still alive and within reach. The two charged the crevice with no hesitation.

The greal holding the club reached the fissure first. It swung its mighty weapon in a downward arc straight at Cestator. He raised his sword in defense, and twisted the blade so the blow would glance off. The club hit his sword and slid down the blade, and hit the rock wall smashing it to bits. Dust and debris filled the air, and Cestator could not see for a few moments. He fought hard to keep from coughing in the cloud, for he knew it would only redouble the pain he felt now.

The greal unable to see him in the thick cloud of dust reached its arm into the fissure to see if it could find him. Seeing an opportunity, Cestator took a swing at the reaching arm and cut deep into the wrist. The greal grunted in pain and pulled its arm back. Cestator raised his sword up in defense as the club came swinging down at him again, and he paid dearly for it. His arm went numb from the vibrations and he nearly dropped his sword.

By this time the air had cleared, and the greal seeing him at a disadvantage swung again. This time Cestator decided against blocking it. He noticed the greal had a wide stance so it could get the proper leverage to swing the huge club. He took advantage of this and jumped through the creature's legs.

The club hit the ground a second later, but as Cestator was going through the greal's legs it caught his ankle. He stifled a scream of pain as he felt bone being crushed in the greal's mighty grip. The greal pulled him back through its legs, and lifted him up so he was looking it straight in the eyes. It smiled at him, and raised its club ready to smash his head like a melon.

Before it could swing the club Cestator quickly raised his sword and drove it straight through the creature's windpipe. Clutching at its throat the greal turned and dropped Cestator on the ground. Gasping for breath it fell to its knees as blood oozed from between its fingers.

Cestator stood up as quickly as his ankle would allow. He stood there a moment, and gave the greal a smirk intending to finish it. "So you're not so tough when you can't breathe now are you." He pulled his sword from the creature's throat severing two of its fingers in the process. He lifted it over his head intending to split the Greal's skull.

Suddenly he heard a grunt from behind him, and Cestator cursed himself for a fool. He did not know if it was due to the pain he was in, or some odd phenomenon but his senses were somehow dulled slightly. The second greal had gotten behind him in the confusion. Nothing like this had ever happened to him before.

He turned around and saw the greal swinging its axe. He quickly spun away from the attack, but because of his ankle he was slightly too slow. The tip of the blade left a large gash in his right side. The brunt of the swing went past him however, and it bit deep into the other greal silencing it forever.

Slightly put out by being denied the right to finish the kill, Cestator roared in pain and anger. He was now determined to finish this one way or another. He lifted his sword and with all the strength he could muster took one final swing, aiming for the greal's neck. He knew it was a feeble attempt, but exhaustion and pain were taking their toll on him, and he no longer cared if he lived or died.

The greal seeing him cackled, and with a large fist it knocked Cestator aside. He flew through the air for a few feet and his sword flew from his hand as he hit the ground. Knowing he would not have much time before the greal was upon him, he decided to abandon his sword.

Remembering the spell Cargon had given him, Cestator quickly uttered the few words to the spell. "Karzanok . . . ralaston . . . necolat." The instant he spoke the last word his hand was engulfed in blue flames. By this time the greal was on top of him. Cestator lunged towards the greal reaching as far as he could manage. He touched the greal's leg and instantly the creature was consumed in blue flames. The fire quickly burned out and the greal was frozen in place. Cestator looked up and saw that the axe was merely a few inches from his head. He cringed at the irony of it all.

Cestator reached up and grabbed the axe trying pull himself up but it broke off in his hands and he fell back on the ground. The moment the axe hit the ground it shattered into hundreds of pieces as though it were made of glass.

Intrigued by this Cestator tapped the greal with a knuckle. Cracks spider webbed out from where he had hit it, and moments later the greal fell to pieces with a loud ringing sound.

He laughed to himself and gritted his teeth from the pain of his broken ribs. He looked up to the sky knowing Valclon would be watching. With a smug attitude he said, "Ha, did you really think I would be so easily beaten? Did you forget who I am? I was the one who made these creatures submit to you." He then tore off his ragged tunic, and tore it into strips to bind off the gash in his side as best he could. Then looking around he found a few pieces of wood large enough to use as a splint, and using some left over strips torn from his tunic he tied them to his ankle to immobilize it.

Cestator looked around to see how far the portal was from where he lay. At first he could not find it, but he kept his composure and looked around to get his bearings. When he was sure he knew where it would be he turned himself in that direction, and a short distance away he saw a shimmering of light reflecting off of a large object.

He tried to get to his feet, but his broken ankle refused to hold his weight. He fell to the ground hard and grunted. The gash in his side was bleeding severely and his ribs pained him. Grunting through the pain refusing to let it beat him. Cestator then dragged himself towards the portal.

After what seemed like an eternity he reached the gateway. When he was finally before it he pulled himself up. His ankle protested severely, and he was weak from the loss of blood, but he was not going to let his father see him slinking away.

Cestator stood before the portal for a moment, collecting himself. Holding his head high, he took a few cleansing breathes to help with the pain. He took a small step forward, and his ankle began to give out on him. He caught himself through sheer force of will, and took a second step. Then with all the pride he could draw from within him, breathing almost in meditation, he took one last step and he was through.

Drean jumped back to avoid the flying splinters of stone. Valclon had shattered the pool out of anger.

"Damn you Cargon, you shall pay for this outrage! Drean find exactly where Cestator landed, and send a shade. I want him dead, and I want it done yesterday."

Drean bowed deeply, his hands shaking in fear. "Yes lord I will get right upon it, this very instant. I will report back to you the moment I have any more information."

"Very well just get out of my sight, and send in one of the slaves on your way out." Valclon said in an infuriated voice as he walked to the desk.

"Yes lord." Drean said as he backed out the door. He quickly walked down the hall and stopped the first slave he saw. It was a young man, someone of no importance. "You there slave," he called out. "Lord Valclon is in need of assistance, go to his quarters and attend to him."

The boy looked frightened, but he nodded, and did as he was bid. A few moments later Drean heard a bone chilling scream coming from the direction of Valclon's chambers. He cringed at the thought that he had just sent the slave to his untimely death, yet he was relieved that today he was not the one having to face the wrath of his cruel and evil master.

Chapter 4
Shepard

Reaching the other side of the portal, Cestator could no longer keep his balance and quickly collapsed to the ground below him. He let out a pain filled groan, for his ribs were bruised and broken, and the pain from them now over powered his shattered ankle. He landed in what appeared to be a shallow forest. The trees were old and large, but there was a good deal of space between them, and there was very little underbrush. He knew from these facts that he had to be near a city. He could hear the sounds of small animals scurrying around on the forest floor, and birds singing in the trees. This told him it was a peaceful place. The smell of decomposing leaves filled his senses. It was not altogether unpleasant for it had a slight sweetness to it. He realized it must have rained recently, for the ground was slightly damp, as the early spring air still had a slight chill to it. It was as though winter was refusing to let go.

Cestator lifted himself up and took a deep breath. The air smelled fresh and clean. The day was coming around to dawn and the glow of the first sun crawling up over the horizon was stunning. He smiled at the irony of it all. This was the first time he had ever stopped to see the beauty in it. Thinking he was dying he took a long look and thought how majestic it all was.

Then from a good distance behind him, he heard a very familiar sound. Holding his breath in anticipation he listened intently, hoping against all odds it was what he thought. Then after a few moments he heard it again. The sound was that of a horse galloping and it was getting closer.

Cestator turned himself around and could faintly see a road through the trees. The sound continued to get louder as the rider came closer. As quickly as he could manage Cestator began to crawl towards the road hoping he could get the rider's attention. He managed to get within a few feet of the road just as the rider passed. He tried to call out to the man, but it came out as a low moan due to his broken ribs, making it progressively harder for him to breath.

As the rider passed he looked in Cestator's direction seeming to have heard him. Seeing this Cestator tried to wave the man down. It did no good however, for the rider merely smiled and rode on.

Exhausted from the loss of blood and the exertion of getting to the road, Cestator collapsed on the ground, not caring if he lived or died. He lay there fading farther and farther, when suddenly he was startled by a strange sound. Somewhere, down the road, there was a rickety cart. It was creaking and moaning loudly as it traveled. Cestator decided that this time he was going to be seen even if it killed him.

He crawled the remaining distance to the road and looked up towards the sound. He chuckled when he saw the cart, it did not look much better than it sounded. The cart was old, and looked as though it would fall apart at any moment. The old mare that pulled it looked tired and ready to collapse, but had an air about her that spoke of training. The man sitting in the driver's seat was old as well, he looked weathered and sun dried with leathery looking skin. Cestator decided that it was likely from working his entire life out in the hot sun.

Cestator noticed something that did not fit that description however. Like his horse the man's outward appearance was deceiving. He could tell the man was quite healthy and strong for his age. Cestator nearly dismissed this for the hard work he must do every day, yet that did not quite fit him. The man's posture, the way he held himself, and moved told of much discipline and training. This old farmer had likely fought in many battles, surely in his king's army.

When the cart came closer and he was sure he would be seen, Cestator pulled himself up using the branch of a nearby tree. He then let go of the branch and tried to wave the man down, and paid dearly for it. The motion reopened the gash in his side, and it bled anew. His ankle unable to withstand any more of this abuse completely gave out on him, and he fell to the ground with a groan of pain. The man appeared to have noticed him for the cart sped up.

The next thing he knew the old man was standing over him saying something he could not hear. All the blood left in his body seemed to be rushing to his head. The pounding in his head was so unforgiving that he could not hear. He caught one thing the man said by watching his lips move, and he answered just as he passed out.

The man in the cart Cestator saw was an old yet burly dwarf known by most as Shepard. He was heading into town for supplies as he did once a month, to get feed for his animals, and anything else his wife decided they needed. He only made the trip once a month because getting into the city was hardly worth the trouble. He despised the crowds and the stuffiness of being packed within the walls.

On this day Shepard was in no mood to deal with the crowds, and all the noise. There was nothing to be done about it however. His stores had run far too low to avoid going into town any longer. Suddenly the cart hit a bump and nearly sent Shepard out of his seat.

"By all tha be mighty! It be high time, I be get'n me self a new cart. Dis ol' bucket jus' won't be do'n it any more. An while I be at it I may well be take'n Stamper out to be pull'n it."

At that the horse whinnied in protest and reared slightly. Shepard chuckled loudly. *"Oh Clinet do'n ye be worry'n I would no ever replace ye, we did be through too much together fer me ta ever be do'n that. Now let us be go'n, I wan' ta be ge'n dis over wit as quick as be possible."*

They traveled down the road a bit farther, and as they rounded a corner Shepard saw something that caught his attention. There was a man leaning heavily on a branch up ahead on the side of the road. His shirt was in tatters, and blood soaked. The man looked as though he were in a bad fight. He let go of the branch and tried to wave, but all he managed to do was swing his arm slightly before he fell to the ground hard.

"Come on Clinet that thar fella be in real trouble from da look o' things. It look though he gonna need da help o' a healer."

Shepard shook the reigns urging the horse to go faster. They reached the man in moments, and before the cart was fully stopped, Shepard jumped down and ran over to him. He bent down to check the man's condition and noticed he was near dead.

Noticing the stranger was barely conscious Shepard asked the man what had done this to him. "Greal," was all that he was able to say before momentarily losing consciousness. Shepard pulled back in shock then shook his head dismissing what he had just heard. There was no way it could have been a greal, there had been no sightings of them in many years.

Shepard loosened up the tattered bandage to see the gash, and the broken ribs. He whistled through his teeth at the sight. *"Oh me, by all that be mighty, boy ye do look'n like ye was on da wrong side o' a mighty blade. Ye be lucky it did no go any lower, ye would no' be lay'n here right now if it had."*

The man stirred and tried to reach up to him. The hand was shaky and weak, and fell before it could reach him.

"Nah lad save yer strength ye be need'n it. I'll be get'n ye some help right quick." With that Shepard lifted the man up onto his shoulder and gently placed him into the cart. He hopped up into the driver's seat and shook the reigns. *"Come on Clinet we be need'n to git dis feller ta town. He be need'n da help o' an ol' friend."*

The horse immediately jumped into action and began to gallop down the road jarring the cart all the more. *"Careful thar Clinet dis lad can no handle too rough o' a ride we need da speed, but if we be shake'n dis feller too much he may star' bleed'n again, an' from da look o' things he do no' have much left in 'im."*

The horse whinnied again and slowed her pace just a bit to try to reduce the bouncing of the cart. *"Right that be good Clinet keep that thar pace it be a bit rough but thar be noth'n can be done 'bout it."*

A short time later the pearl white walls of Cerdrine came into view. The sunlight reflecting off of their polished surfaces made the walls appear to shimmer vibrantly. They were one hundred feet tall and fifty feet thick at the base. There was a small passageway close to the interior of the wall, just wide enough to fit three men side by side within the foot of the structure. This allowed men to travel quickly around the city and exit one of many secret doors branching off the passage way, if ever an enemy found their way in. The two gates into the city were just as solid as the walls themselves. In times of peace only the large iron infused wooden doors were used to seal out the night, but in the case of a siege the main doors to the gates were used. These were two massive blocks of stone that fit seamlessly into the gap in the wall. They floated freely on ingeniously fashioned hinges that allowed the two pieces to settle onto the ground when closed, thusly sealing the wall completely. The only way they could be reopened was with a mechanism below ground that required fifty men to operate.

The only part of the city itself that could be seen peeking over the mighty walls was the palace's twin towers in the very center of the city. Yet even they did not out reach the guard towers on top of each corner of the wall. These structures were the highest ever created measuring nearly one hundred feet over the great walls. Their seamlessly solid construction made them nearly impervious to all mechanisms of war, second only to the walls themselves. The small windows that were set at each level gave a great vantage point for hundreds of archers to unleash a flurry of arrows at any enemy below while allowing them to be relatively safe.

The Dwarvern built city had never been taken in a siege. This was a great tribute to the dwarf heritage, for they were well known for their remarkable constructions. Cerdrine was one of the last signs that the dwarves even existed. After the trial wars they simply disappeared off the face of Trecerda. Shepard being a dwarf himself knew exactly where they had gone, and why they disappeared.

"Well lad thar it be, Cerdrine. Did ye know it do mean Da Light O Da World in Dwarvern? It be da second mos' beautiful sight in all o da world." When he received no answer Shepard sighed and turned to the horse. "K Clinet we be head'n to da wes' gate today. We do no have time ta be waste'n wit all dees bleed'n crowds. Dis lad here would be dead 'fore we even reach da gates."

As they passed the main gate Shepard noticed there was a line of people down the road leading to the docks and fish market trying to get into the city. He shook his head when he saw this. It was exactly as he knew it would be at this time of day. At best it would likely take hours just to reach the gates. Knowing his passenger would never last that long he was gambling that his old student was still at the temple of Cargon.

As they came around to the west gate, Shepard looked out over the stone bridge that spanned the long drop to the ocean waters below. The bridge itself was another of the greatest defenses of the old city. The dwarves had built it in two segments with the seam in the center and giant hinges on either end. These were concealed so well that they were not visible to those without knowledge of their existence. Two massive steel rods were used to keep the bridge in place. They too were hidden within the structure of the bridge. They were counterweighted with two giant stones, and the entire mechanism was hidden within the cliff to keep all unaware of the trap. With the simple pull of a lever the stones would drop pulling the rods out, and in turn splitting the bridge apart dropping anything on it to the rocks far below.

Yet it was not the bridge that brought a tear to Shepard's eye. Instead he was looking upon the doors of the mighty gate. *"It sure has been some time since we did be here las', has'n it ol' girl? It sure do bring back lot o' memory o' da ol' days when we did be more adventurous."*

After a few moments Shepard shook off the haze from remembering times long past. He knew the man in the back of his cart did not have much time left. He walked up to the large doors, which served more as a private entrance for the paladins of Cargon due to the fact that the temple overlooked most of the west wall. Normal traffic was not allowed through which made it easier for the guards to screen all who wished to pass through.

Shepard pounded hard upon the door until it cracked open and a man's head popped out. When the guard saw only Shepard there he opened the door wider. Shepard found this odd, for only a fool would open the door to a complete stranger. There had to be something he was missing. He looked up and found what he was looking for. Atop the wall there were four archers with arrows poised and ready. He also remembered there would be a pair of oxen inside the wall that were connected to a large chain. The chain was hooked into a mechanism that would shut the doors very quickly.

The guard looked at Shepard with a frown on his face, he was certainly not happy to have to deal with this. "This is a private gate," he grumbled. "Only Paladins of Cargon are allowed through here. I have never seen your face before and I have no time to deal with strangers, you will have to go around to the main gate like everyone else."

Shepard did not like the tone in which the guard spoke to him. He scowled deeply and the lines of age and experience enhanced the look. The guard took a fearful step back and began to shut the gate.

"Now ye jus be hold'n it right thar ye young'n. I be due more respect than that. Why I were kill'n all sort o' beasts when yer papa were nurs'n on his momma's milk. An I been visit'n dis place long fore ye were even a twinkle in 'im eye. Now go an fetch Slanoth fer me. Tell 'im thar be an ol' frien' out here need'n 'is help."

The guard shook his head sadly. "I am sorry sir, but Slanoth is not to be disturbed. He is morning the loss of a dear friend."

"Wha' did ye say boy? Who be dead tha I do no be know'n bout? Tell me lad I do be know'n most 'o da people that Slanoth do."

The guard bowed his head in respect before answering. "Master Randor has joined Lord Cargon merely a few days past now. He suffered a strange illness that none could heal."

Shepard flinched as though he were struck. *"Yer mean'n ta tell me that Randor be dead. How do dis be, I did see im but a few month back in da city, an' he were fit an fine."*

"Yes sir I am sorry to be informing you in this way but we all have been mourning his loss. Lord Slanoth has taken it especially hard and has not wanted to see anyone of late."

Shepard closed his eyes and bowed his head. *"May ye fine peace and happiness at Cargon side ol' friend."*

"Once again sir I am sorry I had to inform you in this way, but as I said Lord Slanoth is not seeing anyone at this time so if you will tell me where you will be staying I will send someone for you when Lord Slanoth is ready to see you."

"Oh no young fella ye won' be get'n rid o' me tha' easy. Randor were a dear friend 'o me also, but we be have'n a serious matter out here. Thar be a die'n man here in da back o' me cart here. So go an

fetch Slanoth right quick, cause I be know'n he would be none too happy if ye let a man be die'n cause ye were afraid to be disturb'n 'im."

Meanwhile Slanoth was walking through the temple garden still pondering what Cargon had told him a few days ago. He was deep in thought when he heard a commotion at the gate. It sounded like someone was trying to get in, but the guards were refusing him. When it was not resolved in a few moments Slanoth decided he had best see what was happening.

Slanoth then picked up his pace and headed for the gate. When he arrived he asked the guard what was going on. The guard turned and bowed when he saw Slanoth. "Pardon me for disturbing you Lord Slanoth, but there is a man here asking for you. I tried to tell him that you did not wish to be disturbed, but he is insistent. He also says he has a wounded man here with him."

Slanoth frowned, "well then why have you not allowed him to enter, and come to inform me. I am never too busy to look in on a wounded man."

Hearing this Shepard spoke up, *"now I hear ya talk'n ta Slanoth thar so be move'n yerself outa me way."*

Shepard did not even wait for a reply. He merely bumped the guard out of the way and went through the gate. When he got to the other side he looked around and could not find Slanoth, he turned back to the guard in puzzlement. *"Now I be know'n ye were talk'n to Slanoth. I did hear ye say his name. So where do he be, I do no' be see'n 'im here."*

Slanoth chuckled deeply. He had not seen Shepard in a long time. It felt good having him here at a time like this. "Oh Shepard I should have known it was you. It has been a long time old friend, and it is good to see you."

Hearing his name Shepard turned to the person who was talking to him. *"Now how do ye be know'n . . . ?"* he stopped short when he got a good look at the man who was speaking to him. He saw more age and wisdom in the man's eyes than should be there. *"Slanoth do that be ye, tell me are me eyes fool'n me? Ye look lots like Slanoth but . . ."*

Slanoth smiled and nodded. "Yes Shepard it really is me. I must say that you are truly a sight for sore eyes old man."

"By all that be mighty! What kind o' sorcery be dis? Slanoth ye be like a young man here 'for me, but I be know'n ye be no way near as young as ye look now. What in da heavens happen to ye?"

Slanoth flinched at the curse, it was something he had heard Shepard say thousands of times but he could never get used to it. "Well you have not changed one bit have you old man? It is not sorcery Shepard, it is something quite different, but I will explain that to you later. For now though did you say you had a wounded man with you?"

"Aye that I did, he be in da back o' me cart. I were try'n ta tell dis young guard here that Cestator be knock'n on ol' death's door an' we no have time ta go through da main gate."

It was now Slanoth's turn to be shocked. He stood there for a moment not saying a word. Shepard frowned, and scratched his head. *"Slanoth do ye be ok, yer mouth be hang'n open like ye gone over da edge er something"*

"Yes of course I'm fine Shepard, but tell me did you just say that his name was Cestator?"

"Aye, at least tha' be da name he did give me when I did ask im. Course he were near out o' it when I did. Personally me, I don' know what kind o' people would be name'n thar son such a curse name."

Slanoth cut Shepard off short by putting his hand on his friends shoulder and squeezing tightly. "Shepard I am sorry, but could we continue this later, if this is who you say it is, then we have a serious matter on our hands. Please go inside, and ask one of the servants to show you to my quarters. I will join you when I am done healing our friend there. That is if you do not mind waiting, for we have much to catch up on."

Shepard nodded his agreement. *"I will be meet'n ye thar then."* With that he turned and headed towards the temple.

When Shepard was out of ear shot the guard turned to Slanoth. "Lord who was that old farmer? He seems to know you very well, but I have never seen him before."

Slanoth chuckled warmly. "My son, that man you see there is no mere farmer. He is one of the greatest warriors of all time." He then let the man ponder his words for a few moments. When he saw the man was even more confused Slanoth went on. "That man that you see there is none other than the King's greatest general of all time. My son, that man was General Bear Shepardalious."

The guard's jaw dropped and his eyes flew open wide with shock. "Lord do you mean I spoke that way to General Shepard? Oh I am such a fool."

Slanoth laughed loudly. "Yes my son, that truly is the General, but I would not worry if I were you, the General has respect for you right now. Had you just let him through he would have been upset with you."

The guard looked extremely puzzled by this. "But Lord, he gave me the roughest side of his tongue for what I said to him."

"Oh I would not worry about that." Slanoth said with a smile. "He treats most people like that. Do not take it to heart you did what you felt was right, and that is what matters. Now help me take this man down to the healing rooms."

The guard did as he was bid without another word, pondering what he had just heard. When they got to the room Slanoth sent the man back to his duties and began to heal Cestator.

Shepard paced back and forth, being in this room always made him uncomfortable. This was the head acolyte's quarters, meant for the strongest in their faith. The furnishings were simple yet comfortable, and the room was well lit. A large window looked out over the mouth of the Serrling River creating a spectacular view. The air about the room was warm and inviting and spoke much of Slanoth's personality.

Despite all of this Shepard still could not get comfortable in the room. He had been in this room many times over the years, and most times he had highly volatile conversations with the former acolyte.

Suddenly the door opened behind him and Slanoth entered the room. He looked weary and tired. "I had almost forgotten how exhausting that is, even as I am now. That healing has nearly tapped all of my strength."

"Ha . . . Well what do ye be expect'n, he were near ta dead when I did fine him. He were hurt so badly that I be surprise ye be walk'n right now."

"Yes I can see that, I nearly had to bring him back from the dead. At points I was not sure that I would be able to heal him. By the way did he ever mention what did this to him?"

Shepard looked out the window thinking to himself. A moment later he turned back to Slanoth with a frown on his face. *"Well now that ye do mention it he did be mumble'n someth'n bout a greal when I did firs git' ta 'im. I figured it fer nonsense 'cause 'im did pass out a few moment after I did git thar. I still be find'n tha' ta be no likely, cause I be blasted if thar be a greal round these here parts. Why thar be no mention o' them things since Tha Trial Wars. Why most folk round here do no believe they even exist."*

Slanoth sighed deeply bothered by the answer he had just received. This confirmed everything he had feared since Cargon had visited him. "Unfortunately Shepard I must tell you that it is not so unlikely that he fought a greal. It actually confirms a few things that I have been fearing, and thusly it begins a great many things."

Shepard turned quickly and stared Slanoth square in the face. *"Do ye be mean'n ta tell me tha' thar be a greal here in Trecerda?"*

"No Shepard there are no greal here, at least not at this point. Praise be to Cargon for small miracles."

Shepard dropped into the chair behind him somewhat dumbfounded. *"Wait thar one moment what do ye be mean'n tha thar be none here at this point? What are ye try'n ta say wit that choice o' words, ye be know'n someth'n an' ye bes' be tell'n me what it be. An if thar be none here how could that lad meet up wit' one?"*

Slanoth walked around the desk and sat down across from Sheppard. He sat there for moment, thinking about how would be the best way to tell his old friend about what he knew. In the end he decided to just be straight forward with the old dwarf. "Shepard you asked me who would name their son such a cursed name as Cestator, to answer your question his father did The Dark One himself . . . Valclon."

Shepard jumped to his feet, anger in his eyes. The chair he had been sitting in skidded across the room and hit the wall with a load bang. *"Wha . . . do ye be mean'n ta tell me tha' man down thar be da' real Cestator, Da Dammed One's own son?"*

Slanoth merely nodded in reply not saying a word, he knew it would come to light. He simply sat there looking at Sheppard over his folded hands letting his friend work it out for himself.

"Ye knew dis an ye still heal 'im? No . . . no ye nearly died try'n ta heal 'im. Be ye loose'n yer head er do I be miss'n something here?"

"Yes Shepard I did suspect he was the real Cestator. The one we all know all too well, or should I say the man behind the handy work we know so well. Yet still I healed him, as I would anyone."

"Do ye be mad er something? Why in all o' da world would ye risk yer life fer da likes o' 'im ye know well as me tha' he would be leav'n ye right thar where he found ye ta die. Ye be know'n well as me wha' tha' bastard be capable of. Why he have done kill more people than ten greal, an' most o' them were no jus men he did be kill'n. Lots o' them was innocent women an' children, an' they did be lucky if he did jus' be kill'n them ye done seen da aftermath o' his torture same as I done."

Slanoth sighed deeply understanding his friend's anger, and hatred for Cestator. Had he not been forewarned, he himself would have had trouble doing what had been asked of him. "Yes Shepard I do know all of that, and I know that he ordered twice as many deaths. Believe me I had the same fears and troubles when I first learned of it. This was one of the hardest things I have ever done in my life."

"Well then why do he still be alive right now? Why did ye heal da likes o' 'im? He no be deserve'n our help. We did battle wit' his army on a few occasion he do be da most evil fighter ever I did see. He care not for his own troops never ye mind any others."

Slanoth shrugged his shoulders. "Yes Shepard I remember those days quite well, many of them we nearly lost to him and I would hate to imagine if we had. As to why I did it that is simple, Cargon asked me to. I put my faith in him to see us through this. Yet even if he had not asked me, I likely would have still done it anyway, because it would have been the right thing to do. That is what Cargon teaches us, every man deserves a chance to defend himself against all charges, no matter what wrongs he may have committed.

If he decides to give up that right then it is his choice but we must offer him that choice."

Shepard let out a strong laugh, picked up his chair and sat down in front of Slanoth. *"I should have been know'n Cargon done had someth'n ta do wit' this. 'Im ideal's be way out thar, but me I mus' admit he do git things done, even if they be done in a roundabout way. We dwarves be direct an' to da point we see wha' be need'n done an' we no worry 'bout wha' er who be in da way we jus' git to it. Let me guess then, he be da one behind how ye look thar?"*

Slanoth smiled warmly. "Well what do you think of it? This is his gift for the services that I am to render for him"

Ha . . . an what be da price o' that? Ye be know'n well as me that Cargon never gave out no gif' fer noth'n in return, da whole balance thing he do call it."

Slanoth was shocked for a moment, he had expected many things but this was not one of them. He thought about the question for a moment before answering. "Well I would say that all he has asked of me is that I am to train Cestator to be a true paladin."

"Hmm an ye be think'n he could make it? Ye be know'n better than anyone what it be like. It be sure a hard road ta be traveled."

Slanoth was truly shocked at this point he had thought he would have to argue fiercely to get Shepard to see things his way. He almost did not know how to answer. "Yes actually I think he can. In fact someday he may become one of the greatest if he learns to control his rage."

Shepard nodded, *"ok then I'll be need'n ta git back to me farm an lett'n Bridget an James know tha' I be stay'n here fer awhile. Also I be need'n to git a few things."*

Slanoth nearly fell back in his chair. He was so shocked by Shepard's reaction He could hardly contain himself. Shepard had always been a very critical person and as stubborn as a mule.

Slightly frustrated Shepard glared at his friend. *"What be that look fer Slanoth? Ye should be know'n me better than tha'. Do ye no see that me do have all o' this figured out already? Now me have only one question. Do ye be sure that it were a greal that done that to 'im?"*

Slanoth thought for a moment before answering. "Yes, a greal would fit best. His right ankle was crushed as though something with great strength had squeezed it. There were no teeth marks or torn skin so it was not an animal bite. Everything tells me that it was a greal that did this to him."

"Hmm . . . yes ye be right thar. But me be think'n tha it no were only one greal what done it. Now think on dis a moment. Cestator be one o' da finest blade-masters da world has ever done seen right?"

Slanoth smiled and nodded. He now knew his old friend had put most of the pieces together and probably knew almost as much as he did himself. Slanoth was always amazed how the man's mind worked. It was clear why the king had asked him to lead his armies in The Trial Wars.

Shepard, now pacing around the room did not see his friend nod in answer to his question. He merely went on as though he was explaining it all to Slanoth for the first time. *"Right an any blade-master would no be have'n too much troubles kill'n one o' them. He may no git away unhurt but he would no be knock'n on ol' death's door. Also he would be know'n jus' 'bout everything thar be ta know about them beasts, which would be give'n 'im more an advantage."*

Shepard paused a moment, and walked around the room. He was so deep in thought he did not see anything else that was in the room. Slanoth marveled at this, he could almost see the thoughts burning in Shepard's eyes. Then Shepard suddenly began again as though he had never stopped. *"Yes so thar had ta have been at least two o' them. An if thar did be two o' them, someone did have ta be order'n them to attack 'im. Me I could be see'n one o' them maybe git'n angry and attack'n 'im, but no thar had ta be two. I . . . yes thar were two cause one no would be do'n that ta 'im an three would sure be kill'n 'im. Greal no be smart enough ta work together wit' no guidance. Beside it be a well-known fact that greal no be like'n each other none too much. So they did have ta be follow'n orders, an' who we know would be give'n them those orders? Me guess it would be Drean, cause Valclon would no lower 'im self ta deal'n wit' them. Yet who would be give'n Drean them orders?"*

Slanoth smiled in enjoyment of the moment. "That would have to be Valclon himself of course."

Once again Shepard showed no signs of even hearing what Slanoth had said, he was deep in thought and showed no outward emotions except the fire that was raging in his eyes. *"Aye it would* have been Valclon what ordered it, cause Drean no have da backbone ta be do'n something so foolish o' that without orders. So if da dark one did send da greal then I be guess'n that Cestator did either betray or fail him. In either case Valclon would be want'n 'im dead, an that would only make it logic that Cestator would be run'n here. An da fact that he even be hurt do prove that he no be wit' his father, fer he no be immortal anymore."

Shepard paused a moment and looked out the window at the bay below them. He watched as the waves crashed on the rocks below. He had always admired the power of the rolling sea it was the one thing that was more relentless than any dwarf. He did so love to watch it, but like any other dwarf he was terrified of it. It was a well-known fact that all dwarves could never swim their stocky build caused them to sink like a stone. He shivered at the thought and stepped away from the window. *"It be me guess tha' he did betray Valclon though. What would be 'im reason fer it, that me no can figure but it no matter much. He would know that he would lose all o' his power so he would be go'n ta Cargon fer help an thus he do be here. Do me be right er no?"*

Slanoth still amazed at what he had just heard smiled deeply. "Shepard I must say you never fail to amaze me. You are correct on all accounts as much as I can tell. Please tell me how the king ever let you go."

Shepard chuckled and smiled knowingly. *"Ye know well'n as me do tha' Bridget would be have'n none o' that. She would be give'n Lysandas da rough side o' her tongue fer even think'n o' it."*

Slanoth's smile widened and he laughed heartily. "Yes I do believe she would my friend. Now as far as Cestator, I do believe that he has seen far too much of what his father is capable of. Apparently some young child softened his heart. I do not know the details, but I heard that he killed her entire family yet spared her life for some reason."

"Hmm . . . that be strange fer sure, an I do no be know'n what to make o' tha'. Ye can be sure thar be more to tha' story." Shepard paced around the room a bit longer mulling this over, he looked at it from every angle he could think of but found no logical reasoning for it. *"Well tha' do be beyond me tha' do be fer sure. Though if Cargon have faith in 'im, then I do guess tha' be good enough fer me. Ye*

know though, before I be go'n I sher would be like'n ta be have'n a few word wit' 'im an be figure'n out what his motivations be."

Slanoth nodded, "I think that would be a good idea old man. Could you wait just a moment however there is something I would like you to see." He stood and walked into the back room for a moment. When he returned he held what appeared to Shepard like a large book wrapped in red cloth. "Do you remember when I searched for any written word on the existence of the phoenix?"

"I tha' I do, ye made it yer lifelong quest. Do ye be telling me tha' ye found something now after all these year?"

"Yes my friend, just the other day I found this book in the library I have not seen it in years. When I pulled it out it jumped to this page here."

Slanoth placed the book on the table, and he untied the string holding the red cloth in place. He then unfolded the cloth revealing the deep black cover that was bound in gold. Inlaid into the cover there were golden runes written in language long forgotten. Holding the book closed were two golden claws of a creature that few people had ever seen, and the tips of the claws appeared to be puncturing the pages.

Shepard knew this tome all too well and the moment that he saw it he jumped up out of his chair. This time however it was with a look of fear and anger. *"Where in all o' da worl' did ye fine that blasted thing? Ye should no be look'n inta it, tha' thar damn thing be cursed."*

Slanoth looked at his old friend in shock. "Randor and I took it from Slavendor when he died. We knew it was something that should not fall into the wrong hands, for it seemed to contain great power. It seems as though you know it, have you seen it before?"

Shepard lowered his head a moment, and when he looked back up at Slanoth there was a deep sadness in his eyes. *"Aye I do be know'n tha' book. It be from a time tha' me I would be like'n ta ferget. It be one o' da thirteen items from da dark days."*

"Wait just a moment." Slanoth hastily interrupted his friend, "do you mean to tell me this is one of the thirteen pieces that nearly . . . ?"

"Aye it be one o' da thirteen pieces that Keronoth the Destroyer held when he did rule. Cargon done took it from 'im when he done

imprisoned 'im wit da other Dark Knights. We done hid it away where we thought it could no ever be foun', I guess we did be wrong."

Slanoth stared in shock at his old friend. He had never known this about Shepard. "Wait one moment there, are you telling me that you were there? How could that be possible even dwarves do not live that long that happened thousands of years ago."

"It be tens o' thousands o' years now, me los' track fer some time now. I no be tell'n ye, cause it no be something me like ta remember. I be da only remain'n person alive wha' created one o' them blasted things. That be why I do no make weapons no more. All thirteen o' them things got a mind o' their own an they eventually did kill all their creator. Evil they did be, an me I done created Justice ta counter that bleed'n axe o' mine. That sword were me save'n grace, course Cargon be da one what gave it true magic."

"Slanoth stared in shock at the old dwarf standing across from him, as though for the first time. "I never knew that you had lived through all of that. There is much that we need to discuss, yet we must leave that for another day. For now you must see this that I have found in the book. I know very little of the language, but I was able to pick out a few words. Perhaps you can make out what it is saying." Slanoth then touched the claw like clasps and they released their grip and the book flew open turning to a specific page all its own.

Shepard hesitated a moment before he leaned in and read the words on the page. He knew well anything this book said could be a trick of words that lead the reader to an untimely death.

In a day when the dead walk in an army and the seas roil with danger the people of the grandest place will find nightmares among them. Then in the time of greatest need the people's shining light will fall. A thunderous roar will erupt, and a mighty fire will rage. All that dare to stand against it will be consumed in its fury. Then in the calmness after the blaze the world will stand still, the past will bow their heads in sorrow for their loss, and the stones will weep. Yet in this darkest hour the phoenix will rise up from the ashes and be reborn. The day will be won but an evil unlike anything ever seen will rise to destroy all life. Many will come together to battle this terrible evil, but it is yet to be seen who is to prevail. They will each have to battle their own evils before they can become strong enough to battle that which has chosen to destroy them. The phoenix itself may not be strong enough to defeat this evil. Innocence will be lost, and love will flare then turn to hatred. The only hope for all will be to take the ancient text to the place where even the mighty dragons fear to go.

Shepard looked up shaking his head. *"Fer one thing me no have read dis language in such o' long time it do be almos' har' fer me ta read. Secon' I no like dis much, dis here bloody thing have but one purpose an tha' be to fine all o' the other thirteen pieces. dis here prophecy I can guarantee be not more than tha', though I do say what it do imply can no be good tidings fer Cerdrine."*

"I had feared as much, I had put this thing away never expecting to ever touch it again, but for some reason this thing wanted to be seen. I have passed it many times over and never thought about it, but just the other day I was in the library and I heard a voice and it drew me to the book. When I pulled it out it fell out of my hands and opened to this page. I hoped you may have some insight into it."

"Me advice to ye be ta forget tha' blasted thing. As I did tell ye them things be evil an they do serve theyselves only. Now please git it away from me I can no think wit it here so close. It do bring up too many o' bad memory."

"I do understand your reluctance my old friend, but I must know what it says for the sake of all the people. It has revealed itself to me for a reason, be it for the gain of finding the others or not I must know why. So please if it is not so terrible could you translate it for me?" Slanoth pleaded painfully. "You know I would not ask unless I knew it was important to this situation."

Shepard grumbled something about being forced to remember times long past, but Slanoth could hardly make it out. When he was finished Shepard nodded. *"Alright but ye is gonna owe me a large favor here."* Shepard then grudgingly grumbled to himself knowing he had no other option than to answer such a request as he began to translate. The words that came before Slanoth began to purge up apprehension, with the knowledge of the world was about to come into a new era and not necessarily for the good. When he was done Shepard looked up with a dark scowl on his face. *"Now do ye no be put'n too much into dis here thing. It could no be mean'n noth'n about what be go'n on right now. So if ye would please git this thing outa me sight."*

Slanoth nodded sadly. He knew how hard it must have been for the old dwarf to have to relive such dark times, but this was far worse than he could have expected. He then returned the book to its hiding place in the library. When he returned Shepard was back in his seat finally relaxing a bit. "Well Shepard shall we go and speak with Cestator now."

"I, that do be a good idea, I be think'n. I should no be too much longer away from da farm. Bridget might start wonder'n where I be. We should be gett'n down thar an see wha' our frien' be have'n ta say."

CHAPTER 5

CESTATOR

Cestator awoke to the sound of a gruff voice with a heavy accent. He had no idea where he was and felt groggy as though his mind was in a fog. His head was pounding, and he found it hard to think. The voice was persistent however, and it eventually broke through to him, and brought him out of his fog.

"Come on now ye lad, ye done sleep da day away. It be right time ye be gett'n up out o' that thar bed, an join'n da world o' da live'n. Why it be nigh go'n on dusk."

As Cestator opened his eyes and looked around the room. His vision was blurry, and all he could make out were unidentifiable shapes. He rubbed his eyes and blinked a few times, and eventually he could make out more of what he was seeing. He noticed then that he was in a small room with very few furnishings. He looked over to where he heard the voice. He saw two men standing near him. One was tall and slender, but he seemed to have an air about him that said he was not one to be reckoned with. The man wore a sword at his hip and looked as though he was more than able to use it. Cestator respected that for he did not look over confident like most fighters who were easy to overcome. This man knew his limits and that made him dangerous.

The second man looked worn and weather beaten, but very solid. He had a large bushy but well-kept beard. Cestator knew instantly that this man was a dwarf, and from the looks of him he was just as able to defend himself. "Where am I, and who are you?"

He managed to stammer out after a moment of trying to find his voice.

The dwarf came over and sat beside him. He smiled at Cestator and spoke in the same gruff voice, which had awakened him. *"Ah so ye do still be alive. Well me boy welcome to da land o' the live'n. I be Shepard an tha' feller behind me would be Slanoth. As fer where ye be, well ye would be in da temple o Cargon."*

Cestator shook his head in confusion. "How did I get here? The last that I remember I was on the side of the road waving down a man in a cart"

"Well me boy it were me that ye did wave down. I did spot ya an brought ye here to me old frien' here. Let me tell ye lad that ye be lucky that it did be me that were pass'n cause most folk would jus' leave ye fer dead."

Cestator nodded that he understood. "Thank you for your help, it was very honorable of you."

"Ha . . . it were no have'n any thin to do wit' honor it were merely common courtesy lad. Now since we be talk'n bout these things how bout ye be tell'n me why ye be here."

Not sure if he should reveal himself to this man right away he circled the answer. "You said that you brought me here. What are you talking about?"

"Do no be play'n dumb wit' me ye know what I be talk'n 'bout. What I be want'n ta know is why ye be betray'n yer father, an how did ye get to the side o' the road like ye were? As I sees it ye be lucky ta be alive, if it were no fer me an Slanoth here ye would no be talk'n to us right now. The least ye could be do'n is give'n us a little courtesy, an explain'n ta us why we should be trust'n ye. Yer record wit' us no be so good."

Instantly Cestator knew that Shepard was not one to try and play around, right then and there he decided he liked the man. He began telling his story leaving nothing out. Shepard stopped him from time to time to ask a question about something that was said, but for the most part he merely sat there listening intently.

After a few hours Cestator finished his story and Shepard sat there for a short time deep in thought. After a few moments of grumbling he looked up and smiled. *"Well me boy I believe ye, an I do be glad tha' ye did cooperate. Well since tha' be settled I be need'n to be go'n an gett'n some things settled at home. Ye can bet though that I will be get'n back ta give ye some o' real train'n. Till then though I'll be leav'n ye in Slanoth's capable hands. Ye best be sure ye get plenty o' rest an enjoyment outa the time ye spend'n wit' Slanoth. When I be gett'n back I'll be whip'n ye into shape so ye look like a real man."* With that Shepard stood patted Cestator's shoulder and left the room.

When he was gone Cestator took a moment to absorb what he had just heard, he looked at Slanoth puzzled. "You look much different from our last encounter that I remember. You look much younger, but your wisdom glows in your eyes so I can tell you are who you say you are. Let me guess then, Cargon has done that to you so you will be able to train me, am I right?"

Slanoth smiled pleasantly, but then noticed it was lost on Cestator, for the man still had a dark look about him. "Yes you would be correct in your guess, Cargon did just that. He felt it necessary for me to be able to match you."

Cestator cracked his half smile, and Slanoth flinched inwardly at the wickedness of it. "Well then that would be a good thing. There was no way you could keep up with me as an old man. Now tell me, who was that man there, he seemed to be someone worthy of respect and trust?"

Slanoth smiled and patted Cestator on the shoulder trying to dispel the dark feeling that had overridden the mood in the room. "You have a good judge of character my friend. That was General Bear Shepardalious, and you would do well to trust him. I have known him for many years and he has never let me down."

"Hmm . . . Yes he does fit the part well. I have been on the other side of the battlefield with him a time or two. He does seem quite intelligent, and appears to know much in the way of warfare. I can see he is not a man to be trifled with that is for certain."

"Ah . . . Cestator you certainly do have a gift." Slanoth said with a light chuckle. "Well then enough of that, I must say your story is quite intriguing. I would like to hear more at another time, but for now do you feel well enough to move into regular quarters?"

"Yes so long as they are better than these awful rooms. It may sound strange but I can feel the sickness in this place. Before we leave however, when will we begin this training you speak of? I feel like I have never before, I could start this very moment if you are ready."

Slanoth chuckled, a knowing laugh. "Ah the impatience of youth, you are feeling the after effects of the healing. If you try to stand too quickly you will surely fall. The effects will soon wear off and you will be more tired than you ever have been before. So we should get you up to your quarters as quickly as possible."

"That is not possible I have never felt better. I feel that I could take on those greal once again. Besides that I am older than even Shepard there I know what I can do, so you have no room to consider me youthful." Cestator then turned and put his feet on the floor. He began to stand then fell back on the bed. His legs were too weak to hold him up. "Damn . . . I can hardly stand, what is wrong here. I feel that I should be able to run, but my legs will not hold me."

Slanoth flinched again he really was going to have to teach these people some manors. All the cursing was going a bit far. He walked over to offer Cestator a helping hand. "What I said stands on the grounds that you knew your limits when you were immortal, now that you are not, everything is different. So yes you may be older than all of us but when it comes to things like healing and limits here on this plane you are still a student. Now here take my arm I will help you to your quarters. It is a bit of a walk from here, and you may not make it all the way."

Cestator shook his head gruffly. "No I will do it myself. I am no babe that needs to be carried. I can do this with no one's help." With that he slowly got to his feet, limped to the door, and stepped out of the room.

Slanoth watched Cestator limp past and sighed deeply at his back. "Oh dear Cargon you have brought him to me to train, yet he needs so much more than that. I only hope there is enough time to do what is needed." Slanoth left the room shutting the door behind him. He then led Cestator up to his quarters.

As the door to the healing room closed a shimmering light appeared and a ghostly figure stepped out. "Ah my friend that is exactly why I have brought him to you and Shepard." Cargon said with a smile.

As they reached Cestator's new quarters Slanoth opened the door and turned around. "Now, you will be down stairs in the main dining hall come dawn. Simply ask any of the servants walking around how to get there, they will gladly show you the way. For now however you will go to bed and rest. Is that understood?" Slanoth said in a commanding voice leaving no room for argument. Cestator began to protest a bit, but Slanoth cut him off short. "Good, now that we have that settled I will see you in the morn. Be sure you are not late for there is much to be done and not much time to do it in."

Satisfied that his orders would be followed Slanoth turned and walked away heading to his own quarters. "So it begins," he sighed. "I had not expected it to occur so soon. I certainly do hope that you know what you are doing Lord."

Slanoth reached the end of the hall and was about to turn the corner when he heard a voice from behind him. "Well I am sorry dear friend that it has come upon you so soon. It was quite inevitable I'm afraid. I also do hope that we are doing the right thing for even I cannot see the final outcome of this war."

Slanoth quickly turned around to see who had snuck up behind him. He then saw a ghostly figure standing there. He quickly dropped to one knee before his god.

"Oh Slanoth rise before me, I do so wish that you would stop doing such. You have more than earned the right to stand before me. I need no show of loyalty from you. I have told you before I consider you a close and personal friend."

Slanoth shook his head. "I do it out of respect for you Lord. It is something I shall always do. I also thank you once again for honoring me by calling me a friend."

"Slanoth, we have known each other for a long time now, so of course I am going to call you friend. I do also enjoy talking to you."

"Well Lord I surely do thank you, but do you not have many things to attend to? I know that you are quite busy and must have many things to do."

Cargon smiled. "You asked me a question so I came to answer you in person. Now that I am here is there anything else you would like to ask me?"

"Yes in fact lord there is one thing that I would like to know. Was it you who brought Shepard back into my life? Seeing him once again has eased some of the pain of losing Randor."

"You are quite welcome my friend it worked out nicely that he was so close by. I did what I could to influence it and I was lucky enough that it was timed just right."

"I thank you lord for everything that you have done for me. I do not know how I could ever repay you for everything." Slanoth said with tears welling up in his eyes.

"Oh Slanoth do not worry about any of it. You have more than earned everything. Well then if there is nothing more that you need, I should get on to other things for as you have guessed I am very busy. So I will allow you to rest I know you have much work to do. Remember what you do is for the sake of the world, so be hard on Cestator. I will be watching with anticipation. I want to see him on the ground much over the next few weeks."

Slanoth smiled and bowed. "I will not let you down lord he will learn all of what it is to be a paladin."

Cargon nodded solemnly and waved, then without a word he was gone as quickly as he had appeared. Slanoth shook his head thinking he would never get used to Cargon doing that. He turned and began to walk down the hall to his quarters.

After just a few steps he felt an icy chill grip his spine. The hairs on the nape of his neck stood on end, and he froze in place for a moment. An unexplainable fear coursed through his veins, and his skin began to crawl. He slowly turned around gripping the hilt of his sword.

At the end of the hall a pair of drapes fluttered by an open window. Shadows danced across the floor as the flames from the many lamps set on the wall flickered in the breeze. He began to dismiss the feelings for a cold breeze coming in through the open window, but a deep ache in the pit of his stomach told him it was something more sinister.

He carefully searched the hall with his eyes, checking every shadow, every doorway. Then in the corner by the window he saw a deeper darker shadow. He strained to see what could be lurking there. Yet he could not place any physical presence there, and after a short time of not seeing anything out of the ordinary about it he began to turn away. When it was nearly out of his line of vision Slanoth noticed the shadow move in an unnatural way. The movement was slight but it was enough for him to catch it out of the corner of his eye.

He turned around quickly gripping the hilt of his sword. Thoughts racing through his mind Slanoth began to slowly walk towards the end of the hall. His heart raced with renewed fear as he watched for any more signs of movement.

Up ahead he suddenly heard footsteps coming from around the corner. Slanoth froze instantly and pulled Justice partway from its sheath. As the footsteps came closer he backed up against the wall preparing for any attack that may come. He had long ago learned there was no place that was absolutely safe from all evil.

The footsteps stopped just short of coming around the corner, as though the person was aware of his presence. Slanoth then slowly freed Justice, trying not to give himself away. He ducked into a doorway trying to make himself less visible to anyone coming around the corner. He knew most paladins would stand out in the open or even charge headlong into battle, but Slanoth knew from years of experience that was usually a foolhardy maneuver. He had long since learned to size up his opponents before he tried anything.

He then heard the faint sound of steel scraping against steel, as though someone were pulling out a knife. Slanoth's heart began to race in fear and anticipation. He took a deep breath and held it. His muscles tensed up ready to spring into action.

After what seemed an eternity the footsteps slowly began again. Slanoth prepared himself to spring at the first sign of hostility when this person stepped out. The figure stepped out of the shadows that wrapped around the corner of the hall. Yet even then it was hard to make out much about the man. What could be seen was that he was a tall slender figure that did not appear to be overly imposing. Slanoth however was not one to take any chances so he backed up a little further into the doorway so he would not be seen as he examined the man further.

The stranger did not appear to see him yet, but Slanoth was not about to take any chances. The man suddenly stopped and looked around as though he knew that there was someone else in the hall. In the darkness Slanoth could not see the man's face, but he did hold a strange weapon in his right hand. When the man turned towards the open window Slanoth slipped out from his hiding place intending to find out what this man was up to.

When the man realized Slanoth was behind him and he turned around Slanoth put his sword to the man's throat. Finding the tip of a sword at his throat the man jumped back and fell to the ground, his weapon flying from his hand and making a dull hollow clunk when it hit the ground. "No please do not kill me I am merely a simple servant. Please I beg you."

Hearing the voice Slanoth realized who the man was. It was Bernard an old servant who had been at the temple for many years. Feeling quite the fool he replaced Justice to its sheath. "Oh Bernard I am truly sorry old friend, it would seem that my nerves are on edge here tonight."

"Oh my, Lord Slanoth" Bernard said with a little shock himself. "I did not know you were about this evening."

Slanoth let out a sigh of relief, and offered Bernard a hand up. Happy to still be alive, Bernard took the hand and wiped his brow trying to slow his heavy breathing.

"All is well lord." Bernard said with a still shaky voice. He then bent down and picked up the oil can he had dropped in his fall. Then shook his head when he saw the oil stain on the floor.

"Bernard," Slanoth said with a smile. "I do apologize for startling you I feel such the fool, but tell me have you seen anyone else about this night?"

Bernard waved off the apology. "Worry not lord we have all been on edge lately there seems to be something in the air. There was no harm done, save for my heart racing and sadly the new stain there on the floor. I will have to get it cleaned on the morn, but to answer your question, no lord everyone is in their quarters. I was filling the oil lamps and I was going to turn in myself, but I have not seen anyone else in some time. Why is it that you ask?"

Slanoth waved off the question. "Oh it is nothing I have just been letting my imagination get the better of me. Well then thank you Bernard, and I am surely sorry for startling you, but I had best be getting some rest myself, so good night." With that he headed off to his quarters.

Slanoth disappeared down the hall and Bernard filled the last of the lamps. He shivered as a chill overcame him. He rubbed his arms trying to dispel the cold and turned towards the source. He noticed the open window rubbed his arms again then walked over and closed it. Looking around and seeing nothing more to do for the night he yawned and headed off to the servants quarters.

In the quiet of the empty hall the dark shadow in the corner stretched out to the window. Ever so slowly the window opened and the shadow slipped out disappearing into the night.

Chapter 6

Training Begins

The next morning Cestator awoke the moment the sun crested the horizon, and its light shone into the window of his room. He was surprised to hear that there was quite a bit of activity outside his door. He got up and dressed quickly remembering Slanoth's orders the night before. He opened the door and to his surprise there was a tall servant standing outside.

"Ah sir you are awake," the man said when Cestator emerged. "Come, follow me Lord Slanoth awaits you in the main dining hall." He turned and began to head down the hall not looking back to see if Cestator followed.

"Wait just a moment there," Cestator called out. "How long has everyone been awake? The sun has only been up for a few moments now."

"Why, Lord Slanoth has been in the dining hall for some time now. The day starts quite early here in the temple. I was sent to fetch you just a few moments ago. I would have woken you, but I was told you needed to rest. Now please follow me for everyone wishes to speak with you." With that the man continued down the hall.

Cestator was slightly intrigued as to who these people were that wished to speak to him. Knowing well how this could turn out he smiled, most of the men here would know by now who he was. He followed the servant thinking that things were about to get interesting. As they approached the doors to the dining hall Cestator heard men laughing and talking. The servant opened the door and motioned Cestator to enter.

Without a word Cestator walked into the dining hall. The moment he stepped through the doors, the room became deathly quiet. Everyone was staring at him, and some of the men were whispering to others near them. He had no doubt what they were discussing.

Slanoth was the first to break the silence. "Ah Cestator come in, sit and eat." He said as he motioned to an empty chair beside a large burly man with a scar that ran from his right cheek across his nose and up to his left temple and from where he stood Cestator would guess the man's left eye was missing. This did not appear to inhibit him in anyway however for he sat at Slanoth's right hand, which made him of some importance.

Cestator looked at the chair for a moment. A frown lightly touched his face but just as quickly it was gone. He shrugged and walked over to the chair then sat down. All eyes followed him, the silence felt like a physical entity and his footsteps were disturbing it.

When he was seated Slanoth stood and addressed him. "Now then Cestator since you know no one here. Allow me to introduce everyone." Slanoth then began to introduce everyone around him. Cestator looked at each man as Slanoth named him and made a mental note of each, especially as to which of them scowled at him. When Slanoth finally reached the large burly man beside him Cestator paid extra close attention. "Finally this large fellow here between us is Braggor. He trains all of the men who come through here, I have asked him to begin your training for me."

Cestator jumped from his seat angrily, and his chair skidded across the floor. The anger burned in his eyes, he felt somewhat betrayed. "Slanoth I did not come here to train under this ox. If I wanted to get training from an oaf like him I would not have come here. I came here to train under your guidance."

Instantly Cestator was surrounded with steel. All of the men stood drew their swords, and held them at his throat. Bragger spoke up saying what every other man was thinking. "Call me what you will I do not care, but if ever I hear you take that tone with Lord Slanoth again I will personally separate that arrogant head from your shoulders."

Cestator smiled at them showing a confidence in his abilities, and that he had this situation under his control glimmered in his eyes. Bragger was the only man who kept his composure under that look. The rest of the men took a step back, losing some of their confidence. None of them quite understanding, what had just happened.

Suddenly the ring of steel echoed throughout the hall. Everyone looked back to see what had happened. They stared in shock at what they saw. Slanoth had drawn Justice, and he held the sword hilt up and was praying upon it. He then laid it upon the table point facing him.

The men feeling ashamed of what they had done lowered their swords. Each muttered an apology to Slanoth for their foolish actions.

Slanoth scowled at them. "I am not the one you should be asking forgiveness from. Your apologies should be directed towards Cargon and our guest there."

The men mumbled a short prayer to Cargon asking for his forgiveness, and then returned to their seats. Cestator smirked knowing he would never get any kind of apology from any of the men. He was not surprised in the least. He would have done the same if the positions were reversed. Without a word he pulled his chair back up and sat down.

"Now Cestator please trust my judgment in this matter, Braggor here is highly experienced in training men. He has trained all but the oldest of the men here in the temple. Oh yes and I do believe that Shepard wishes to take part in your training as well."

Braggor's eyes opened wide with surprise. "Lord Slanoth, please pardon the interruption but did you say that General Shepard will be taking part in his training as well?"

"Yes Braggor, that is correct. The general was the one who had brought Cestator to us last night, and he has taken him under his wing. Shepard has gone home to settle a few maters then he will be returning."

Braggor smiled then turned to Cestator. "A word of advice to you, General Shepard is the best there is. He is hard but he is fare. Do not try to argue his word for he will show you to be lacking."

Cestator nodded not quite understanding what the man meant, and not really caring for he had never known anyone who could best him. "Right, well if it is the same to everyone else here I would just like to get started right away."

"Now that is what I like to hear, someone ready for a good hard day. Good we must first get approval from Lord Slanoth, but I have no troubles with starting now." Braggor then looked to Slanoth for approval to leave.

Slanoth nodded. "That would be just fine. In fact I think it is time everyone returned to their duties. There is much to be done today."

Everyone stood, and began to leave saying their thanks to Cargon for the meal. Just as Bragger reached the door Slanoth called to him.

"Braggor could you stay a moment please, I have something to discuss with you in private."

"Of course Lord Slanoth I am at your disposal." Bragger then turned to Cestator. "Wait for me out in the courtyard I will join you in a few moments."

Cestator not happy about being dismissed in such a manor frowned but did as he was bid. Braggor turned around and shut the door behind him. He returned to his seat beside Slanoth bowed slightly and sat down.

When he was finally seated Slanoth went on. "Braggor when you train him I want you to push him to his limits. I want to know how far he is willing to go. I do not want him to take this lightly."

Braggor smiled and nodded. "I understand Lord Slanoth. Fear not he will learn to respect your decision."

"Good, now I think you should not keep our guest waiting. Thank you again Braggor, I know how difficult it is for you."

"Think nothing of it Lord, I can get past it for the sake of all, and it is my duty to serve you, and Lord Cargon in any way that I can."

A warm smile touched Slanoth's face. "I am glad you can my friend, for I know it will be difficult for many of the men here. Your willingness to help may make it easier for them."

"It is my honor to serve Lord." With that Braggor stood and left the dining hall shutting the door as he went. When the door closed and he was alone Slanoth sighed in relief. It occurred to him that he was doing that quite often lately. He looked up at the statue of Cargon and smiled. "Well Lord you certainly did not say that it would be easy. I certainly do hope that this works out better than what we have seen so far."

Suddenly there was a knock at the door, and Slanoth called for the person to enter. The door opened and a tall well-built man entered.

"Lord Slanoth may I have a word with you for a moment?"

"Yes of course William what it is I can do for you? I am always here to help anyone in need."

William walked in and sat next to Slanoth, bowing before he took his seat. "Lord I must apologize for my actions earlier. I know the wrong I have committed, and I feel ashamed, but it felt so good having Cestator at the tip of my sword. As you well know, Cestator brutally murdered my parents, when I was a boy!"

Slanoth nodded sorrowfully, for he knew the circumstances behind their deaths, and how William felt. There were many men in the temple with similar stories, but none as gruesome as his. Slanoth worried about him the most for that reason, he never truly fit in with the other clerics and was always was mistrustful of them, yet through it all, William had always shown the most promise.

"Yes William I do remember. Yet we must always remember that Cargon calls us to forgive those who wrong us. It is hard I know but Cargon will help you if you ask. Now please go on. What is it that ails you this day?"

"You know that I came here for many reasons, but what drove me the hardest was that perhaps one day I would get my chance to kill Cestator. When we all had our blades at his throat, he did not even react. Instead he simply smiled and looked at us, as if he were the one in control of the situation, it frightened me, my Lord. To be truthful I have not been that scared and angry since the first time I faced him. I have heard the tales of him and the things he was said to do, but those were stories to frighten children, or so I thought until he visted my home."

Slanoth had seen this quite often. Where men were confident they had a situation under control only to realize they were wrong, yet sadly the outcome usually was far worse. He patted William on the shoulder to try and reassure him. "It is quite all right that you were frightened and angry. William, no man who ever faced

Cestator would ever blame you. Just know that what he did however was not very special it was simply a tactic to intimidate you. The moment you backed away from him would have given him the time to take over. He did it out of pure habit, but he did restrain himself. That look also would have served as a way for him to keep the chaotic creatures of evil in line."

"I see, well I do thank you Lord for helping me. I do believe that I have much to think about today. I must make some decisions about what I feel, and do some praying to Cargon for forgiveness and guidance."

"That is good William, I truly am happy you are so understanding. Now then, are there no other things that you must be doing as well?"

"Yes of course lord thank you again for your time I do appreciate it. You have helped me make amends with my past."

"That is quite fine William that is exactly why I am here, to help those in need. Now go out to the yard and tell the men I will be there shortly."

"Yes of course, my Lord." William said as he left, and shut the door behind him.

After leaving the dining hall Braggor headed to the stables. He stopped a young boy working there, and told him to saddle his horse quickly, for he was quite busy. The boy went to his work as told, and a few moments later he came out with Braggor's chesnut mare. Braggor smiled impressed with the boy's swiftness.

"Is that all you require master Braggor?" The boy asked with his head down so he would not have to look up into Braggor's face.

Braggor frowned and took the boy's chin in his large hand and lifted his head to look into his eyes. "What is your name lad?"

The boy was small and looked a bit underfed, but Bragger could see beyond that. He could see that this little boy could someday be a good strong man with the proper guidance.

The boy flinched slightly at the scar on Braggor's face but he found his voice after a moment. "My name is Jonah sir, but I am just a simple stable boy. My mother died and my father could not take care of me so he brought me here. Master Higgins took mercy on me and gave me this job and a loft in the barn."

"Hmm . . . I see, well lad gather your things and go to the servants entrance and ask for Bernard. Tell him that I would like him to get you some squire's clothes, and to find you a room. I will not tolerate my new squire sleeping in hay lofts and dressing in those rags."

The boy stood there dumbfounded for a moment, not sure what to do. "But master Bragger, what of master Higgins he will wonder where I have gone?"

Braggor smiled. "Worry not, upon my return I will tell Higgins that I have made you my new squire."

A large grin spread across the boy's face as he ran to get his belongings. Braggor smiled and mounted his horse. Not wanting to waste any more time he rode off to where Cestator awaited him. When Braggor finally reached the courtyard Cestator was pacing, and mumbling under his breath. Braggor rode up and stopped beside him. "Are you ready for a nice run today?" he asked with the smile still gleaming on his face.

Cestator scowled at this, not very happy that he was left to wait for so long a time. He had wanted to do much today and this big oaf was off doing who knew what. "What kept you I was starting to think that I was going to have to find something else to do? In the time it took you to get here I could have run around this courtyard a dozen times already."

The smile faded from Braggor's face. He was really beginning not to like this man. He was cold and cared for no one, but himself. "Well then, I will take that as a yes, so follow me and do not fall behind or I will have to drag you." With that Braggor trotted his horse out the gate and over the bridge not looking back to see if Cestator followed.

Cestator grunted and scowled deeply at the man's back then followed. As he was running over the bridge he noticed something odd. Down on the water below, there appeared to be an island but it was shrouded in a deep darkness. He decided to ask about it at a later time, and he continued after Braggor.

After several miles Braggor looked back and saw that Cestator was still not far behind. He was quite surprised to see that the man seemed hardly winded. They had been running for most of the morning and noon was just around the corner. Braggor decided that it was time for a rest, and he knew of a small clearing not far from where they were. He slowed his horse to a walk so she could cool down before stopping.

Cestator caught up to Braggor then began walking alongside the horse. "Why have you slowed down? I could have run much farther than this."

Braggor looked down at him and shook his head. "There is a clearing up ahead where we can rest for a spell and refresh ourselves. You may not show it outwardly, but I can see you are winded. Do not try to dismiss it. You put up a good front I admit, but I have done this for many a years and I can see it in your eyes. Also let me tell you something about all those who serve Cargon. We are all brothers, and we do not hide things from each other, that's how men get killed. It is wise to hide such things from your enemies I agree, but it is unwise to hide it from your friends. Do you understand the wisdom of this?"

Cestator nodded back. "Yes I can see what it is you are saying. It is however difficult to change so rapidly, as I am sure you know. So if that is how it is to be, where is this clearing of yours I certainly could use a bit of a rest?"

Braggor smiled, this was the first time he had seen the man soften at least slightly. "So you are not made of stone." He chuckled. "The clearing is merely a few paces ahead."

A few minutes later they reached the clearing. Braggor jumped off his horse and tethered her to a tree by a small brook running through the clearing. Braggor then took a drink from the brook. The water was icy cold and felt good. He splashed some up on his face to clear the dust from the road. The frigid water was shocking at first and he gasped for air, but after the initial shock, it felt refreshing.

When he was finished he walked over to a log lying on the ground and sat down. He looked up at the bright sun shining above. It felt warm and comforting, and that raised his spirit further. When Cestator finished freshening up he sat down across from Braggor.

Braggor stared at the man for a moment wondering what the man was up to. "So tell me, now that you have seen most of the men in the temple what do you think?"

Cestator smirked at the question. "They look like a group of farmers who have had a bit of training. They are certainly unlike any knights that I have ever seen."

Braggor laughed heartily at this. "Well that would be because most of them were farmers, or something of the sort at one point or another. All the men who train at the temple are common men. Not one of them is of high standing blood, as a knight of the crown would be."

"In many ways that puts us at an advantage however. Think on it, which makes a more dangerous opponent, a man looking for glory and gold, or a man defending his homeland and family. Also because we all were commoners most of the people are more willing to give us a place to rest for the night."

Cestator frowned, he found the man's words logical, but he was having a hard time picturing Braggor working in the fields. Everything about the man spoke of him being a soldier. "So are you telling me that you were a farmer at one time in your life? I said most of them looked like farmers, but I just can't see you being one."

Braggor chuckled heartily. "No, not quite, I was the son of a Thatcher, until my family was taken by the plague, I by Cargon's good graces survived yet it left me this scared body you see here. So then orphaned and alone I lived on the streets making a living how I could. Then one day General Shepard caught me and brought me to the temple."

"What of the scar on your face, how did you receive that may I ask?" Cestator asked intrigued by the man's tale.

Braggor's face went instantly dark and a scowl touched his lips. Cestator knew instantly what had happened and before the man could say a word he spoke up. "I am sorry for all transgressions I may have had against you in the past. I find myself regretting much of what I have done."

Braggor shook his head and the smile returned. "One thing I have learned from this." He said as he pointed at the scar. "Is that you should never have regret in your heart. It is a wasted emotion and can do you no good. The best way to make up for the things you have done is through your actions. If you do good things for others, people will begin to forget the past."

Cestator gave Braggor his half smile and nodded. "Thank you for that, I will keep it in mind. So if everyone in the temple is of common blood then what is Slanoth's story? He of all I would have thought would be of noble blood."

Braggor's smile faded for a moment but returned quickly. "That is a good question, if you could figure that one out you could be a rich man. For no one knows, but the few people who knew him when he was young and now the only one alive would be the general. In fact many men have put out a bounty on the information, but if there is anyone who knows they are not talking. The latest thought is that he is the unnamed son of Cargon."

Cestator scoffed at the thought. "That is foolish Cargon has no children that I or my father know of. That I can say with the utmost confidence for we have watched this very closely," Cestator thought about it a moment then decided it was not worth the trouble. "So if what you say is true, then what separates the Paladins of Cargon from the average men who serve him?"

Braggor's face instantly darkened and he seemed haunted by some far off memories that cut deeply. After a few moments he appeared to return from the memories, but the frown did not leave him. "Well I guess that you do need to know, so I will tell you." He paused again seeming to be haunted by those memories, then after a moment he answered. "All Paladins of Cargon have faced the trials of the isle."

Cestator frowned not sure what Braggor meant. Then he remembered the dark island he saw on the bridge. "Do you mean that dark island out in the bay, the one that can be seen from the bridge?"

Braggor nodded solemnly and his voice seemed haunted when he spoke. "Yes that would be the one. You see, to become a paladin you must face the trials it brings, and it is different for each man." Braggor then reached into his shirt and pulled out a pendant. It was made of the rare red platinum, and wrought in the shape of the mighty phoenix. "Finally all those who successfully face the trials receive this upon leaving the isle. It is as you might say a reward and proof to all that you have become one of the few."

Cestator jumped to his feet with the intent to begin the trials at that moment. "Ha . . . if that is all there is to it then I will face these trials now. Take me there so I may finish this, and become what I have come to be."

Braggor shook his head firmly, and motioned Cestator to sit. When the man was sitting again he went on. "No I will not intentionally send you to your death, no matter who you are."

"I have faced things far worse than anything that could be there, and yet here I am before you." Cestator said with his trademark smirk upon his face.

"There is your first mistake which would kill you. If you are to face the trials you must first discard your arrogance. Also your faith in Cargon must be strong. You must be able to let him guide your thoughts and actions. It will test this to the limits and far beyond. All the men who come out of there are never quite the same again, it changes you. Those who fail however, rarely ever come out alive, and those who have would have been better off if they had not."

Suddenly Braggor's horse whinnied slightly, but loud enough to catch the two men's attention. Then the horse's nostrils flared, and she snorted. Braggor looked at her confused at what could be bothering the warhorse. "What's wrong with you girl? What has got the burr under your saddle? Calm yourself there." Braggor walked over to his horse and tried to calm her down, but she only seemed to get more agitated. He had never seen her act in such a way.

Cestator's demeanor instantly changed to a dark and deadly one. He turned into a completely different person than he was but a few moments before. "Get on your horse and keep her under tight reign. We're being surrounded by orcs."

"What, how can you tell that? That is not possible there is nothing more dangerous than a lynx in this forest. The city guards' patrol here every day to be sure it is safe for travelers."

"Well I don't know about whether they do or don't, but I am telling you there are orcs out here. The first sign was how your horse is acting, you see horses hate orcs. The mere smell of orcs in the area drives them crazy. Also I can sense them in a way. It is as though I can feel the wickedness of them. I have been around them so much that I know how they smell sound, and act. Your horse has never faced them before that is obvious. I guarantee if you don't hold her tight she will bolt. I have seen it countless times."

Braggor did as Cestator instructed without a word. He took hold of his horse's reigns tightly and close to her neck not giving her room to do anything he did not want her to. With his free hand he pulled out his sword and readied himself.

He looked down at Cestator to see what the man was doing. What he saw made his blood run cold. Cestator had his dark sword out, and at the ready, his posture was that of a viper ready to strike. The man looked like death incarnate. Braggor shivered at the thought. Suddenly his horse became frantic, and tried to run, but he held her still with every bit of strength he had.

"Hold her still, if you let her run she will keep going until she runs herself to death under you. I will try to keep most of them away from you. It will be hard to hold her when they attack but you have got to be steadfastly in control."

Then as though Cestator had brought it into being the horse went wild. It took everything Braggor had to keep her under control. Then suddenly they appeared. The disgusting creatures were a dark green in color and had warts and scars all over, and were the size of a large man. They wore old dented, and rusty mismatching armor. Likely pieces they had gotten from previous victims. Then Braggor got a good whiff of them. The stench of the creatures made his nostrils burn and his eyes water. They grinned wickedly showing off rotted and broken teeth.

Braggor looked around to see their odds and saw that there were ten of the creatures. He knew then they were in trouble because he was having a difficult time keeping his horse under control. Then the attack came, four charged straight at him. He worked hard to fend them off. In skill he outmatched them, but their number and the fact he had a wild horse below him made matters difficult.

Then his horse bucked and kicked out with her back legs and caught one orc in the jaw. The creature flew across the clearing and fell in a heap on the ground. Braggor patted her on the side with his knee letting her know she did well. Then as though that brought the horse to her senses she calmed down. Braggor immediately took advantage of this and made short work of the remaining three creatures. He then looked to see if Cestator needed help. What he saw however shocked him. He saw what seemed to be five orc bodies lying there though he could not be sure because they were cut to ribbons. Cestator however, was nowhere in sight.

Then from behind him Braggor heard something rustling through the woods. He quickly turned his horse to face the new threat. He sighed in relief as Cestator stepped out from the tree line. "I surely am glad you are on our side here. I feared you were another orc or something. So what happened here?" Braggor asked as he pointed at the bodies lying on the ground.

Cestator smiled, "A little practice. Orcs may be mean and ruthless, but they are quite unskilled in the dance. One ran off and I saw that you had it under control so I went after it. It was trying to get help. This was only a scouting party. There is another group of about twenty orcs off to the north. You should return to the temple and warn the others."

"I agree, we cannot allow those creatures to run wild out here, there are many farms nearby." Braggor then reached down for Cestator to take his hand. "Here get on. It will be faster if we ride."

Cestator shook his head and waved Braggor on. "No go on, you can get there even faster with only one person on your horse. Don't worry about me I will be right behind you."

Braggor nodded snapped the reigns and his horse began to run back to the city. After a short distance he looked back and did not see Cestator anywhere. He cursed himself for a fool at letting the man stay behind, but kept running hoping that Cestator did not do anything foolish.

Cestator watched as Braggor rode off towards the city. He smiled wickedly then turned back to the orc party. He carefully worked his way through the trees being careful not to alert them. When he found the orcs once again they had traveled a surprising distance. This troubled him greatly, they were after something and he intended to find out what it was.

He let the orcs pass before he moved out onto the road again. The creatures did not seem too concerned about anyone following them, for they did not even look back or notice he had gotten behind them. Cestator found this odd and he wondered what could be driving the creatures so hard that they were oblivious to their surroundings.

Cestator ran up behind the creatures and stabbed the last creature in line. The orc looked down and saw the end of Cestator's blade protruding from its' chest. It tried to scream as he pulled out the blade, but all that came out was a gurgling sound since its lungs were filled with blood. At that moment the others turned around to see what was happening. Only then did the orcs realize he was behind them.

Cestator decapitated another orc as it began to turn around. Before the creature hit the ground he severed the hands of another that was reaching for its weapon. He turned away from that creature, stabbed another, and split it open from navel to neck. The orc watched in horror as its innards poured out onto the ground. It looked up at Cestator and he smiled at it then shrugged as it fell to the ground.

As the creature fell Cestator moved onto the next, this one was slightly more prepared yet that did not help it survive any longer. The creature swung a rusty sword in a downward arc intending to split his head open while he was turned away. He easily blocked the wild swing with his sword, then with his other hand Cestator pulled out his dagger, and stabbed the creature in its thigh. The orc roared in pain, but Cestator quickly silenced it driving his sword up through its jaw into the orc's brain. Blood spilled out onto his hand but he ignored it and moved onto the next creature.

The handless orc then charged him barring broken and rotted teeth. Cestator simply swung high and using the creature's momentum he gave it a permanent smile then the top half of its head slid off and fell to the ground. By this time the creatures regrouped, their initial shock of being attacked by a lone man had faded. In their stance Cestator could see that they were overly confident in their numbers, and that was their greatest downfall.

One of the creatures in the back grunted some kind of orders, and three of them charged at him. Using his sword Cestator cut the legs off of one at the knees, and it toppled to the ground. At the same moment he drove his dagger into the second orc's eye burring it deep into the creature's brain. Then with one fluid motion he brought his sword around and gutted the third, and split the legless creature's skull.

Again the orc in the back barked out orders to the rest. This time the others hesitated a moment before six more charged at him. That moment's hesitation was more than enough time for Cestator to put down his sword and dagger, then pull out the two throwing knives he had in the top of his boots. With just a flick of his wrists the knives flew through the air directly towards their targets. One buried itself in the throat of the first of the six that were charging at him. The second blade found its home between the eyes of the leader, and he dropped where he stood.

Before the blades even found their marks Cestator had his sword and dagger in his hands. He was instantly on the move running towards the rest. As he reached the first he swung his sword in an upward angle cutting the creature in half from left hip to right shoulder. It stood there for a moment not quite realizing it had been wounded, but as Cestator ran by its' eyes glazed over. The top half of the creature slid down, and the legs crumpled to the ground. Even then Cestator did not pause. He stabbed the next creature in the gut with his dagger, and pulled up until the blade lodged itself in the orc's upper jaw. He let go of the blade and turned to the next creature. This orc was far more prepared than the others, yet it was terrible at the dance. The beast swung its blade in a wildly wide arc. Cestator easily blocked the swing then kicked the creature's knee out breaking it. The orc fell to the ground screaming in pain, clutching its leg, and rolling around.

Cestator ignored the creature at that point for the final four orcs joined the two that were already after him, and they now surrounded him. They feared his abilities, and thusly remained just out of his reach. Any time he tried to strike one it would jump back, and one behind him would jab at him. This was a very simple rudimentary tactic, and he was far too skilled to fall for something like it.

Cestator feigned an attack at one of the creatures. It predictably jumped back away from him, and as expected one of the creatures in the back tried to stab him. Instead of dodging however, he quickly turned around just barely avoiding the blade and faced the attacker. He grabbed the creature's wrist and pulled it towards him making the orc lose its balance. Cestator smashed the pommel of his sword into the creature's face and it dropped to the ground. He did not let go of the wrist however, instead he severed the arm and wrenched the sword free. Wasting no time he threw the blade piercing another of the creatures through the heart.

The remaining four grunted amongst themselves in hushed tones as they circled Cestator in hopes that he would not hear them. He did however catch a few words from them, and he could tell they wanted to run, but there was some greater force driving them. After a moment's hesitation all four rushed him swinging as they came. Cestator proved to be faster however. He backed away from the three that he could see, and directly in towards the one behind him that was swinging its sword up over its head. He flipped his sword back and stabbed the orc in the gut, then twisted the blade and pulled it around to the right splitting the creature's belly open.

The final three had to pull back their swings to avoid hitting each other. One of them was more nimble than the other two and it redirected its swing. The orc's blade pierced Cestator's left shoulder, and he roared more out of frustration that he was sloppy enough to allow it than he did out of pain. As he pulled the blade from the orc behind him he brought it around and severed the arm of the creature that had struck him. The orc stared dumbly at the stump that was left of its arm, and did nothing to stop its life giving blood from pouring out on the ground. The creature then fell to the ground headless, and Cestator moved on.

The two remaining orc's stared at him their eyes wide with fear. That fear of him now overcame whatever was driving them, and they turned to run. Cestator immediately took advantage of this. Showing no mercy he swung his sword low cutting the trailing creature's legs off mid-thigh. He then stepped over to the orc and drove his sword down into its screaming mouth pinning its head to the ground.

Cestator left his sword there and walked over to the leader's body and pulled out his knife and threw it at the fleeing orc. His aim was true and the struck the creature at the base of its skull. The orc's momentum made it fall face first into the ground.

Cestator turned back pulled out his sword and walked over to the last living orc. The creature was still writhing around on the ground screaming and clutching its shattered knee. He kicked the orc in the side, and put the tip of his sword under its chin. The orc's screams stopped, and it stared up at him defiantly.

"Why are you here, and who sent you?" Cestator asked the creature in the old language.

The orc snarled and started laughing at him, and answered him in a more guttural and harsh version of the same language. *"I not tell you. You go die miserable human. You threaten to kill me, I no care better me die now than stay alive and fail."*

Cestator frowned in frustration then quick as a flash he moved his blade and pierced the creature's right eye. The orc screamed in pain and spat out the worst obscenities it could come up with at him. He kicked the creature again and put the tip of his blade back under its chin. *"Who said I was going to kill you. I would rather make you suffer. So if you wish to avoid any more pain I would suggest you tell me everything I want to know."*

"Foul human you will no survive. They come for you. You die when others come." The orc then began laughing hysterically. *"You wait they find you and you die."*

"What are you talking about?" Cestator demanded. "What others, tell me or you are going to lose more than just an eye."

The orc spit in his face and snarled at him. *"I tell you nothing. You see when others come for you. They kill you good."*

Frustrated with the situation Cestator decided there was nothing more he could learn from the creature. He grabbed his dagger and threw it down. The blade buried itself in the orc's belly. It roared in pain and feebly tried to swing at Cestator. He easily blocked the swing, and pierced the orc's shoulder. He then bent down and pulled out his dagger. *"I was going to make it quick for you, but now you can suffer,"* Cestator said as he turned away.

He headed back to the temple avoiding the main road not wanting to be seen and have to answer any questions. When he was about half way back he heard a large group of soldiers ride past him towards his handy work. Cestator smiled wickedly and ran onward. "They are in for quite a surprise," he chuckled as he ran. Then without another thought or consideration he ran back to the temple.

Chapter 7

The Dance

After what seemed the longest ride he had ever taken Braggor saw the walls of Cerdrine. When he was close enough to be heard he shouted to the guards at the gate. Seeing who it was and hearing the urgency in his voice they let him pass without a word. He rode straight to the king's palace and demanded an audience.

When he told the guards at the door what had happened they quickly brought him before the king. Braggor bowed then explained the situation to the king and what had happened. Outraged that orcs would be in his kingdom Landren called for his guards, and had them send the army to deal with the creatures. He thanked Braggor, and dismissed him.

Braggor returned to the temple to report this news to Slanoth. He found Slanoth in the courtyard training the men. "Braggor, why have you returned so soon and why do you look as though you had the dark one himself on your tail." Slanoth called out to Braggor, when he saw the man.

Braggor stopped quickly and jumped off his horse. He ran the remaining distance to Slanoth. Curious of what was transpiring with Braggor's abrupt appearance the men in the yard stopped what they were doing and stared. Braggor scowled deeply. "Get back to work, or you will be doing an extra measure of work tonight."

Hearing this, they instantly went back to their training, but with one ear open trying to hear the news. Braggor stood there a moment and watched them, and when he was satisfied they were not going to stop again he motioned Slanoth to move over to the side a bit.

When he was satisfied they would not be overheard Braggor once again scowled at the men for acting like a gaggle of women listening in on the latest gossip. None of them directly saw the look but all felt his burning stare. He turned back to Slanoth and began to relay the news. "Lord Slanoth, we ran into a group of orcs out by the creek. We had stopped for a rest, and we were ambushed by the creatures. We dispatched them fairly easily, but there was a larger group to the north. I rode to the palace to inform his majesty Lord Landren, and then I returned here."

"Landren sent men to deal with them of course?" Slanoth said more as a statement than a question.

Braggor nodded in reply. "Yes of course milord. This does not bode well for us however. These are surely troubling times if orcs dare come this close to the city."

Slanoth pondered this for a moment knowing now that the battle had truly begun. He feared this was not to be the last incident like this. After a short pause Slanoth looked up with fear in his eyes. "Braggor tell me where is Cestator?"

"He stayed behind saying he would follow. I had offered him to ride with me but he refused. And when I looked back he was nowhere to be seen. I hope he did not do something foolish and got himself killed."

A frown lightly touched Slanoth's face, then was instantly gone again. "No I feel that Cestator would not do anything rash. He is far too intelligent for that."

Then suddenly, as Braggor was about to say something there was silence in the yard signifying that the men had stopped training. Braggor looked up and was about to scold them when suddenly one of them spoke up. "Look there The Tiger goes to face the Demon. This should be a good show."

Braggor looked where the man pointed and saw Cestator standing there covered in blood and some appeared to be his own. The man looked exhausted, nearly to the point of collapsing, but he stood tall with pride trying to show no weakness.

Then Braggor saw William walking towards Cestator. He instantly knew this was going to be trouble. Of all the men in the temple William was the loner, and the one who had the most to hate Cestator for. "William, hold there. I don't want you starting any trouble here." He called out trying to defuse the situation.

William turned and looked to Slanoth. For a moment he looked somewhat sad, but then he smiled. Slanoth saw peace in the man's smile. The same free smile that had been there before, and this time it even seemed to touch his eyes. For the first time in the many years he had known William, the man looked to be at peace. "Go on William, it is quite alright my son." He called out to the man.

Braggor looked at him questioningly, but said nothing out of respect. He decided that Slanoth in all his wisdom must have seen something he had missed.

Not waiting for any other approval, William continued his trek towards Cestator. Everyone in the yard held their breath in anticipation of the fight that was surely about to break out.

Cestator stood there watching this all transpire. He remembered the man from earlier in the morning. He was well built and looked to be strong, at least stronger than most of the men here in the temple. The man wore a sword at his hip and from his posture Cestator could see the man knew how to use it. He watched as the man drew closer, Cestator was exhausted and he knew if this man wanted to kill him he would be hard pressed to stop him. Then the man reached him, and smiled. The smile somehow seemed out of place, as though the man had not smiled in some time.

"So you are the one I have been chasing all my life. You are the dreaded Cestator son of the dark one. Well you don't look so bad to me."

Cestator smiled back at the man's sarcasm. He knew then at that moment there was nothing to fear from this man. "Yes that would be I, is there something that you want of me."

Williams smile faded slightly. The smile upon Cestator's face seemed cold and untrue, but he went on. "Yes . . . there is one thing that I ask of you. I ask you to forgive me my actions earlier today. I acted out of anger and hatred, and I was wrong. Lord Cargon teaches us better. So allow me to be the first to offer you my hand in friendship." When he finished William extended his arm out to Cestator, his smile returning in full force.

Cestator stood there a moment sizing up the man, deciding if he was being truthful. He looked into the man's eyes and saw that the smile was there as well. Slightly puzzled by this he looked down at the man's extended arm. He then smiled back and took the man's arm grabbing it close to the elbow in the sign of true friends.

William slightly surprised by the bold gesture gripped Cestator's arm in return and smiled brightly. "Well if you do not remember, my name is William. Now you look as though you have had quite a hard day, what say you we go inside and get cleaned up some?"

Cestator looked down at himself and realized how much blood he actually had on him. "You know that likely is the best offer I have had today." He said with a laugh.

William laughed as well, he offered Cestator help, and they walked to the temple talking and laughing.

Braggor watched in amazement as the two men grasped arms, and walked towards the temple as though they were old friends. "What has just happened here? Do my eyes deceive me or have I gone mad?"

Slanoth smiled at the question. It was a soft and reassuring smile that could put even the most raging person at ease. "It is nothing to be concerned for my son, William has finally found Cargon, and I think most importantly he has found himself. Enough of that though, tell me now what happened out there."

Braggor scratched his head in confusion. At one point he had known there would be trouble, mixing Cestator with the other men, but now he was unsure. Deciding it was not something to bother with at this time he turned to see what the others were doing. He found the other men standing there staring in the direction the two had gone. "Get back to training! The event is over now, so I want to hear some noise unless you want me to find something for all of you to do." The men in the yard instantly found something to do. Satisfied that the men were busy, Braggor turned back to Slanoth.

"Lord all I can say of this man you have brought us is that there is nothing that I can do to help him. When those orcs attacked he became the spirit of death in the flesh. I have never seen anything of the like. I would say he is a master of the blade. There was near to nothing left of the foul creatures from what I saw. I could hardly tell one part from the other."

Braggor paused a moment to remember the scene. "I still have trouble believing what I have seen. Though I did see some faults in him. He is quite arrogant, and is over pompous about his abilities. He also has little faith in others and is very mistrustful. Physically I have seen very few who could match him, but spiritually he is quite lacking."

Slanoth nodded his assent. He had known what the result of this test would be, but it was one that he knew had to be performed. "Thank you Braggor I do value your opinion in this. I had thought that it would take a bit more time than this, but it would appear we are being somewhat rushed along here. So I will take over his training come morning."

"Yes Lord Slanoth as you wish. If that is all that you need I will take over the men's training for you now."

"Yes of course Braggor that is fine, and thank you again for your help. I have much to prepare for tomorrow." Slanoth turned and started back towards the temple, and then there came a disturbance at the gate. He sighed and turned back to see what was wrong. It seemed life had become more eventful since he had agreed to do this.

After a few moments one of the kings Guards came through the gate asking for Braggor or Slanoth. The man looked worried and distraught, as though he had seen something very disturbing. Slanoth was the first to approach the guard. "What is it that I may do for you my son? You look that you have seen the seven gates."

The man bowed out of respect for whom stood before him, and at first the man could not find his words. "I . . . beg your pardon lord for interrupting you, yet this is of utmost importance. I was with the group of men sent to deal with the orcs out in the wild. However when we found the creatures they were all dead. No it was far worse, they were slaughtered violently. General Albrecht sent two of us to warn the king and yourselves of the impending danger. He fears there is something far more dangerous in the forest. At this very moment he hunts it."

Slanoth looked back at Braggor who was standing just behind him. He did not have to ask the question on his mind. He could see plain as day that Braggor was thinking the same thought. He looked to where William and Cestator had gone. Cestator looked to be more tired and bloodied than he should have been from Braggor's description.

Slanoth turned back to the messenger, and told him to inform the king and the general that he knew what had done this, and that he had it under control. He also asked the man to apologize for him for concerning everyone, and that he would explain everything at another time. He then dismissed the man, and turned back to Braggor. "Shall we find the story behind all of this?" He asked as he motioned towards the temple.

"I surely think that we must." Braggor said as he turned and headed for the doors.

As William helped Cestator along they grew to be better friends. William learned that Cestator had never known any man that he would trust enough to call friend, so he was honored to be the first.

As they walked down the hall to the baths they passed a group of servant girls. One of them ran up to them, and began walking beside them. "Hello William where are you headed at this time of day, should you not be training?"

William looked over at the girl. He had known who it was just by the ring in her voice. When he saw her however he could not help but smile, the girl was beautiful, her big brown eyes sparkled, and her full lips were in a bright smile. "Hello Ciara, how are you. Yes I would be training at this time, but as you can see my friend here has gotten himself, and I quite bloody so we are going to bathe."

Ciara's smile broadened at this. She looked Cestator up and down, and her eyes sparkled all the more. "Well then I shall draw the water for you." She said with a pleasant laugh.

Before William could say a word, she turned and ran off towards the kitchen. He looked back and watched her until she turned the corner. He looked back to Cestator and smiled. "Well friend you have just met the beauty of the temple. It is best if you do not try to argue with her. You will not win. When she gets something to her mind she is quite stubborn. So shall we get to the baths?"

Cestator nodded his consent, and they both walked the rest of the way to the bath chamber. They removed their soiled clothes and stepped into the baths. The water in them was cold but it felt refreshing nonetheless.

A few minutes later Ciara came in with two steaming buckets of water. She smiled deeply when she saw they had already gotten in. "I have some hot water here for you two. Would you like me to warm your baths?" She said with a flirting smile.

William smiled grandly, and lightly laughed. "Thank you Ciara could you just put them on the benches here?"

"Oh William you truly are humorous, I can add the water for you. Don't worry I will not scald you." Ciara went to the foot of the bath William was soaking in and slowly poured the hot water in.

William sighed as the heat spread throughout the tub. He looked up at Ciara and smiled. She smiled back at him and his heart fluttered for a moment. "Thank you Ciara that is exactly what I needed. It has been quite the hard day."

Ciara's smile brightened and she told him it was her pleasure as she turned away and headed towards Cestator's bath. When she came around to the foot of Cestator's tub she saw that his eyes were closed as though he were deep in thought.

She giggled softly, and he opened his eyes. She gasped at what she saw. This stranger had deep piercing green eyes that seemed to see right through her. He was well built and muscular, and he had a deep gash on his right shoulder. She was quite taken by him, but she quickly recovered her confident demeanor. "Why hello sir, I do not believe we have met, I am Ciara who might you be? I had thought that I knew every intriguing person here."

Cestator looked up at her with no expression upon his face, and she found this interesting. This man here before her was not the average would be hero who came through here. William was the first to speak however much to her dismay. She had so wanted to hear this stranger's voice.

"I am sorry Ciara I did not realize that not all knew of our friend's coming. The man there before you would be Cestator newest cleric of Cargon, He has traveled far and has done much to get here."

"I see . . . well Cestator It looks like you have gotten into a little trouble today, so allow me to help you." Without waiting for consent Ciara poured the hot water into the tub. Cestator did not so much as flinch as the scalding water rushed around him. He merely closed his eyes, and enjoyed the heat.

Ciara then walked around to the right side and sat down on the edge of the tub. Her heart racing, she then took a damp cloth and reached over to clean the wound on Cestator's shoulder. She nearly fell back when suddenly he gently grabbed her wrist stopping her. He opened his eyes and frowned. The frown made her heart race even faster. She was becoming quite intrigued with this man.

"What do you think you're doing?" He asked in a hard and very masculine voice that she found compelling.

"Your wound there, it is deep, and it is dirty. I was going to clean it out. You know if you do not do so it will go bad on you, and I would hate to see anything happen to you." He looked deep into her eyes. It felt to her as though he were looking straight into her soul. It chilled her for a moment and her legs went limp. The more time she spent with this man the more she wanted.

"It is fine I have had worse and lived. Now if you would not mind I would like to be left in peace for a time."

He released her and closed his eyes once again. Ciara stood a pout upon her full lips in all her eighteen years she had never been rejected. William watched as this transpired somewhat amused and somewhat shocked.

Suddenly a knock came upon the door, and a moment later Slanoth and Braggor walked in. Ciara quickly curtsied when she saw them. "Lord Slanoth, Master Braggor, how might the two of you be this fine day, is there something that I may help you with?"

Slanoth smiled at seeing the girl. "Hello Ciara. We are faring well today, but Braggor, and myself need to talk to these two gentlemen privately if you don't mind."

Ciara curtsied once again. She had always liked Slanoth because he had always been kind to her. She looked up to him as a favorite grandfather. "Of course lord Slanoth I was just going to take their clothes to be cleaned, and fetch them some new ones."

Slanoth's smile broadened. Ciara always liked that smile. It was warm and inviting, and it had always made her feel safe. Slanoth was the only man she knew that she could confess her deepest and darkest fears to, and he would understand and help her. Had he not been more than thrice her age she would have pursued him. Yet as it was she thought of him as the grandfather she never had. She then headed for the door. She paused a moment as she opened it and looked back at Cestator. Her smile broadened at the thought of the new conquest. She walked out and closed the door behind her.

As soon as the door closed behind the young girl, Braggor stepped up to Cestator, with anger burning on his face. "Who do you think you are? Do you have any idea, what kind of trouble you have caused? I told you to return to the temple, and you disobeyed my orders. That is not how a paladin of Cargon acts."

Slanoth walked up and put his hand on Braggor's shoulder. "Calm yourself Braggor it is alright no one was harmed today, praise be to Cargon. Let us hear what Cestator has to say about his actions before we condemn him for them. Lord Cargon teaches us not to cast judgment too quickly."

Braggor bowed his head in consent. He knew well Slanoth was right. "Yes of course Lord Slanoth you are correct, I have forgotten myself. I just worry about the men, and what could have happened."

Slanoth smiled and squeezed Braggor's shoulder. "It is all well my friend worry not of it." Slanoth then turned to Cestator and looked directly into his eyes. The smile faded from his face as he began to speak. "Now Cestator tell me why it was that you felt it necessary to battle a large group of orcs alone, even after Braggor told you to return to the temple?"

Cestator looked up without a shred of emotion on his face. The coldness of the look chilled Slanoth even in the hot steamy room. For a short time Cestator did not say a word. When he did speak however the words were even colder and devoid of emotion. "When I saw the creatures I knew there was only one reason they were here. It was no coincidence that they happened to appear where they have never been, at the exact time we were there. So I decided to give them what they wanted."

A cold smile then appeared upon Cestator's face. It was the half smile that all would soon come to know very well. "Of course I was not about to give it to them freely, and as I had told Braggor before, orcs may be strong but they are unskilled in the dance. Also I felt there was no reason to endanger the lives of anyone else for my fight."

Hearing this Braggor exploded. "Your fight, we were upon the king's lands, if there are any creatures such as the orcs upon the king's lands it is for us to inform his majesty of them, and if he deems it for us to deal with, then and only then do we deal with them. I headed straight to the palace and warned him of the orcs, and he sent out the army. They found what you had left of the creatures and sent word back that there was something far worse in the forest, whilst the rest of the men hunted it down. Do you understand what it is you have done? We now must clean up your mess. There are reasons why we do the things we do, and you must come to understand that."

Once again Slanoth placed his hand on Braggor's shoulder to calm him. "Braggor it is alright we must remember now that Cestator here has come from a place where the rules are quite different."

"But lord Slanoth that makes no matter, all men must learn to obey orders or there will be chaos."

"Yes Braggor I know. Worry not I share your concerns" Slanoth then looked at Cestator and went on. "I am not excusing your actions today. Braggor is correct, there is no place for that kind of behavior here. As disciples of Cargon we must work together for the common good. We must not act alone for personal matters, because what is done unto one is done unto all. Now do you understand this?"

The smile faded from Cestator's face, and was replaced by a look of puzzlement. "What do you mean by this, I was the only one who fought in that battle with the orcs? I received this wound and no other man I have seen has a wound."

Slanoth sighed deeply and looked up to the sky for some kind of answer, but did not find one there. He turned to Braggor and

The Dance

whispered to him. "I now understand what it is you were saying of his training."

Braggor nodded in reply. Slanoth turned back to Cestator and shook his head. "Cestator I know you to be an intelligent man, so I am not going to give you the answer to that. I am going to leave you to ponder the question on your own. When it is that you know the answer to it you will then be ready for the final trial. I know Braggor spoke to you of it. For now however we are glad that you are well, but you must promise to me that you will not do anything so rash ever again. I will now let you finish what you are doing and I expect you in the dining hall at first sun set for evening meal."

Slanoth turned and headed for the door. Braggor scowled at Cestator for a moment then followed.

When the door shut behind the two men William turned to Cestator, amazement shining on his face. "Did you really do as they said?"

Cestator smiled and nodded back. "Yes what they said was true, I killed about twenty of the creatures."

William whistled through his teeth, shaking his head in disbelief. "You mean to tell me you battled twenty orcs alone, and only came out with that cut on your shoulder. I say you must be a master swordsman. Even on my best day I could not accomplish such a feat."

"With those thoughts, no you would not. You see as I told Slanoth orcs may be strong, but they are unskilled in the dance. Any Blade Master could accomplish such a feat easily."

William sat there a moment and pondered what Cestator had just said. He found himself slightly confused. "Now wait one moment I have noticed that you call swordplay, the dance on more than one occasion, why is that?"

"The answer to that is simple." Cestator said with a smile. "You see, when you become one with the blade the movements become a part of a grand dance. If you ever watch someone who has truly mastered it, the dance of the blade can be a beautiful thing. I will show you if you would like."

"Yes I would much enjoy that, and I would like to learn if you would teach me."

Cestator nodded and smiled warmly. "Very well then, Slanoth has given us until dusk to do what we will, what say you we start now."

Without waiting for an answer Cestator got out of the tub, and looked around for his clothes. "Ah where is that damn girl with our clothes? What takes her so long?" Cestator then headed for the door mumbling about poor service. When he reached the door he tore it open, and Ciara was standing on the other side.

When she saw Slanoth and Braggor leave the room Ciara picked up the men's clothes and headed to the bathing room to give them to William, and his interesting friend. Just as she reached for the handle the door flew open. She jumped slightly and made a small squeak. When she saw the tall stranger there she blushed slightly. She looked up into his eyes, which were now a slightly blue, and this intrigued her all the more. She slowly lowered her vision tracing every line of him. His muscles were well formed as though they were chiseled by an artist, and he had an air about him that made her shiver in delight. Then as her vision moved down further the clothes fell from her arms and she stood there in mute shock. The man had gotten out of the bath, and not bothered to grab a towel.

Cestator watched, as the young girl looked him over. He frowned when the clothes fell to the floor. He bent over picked them up, nodded to her then turned and shut the door on her.

William watching all of this from his bath chuckled slightly. "You know Ciara appears to have taken a liking to you there. You may have just given her more of a reason to pursue you."

Cestator looked back at the door and snorted. "Bah I have no use for young girls who think they are every man's dream. For that matter, I have no use for any of the womankind they merely get in the way of important matters."

William looked at him in shock. He could hardly believe what he had just heard. He did not say anything else on the matter however. He could see it was not something the man liked to speak of.

Cestator walked over and handed William his clothes. They both dressed quickly, and left the room. As they walked down the hall towards the courtyard, they saw the same group of girls standing down the hall that they had passed on their way in. This time however the girls were whispering among themselves and giggling.

The Dance

When they got out to the courtyard there was still a good hour before sunset. Cestator stopped in the middle of the large pillars holding up the vaulted ceiling of the entryway, and turned to William.

"I will show you the dance first so you may see it when it is done correctly. Watch closely at how the movements flow into one another."

William nodded his assent anxious to see what the man spoke of. Cestator then drew his dark blade from its scabbard. William whistled at the sight of it. He had never seen any sword like it. The blade was black as a moonless night, and was of such quality that it rivaled even Slanoth's.

For a moment Cestator merely stood there with his eyes closed and his sword resting across his palms. Then suddenly without warning Cestator began. William nearly missed the first movements, and he was unsure if the blade had ever been at rest. William watched as Cestator's sword danced through the air, and he could think of no other way to describe the fluid movements of the blade. He watched as Cestator moved the sword from one hand to the other. It was done so smoothly that it almost seemed the sword had never changed hands. After a few minutes the sword once again came to rest upon Cestator's outstretched palms.

William stood there in stark amazement, he had never in his life, seen such grace and movement with a sword. "I can find no words to describe what you have just shown me. I do now see why it is you call it a dance. That was beautiful, yet how does it relate to battle?"

Cestator smiled at the question. It was one that he had heard numerous times. "The dance helps you learn to control your sword. It is the first step in becoming a master blades-man. It teaches discipline, and every attack and block will root from the dance. You will find when you begin to do it that it uses everything you have ever learned about using a sword, and much more."

"Now let us begin. Start with your sword resting upon your left palm, as I have mine here."

William drew his sword and rested it on his palms as he was instructed. He placed his left palm under the center of the blade and the hilt in his right hand.

"Good now using your left hand flip your sword around the back of your right hand, then catch it as it comes back up. This is one of the most difficult maneuvers so do not become frustrated if you do not get it for some time."

William watched as Cestator showed him the technique. William decided it did not look too hard, and he tried. His sword flipped up and flew to his right landing a few feet away.

Cestator smiled and shook his head knowingly. "You are trying too hard. You want to only give the blade enough force to get it to go around. And twist your right hand to guide its motion."

William picked up his sword and tried again, and once again it flew from his grasp. It took him many tries but when William finally mastered the first maneuver they moved on to each step in turn with Cestator giving him hints on what he was doing wrong.

As the sun began to set William had mastered the first half of the dance. He looked up and frowned, upset that they could not finish. "We had best get to the dining hall. Lord Slanoth does not take kindly to us being late."

"Yes I agree we should return. You have done well too have learned so much in as little time that we had. You should practice what you have learned more when you can for the rest only gets harder." They both headed for the dining hall, talking about the dance. When they entered the hall everyone was just sitting down.

Slanoth smiled when he saw the two deep in conversation. He had hoped that Cestator would find a place here. When dinner was over Slanoth called Cestator over, and told him that he would be taking over his training. Cestator said that he understood and excused himself, and returned to his quarters.

When morning came Cestator awoke to the sound of someone banging on his door. Frustrated he quickly dressed and pulled open the door ready to curse someone. The words froze upon his lips when he saw Slanoth standing there with a frown on his face.

"I know what you were thinking, and that will not go well here. I told you that I was going to take over today so follow me."

Cestator did not try to apologize. He simply did as he was bid, and followed Slanoth out to the courtyard. When they got there Slanoth turned to him and handed him a scarf.

"What am I to do with this?" Cestator asked.

"Cover your eyes with it, I wish to test your ability to trust in Cargon to guide your hand." Slanoth waved at one of the men standing over to the side. The man came running over with a long staff in hand that was padded on each end.

Slightly confused Cestator did as he was told. When he had the scarf tied over his head Slanoth asked if he could see.

"All that I see is the back of this damn scarf you had me tie around my head." He replied.

Slanoth frowned at the comment, but took it lightly. "Good, now I want you to block."

Cestator was just about to ask what Slanoth was talking about, when he was hit in the stomach with one of the padded ends of the staff. It knocked the wind out of him and he bent slightly over. Then the staff hit him on the back and knocked him to the ground.

He heard laughing coming from where the other men were standing, He became furious and quickly got up. Just as he got to his feet the staff hit him in the chest, and then the other end got him just behind the knees and he went down again. He felt it lightly touch the side of his head.

"Get up and take that blindfold off, you have failed." He heard Slanoth say with a scolding tone.

Cestator jumped up, and tore off the blindfold extremely frustrated at this point, and it showed strongly upon his face. "What kind of test was that? You said nothing of this kind of thing."

Slanoth shook his head in disappointment. "There are three reasons you failed the test so miserably. What do you think they are? You speak of the dance yet you cannot stop those attacks, why?"

"My senses are dull there is something wrong, and I could not see anything behind the scarf."

"Wrong . . . that is irrelevant. Your senses are the same as all of ours now. You failed for the same reason you have that wound on your shoulder. Because you did not look to Cargon to guide your actions, and you let your anger rule you. You must learn to put your faith in Cargon. Look to him for guidance. He sees all, even when you cannot. You must learn to let him be your eyes when yours do not show you the truth, and finally your arrogance gets in the way of your judgment. You must learn to overcome it. If you do not learn to, it will be the death of you one day. Someday there will come one who is faster and better and you will not see it for you will be too blinded by your arrogance, and they will kill you. Now stand and follow me, that is if you wish to learn something."

Cestator quietly followed slightly curious. Slanoth lead him back into the temple, and down into the catacombs below it. After some distance Slanoth stopped before two large doors. He turned to Cestator and put his finger to his lips. "We are about to enter a very sacred place, so if you speak do it in hushed tones." Slanoth then placed the torch he had been carrying in a scone outside the door. He opened the two large doors and stepped through.

Cestator quietly followed and was in awe at the sheer size of the room. The chamber was well lit yet he could not find the light source. On either side of the room there were massive statues of proud looking men. "What is this place? I have never seen anything like this."

Slanoth smiled patiently. "That would be because there is no place of its like. We now stand in The Hall of Legends. This is the place where all of the greatest of Cargon's paladins rest. Each statue you see here was made in their likeness. Now come follow me."

Cestator looked up at each statue wondering, whom each man was. He recognized an occasional one from ages past, but most outdated even his many years. He thought to ask Slanoth who the men were, but it seemed it would be blasphemy to disturb the peace in this sacred place. When they finally reached the end of the long chamber Slanoth knelt, and motioned for Cestator to do the same.

Cestator did as he was bid and waited there a moment until Slanoth stood, and he followed suit. He then looked up at the final statue at the very end of the hall. This one he did recognize it was a semblance of Cargon himself.

"You may be wondering why I have brought you here." Cestator jumped slightly at the sound of Slanoth's voice. The sound felt out of place here. He looked back at Slanoth and nodded not wanting to disturb the awe-inspiring peace here.

"I have brought you here so you may find yourself and perhaps Cargon as well. I come here often when I feel lost. This is a place of prayer. There is much wisdom here in this hall. The essence of the past is very strong. You would be wise to listen to what the past has to say. You may stay as long as you like, and return to us when you feel you are ready." With that Slanoth left Cestator alone to ponder.

Cestator remained in the hall for five days. William came down to bring him food, yet he left it untouched so William stopped. On the eve of the fifth day he returned from the catacombs. Everyone was in the dining hall having the evening meal. Slanoth stood when he saw Cestator enter the room, and each man stood in turn. With a bright knowing smile Slanoth motioned for Cestator to sit and eat.

Cestator found his chair next to William still vacant as though his friend had held it for him awaiting his return. He smiled at this. He had learned much in the five days he had spent in the chamber. He also found what Slanoth had said about the past being strong correct. He had felt the presence of many of the men that resided there sharing some of their wisdom with him. He now felt he could easily pass Slanoth's test.

Cestator walked over to his seat and William griped arms with him and the two shared a friendly smile. Slanoth motioned everyone to sit, as the attention was drawn off of Cestator the conversations began again.

William was quite enthusiastic about asking Cestator about his experience in the hall. Cestator however was somewhat shady on the details, which he explained as being something not easily described. William took it at that and changed the subject understandingly. "I have been practicing the dance with every free moment I have. I have become quite skilled at the first half. I hope you are still willing to teach me the rest."

Cestator smiled at his friend, remembering when he was first learning, he had had the same enthusiasm. "Yes of course I am still willing to teach you, my friend. I am more than glad to help you."

The meal went on for a bit longer with them speaking of many things. When everyone was finished, and they began to head to their quarters Slanoth called for William and Cestator to stay a few moments. When everyone was gone the two sat near to Slanoth and waited for him to speak. "I have noticed that the two of you have bonded well, this makes my heart shine. I have also noticed that Cestator, you have been teaching William here something not well known."

William quickly spoke up not wanting Cestator to take the blame. "Lord . . . it was I who approached Cestator with it, and asked him . . ."

Slanoth raised his hand silencing William. He smiled and shook his head. "Do not fear William I am not displeased. In fact I am quite glad that he is willing to teach you the dance. I have seen the potential in you for some time now, yet I have been far too busy to teach you myself. So in this case I have made a decision. I am going to allow the two of you to have the entire day for yourselves tomorrow, on one condition. You must spend it working on the dance. Is that understood?"

William heartily agreed to the terms saying he would do just that. Cestator also agreed to the terms, and found himself respecting Slanoth all the more. The man was fair, and wise.

Slanoth dismissed the two and lay back in his chair, and sighed. He hoped what he had planned for the two next would work out well. He heard the door closing behind the two when suddenly he felt a chill. It was the same sort of feeling he had the night when Cestator had first arrived, in that lonely hall on the way back to his quarters. Only this time there were no windows. He looked around for anything out of the ordinary, but could find nothing.

As Slanoth looked around the room, a dark shadow slipped slowly along the wall moving carefully so it would not be seen. It had watched as the men all had their meals, and laughed. Always it had its eyes focused on its target. It was here for one purpose and one purpose alone, to kill the biggest threat to its master's plans. The shade watched as Cestator and William sat alone with Slanoth, fearing that it might be noticed. It knew that Cestator was well attuned to noticing creatures of the dark. Now that they had left, the shade saw its opportunity to complete its dark mission. It silently moved from shadow to shadow working its way around the room so it could get behind the legendary paladin.

Cestator was shutting the door behind him when he felt it. He knew instantly what it was. He turned to William and told him to remain where he was. When William asked what the problem was Cestator simply said, "a shade." Confused William did as Cestator instructed, and did not move.

Cestator slowly drew his sword, and quietly opened the door. Cestator quickly found the shade, it was rising up behind Slanoth its claws out ready to rip Slanoth's soul from his body. "Slanoth get down!" He shouted.

Slanoth hearing Cestator's yell quickly fell to the floor. With Slanoth out of the way Cestator did not hesitate. He threw his sword directly at the center of the shade. The blade struck home and for a moment it looked strange. It appeared to be a sword floating in the air piercing a dark shadow. Then suddenly the shadow dissipated and Cestator's sword fell to the floor.

William wanting to help if Slanoth was in trouble, arrived in the doorway just as Cestator threw his sword. He stood there in shock at what he saw. "What in the name of Cargon was that?"

Cestator looked at him and frowned, but the frown did not last. He knew the man was there to back him up. "As I said it was a shade, and by no means is it by Cargon. It is a creation of Valclon. He created them to be his assassins, and they are masters of their art."

By this time Slanoth had stood and picked up Cestator's sword. He carried the weapon gingerly. He could feel the inner darkness of the blade. When he reached the two he handed Cestator his weapon. "I thank you Cestator. I must praise Cargon for your quick wit and fast hand. Yet I do hope someday you will rid yourself of that darkness."

Cestator caught Slanoth's subtle remark of his sword, and grunted in reply. He knew well what it represented, but it had become an old friend over the years. He knew that to truly be a paladin of Cargon he would have to rid himself of it, but at this time it would be like giving up his right arm.

With that Slanoth bid the two good night, and headed for his quarters. When he arrived at his chambers he decided not to go straight to bed. Instead he went to his private shrine to pray. As he knelt down before the altar he groaned in remembrance of old pains. He then looked up and prayed. "Lord Cargon, I beseech you. Help me see how it is that we are to prevail in this when Valclon has already found us, and sends his beasts after us. Cestator has much to learn, and it would seem very little time in which to learn it. I know surely that the lord above who watches over all would not allow this to go on without reason. So I ask of you, if you would know what his intent is, help me to understand."

Not getting an answer, and truly not expecting one Slanoth sighed and stood. He had known what the answer would have been, but he needed the comfort in asking. He then praised Cargon and thanked him for listening and went to bed.

For the first time in ages the morning sun found Slanoth still in his bedchambers. He had been up for some time, because the events of the night before had made it hard for him to sleep. Seeing the first sun was rising he decided he should join everyone in the dining hall. When he arrived there he noticed there were two vacant chairs. When the men saw him coming in everyone rose and waited for him to sit before returning to their seats. When everyone went back to their conversations he turned to Braggor. "Tell me, where has William and Cestator gotten to at this time of the day?"

"They came early this morn, Lord. They said that they wanted to get an early start on their day. They also said you had told them they were allowed to do some of their own training today."

Slanoth smiled despite his dire mood. "Yes I certainly did tell them that, I guess they were even more enthusiastic than I had thought."

Braggor looked puzzled for a moment. He was unsure of what Slanoth was talking about. "Well I had tried to stop them until they said you had arranged it with them. I allowed them to leave in such a case, but I must ask what is it they are training for?"

Slanoth's smile deepened. He was glad to be able to get away from last night's events, though sitting in his chair was a cold reminder. "Cestator has decided to teach William the dance of the blade. I have seen William practicing the past few days, and he has gotten rather skilled at the portion Cestator has taught him so far. It should be interesting how much William knows by the end of the day." Braggor agreed that it would be something to see then returned to eating.

Slanoth not feeling quite hungry picked at his food, after a short time he stood and stepped away from the table. The men all began to stand as he rose, but he waved them down. "No . . . no do not rise please finish your meals, I have much work I need to do. Do not worry yourselves with me."

With that Slanoth headed for the door. The men went back to what they were doing without another thought. All except Braggor, there was something wrong and he didn't know what. He had never seen Slanoth act this way before and it bothered him greatly.

Slanoth went out to the courtyard and found Cestator, and William practicing. He stood there for a time and watched. William appeared to be doing quite well for he had nearly gotten it all down. He smiled at the sight of the two. No one would have ever thought that these two men would become so close. Both of them loners at heart yet they seemed to find strength in each other, and he marveled at this.

As he watched them he began to see what Braggor had meant about Cestator being death incarnate. The man moved like a viper, every move flawless. He also appeared to be a good teacher. It seemed he was learning patience, which was partly what Slanoth had hoped for.

After a short time he approached them and asked if they would mind him joining them. They both agreed that it would be a pleasure to have him join them. Slanoth then drew his sword and began to help Cestator in teaching William the dance. Having two teachers William picked it up very quickly and by midafternoon he had it down. Slanoth was quite impressed by how fast the man learned. He had the makings of a true Master Blades-man. Once William had it down they went through it from beginning to end many times over loosing themselves in the dance.

When finally they did stop they heard a grand applause behind them. They turned and, the three saw that the entire population of the temple was in the courtyard watching in awe. Many of the men came over to them asking many questions about what they had seen. Some of them wanting to learn others just wanting to see it again, and some just felt inspired. The three took the questions and comments in good stride, but after a short time Slanoth raised his hand for silence. When all was calm he told everyone the three of them would be going out to the city for a time, and with that he herded Cestator and William out to the city gate.

When they were free of the crowd Slanoth smiled at his two companions. "I am not sure of the two of you, but I need to get away for a short time. I had just thought you might need a bit of a rest as well."

William and Cestator both agreed that they could use some time away from the crowd. Slanoth led the two through the city in a winding path. After a time William became curious of their destination for they had started to get into a hard part of the city. "Lord I mean no disrespect, but you seem to know where we are headed, and this is not a part of the city to be wandering. I was just wondering where we might be headed."

Slanoth laughed softly and waved his hand over his head unconcernedly. "Fear not William. I do know where we go and the way is not as dangerous as you may think. As for where we are going, I know of a small pub with the finest ale you will find around. I thought we all needed a breath away from the troubles we have seen."

William stopped where he was, a look of shock painted across his face. Meanwhile Cestator watched all in slight amusement. "Lord I did not think you were one to drink ale, it is for the common folk."

Slanoth laughed heartily at this. Remembering how the men of the temple thought of him. "William I may be close to Cargon, but remember I am still a man. And I have in my days spent many a day and night in the wild. So of course I have had ale, in fact where I am taking you, has some of the best here in Trecerda."

Slanoth turned and began walking again. William looked at Cestator with a puzzled look, and Cestator shrugged his shoulders then followed. William thoroughly confused at this point looked at the two men's backs shrugged and followed.

A short time later they arrived at the inn, and Slanoth led them in. The place was filthy and noisy. It was not somewhere William would have chosen to go. When he tried to mention this to Slanoth, he only shushed William and told him there was a test he needed to perform here, and told him not to drink too much.

They found a table in the back of the bar and they sat down. The barkeep came over and asked what they wanted. Slanoth told the large man to bring them three Dwarvern ales, and then slid a large gold piece across the table. The man looked down at the coin smiled then snatched it up quickly. A few moments later the man came back with three frothing pints and laid them on the table before the men, then went about his business.

The three sat and talked a while about many things. Slanoth and William both drank slowly being sure not to get intoxicated while Cestator drank heartily. He asked them once why they were taking their time and Slanoth avoided the question by speaking of other things and after a few pints Cestator had forgotten about it.

When he was sure that Cestator was drunk Slanoth called the barkeep over. When the man came over Slanoth motioned him to come closer. He whispered to the man so as not to be overheard. "My friend here has a message for that big burly man over there. Do you know him?"

Slanoth pointed to the largest man in the bar, a large gruff and violent looking man. The barkeep nodded that he knew him, and asked what the message was. "My friend here says that the man is a disgusting swine, and that his presence is turning this ale into foul tasting pig waste."

"Are you mad? I am not going to tell him that. That is a sure way to get him angry and start a fight. I don't want any fights here."

"I can assure you my good man, there will not be much of a fight, and the damage will be minimal. Yet if there is I am sure this will be more than enough to repair any damages to your establishment." Slanoth then handed the man a small bag that was heavy with gold. The man looked in the bag and smiled. He nodded to Slanoth then walked over to the large man and bent down close to him and pointed at Cestator.

The large man jumped to his feet with a loud roar. He came stomping over to the three. He stood behind Cestator and tapped his shoulder roughly. Cestator turned his head, and looked at the man coldly. "If you ever touch me like that again I will remove your hand from your fat arm."

He turned back to William. The large man now fuming grabbed Cestator's shoulder, and pulled a knife. "I'm going to gut you like the pig you are, you puny little mule dropping."

In a flash Cestator was on his feet and had the man's arm pulled up behind his back, and the dagger at the man's throat. "I warned you about that, now you will pay with your life you fool."

Slanoth quickly jumped up knowing what was about to happen. "Cestator stop, you are better than this." He turned to William. "Get him out of here I will take care of the rest."

Frustrated Cestator growled and pushed the man's arm up until he heard the shoulder pop. The man screamed in agony as his arm fell limply. "Consider yourself lucky, had Slanoth not stopped me you would have had more than a dead shoulder."

Cestator pushed the man down and walked out of the bar with William. The only sound in the room was the man screaming in agony. Everyone there was in shock at what they had just seen. Slanoth was the first to move, he quickly went to help the injured man. He laid hands on him, and felt that familiar warmth of healing, and then he felt the man's shoulder slip back into place. When he was finished he thanked the man, and handed him two gold pieces for his trouble then left.

Slanoth walked out the door. Cestator and William were outside waiting for him. Cestator was pacing back and forth growling about something incoherent. Slanoth looked to William, and William shrugged his shoulders. "I don't know he will not speak to me. He has been doing this since we came out here."

Hearing William speak to Slanoth, Cestator looked up. His upper lip was curled up in anger, and his eyes had a dangerous fire burning behind them. "What was that all about? I had that buffoon under control. Why did you stop me? Any fool who picks a fight like that deserves what he gets."

Slanoth did not even flinch at the words, even with Cestator in his face. He simply frowned back, and placed his hand on the man's chest gently pushing him back. "I was the one who provoked him. I wanted to test your reaction, and I found you were no better than him. You still have not gained control of your anger I am afraid."

Slanoth turned away in disappointment, and began heading back to the temple. He motioned William to follow, and told him not to look back, no matter what Cestator said.

Cestator watched as Slanoth turned from him, and pulled William along. Their silence infuriated him. "Wait, where do you think you're going? I am not finished." When they did not stop, or even look at him he became even angrier. He ran past them and stood in their path. "I said that I was not finished!"

The Dance

Slanoth stopped and looked him strait in the eye. The fire behind those eyes roared with furry, yet Slanoth did not look away. "Perhaps you are not, but I am." Slanoth said nothing more and walked around Cestator, and he did not stop. Cestator stared at the two men's backs feeling slightly foolish, and beginning to wonder what he was truly angry for. After a short time he forgot he was even angry, and began to follow. When they returned to the temple Slanoth convinced Cestator to go to his quarters to rest, and think about what had happened this afternoon.

Chapter 8
Shepard's Farm

The next morning Shepard returned, and met Slanoth in his quarters after the morning meal. *"So whar be our lad on dis morn? Do he be out thar train'n wit' da rest o' da men?"*

Slanoth chuckled despite himself. "My guess would be that he is still in his quarters getting over a hard evening. He had a bit much to drink last night, and got into a small squabble with a large ruffian."

Shepard laughed loudly. *"Wha' did ye do, go out an git 'im drunk, then pick a fight wit' da local bully?"*

"As a matter of fact, yes I did."

"Aye I should have been know'n ye would be do'n someth'n like tha'. So wha' did ye be give'n 'im ta drink?"

"Dwarvern ale of course, I needed him good and drunk. I did not want there to be any doubt."

"No doubt! By all that be mighty, ye were no try'n ta git 'im drunk ye were try'n ta kill 'im. Why I would no be surprised if da lad no be blind. Well we should be go'n an check'n up o' 'im, an make'n sure he do be ok."

Slanoth agreed, and the two headed for Cestator's chambers.

Cestator woke up to someone singing, and the sound seemed to be splitting his head in half. He opened his eyes to see who was there, and the light only made things worse. He groaned loudly at the pain. The person in the room must have realized he was awake for the singing stopped. He heard light footsteps heading towards him. When they stopped beside his bed he slowly tried opening his eyes again.

At first his vision was a blur but it cleared quickly and he saw Ciara standing there smiling at him. She was wearing a tight dark blue dress that was very low cut in the chest and did not leave much for the imagination.

"Good morning Cestator." She said in a bubbly voice. "You had quite a night. William told me all about how you beat that big brute." She reached down and traced her hand over his arm, and smiled even more brightly. "I just love to hear about things like that. You must be quite a strong man to face someone as big as that."

Cestator snorted and batted her hand away. He quickly got up and looked for his clothes, and found them on a chair behind her.

Ciara walked up to him, and pressed herself against his bare chest, and reached up and touched his face lightly. "You are so strong and handsome. It's a wonder no woman has claimed you for their own. I would be willing to show you what a woman can do for you."

Cestator frowned and grabbed her wrist tightly, and lifted her up. She squealed in pain and tried to wiggle her way out of his grip, but he was too strong. Cestator tightened his grip on her and lifted her to eye level. When she stopped squirming he spoke. "Do not try your foolish little girl games on me. I have no interest in the likes of a little whore like you."

Ciara gasped in disbelief and anger. No one had ever dared call her that. With her free hand she tried to smack him across the face, but he caught her wrist and squeezed hard. She gasped in pain and he let go of her left wrist. "If ever you try that again I will break it for you. I do not know if it is your custom to spread your legs for every man who comes along, but it is wasted on me. If I were you though I would watch who you do such for, you may just get what you ask for, but not in the way you want it."

He then dropped her onto the hard floor and she fell crying and rubbing her bruised wrists. Cestator then walked past her and dressed, he headed for the door out. As he reached for the door handle he turned back to her. "I have a word of advice for you. There is someone here who does fancy you. It may be a surprise, but you should try looking at someone who you might not see."

He turned back and opened the door and began to walk out. Just as he stepped out the door he heard her call to him between sobs. "Wait . . . oh please wait . . ."

Cestator stopped and turned back to her. The half-smile touching his face he had guessed her right. She was desperate for attention. "Yes," he said in a cold voice.

She did not appear to hear the sarcasm in his voice for she went on when she saw him turn back. "Who . . . you say someone fancies me who is it? Please I beg you tell me who it could be."

"As I told you it is someone that is right in front of you, but you do not see him. You befriend him, but you do not see the glances he sends your way. He burns for you, but he will never say." Cestator then walked out into the hall and closed the door behind him. As he walked away he could hear her calling to him to tell her who it was.

Cestator knew that morning meal was well over by this time so he headed for the kitchen to see if there was something there that his stomach could handle. The ordeal with Ciara had nearly made him forget his pains, but not quite.

On the way to the kitchen though, he ran into Slanoth and Shepard. The two apparently had been looking for him, for when they saw him Slanoth called out to him. "Cestator hold there a moment. Shepard and I must have a word with you."

Cestator sighed and waited for them. His stomach gave a loud rumble of protest but he ignored it.

"Ah Cestator we were just headed for your chambers to wake you, and see how you fared this morn." Slanoth said in an unsualy chipper voice.

"Other than my head feeling like I had just been hit, and a bit of hunger I am faring well. I was just heading to the kitchen for something to break the fast."

"Ah I would no be advise'n it lad, wit' wha' ye had ta drink las' night tha' thar food in thar would make ye more sick. I know jus' what ta be give'n ya fer tha'."

Cestator nodded his assent. "Yes . . . I was thinking to get a loaf of bread or something but if you know of something better." He paused a moment then before going on. "So what is it the two of you wished to speak with me about?"

The two men looked at one another for a moment as though they were deciding who would tell him. When they looked back at him Shepard was the one who spoke. *"Lad . . . now Slanoth did tell me that he spoke ta ye about me help'n in yer train'n, but thar be one little catch. Ya see it be plant'n time now, an me I no can be away from me farm fer too long . . . So me an Slanoth here, did be talk'n and we decided that some good ol' hard work would be do'n ye good."*

"So you're telling me that you want me to work on your farm. What good is that going to do?"

This time Slanoth stepped forward, a large grin spread across his face. "It will teach you the meaning of a good honest day's work. It will also teach you humility and respect."

Cestator frowned not quite sure how working on a farm would make any difference. He decided though that he would let them do what they felt was necessary. "Very well then if that is what you feel is proper, who would I be to disagree?"

Shepard and Slanoth both caught the sarcasm in the words. Slanoth shook his head seeing that the arrogance was still there. Shepard looked at Cestator, frowned for a moment then burst out laughing. *"Lad did I no tell ye that while ye were here that ye should rest up 'cause when I did get back yer real train'n would be start'n? Well ye bes' git ready fer some really hard days. Ye best be ready 'cause I will no be easy on ye as Slanoth were."*

Cestator frowned. He doubted that working on a farm would be as difficult as Shepard was making it out to be. "Ok then when do we leave?"

"Right now if ye be up to it."

Cestator simply nodded.

"Good," Shepard said, and then turned to Slanoth. *"Do ye be come'n wit' us, or do ye be need'n ta stay here?"*

Slanoth smiled brightly at the question. "But of course I am going to come along. We have so much to catch up on. Besides it has been some time since I have seen Bridget. I was wondering if she remembers me better than some folks."

"Bah . . . I did know who ye were da moment I did lay me eyes on ye."

"Mm . . . Hmm, Yes I know." Slanoth said his smile broadening.

Shepard scoffed again turned and waved them to follow. Slanoth looked at Cestator, shook his head and chuckled. Cestator not quite sure what they were talking about simply smiled. The two then followed Shepard out to the courtyard. They found Braggor training the men as usual. Slanoth let him know that he would be going to Shepard's farm, and he was leaving control of the temple to him until his return.

With that done the three headed for the gate where Shepard's cart was waiting for them. When Slanoth saw it he laughed even harder than before. "You still have the same old cart I see, and is . . . Why yes she is." Slanoth walked over to the horse and patted her nose. "Hello Clinet. It has been a long time since I have seen you old girl."

The horse whinnied in response and nuzzled Slanoth's hand. Shepard chuckled, and hopped up onto the cart. *"Well if ye be done thar we really should be go'n."*

Slanoth nodded and hopped up onto the other side of the cart and looked at Cestator who was still standing there. "Are you not going to join us?"

Cestator frowned at the cart and said that he would rather walk. Shepard scoffed and snapped the reins lightly and they were off. Evening was coming around as they neared the farm and Shepard pointed in pride. *"Ah here we be. Lad ye best be enjoy'n da sight now, fer ye soon will be regret'n come'n here."*

As they approached the farmhouse they saw Bridget was standing in the door, and she was not looking happy. Shepard stopped the cart in front of the barn, and unhitched Clinet and brought her inside. While Shepard was taking care of Clinet, Bridget came over to Slanoth, and Cestator with a frown on her face. "Now then since Shepard has decided to take you two in I guess I should feed you as well. Please come inside."

Slanoth then looked at Cestator and frowned. "I guess she does not."

Just as Slanoth said the words Bridget turned and smiled at them. "It is nice to see you again Slanoth, it has been too long. Next time, don't wait so long to come visit us."

Slanoth chuckled. Bridget had not changed a bit. "I must ask your forgiveness Bridget, but life has become very difficult in the past few years. I have had little time for myself."

"Yes Shepard told me that you are now the head acolyte of Cargon. I do feel for you. So then who might this other young man here beside you be?"

"I am Cestator. And I am not . . ."

Slanoth silenced him before he could finish what he was about to say. Bridget smiled at this. She knew well what he was going to say, and she also knew well whom he was, but she wanted to hear it for herself. "Welcome Cestator, to our home. Try not to let Shepard frighten you too much. He really is a big pushover."

"Ah, only fer ye me dear wife." Shepard chuckled as he walked up to the house.

Bridget frowned again when she saw Shepard coming up to them. "Your late Shepard, you should have been back before first sunset."

"Ah I do be sorry Bridget, but Slanoth here took da lad out las' night fer a few drink an we had a hard time try'n ta git 'im out o' da temple."

"Mm . . . hmm, a likely story Shepard. Well since your back your meals are waiting for you inside and they are getting cold so you should get to them."

With that they went inside for the dinner Bridget had prepared. When they were done Shepard showed Cestator to a room and told him to get some rest for there was much work to do in the morning.

Cestator awoke instantly when he hit the floor. He looked up and saw Shepard standing over him with a large grin on his face. *"I done warned ye lad. Ya did no feel ta git up so ye met da floor. Now git up an git yerself dressed, we've lots ta be do'n."*

"Bloody old man, I should show him what I think of his work." Cestator cursed under his breath.

Shepard walked out chuckling loudly. He did not have to hear Cestator's words to know what had been said, he had been in this position may times before.

Cestator quickly got dressed, and went out to the kitchen, where Bridget was cooking. She smiled at him and pointed at the door. "Shepard and Slanoth have already gone out. I believe they are waiting for you."

Cestator smiled back thanked her, and went outside. He found Shepard and Slanoth standing by a large pile of stones. Shepard saw him, and called him over. Cestator walked over to them and frowned. "So what is it you would like me to do now?" He said in an irritated voice.

Shepard smiled not seeming to notice Cestator's tone, or he just chose to ignore it for he went on in a joyful voice. *"Ah lad I has da perfect job fer ya. Ye should build a good sweat today. I be need'n these here stones moved on over there by tha' wall thar."*

Cestator looked where Shepard pointed and saw an unfinished stonewall. "I suppose you will want me to finish the wall, as well then."

The sarcasm was very heavy in Cestator's voice this time. Once again however, Shepard went on as though he did not notice. *"Well since ye be offer'n tha' would be might fine o' ye, but ye best be do'n a good job o' it, Bridget thar she dona take kindly ta jobs half done, er done bad."*

Cestator grunted at them then went to the task at hand. Every now and then he stopped and looked over at Shepard and Slanoth to see what they were doing while he slaved in the hot sun that even the cool air of early spring could not relieve. Each time he looked, the two were busy doing other tasks that had to be done after a long winter.

About mid-morning Bridget yelled out for them to come and eat. Cestator brought the stones he was carrying the rest of the way to the wall and placed them on the ground. He grabbed his shirt and headed for the house. When he arrived he noticed everyone was waiting for him. Cestator found a seat next to Shepard's son and sat down.

"So lad, how be da wall come'n thar?"

"It is growing slowly. Though I do not see any point in me doing this. It is a complete waste of time."

Slanoth tired of having to hear this spoke up. "If you could forget your anger and put a little trust in us then you would see the good in everything we do. Have you not been told that every man in the temple of Cargon started out doing much the same as this? You will not find the use in anything if you continue to be so unwilling to see. Open your mind and learn from every experience. Only then will you find the answer to the question you asked."

"What . . . why do you talk to me in riddles? I thought you were here to teach me to be a paladin, and all you have done is given me riddles to figure out."

Slanoth sighed shaking his head in dismay. When he looked back to Cestator there was a deep sadness in his eyes. "Do you not understand Cestator? I am not here to teach you, I am here to guide you. You see, the answers you seek are already inside you I am only here to help you find them. You have proven to be a most capable fighter, but that is not all that a paladin is. You see if I gave you all the answers to these questions you would not grow. You must work to find the answers. That is the only true way to find enlightenment, to be given the answers is the dark path. The road of good is long and hard, but the rewards are great. Allow me to tell you a story, to show you."

Cestator nodded in assent. Shepard smiled knowing what story it would be, and remembering telling it to a young hot headed upstart himself.

"This is a story that happened may ages ago, about two brothers, Verslin, and Dorgoth. You see the two were complete opposites. Verslin was kind and gentle always working hard for his living, while Dorgoth was a bully and never worked. He would live off of his brother always taking the easy way out."

"One day their home burned to the ground and they lost everything they owned. Verslin tired of supporting his brother left town and found work on a farm. He worked hard for many years doing most of the work for the old family who owned it. They could never pay him for his wares for they were poor, but he worked for a place to stay and food to eat, and he was happy."

"Then one day the Baron was passing the farm and saw Verslin working the fields, He found this strange, for he was a man who knew well the people tending his lands and he did not know Verslin. He stopped and asked Verslin why he was tending the farm. Verslin explained the situation, and the wise baron smiled upon him. The baron then called Verslin over to him and handed him a bag filled with gold. Verslin looked into the bag and thanked the baron kindly, but told him he had done nothing to earn the money and tried to give it back. The baron even more pleased with Verslin told him to accept it for payment in working his lands, and also told Verslin to expect just as much each season. After time Verslin saved his money and became wealthy and was granted land, and he was loved by many and he lived a ripe many years."

"Dorgoth finding himself homeless and without his brother to support him went to a life of crime. He knew nothing of how to work or had any want to. He found he could quickly get rich by stealing from others. Soon he became a wealthy man and forced his way into a large portion of land. He became a tyrant and his people despised him. Then one night as he slept a group of men entered his keep and kidnapped him and, they tortured and eventually killed him."

"So you see the easy way is not always the best way. As I am sure that you well know the evil side has its appeal in that it does not take much work, but the prizes are short lived. However traveling the road of righteousness is a hard road, but the rewards for it are many and long lived."

Cestator listened intently to Slanoth's story and found some wisdom in it. Yet he could still not find the meaning of it as pertained to his situation, and he voiced this concern.

Shepard burst out laughing at this. *"I . . . ye do sound like some other lad I did once know, who said much da same when I did tell it to 'im. Time do seem ta repeat itself eh Slanoth?"*

Slanoth smiled. "Quite," he said in reply. "And do you remember what you said in response to that Shepard?"

"Aye that I do, I did tell da lad tha' it did no matte,r him still had ta do da work. I also did tell 'im ta think on it fer awhile an he would see sooner, er later what I did mean by it."

"Yes that is what I remember as well." Slanoth said with a chuckle. "So Cestator if you are finished eating I would advise you to do just that."

Cestator grunted, stood and went back to work. The sun had fallen well below the horizon when he finally finished. He was so exhausted that he refused food when he returned to the hous,e and instead went right to bed. When morning came Shepard woke him, yet Cestator felt in no way ready to get up. He tried to explain this to Shepard but he would not hear any of it.

"Bah lad ye just be tight from work'n yer muscles yesterday. Once ye start move'n an work'n again ye'll be right fine, now get up or I'll be have'n ta send Sniffer in on ye."

"Sniffer?" Cestator asked confusedly.

Shepard smiled then turned and whistled. *"Sniffer come boy git 'im."*

Cestator then heard a loud barking, and something running through the house. A moment later a large furry dog jumped up on his chest and began liking his face. Cestator tried to swat the animal away, but the dog thought he was playing and became even more excited. Meanwhile Shepard was standing in the doorway laughing heartily.

Cestator highly annoyed quickly jumped out of bed. He gently pushed the dog out of the way and scowled at Shepard, which only accomplished to make him laugh even harder.

"Lighten up lad. I did warn ye, an it did get da reaction what were needed. Meet me out in da field when ye be done play'n wit' Sniffer." With that Shepard left. Cestator could hear him laughing as he went. After a few minutes Cestator got the dog to calm down enough for him to get out of the room, and he met Shepard and Slanoth out in the field. Shepard had two plows out and was hitching a horse to one of them. When he was done he turned to Cestator and told him to take the harness of the other plow and start pulling it.

Cestator frowned deeply. "I am no beast of burden why with Slanoth on that thing it must weigh more than your horse there. Not speaking that it is in the ground. I have no cause to do something like that. Why look at you. You ride on the back of the other while the horse does the work."

"Bah . . . so ye no be think'n it can be done, well I'll be show'n ye then. Slanoth git down off tha' thar plow an Cestator git on."

Cestator smiled. "This should be interesting," he said to Slanoth as he stepped up onto the plow.

"Yes well, I have a word of advice. You had best hang on tight." Slanoth answered with a bright smile.

Shepard picked up the harness and called back to Cestator to ask if he was ready. Cestator chuckled and said that he was. Shepard then began to pull on the harness, for a few moments nothing happened. Cestator turned to Slanoth and smirked shaking his head. Then suddenly the plow jerked into movement and Cestator fell onto his back hard. When the plow moved too easily Shepard turned back and saw Cestator lying on the ground.

"Lad what ye be lay'n down thar fer, I did tell ye ta git on da plow, now do it. I no did be joke'n wit' ye."

Cestator not happy being made to look the fool got up and stood back on the plow, and this time made sure he held tight. When Cestator was situated Shepard pulled again and the plow began to move. He pulled the plow up to the end of the field, and back before stopping.

"Thar ye be lad, now I did some o' yer work fer ya. Ye be have'n lots more ta be do'n so ye best git to it."

Cestator frowned and picked up the harness. "Cargon never said anything about being a beast of burden."

Slanoth chuckled. "Get accustomed to it, there are many things you will do that Cargon happens to fail to mention. He has quite the sense of humor."

Cestator grunted in reply then pulled on the plow. At first it would not budge then slowly the earth began to give into the pressure and it moved. He found that once he had the momentum the plow moved easier, but if he stopped it became hard.

By the end of the day Cestator was exhausted and his muscles ached severely. Bridget gave him some bad tasting tea and told him to rest. She told him he would be fine by morning as she chuckled under her breath.

"Don't let Shepard get to you. He really does like you, trust me I know him. He pushes you to see how far you will go, but he would never ask you to do something he would not do himself. I know he can be hard, but really he is just a big pushover."

Cestator gave her a warm smile and thanked her for her consideration, and the tea. He then went to bed. Over the next few weeks Cestator learned much about hard work, and he gained much more respect for those who lived the life.

Slanoth awoke with a start. The sound of wolves, and panicked horses broke through his sleep. *"What is going on here,"* he thought. He quickly dressed then headed for the door grabbing Justice on his way. As he opened the door Shepard was running by.

"What is happening around here?"

Shepard did not waste time looking back, and he answered on the run. *"It do sound though it were wolves be attack'n me animals."*

"I agree but, are you sure Shepard. There has not been a wolf in this area for some time now?"

"Well I no be sure o' anything, but I no gona let whatever it be ta kill all me livestock"

Agreeing with the logic Slanoth followed without another word. When they got outside the sun was just cresting the horizon. Everything was deathly quiet. Then they heard Clinet whinny loudly from within the barn, and suddenly something flew out of the barn and landed just outside the door. It landed in a heap as though Clinet had kicked it and likely killed the thing. For a few moments the creature did not move, but then slowly it began to stand. What they saw was indeed a wolf but there was something not right about it.

After a moment of looking at it Shepard gasped in shock. *"By all that be mighty, tha' thing be dead. Wha' in da name o' the dark one be happen'n here. It be a bloody zombie beast."*

"May Cargon protect us, I think your right old friend."

As though hearing the mention of the gods name the creature turned to them. A rumbling growl came from it, and a green glow appeared in its empty eye sockets. It howled then charged at them.

The two had fought side by side many times before and reacted as such. They both drew their weapons quickly turning away from the creatures leap.

The zombie beast landed between the two men and growled loudly. It looked at each of them in turn. It howled, and charged at Slanoth. The moment of hesitation however gave Slanoth just enough time to pull the phoenix emblem from his shirt and start a prayer.

"In the name of Cargon, I command you foul beast to be gone. Go back to the depths of the hell which spawned you." Instantly after the last word was spoken the beast burst into flames. Slanoth quickly moved out of the way of its charge and it fell to the ground next to him.

"Ha . . . me I did always like tha' about ye. Them dead beasties no have a chance against it."

"Yes, it is a good benefit to being a paladin, but my question is. Where did this thing come from? First orcs and now a zombie hound, this does not bode well for us. We must figure out what is happening here."

Shepard walked over to the flaming creature and kicked it. The beast fell to pieces and quickly tuned to ash.

"I tha' do be a good question, but it be more than just tha'. Some few weeks back I did find a large group o' animals all dead. There were all sort too. It were like someone did kill 'em then dropped them there to rot. I did think it strange then but I done dismissed it fer some illness hit'n 'em."

Suddenly from behind the barn the two heard a loud raspy roar. The ground below them began to shake as though something very large was headed for them.

"What in da name o' da almighty be tha'?" Shepard asked as he looked to Slanoth hoping for some answer.

Slanoth looked just as confused and shrugged. "I do not know but we had best be ready for it, because it's about to come around the barn there."

Just as Slanoth said the words and pointed, the creature appeared. It was a massive beast standing nearly twenty feet tall. It walked upon four short legs compared to its massive body and tail.

Yet its size was not what made the two men gasp in horror, that was caused by the sight of the seven serpentine heads.

"**BY ALL THAT BE MIGHTY!** *What on all o' Trecerda be that thing? Why it be have'n more heads than one o' them bewitched folk who do talk wit' themselves.*"

A few days after the three left William was practicing the dance that Cestator had taught him in the courtyard of the temple. He found himself doing it quite often since Cestator had left with Lord Slanoth two days ago. It helped him focus on something other than what the two had spoken of before Cestator left.

Suddenly there she was, the sun glimmering on her red hair and lighting her fare face. There was a glimmer in her eyes. Ciara seemed to be looking for someone. Then she looked straight at William and smiled. That smile made his heart do flips and he lost his concentration and his sword flew from his hands. She giggled at this then started towards him.

William suddenly broke out into a sweat. He truly wished Cestator had not confronted him about his love for her. It was so much easier for him to put the thoughts aside when he was not faced with it.

Since that day whenever he even saw her he became nervous and could hardly speak, and now she was headed right for him. He stood there nearly paralyzed as she approached. He watched her intently taking in every curve, and how she seemed to float upon air.

As she neared him she bent down and picked up his sword, then stepped up to him. She then slid his sword back into its sheath and ran her hand up his side to his cheek and played with a stray lock of his hair. Her smile brightened and his heart fluttered.

She had a slight hint of jasmine and lilies about her and William took a deep breath of her and sighed. He took her hand into his, and got down on one knee. He looked up into her big brown eyes and knew he could happily lose himself in them.

"Ciara." Saying her name sent chills up his back, and gave him warm feelings inside.

Ciara's smile brightened, her heart was racing. She had never before felt this way. She had flirted with many men, but none of them ever made her feel as though she were floating on air. She had known William for a long time but she had never been interested in him in that way.

He was her best friend and she never looked at him like that, at least not until Cestator had said something. Since that day she had noticed William looking at her longingly. She also began to notice how handsome he was, and standing here with him down on one knee before her holding her hand was shear bliss. She had never been with a man, but then he softly said her name and she melted, and she suddenly had a great longing for him to take her into his arms and make love to her.

William watched as her heart fluttered when he said her name. She closed her eyes and seemed to gain pleasure from his touch. Seeing this he became braver and decided to take advantage of the moment.

"Ciara" he said again. This time she seemed to get some physical pleasure from it for she tilted her head back and moaned softly. She opened her eyes and looked directly into his.

"Yes William," she said sweetly.

"I love you Ciara. I have loved you since the first day I laid eyes upon you. I have just always been afraid to tell you."

Ciara's smile deepened and she pulled him up to his feet. She wrapped her arms around his neck, and pulled his lips to hers and kissed him deeply.

"I love you as well William. Now take me for I cannot contain it any longer."

William did not hesitate a moment. He lifted her into his arms and kissed her. Her lips tasted so sweet. She seemed to melt into his arms, and every part of him screamed to be with her. He took her to his private quarters and there they became one with each other.

Slanoth looked up at the giant Creature and was amazed. For a moment he nearly lost himself into its dancing gaze, but quickly caught himself. "I do not know what this thing is, but do not look directly into its eyes it seems to have a strange effect."

"*Aye I got tha' but how is we suppose ta be fight'n something wit' seven bloom'n heads on it. I mean I have done fought some strange things in me day, but I ain' never fought no seven headed lizard 'fore, 'specially one that outsize a greal.*"

"Well I am not sure, but my best guess would be for one of us to keep as many of those heads busy while the other tried to take a few off."

"Aye *tha' do soun' good ta me, so who gonna be da bait?*"

"It does not matter which of us acts as the decoy. We should split up and see which one of us it comes after, and then the other can come in, and even the odds a bit."

Shepard nodded his agreement not wasting time on words, for the creature was coming at them fast. They waited until it was only a few feet away then they ran in opposite directions. Three of the heads turned towards Shepard and hissed in anger as the other four went for Slanoth, narrowly missing him. The body and the rest of the heads turned and chased after him.

Shepard quickly noticing that it had forgotten him stopped, and turned back. He saw Slanoth a few yards away doing all he could to fend off the attacking heads. It was almost amazing to watch this beast fight. Shepard would have thought that something with so many heads would have trouble controlling them all, but each head seemed to work in succession with the others.

He did not waste much time pondering this however, for he knew that sooner or later Slanoth would miss a block, and it was likely going to be sooner. He quickly ran up behind the creature and two of the heads turned towards him, and hissed.

"*By all that be mighty thar be no way ta be sneak'n up on dis god blasted thing. Hold out fer just a short while Slanoth I should be able to git one o' these blasted things.*"

Shepard had no trouble fending off the two heads of the creature, and he quickly found an opening to get a clear shot. He swung his battle-axe and it cut clean through, and the head fell to the ground.

Much to Shepard's surprise though it did not die, it simply roared at him, and then there appeared to be something pushing its way out of the wound. He stared in shock for a moment then looked at the severed neck and saw two new heads sprouting from it.

"Wha' in da name o' the almighty! It be grow'n two new heads. How is we suppose ta kill dis thing if'n it jus' keep a grow'n back it heads?"

"I think that was the intent old friend. We are not supposed to kill it, at least not according to whoever sent it."

Suddenly the creature turned away from them seeming to forget them. All the heads and the body turned towards a figure coming out from the tree line. They roared simultaneously and the creature charged at the man.

Shepard at a better vantage point was first to notice the figure was Cestator. "Lad watch yerself tha' nasty beast do grow back body parts. It can no be kill wit' a sword."

Cestator frowned when he heard Shepard's words. He looked past the charging beast and saw that they had made the same fatal mistake everyone did when faced with a hydra for the first time. They had cut off a head.

He quickly pointed at the severed head now beginning to grow a body, and shouted to them. "Burn that thing any way you can before we have two of these things to deal with."

Shepard acted quickly and ran into the barn and brought out two lit oil lamps and smashed one on the growing head. It instantly burst into flames and in moments it was nothing, but ash.

By this time Slanoth was running to help Cestator fight the beast, Justice ablaze in its magical fire. Shepard looked at the beast then at the remaining lamp in his hand and doubted it would be enough to kill this large beast then dropped it and ran over to help.

When the two men reached the beast some of the heads turned towards them and hissed. Cestator warned them off telling them to hold back for a moment. Slanoth was amazed at how this creature could control all of the heads at the same time and have each one work independently from the others.

"Cestator you seem to know about this thing, how do we kill it? It is most obvious that it grows back anything that it loses."

Cestator using all of his concentration trying to fend off the creatures attacks did not answer immediately. "The only way that I know of to kill it is to strike its heart, but to do so you must climb under the beast and strike it from below. The trick is getting under there without getting bitten, for its bite will turn you to stone."

"Well tha' no be very promise'n. Da blasted thing got more heads than I ever did see on one beast, an it can work all o' them separate."

Slanoth nodded in agreement. "Yes I must agree with Shepard each of those heads work together yet they seem to be able to work separately as well"

Cestator laughed coldly at their words. "I never said it would be easy. You should know by now, my father is no fool. Why do you think that he sent it?"

Slanoth frowned frustrated at this point. Shepard tried a few times to get in under the creatures guard, but every time one of the heads would snap at him, and he would jump back narrowly dodging it.

"Ah what we be need'n ta do is git rid o' some o' them heads. Thar be no other way ta git in thar.

"Yes perhaps, but you saw what happened the last time you did that, don't you remember?" Cestator sneered.

"No Cestator Shepard is right. Now fire killed the head that Shepard cut off earlier correct."

"Yes that's right, but you would need a lot more than a lamp to kill this thing."

"Yes I know, but if I use Justice against it, the flames should stop it from healing, at least for a short time, and perhaps if I can get enough of them down one of you could get below the creature and kill it."

"Aye I do agree if'n ye could git three or so I do be thinking I could git in thar an kill it."

Cestator frowned deeply. "Well whatever you are going to try do it quickly. I cannot hold them off for much longer."

Without a word Slanoth moved in, and two of the heads turned to him. He quickly dispatched them, and as he had hoped the fire sealed the wounds, and the necks swung around wildly. Meanwhile the severed heads snapped at his feet. The creature stunned and in shock turned to him and roared with its remaining heads completely forgetting Cestator and Shepard.

Shepard quickly taking advantage of its distracted state ran under the beast. Realizing he did not know where to strike he turned to Cestator. *"Lad where do it be, where on dis blasted thing do I need to hit it?"*

Cestator nearly collapsed from exhaustion, but he caught himself through shear will. Instead he sat down hard, and then he heard Shepard call out to him from below the creature, asking him where to strike it. He pointed and shouted to Shepard.

"There towards the front of the beast just behind the place where the necks touch the body. You will have to work fast for the heart is buried in deep and it will quickly forget Slanoth and try to get to you. If you stay just behind there though they will not be able to reach you, it will not stay in one place however so move quickly."

Shepard quickly went to where Cestator had pointed out, and swung his ax with all his strength. The creature roared loudly and as Cestator had said it forgot about Slanoth and tried to get to him. When it could not reach him it tried to move and get a better angle. Shepard however was quick on his feet and moved with it and swung again his axe going deeper this time. Once again the beast roared and tried moving to get to Shepard.

Slanoth seeing the creature's attention was off of him ran up from behind the beast and joined Shepard below it. Just as he arrived Shepard swung again and cut deeply, the wound was spewing blood and covering Shepard, but he paid no mind to it and quickly pulled out his ax and moved out of Slanoth's way.

Taking the opportunity left him Slanoth drove his sword up into the wound Shepard had created. "Cargon guide my blade and let it strike true." He prayed as he stabbed upward. The sword drove its way up past the hilt and cleaved the creature's heart. Suddenly the creature's heads went limp and they fell.

"Aye ye did it, but me thinks we should be gitt'n out o' here for it come down on us."

Just then the creature's tail hit the ground and its legs began to buckle. Slanoth quickly pulled out his sword and the two of them ran out from below it.

The two looked at each other and began to laugh. Then suddenly they heard Cestator's gruff voice from behind them.

"I would save the celebration for later the hydra was only the least of our problems. There is an army moving in on us as we speak. So I would gather all your things and head for the city."

"What . . . how do ye be know'n tha'?"

"What do you think I was doing out there?" Cestator asked as he pointed back from the way he came. "I felt there was something wrong out there so I went to check and there is a large army headed this way. They appear to be headed for Cerdrine."

"Ah we be need'n ta warn me neighbors."

Cestator shook his head regrettably. "It's too late, their farm was taken and everyone was killed. The hydra was sent here to kill us before they came, but it won't be long before they get here."

Slanoth quickly took control of the situation. "Ok Shepard, go inside and wake the others. Cestator and I will gather the horses and hitch the wagon. We must be long gone before that army arrives. We will not do Cerdrine any good if we are dead."

Shepard nodded. *"I ye be right thar."* He ran into the house to get the others.

A short time later Shepard, Bridget and their son came out of the house and Slanoth had the cart waiting with Clinet hooked up.

"Stepper?" Shepard asked.

Slanoth shook his head regrettably. Shepard cursed and punched the door jamb then threw all that he had into the back of the wagon and jumped into the driver's seat. Bridget joined him on the seat and the others got in the back and they headed for the city.

Chapter 9
Trouble on the Horizon

As they approached the temple gates Slanoth called out to the guards, and seeing who approached they immediately opened the gate. The moment they were inside, Slanoth jumped down and called one of the guards over.

"An army approaches, go and tell the king that in no more than two days they will be at the city gates. Now go quickly there is much to do and little time."

The guard looked shocked but he nodded and ran off. Slanoth called Braggor, Cestator and Shepard to follow him to his quarters. They stayed there for many hours discussing what needed to be done, and learning what Cestator knew of the army being the only one to have seen it.

King Lysandas dismissed the messenger thanking him and telling him he wished to speak with Slanoth, but that he would send word when he needed him. He called in his advisor. The man came skulking out of the shadows behind the throne.

"Gorloan where is General Albrecht at this time, and why has this army gotten so far into my lands and no one has known of it? I thought you had your spies out there watching for such things. And what of your magic has it not shown you anything?"

The man bowed deeply, his dark hood concealing the smile that spread across his lips. When he spoke it was in a dry raspy voice.

"The General is currently out searching for any stray orcs lurking to the south. As for this army, I fear your majesty that they may have found a passage between planes, which would allow them to travel, undetected."

"What . . . how is this possible. Why have I not heard of such things, and if you knew of them then why did you not watch them as well? That is after all why you are here."

Gorloan's smile grew intensely everything was going according to his plan. The deal he had made was about to pay off.

"I do apologize, your majesty but I did not know of any entrances nearby. Had I known, I would have tried to stop them from coming through. The entrances however are difficult to find even if one knows the general area in which they reside."

Lysandas then looked back at his advisor, and scowled. "Gorloan you know well how I do hate when you wear that cloak over your face. Remove it at once!"

Gorloan's smile vanished as he removed the hood and he bowed. "I beg your majesty's pardon it is hard for me to see in the brightness of the hall."

Lysandas waved this off not wanting to hear excuses. "Leave me then, and find this portal and seal it. I want no more surprises."

"Yes your majesty," Gorloan sneered as he disappeared into the shadows. He laughed to himself as he went down into his laboratory. "Soon your kingdom will be mine, and you shall beg for mercy of death as you lose everything, but I will not give it to you. You will live to see your mighty kingdom fall, and you will rot away in your dungeon.

When he was sure Gorloan was gone Lysandas called one of the guards, and told him to sound the horns calling in the army. The man nodded and ran to do as he was ordered.

When they were finished Slanoth sent Braggor and Cestator out to begin preparations for the defense of the city. The guard he had sent to warn the king was patiently waiting outside. He called the man in and asked the news. The guard told Slanoth what Lysandas had said and Slanoth dismissed him.

When the guard left, Slanoth looked to Shepard. "So old man what do you think of this?"

"This do no look good fer us. I do smell something wrong here. How in all o' Trecerda did dis army git here wit' no one even know'n? Thar has ta be someone who do know something here. Thar be no way to be move'n an army too far wit' no one notice'n. I do still have some folk I can trust in da city, I do think I should be see'n what they know."

Slanoth nodded in agreement. "Yes I think you are all to right there old friend. Be wary though, times are strange."

"I tha' they do be." Shepard said as he left the room.

When Shepard was gone Slanoth sighed tiredly, and leaned back in his chair thinking on the events of the day. He sat there for a short time resting his eyes. Suddenly there was a soft knock on the door.

Slanoth sighed at the sound. This was truly becoming a long and hard day. "Yes who is it?" He called after a moment.

The door cracked open and Ciara peeked in. "Lord Slanoth may I speak with you for a few moments please?"

Slanoth smiled warmly, seeing who it was warmed his heart. He thought of the girl as his own grandchild. "Yes of course child, come in. My door is always open to you when you need someone to talk with."

Ciara opened the door further and entered the room and sat before Slanoth's desk. The girl seemed troubled and this truly bothered him. The girl had always been bubbly and happy, but now something was eating away at her.

"You look troubled child. What bothers you so, and what is it that I can do for you?"

Ciara paused for a moment before speaking. "I do not know how to say this." She paused again before going on. "I guess the best way to put it is that I have fallen for someone. It is almost surprising for I had never thought of him in that way. He has always been my friend, but I have never seen him look at me as the other men do. I would guess that would be because he was looking not at what I was, but who I was."

Slanoth smiled warmly. This was the kind of news he did not mind hearing, in fact it did much to ease his heart. "Why child this is a wonderful thing. Whatever could be wrong with being in love, and may I ask who this special man may be?"

Ciara closed her eyes, and took a few deep breaths. She appeared to be collecting herself for more difficult news. "I have fallen for William, Lord. Yet I fear that is not all. A few weeks back I faced him with my feelings, and we spent the night in each other's arms."

She looked down at this point, and absently rubbed her belly. Slanoth seeing the fear and shame upon her face chuckled softly.

"Oh dear child fear not, if what you did was in the name of love Cargon will give you forgiveness."

Ciara looked up at him, a small tear running down her cheek. This almost tore Slanoth apart. "That is not the reason that I come to you Lord. I have come to you because I carry William's child.

Slanoth fell back in his chair. "Are you sure of this my dear?"

Ciara nodded vigorously. "Yes I am all too sure of it, but I cannot find how I should tell him. I came here to ask if you could tell him for me."

"Oh my dear it is not my place to tell him. This is a great blessing, and he should hear it from your lips."

Ciara smiled brightly. "Yes I know it is, and thank you Lord I just needed your reassurance to give me the courage."

She stood and walked over to Slanoth and hugged him tightly around his neck. "Thank you again grandfather. I love you." She whispered to him.

Slanoth hugged her back gently. "I love you also granddaughter, and you are quite welcome, but do me a favor child."

Ciara let him go and stood back. "Of course I would do most anything for you. What is it?"

Slanoth smiled brightly. "Love him and do not let him get away."

Ciara giggled softly behind her hand. "That is one promise that I will surely keep." She then left Slanoth to himself.

Slanoth sat there for some time pondering what he had heard, and he was amazed. Through all the troubles and turmoil going on around them, there were signs that life goes on. He said a prayer to Cargon to watch over the two lovers, and their child.

Sometime later there was another knock on his door. Slanoth sighed deeply. He was beginning to wonder if the day would never end. Then the person knocked again just slightly harder this time. "Yes come in." Slanoth called out.

The door opened and William stepped in. "Lord my I speak with you? I have an important matter to discuss with you."

Slanoth smiled, he had a good clue as to what William had to say. "Yes of course William come sit down. I am always willing to help. What is it I can do for you?"

William sighed deeply, his hands were shaking terribly, and his heart was racing. Slanoth noticed tiny beads of sweat forming on the man's forehead, and he placed a reassuring hand on Williams shoulder. "It is alright William, take it slow and breathe."

This appeared to calm him, and Slanoth smiled. After a few moments William found the strength to speak. "Lord I have fallen in love with Ciara, and I believe she feels the same for me. A few weeks past we spent the night in each other's arms." William then bowed his head in shame.

"William, do not fret if as you say, that each of you loves one another as deeply as I see in your eyes. I do believe that Cargon has blessed the two of you."

William lifted his head and smiled skeptically. "Thank you lord, yet that is not the only reason I wish to speak with you. I wish to ask Ciara for her hand in marriage, but her parents being unknown it is hard to ask them. She has told me countless times that she looks to you as her grandfather, so I have come to ask you for permission. Also I would ask if you would perform the ceremony for us."

Slanoth was taken aback by this. It was more than he had ever expected. A tear of joy rolled down his cheek. "William you both have my blessings in your marriage, and it would be my honor to perform the ceremony for you. Go and speak with her and we will set the day after this trouble is over."

William smiled brightly. "Thank you Lord you have given me the greatest gift anyone could hope for."

William stood and left Slanoth in peace. By this time nightfall had come and Slanoth was near exhaustion. He felt as though he had the weight of the world resting upon his shoulders. He decided that he would try to get some rest, but as he stood to retire to his sleeping quarters Shepard burst into the room.

"*I do be tell'n ye dis juz be madness. I can no believe half o' what I did hear.*"

Slanoth closed his eyes and chuckled tiredly, then fell back in his chair. Shepard looked at him and frowned. "*Slanoth what be wrong wit' ye? Ya be look'n though ye were 'bout ready ta fall over dead.*"

Slanoth's smile began to fade. "I have not felt this old since the day that Cargon visited me. This has been a long and hard day."

"*Aye ye do be look'n like ye been work'n too hard today. I can go an let ye be, so ye can rest some if'n ye like.*"

Slanoth shook his head. "No my old friend, if I am reading you right, things need attention immediately."

"*Aye, but I can be take'n care o' it if ye need me to.*"

"No I will find some time to rest later, for now there is much that needs to be done. Besides I want to hear what news you have heard."

"*Ah it do be hard ta swallow that. From every tale that I do hear da blasted army did jus' appear out o' thin air, an rumors do be spread'n. People is start'n ta git a bit nervous an such, soon I do think tha' riots may start. Word do be go'n round that da army be of evil spirits. I did hear lots o' word o' people want'n ta leave da city, but o' course da gates be locked down tight.*" Oh an da army do still be out to da south o' here. Lysandas did call them back, but they will no be here till morn. Da city guards be hold'n things down but if things git much worse they will no hold fer long.*"

Slanoth shook his head and rubbed his temples. It had been some time since Cerdrine had been under siege. Most of the people who lived there now were too young to even remember. Slanoth knew as well as Shepard what would happen if the people went into a panic. "Ok go and gather what men that we can spare to help in the situation, and meet me at the city gate."

Shepard shook his head vigorously. "*No you go an git some rest. I can go an handle da troubles out thar.*"

Slanoth smiled at his friends concern. "Shepard you know me better than that. You should know that I will not be able to rest so long as there something I could be doing out there. I must do everything I can to prevent innocent people from getting hurt."

"Aye I did be afraid ye would say tha'. Alright then if ye need ta do dis I'll be meet'n ya thar."

When the door closed behind Shepard, Slanoth bowed his head for a moment trying to collect himself. "Cargon if you are listening now, I ask you to lend me strength to see this through. This surely has become a trying day."

Slanoth then stood and headed to the back of his office to a large cabinet. He stood before it for a moment thinking about what resided within. He said the few words to the spell that unlocked the cabinet then opened it, as he did so light began to shimmer from inside. Slanoth was almost surprised to see that the contents were still there. The second gift that Cargon had given him so many years ago, it was Cargon's own armor that belonged with his sword. He smiled at the sight of the armor for it brought back many fond memories. He took it out and adorned it. The armor felt light for field plate and it did not restrict his movement. The weight of it felt comforting to him.

Slanoth then headed for the gates leading to the city. When he arrived Shepard was waiting with more than a dozen men, Cestator and William among them. Slanoth looked them over and nodded, all the men there were experienced and could handle themselves. "Now we are going out there to help control the crowds and to prevent a riot. Remember now that these people are panicked. Rumors have been running wild, and things can get out of hand quickly. So keep your heads and remember they are common folk with fear driving them. You may even know some of them, but do not forget your training. This may be hard for some of you, but remember Cargon is with us. Now are you prepared?"

The men loudly voiced their agreement. Slanoth smiled at them then ordered the gates opened. As they stepped out they noticed that the streets were unusually empty, a sure sign of impending danger. Then after a short time of walking the empty streets they heard a commotion from the south. Slanoth looked at Shepard worriedly.

Shepard nodded, a troubled look upon his face. *"Aye it do sound like trouble at da main gate."*

Slanoth was in agreement, so they picked up their pace and headed for the gate. When they arrived there they saw a large group of angry and frightened people. The city guards were hard pressed to keep them at bay. One of the guards was standing upon a makeshift dais trying to calm the people down, but his efforts were lost in the commotion of the mob.

Slanoth saw this and looked to Shepard. "Get the men out to the front and help the guards. I am going to get up there and try to calm this crowd, and make them listen to reason."

Shepard nodded and began giving orders, and the men began to push their way through the crowd. Slanoth followed just behind with William on his left and Cestator on his right acting as his guard.

When they reached the front of the crowd Slanoth stepped up onto the dais. The guard atop it was more than happy to relinquish it. At first Slanoth just stood there taking in the situation. Things did not look very promising, but he could not allow these people to panic.

"Everyone please, calm yourselves." Slanoth called out in his strongest voice. "Everything will be fine. I say to you, the safest place for you at this time is within these walls."

The crowd began shouting at him with questions, rebukes and curses. They had yet to realize who stood above them. Suddenly the light from the lamps set above caught Slanoth's armor and shined brightly. It gave them the illusion that he was glowing. He took off his helm and the people all stared in awe.

Slanoth quickly took advantage of the silence. "In the name of Cargon hear me people of Trecerda. I know of the rumors you have heard about the approaching army, but I say they are just that. It is not made of evil spirits. Yes there may be creatures of darkness among it, but I assure you as a paladin of Cargon that there is nothing that these walls have not faced and turned away. I also say to you that Cargon's graces are with us in this time of need. I am also here to remind you that Cerdrine has never fallen to a besieging army, even in The Trial Wars . . . and I say that it never will."

The people began to cheer and chant "Cerdrine . . . Cerdrine." Slanoth smiled and let this go on for a few moments then raised his hands for silence and the people quickly calmed down. "Now all of you can be of most help by going back to your homes, and if you have the space take in those who do not have a place to stay. The streets are not a place to be at a time like this. Prepare for this as you would a large storm. If you are needed for any reason messengers will be sent to you. I thank you all for your time here, now please return to your homes, and may Cargon watch over us all."

A loud cheer went up and the people began to disperse. When everyone was gone, Slanoth stepped down from the dais and all the guards stared in shock before thanking him. He waved to them saying it was Cargon's words that had calmed the crowd.

Slanoth called Shepard over and told him to take the men and patrol the streets to be sure everything was quiet. Shepard nodded, and went to do so. Cestator and William joined Slanoth to escort him back to the temple. Slanoth looked at each in turn and smiled. "I can take care of myself, you two do know that do you not?"

William bowed his head slightly, but had a stern look about him. Cestator however frowned and leaned in close so he would not be overheard. "We are here for your protection. It would not matter if something were to happen to us. If you were hurt however, it would make a great impact upon the men."

Slanoth's smile broadened at this. "Now my son you think like a paladin, putting others' lives before your own."

"Ha . . ." Cestator scoffed, "and is it a trait of a paladin to lie to the people and give them false hopes?"

Slanoth looked at Cestator and frowned. "I did not lie to them. I told them what we know to be the truth. I also gave them some hope, it may be a false sense of hope, but it is hope, and that is better than the despair that they felt before. You see, people with hope in their hearts will fight even if it means their death. Those without hope will flee and surely die. So I gave them a reason to fight."

Cestator simply shook his head and they walked on. When they arrived back at the temple everyone was busy doing everything posible to prepare for the attack. Slanoth found Braggor in the main courtyard directing things. "Braggor, how do the preparations fare?" Slanoth asked as he walked up to him.

"Ah lord Slanoth, you have returned. Everything fares well for the most part, but there are a few things that need to be worked out."

Slanoth smiled, pleased with what he heard. "That is good and now that I am here I will help with this."

Braggor nodded and looked at William and Cestator then frowned. "What are you two doing just standing there? There is much work still to be done now get on it."

William flinched as though he had been struck, then ran off to help in the efforts. Cestator however frowned deeply at being scolded. He turned to Slanoth for retribution but found none there, so he strode off to do what he could.

Braggor looked after him and shook his head. "That one still has a burr in his boots eh."

Slanoth sighed and shook his head. "Yes, unfortunately every effort I try to rid him of his rage fails. He has too much pride in him. I fear it may mean his death one day."

Braggor shook his head disappointedly. "What a shame he has so much potential in him. I hope that we do find some way to break down his walls."

"Yes Braggor I do agree, and I pray to Cargon every night that we do find the way."

Braggor shrugged his shoulders. Slanoth laughed lightly at this and the two went on speaking of what was left to be done. Sometime later Shepard returned and joined them adding his thoughts, and this went on through the night.

As dawn arose it found the three men still in the courtyard working on the defense of the city. Slanoth rubbed his tired eyes and stretched. The temple was secure and they were helping with the city, but even that was in the final preparations.

"I am going to try and get a bit of rest I have had little sleep the past few days."

Shepard smiled and nodded. *"Aye go right on Slanoth. I would be join'n ya, but me I can no rest when thar be action go'n on."*

Slanoth smiled back at him. "Yes I know Shepard. You always have been one to take action." Slanoth then headed for his chambers. When he got there he took off his armor and began to lie in bed. Just as he laid down there was a knock on the door. He laughed at the irony of it then got up.

"Yes come in." Slanoth called.

Bernard entered the room and bowed deeply. "Lord I am sorry for disturbing you, but the kings messenger has arrived and

Lysandas is asking Lord Shepard and yourself accompany him at the palace."

Slanoth nodded. "Alright Bernard tell him that I will be there in a few moments."

Bernard bowed once again and left Slanoth alone. He quickly adorned his armor and went back out and met Shepard in the courtyard.

"Did you get the summons as well?"

"Aye that I did Albrecht do be back, an Lysandas do want all o' us to go over what we should be do'n."

"Yes I had thought it would be that, so shall we go?"

Shepard nodded and the two headed for the palace. When they arrived they were quickly brought to the king. He was speaking with the general when they arrived in a private room.

When Lysandas saw them he called them over. "Albrecht tells me that the army is less than a day from here and it consists of about one thousand men plus some odd creatures of different sorts."

Slanoth frowned at this. "Yes we know about the creatures. We had faced one just yesterday. So what is the count of the creatures we are faced with?"

Albrecht frowned and shook his head. "I cannot say we ran into the outskirts of the army, and I lost a few men, but there is no telling how many total. My scouts came back talking of things out of your worst nightmares."

Slanoth and Shepard both nodded, but Shepard was first to speak. *"Aye that do sound like da army tha' Cestator did say were come'n.*

Albrecht looked at Shepard in shock. "Did you just say Cestator told you?"

"Yes that is correct Albrecht. I will explain the situation later for now though let us focus on the defense of the city."

Albrecht nodded to Slanoth, and they went on filling each other in on the situation. A few hours into their planning they heard the warning horn sound.

Lysandas looked at Albrecht questioningly. "The army is within sight of the walls." He said answering every ones question and confirmed their fear.

"Well then we should be git'n out thar an see what we be face'n."

Everyone agreed with Shepard's logic, and they all headed for the walls. When they arrived, there were men across the entire length of them. As they looked out over the field everyone gasped in fear. This was no normal army with just a few creatures mixed in. What approached the walls, was an army of the undead. It was a chilling sight to see even for the paladins, for there was no way they could turn so many creatures.

"By all that be mighty, may Cargon protect an guide us, cause we sure'n do be need'n his help."

Every man within earshot of Shepard's words agreed, each saying their own prayers. Slanoth looked out over the rows of the creatures and remembered the prophecy in The Tome, and knew it had come to pass. His greatest fears had come to life before him. As a paladin of Cargon and a warrior of the light he despised the undead and all those who dabbled in the black arts. Yet, he also knew what the walking dead could do to those that had never faced them. The damned creatures could strike fear in the heart of the bravest men. An army of them however, was sure to cause wide spread panic.

Slanoth then turn to Shepard "We must not allow them to get near here. If any of those things get inside the walls, there will be chaos."

Shepard nodded, knowing well the disaster that would befall them if that happened. *"Aye ye be right thar but what do we do? Arrows be no use against them bloody things, an we no have enough men here to be turn'n all o' them."* Shepard then took one more look out at them and gasped in fear. *"Bloody hell I do hope that prophecy no be come'n true."*

"I agree." Slanoth sighed as he looked out over the field. "It will be some time before they get here and we must discuss this, and figure out what we are going to do about this problem."

"Aye that be a good idea, thar be much to figure on here."

Lysandas and Albrecht looked at the two men with wondering eyes. Slanoth noticed the look and spoke softly so no others could hear. "We found a prophecy in an old book that spoke of this situation, and now it seems that it is coming to pass."

"And what did it say?" Lysandas asked quietly.

"Nothing we should be dicuss'n right here. Da prophecy do be vague an thar be too many ears here."

Lysandas nodded, and spoke up so all would hear. "Very good then, that sounds as though this army will be breaking their bones against these impervious walls. Now close the main gates and seal them out."

A few moments later they felt the ground shake as the two massive stone doors settled into place sealing the wall completely. "Very good now that we know what we are dealing with we can work on destroying this army. Come Slanoth, Sheppard, and Albrecht there is much planning to do." Lysandas said in the most confident and strong voice he could muster.

With that they headed for the stairs to the ground below. As they reached the bottom William came running up to them. He appeared winded, but when he caught his breath his voice was full of concern. "Lord Slanoth, General Shepard, and Your Majesty he said as he bowed please come quickly. Cestator has sent me to fetch you. There is something you must see over the north wall."

Shepard shook his head angrily. *"Lad we no be have'n time fer look'n out at da water. We do be have'n an army o' the walk'n dead ta be worry'n bout out thar in da field."*

Albrecht nodded in agreement. "We do not have the time here. There is still much more that needs to be done. We had not planned on having to face an army like this."

William looked at the two men and shook his head. "I mean no disrespect Generals. I do understand that, but there really is something more important at the north wall."

Slanoth heard the concern in William's voice, and put a hand on Shepard's shoulder to stay any rebuttal "Alright William lead the way we will be right behind you."

Shepard looked at Slanoth questioningly, and when William turned and began running back to the north wall Slanoth answered the unsaid question. "The man was frightened. In all the time that I have known him, I have never seen him so frightened."

The three other men trusting Slanoth's judgment nodded then began running after William. Slanoth looked up to the heavens and prayed to Cargon for help then followed.

When they arrived at the north wall Cestator was looking out over the horizon. Shepard was the first there, and he was not happy, and it reflected in his voice. *"What be the blasted problem that ye make us come here fer?"*

Cestator did not say a word, he merely pointed out at the horizon. The four men looked out to where Cestator pointed and saw several dark ships with black sails.

"Ah so thar be ships out thar. Thar be no reason to be worry'n, thar be noth'n can be gitt'n up da face o' dis wall."

"Shepard is right Cestator. There has never been anything that could ever get past the sheer rock face. It is nearly five hundred feet to those waters below. No catapult stone could even come close to reaching these walls." Lysandas said without concern.

Cestator frowned and shook his head in despair. "That may have been true at one time, but do you see the symbol upon those sails?"

Slanoth who was watching the ships intently answered. "Yes there is a large red diamond with something in the center."

Cestator nodded. "Yes and if you could see it closer you would notice that in the center is a black web. That is the symbol of the Angorian fleet. They come from a large island across the sea. They have somehow bread giant Spiders, which they ride into battle."

"May the almighty have mercy upon us?" Slanoth sighed in disbelief.

Shepard looked to Slanoth in shock. He had never heard his friend speak of the almighty.

When Slanoth saw the look on Shepard's face he shook his head. "Shepard, think what special abilities do spiders have?"

"Well they do spin webs."

"Yes and."

Shepard stood there for a moment, thinking. *"By all that be mighty, an da Lord in da heavens above!"* He looked down at the wall below him. *"They'll be climb'n dis wall like it were a flight o' stairs."*

Slanoth nodded fear shining in his eyes. "I think the prophecy may be true Cerdrine may fall."

Chapter 10

The Hunt

Angion and Creashaw knelt behind a large stone. The crisp air was filled with the smell of the animals they were hunting, and the grass waved slowly as a cold breeze softly flowed back past the two. The jerusom were peacefully feeding on the tall grass that reached nearly to their shoulders.

The animals made up a large part in the lives of the plains people. One large jerusom could feed most of their village. Their hides were tough and quite resistant to the weather. If cured properly it made a very soft material. Being very large animals some weighing over five hundred pounds they could also be very dangerous. The three horns coming out of their heads made the animals even more so. The long black hair upon their backs was often used for making rope or as thread. If attacked the animals would usually run unless cornered or with a young one, at that moment they become fierce fighters. Most hunters avoided a mother with her calf for this very reason.

"Ah see here the wind carries our scent away from them. This will be a good hunting day." Angion said with a smile.

This was Crenshaw's first hunting trip. He had just turned fifteen, the age when he was becoming a man.

"You see there, how the large bull watches over the rest of the herd?" Angion said as he pointed at the largest animal. Its horns measuring nearly two feet in length made it a menacing animal. The bull's ears continually twitched listening for danger, and it ate only the top shoots of grass while it kept a close watch over its herd.

"How will we get near them when the bull is watching over them so closely?" Creashaw asked quietly.

"Stay close to the ground and follow my lead. Only move when I move. We will do well if you heed this advice. The bull may be alert but the jerusom are thick skulled." Angion said in answer. Then at the first opportunity he was on the move.

Creashaw followed if a bit more clumsily, and he watched in amazement as Angion moved through the grass. Even at nearly seven feet tall and heavily muscled Angion seemed to meld into his surroundings. Creashaw found it hard to follow his steps. He had heard stories from the other hunters of Angion's abilities, but none of them gave justice to what he witnessed. Angion was like a ghost. He made no sound, and left little if any trail of his passing.

Creashaw was proud to be learning from the best, but he could not help but feel a little sadness. Down deep he wished it was his own father that was teaching him. His father however had died when he was young, and Angion was now the closest thing he had to one. Creashaw had few memories of his father, but those he did have, he cherished dearly for they were all of happy times.

When Angion was within one hundred paces of the jerusom he ducked down and waited for Creashaw to join him. By the time that Creashaw reached his side Angion had already picked out a target. A young bull had wandered away from the herd a short distance, and was well within range of their spears. As Creashaw knelt down beside him Angion pointed at the bull and whispered. "There, do you see that young bull? We will . . ." Angion stopped suddenly when he got a sinking feeling, something was amiss, and he looked back the way they had come.

"What's wrong Angion? Did you hear something?" Creashaw asked somewhat puzzled by the short stop.

Angion pressed his index finger to his lips calling for silence, as he searched the area behind them. Creashaw nodded gripping the shaft of his spear tightly. A bead of sweat rolled down his forehead, but fear kept him motionless. He was not sure he wanted to know what could get Angion to look so troubled.

Angion watched and listened intently to see what made his hair stand on end. Then suddenly from far behind them, where the other hunters awaited them, he heard the sound of a crow cawing. He laid down his spear and removed his axe from its harness on his back. The blade of the axe measured two feet across with a sharp hook on the other side to balance the weight. The handle was made of ironwood with silver wire inlaid upon it for better gripping. Angion was the only man in his village strong enough to even lift the mighty axe let alone wield it.

He held the axe in both hands feeling the weight settle. It felt good in his hands, as though it belonged there. Angion had used it many times over the years, and it was like an old friend that he knew he could always count on.

He quickly found what the warning was for. He saw an undulating line and a large gray-scaled back moving through the grass. It looked as though there was a giant snake slithering along. He knew then what was coming their way. With this realization he turned and looked at Creashaw with great concern. At that very moment, he felt an overwhelming sense of despair, he knew that not only were they in danger, but their entire village would be condemned to a horrible fate. This creature that was coming through the grass was a belath.

Creashaw looked back and saw the blades of the grass parting like a raging river was roaring towards them. He knew then something large was headed their way. With a puzzled look on his face he turned to Angion, to ask if he knew what this thing was. Before he was able to utter a word their eyes locked for a moment, and he saw a glimpse of what this creature had done. Creashaw decided it would be best to stay his questions until Angion was ready to discuss the matter.

The belath then came into view. It looked much like a massive lizard. Its head was elongated and came nearly to a point, with a large mouth brimming with teeth that dripped revolting green venom. It walked on six legs, and the front two were longer than the others. Each of them was tipped with claws that could rip a man to shreds. The body of the creature was long and slender, and it measured about fifteen feet long. The last twelve inches of the creatures tail, was covered in long jagged spikes.

Watching it Creashaw would have sworn that the creature floated on air, for it was so swift he could hardly keep up. He wondered how anything so big could move so quickly, and smoothly. He was in shear awe of it.

Angion then leaned over and whispered to him. "Do not move or make a sound. We are lucky it has not noticed us. This is only a hatchling so somewhere nearby will be the adults so at the first chance we get we must move away."

Suddenly the jerusom sensed the belath was near and they turned to run. They did not get much farther than a few feet before the belath was among them. It attacked ferociously with teeth claws and tail all at once. It killed half a dozen jerusom before they knew it was even among them.

The rest of the jerusom scattered quickly and got away from the beast. All but one fled to safety, the largest bull remained to fight the beast. It snorted and pawed the ground angrily.

The young belath turned to it and seemed to smile, but the smile was insidious with the long sharp blood coated teeth. It screeched an ear-piercing roar at the jerusom in a challenge. The jerusom seeming not to realize it faced its own death charged at the belath. This only seemed to excite the young belath more for it screeched again. Then just as the jerusom was about to impale it, the belath moved to the side slashing with its claws, and cut deep into the side of the jerusom. Even then the animal did not seem to realize what it faced for it snorted and pawed the ground once more readying to charge.

Creashaw looked over at Angion in shock. "What is wrong with that jerusom? It seems to not be running. I've never seen such a thing before."

Angion pointed to the jerusom. "That is the alpha male he stays behind to give the others a chance to flee even at his death."

Angion's words were cut off by another screech from the belath. The two animals looked into each other's eyes both knowing the outcome of the match up, but that did not stop the jerusom. The animal charged the belath once again this time the belath moved away sliced with its claws and brought its tail around, and caught the jerusom in the head.

The jerusom instantly fell to the ground and tumbled towards Angion, and Creashaw stopping ten feet in front of them. Creashaw covered his mouth to stifle a scream at what he saw. The dead jerusom was facing them, and it had a large gaping hole in its head. Blood flowed freely from the wound and the animal's haunting eyes stared at him. The belath then stood over one of the jerusom it killed and roared loudly as though it were calling to someone.

"We should leave here. There will be more belath here in moments. Being so young this one is likely just learning to hunt. It is likely calling for the adults. We should not be here when they arrive."

Creashaw then looked at Angion in shock, he could not believe what he had seen and just heard. "How could such a thing be? If this one is just learning to hunt, and it did this, how much more could an adult do? Look there at what it did to those jerusom. The animals did not even have a chance to run."

Angion shook his head. "Yes there is no doubt it is still learning, this one is somewhat crude in its methods. I have seen a belath in action once before, and it was more decisive about how it killed. This young one seemed to just be playing. As for killing one . . . well that is the kind of thing that creates legends."

Creashaw sat there staring in shock, then nodded and began to move. Before he could get up however Angion pushed him to the ground and pointed to the scene of the carnage. He looked where Angion pointed and at first saw only the young Belath standing over a jerusom. Then suddenly two more belath burst from the grass from either side. One looked much like the young one only larger, but the other was a thing from Creashaw's worst nightmares.

It was shaped much like the others, but the resemblance stopped there. This creature had large hard scales on its back that somehow slid below one another and did not seem to impair its movement at all. It was about twenty five feet long and had three horns protruding from its head much like a jerusom, and its two canine teeth protruded down below its lower jaw. Creashaw gave up trying to discern the color of it for it continually shifted confusing his eyes. Then Creashaw saw its eyes, they were a golden color with small slits like that of a cat, but that was not what scared him. In those eyes Creashaw saw something of pure evil.

Creashaw then looked at Angion fear raging in his eyes. "Can we go now?" he whispered.

Angion nodded somewhat uneasy himself. "Yes, but move as the grass moves and make no sound."

Creashaw had no trouble understanding, and he began to back up when the grass waved in the wind always watching the belath to see what they were doing. Then suddenly the big one turned and stared right at them. Creashaw froze, as did Angion.

The beast flicked its forked tongue out like a lizard and then growled, only its growl sounded like thunder rumbling through the mountains. The belath then began to charge at them. It took everything he had, as well as Angion's strong arm to keep Creashaw from getting up and running. He was terrified beyond words.

When the belath got to the large bull jerusom it snapped its head down and bit deep into the animal. It flicked its head up lifting the large animal off the ground as though it weighed nothing and throwing it within a few feet in front of them. The belath then arrogantly crept towards the two. When it reached the jerusom the creature then began ripping the carcass to shreds throwing pieces at them, and splattering them with blood, as though it were warning them they would be next.

For a moment it stood there on four legs staring at them looking straight into their eyes. The two could feel its hot, putrid breath on their faces. Creashaw covered his mouth so he would not scream in terror. He could see the hatred that this beast held for them, the thing seemed almost mad. Then the beast seemed to smile at them, only the smile was insidious and frightening, and then it let out a deafening roar. Creashaw truly wanted to scream at this point, but he thought that if he did they surely would be dead. Surprisingly however the belath seemed to forget them, and it turned and joined the others.

"I think that was our warning to leave now." Angion said as he began to move away.

Creashaw was in agreement, but he was paralyzed with fear. It took Angion pulling him along to get him moving again. When they were a good distance away from the creatures Angion stood and told Creashaw to do the same. They then headed to where the other hunters waited.

THE HUNT

Angion looked at Creashaw and sighed. "I hope now you have respect for the creatures of the land. You see many men have come through here in search of things like the belath, to try and make a name for themselves, and more times than not they just get themselves killed."

Creashaw shook his head vigorously. "I promise Angion I would never disrespect the powers of the animals around us. But what is it that makes a man a legend like The Mighty Slanoth?"

Angion smiled, he was glad the boy searched for knowledge and not fame. "Men like Slanoth care not for fame. They do what they do because it is what is right, and for no other reason."

Creashaw looked up at Angion, eyes beaming with pride. "I hope someday that I may get the chance to help people as Slanoth did."

"That is a good goal to have Creashaw, and as long as you remember that glory will not feed you, you should do fine. You must remember one thing however, never forget where you come from, and never forget those who love you. They will be there for you no matter what, even when no one else is."

"Oh Angion I would never forget. I am proud of who I am, and where I come from. No one will ever take that from me."

"Good . . . for you should be. Our people have strong roots here. Our people reach farther back than any other people that live upon this land. Our way of life has survived for many ages."

Angion and Creashaw then came upon the place where the other hunters hid, and they all stood. Cerndrose one of Angion's closest friends walked up to them and asked what happened and why they were covered in blood.

Angion sighed and shook his head. "It was a young belath. It killed a few jerusom then the adults appeared. It is not safe here, but we cannot return to the village without a kill. Our food is nearly gone. If we move quickly and stay far from the belath we could get at least one jerusom they may be frightened, but they should also be tired, if we can get one or two we would do well."

Cerndrose agreed with Angion's logic, and the hunters headed in the direction where the jerusom had fled being sure to give the belath a wide berth. They wanted to avoid the creatures at all costs, and they had some distance to travel.

As they approached the place where the horned animals gathered Skreal sensed something hiding in the grass ahead. He called out to his mate, and their hatchling to hold for a moment.

He flicked out his forked tongue tasting the air. He knew what was out there and it was nothing to fear. All that was ahead of them was a group of two-legs. Knowing the two-legs would avoid a confrontation with them Skreal told Thrash to head straight for the horned animals while he and Terial would go to either side and flank them. With a screech of agreement they split up.

The excitement of being on these hunting grounds flooded him with memories of times before. They held sentimental value to him. Some time ago he had killed a large group of two-legs here. He had truly enjoyed the smell of their fear, and the excitement of the hunt. He sighed at the thought of how sweet their blood tasted. They were no good to eat, because they had little meat on them, but the blood was sweet and he began to crave it.

Then there was the memory of the one two-leg that had hurt him. This enraged him for he had shown weakness to the puny creature by running. At that time he had never felt pain and it had confused him. He began anticipating the kill ahead, and the more he thought about it the more he wanted it.

Skreal then decided upon a whim that he was going to find where these two-legs were staying and he was going to kill them all. He was also sure that there would be more than the few he smelled out here, the foolish creatures tended to stay in large groups, of mixed types. Skreal had come across such places before. He again smiled at this memory, killing those was even more pleasurable because they feared him more, especially the small ones.

"Yes . . . that would be good. These two-legs will pay for the pain the one had caused me. I will enjoy hunting them."

Skreal was then torn from his thoughts by the sound of the jerusom being stirred up. *"Thrash is as stealthy as one of those horned animals."*

The young belath learned quickly, but he was still clumsy and loud. The sound of the frightened jerusom went on for a short time, and Skreal could hear them running away. Then after the jerusom were gone he heard Thrash screech in challenge. Skreal smiled at this. He could see through his hatchlings eyes that one of the horned beasts was standing its ground.

"This should be amusing." Skreal then spoke to thrash in his mind. *"Wait for it to charge at you, and toy with it. Watch how it moves and attacks. Then kill it, and it will be yours to feast on."*

Skreal then broke the link, and headed for the feast. A few moments later he heard Thrash screech in triumph.

Skreal and Terial then burst into the opening at the same moment, and they saw Thrash standing above one of the creatures he killed. Skreal was proud, but also a little put out that all the animals had fled. Terial began congratulating their hatchling while Skreal looked out over the kill.

He knew that the two legs were somewhere nearby he could sense them, but he could not see them. He flicked out his tongue to taste the air, and he picked up a scent he knew from long ago. Skreal roared in glee. The two-leg that had hurt him was nearby. He looked around the clearing made by the struggle, but could not find the two-legs. Then suddenly he caught a hint of movement near the large horned beast that had challenged the young one. He looked there and saw that there were two of them.

He had a strong urge to just charge after them and kill the larger two-leg for what it had done to him. Skreal had a better idea though. He decided he was going to teach his son how to viciously toy with them instead. He was going to make it the last he killed, for he wanted to savor its fear, and anguish.

Skreal looked straight into the eyes of the two-legs, smiled and charged at them. When he reached the horned beast Skreal quickly bit into the side of it. He paused there a moment taking in the smell of their fear, and he reveled in it

Skreal threw his head up lifting the massive animal, and hurled it at the two-legs, showing them his strength. He then headed for them making sure each of his steps was deliberate, showing off his prowess. He wanted these two-legs, *men they called themselves from what Skreal had gotten from their minds,* to know he was the one in control of this situation. When he reached the horned animal he plunged his front claws into it, and brutally ripped it in half making sure to spray the two men with as much blood as possible. He snapped up the lower half of the animal in his massive jaws, and began shaking his head back and forth shredding it between his razor sharp teeth. With the violent twist of his jaws he ripped and tore chunks of flesh and bone that flew at them. When he was finished with that he stepped on the head of the fallen animal crushing it like a grape, and sprayed blood and brain matter everywhere. As a final show of his strength Skreal ripped into the remainder of the animal tearing through flesh and bone alike and tossed the shredded remains in every direction.

When he was finished Skreal stood up on his back legs and stared at the two men. He could smell the terror pouring off the smaller one and he enjoyed every bit of it. To add to their fear Skreal smiled at them showing off his blood stained teeth. He quickly grew tired of the game, and he roared at them telling them to leave, then turned away and joined in the feeding.

After a short time he saw the two-legs . . . men skulking away. He reveled in the smell of fear that was rolling off of them. When they were out of sight he went on feeding and partly forgot about them.

After feeding the three belath returned to their den. Skreal had chosen this place because it was where he had killed all those two-legs so long ago. As he stood there he smiled wickedly. The scent of their blood still lingered here even after so long, a testament to the deed he had done, and to Skreal's delight the stains were also still there. Seeing and smelling this brought back fond memories for Skreal, and he decided to have some fun. Terial was relaxing in the diminishing sunlight while Thrash played and practiced his skills. So he left them to do what they would.

Skreal returned to the place where they had fed and quickly found the men's trail. He followed the first two's to a larger group of them. The trail then headed in the direction of where the horned animals had gone.

"So they follow the horned beasts. They must be here to feed as well." Skreal smiled wickedly as he thought of an insidious plan. *"They will not eat well when I have finished."*

Skreal knew exactly where the jerusom had fled. He could smell their fear that still drifted in the air. The scent was strong enough that he could find them blindly. So without wasting any time he moved off in another direction away from the two-leg's trail intending to flank the jerusom.

When Skreal found the herd of jerusom he could smell the fear and agitation around the animals. This pleased him for it would make his plan all that much easier. Instantly all of his hunting instincts came into play and he cautiously stalked the animals. His scales flickering, and changing colors almost seeming to flow with the grass made him nearly invisible. He patiently awaited the hunters as he searched for the best point to attack.

His patience soon paid off. His keen eyesight easily picked up movement out beyond the jerusom. The hunters were stealthy enough to fool the slow witted animals, but to Skreal they were easy to spot.

Out of curiosity Skreal decided to watch them for a moment to see how they moved and what tactics they used. He wanted to know more about them before he killed them, so he could do it more efficiently, and gain the most pleasure from it.

Skreal noticed the hunters were cautious about their movements and that they moved slowly. Considering their small size compared to the horned beasts this showed that they had some intelligence. He watched as they singled out one of the foolish beasts that had wandered aimlessly away from the herd. Then it happened, the small hunter threw his spear at the jerusom and wounded the animal, but the beast did not go down. This startled the rest of the herd and Skreal knew it was his time to act.

Skreal roared in glee, and charged right into the animals in the opposite direction. The already panicked animals, finding another belath among them was too much for them. They bolted wildly, with no regard for anything, not even their young all that they knew was they had to get away. Skreal was overjoyed with the results, and he drove the panicked creatures straight at the hunters, killing a few animals just for the sheer pleasure. The men fled from the stampeding animals, trying not to get trampled.

As the last of the jerusom passed the hunters Skreal saw one of the men get knocked down by one of the animals. It appeared that one of the man's legs was injured. Skreal roared in joy at his find. He quickly ran up to the hunter and stood above him a moment taunting him. The man screamed in terror at the sight of Skreal looming up above him

Creashaw forgot his fear of the belath as they stalked the jerusom once more, the thrill of the hunt had overtaken him. Angion pointed out an animal at the outskirts of the herd that was large enough to feed their village for many days. Creashaw felt proud to be able to provide food for his people. This would be his first kill and he prayed silently to the great spirits to guide his hand, and his spear. Then he prayed to his father, and asked for his help.

The moments seemed to pass slower than they had ever before, and Creashaw could hear his heart beating in his ears. The anticipation was making him shake. Then Angion gave him the signal, and said something that he could not hear over the pounding in his ears, but he did not hesitate. He ran crouched as low as he could get until he was within range, then he stood and with all of his might Creashaw threw his spear.

The spear struck home and wounded the animal grievously, but it did not fall. It reared up in pain and shock startling the rest of the already nervous animals. Then the other hunters quickly jumped up to assist Creashaw.

The others had just reached his side when it happened. Suddenly and with no warning the large male belath, the creature that would haunt Creashaw's dreams for many nights to come, attacked the jerusom from the opposite side. The moment the creature attacked, the jerusom went wild and stampeded straight towards the men. Creashaw stared in shock for a moment, but Angion quickly brought him out of his daze by grabbing his arm and yelling for him to run.

Creashaw did not hesitate a moment longer. He ran as fast as his legs would carry him. The thunderous sound of the stampede made it impossible to hear anything, and he quickly lost track of Angion and most of the other hunters in the crowd of animals.

Then as the number of animals began to diminish he saw one of the others, Jeddah a close friend of Angion's. Jeddah spotted Creashaw a moment latter and waved to him, but when he did so, one of the jerusom ran into him knocking him down and injuring his leg.

Creashaw could see that Jeddah would not be able to stand and run without help, and laying there on the ground would surely mean his death. Without a second thought Creashaw began to run to Jeddah's side. Before Creashaw could reach him however, the belath was upon Jeddah. It stood above him, and he screamed in terror. Creashaw stopped instantly. It was as though his muscles had frozen, he could not even look away. He watched in horror as the belath tormented, and tortured Jeddah. The monster almost seemed to be enjoying the man's screams. Creashaw thought he could hear its thoughts, and what he heard horrified him, this thing was purely evil. Creashaw wanted to run to help Jeddah, but his body refused to move.

Moments later the others arrived to help, but the belath kept them back with its slashing tail and claws. A few of the hunters threw their spears at it, but they simply bounced off of the creature's scaly hide. Everything inside Creashaw was screaming for him to try and help, yet his muscles still would not let him move. The belath then desecrated Jeddah's now dead body by tearing it in two, and throwing the two halves at the other hunters.

This was more than Mealeth could take, and he threw his spear at the monster then charged at it with his knife, only to share his brother's fate. When the creature was finished with Mealeth, it tossed his broken body aside and roared in challenge to the hunters. None of the men dared get too close however, and when the belath realized there would be no more challengers it turned away and somehow disappeared into the grass.

When they were sure the belath was gone the hunters all stood above their fallen comrades, in shock of what they had just seen. None of them were quite sure what to do next. Angion was the first to act, kneeling down and praying over them, he asked the good spirits to take them to the grace lands. The rest of the men then began following suit, all but Creashaw.

Creashaw had fallen into a heap where he had watched the entire ordeal. It was all that he could do when his tightened muscles had let go. He sobbed heavily and tears ran uncontrollably down his face.

When Angion finished his prayers he looked at Creashaw and shook his head. He walked over and knelt down beside the boy. "Creashaw you mustn't cry for them. You will bind them here and they will not be allowed to move on. We must celebrate their life before we mourn their deaths. They were good friends to us all, but the great spirits beckoned them, and none can fight back from that."

Creashaw looked up at Angion with tear filled eyes. He sniffed back his sobs and wiped his nose with his sleeve and shook his head. "No . . . that . . . that is not why I cry. I saw it Angion. I saw everything. Jeddah was just to the side of me."

Creashaw then broke into another fit of sobs, and Angion put his arm over his shoulder, trying to calm him. "Yes Creashaw I know. We all saw what happened. It will be alright, we will return them to the village for a proper burial."

Creashaw shook his head vigorously. "No Angion you don't understand. I saw everything that happened to him. We were running from the jerusom and one knocked Jeddah down. I was going to help him, but the belath reached him first. I can still remember his screams of terror as it stood over him. I wanted to go and help him. I did not know how I could, but I was not going to do nothing . . . only when I tried to move I could not. I could not even call for help. I felt as though my body were made of stone."

Creashaw paused again as another fit of sobbing overtook him. "Jeddah tried to get away but the belath played with him, causing him much pain for the fun alone. I could see into its eyes, it found his screams pleasurable. Jeddah died because I was afraid to do anything."

"No Creashaw. That is not so. If you had tried to do anything we would have three dead and not two. The Great Spirits held you back, for what reason only they know, but do not question their wisdom."

"But Angion a warrior always fights for what is right no matter what the cost. You told me that yourself."

Angion shook his head sadly, and he paused looking at the scene before them. When he finally answered his voice was touched with sadness, and what sounded like a touch of fear. "Yes Creashaw I did tell you that, but you must also remember that a true warrior knows his limits and he gives his hand where he may do the most good. It is hard at times for you cannot save all, but those that you can make it worth the while. I will not lie to you, you will never forget what you have just seen, but you must move on."

Creashaw sighed deeply, and nodded. "I understand Angion. Thank you for your help, but I would like to be alone for a time."

Angion smiled and patted the boy on the back. "Yes of course, take all the time you like. We must make camp here for the night we cannot travel at night with the belath out there." Angion then left Creashaw alone to think about what had happened, and let him deal with it how he needed to.

Cerndrose approached Angion questioningly. "The boy, will he be well?"

Angion looked back at Creashaw and sighed. "I pray to the spirits that he will. He has seen things I would not wish upon any man."

"He is strong like his mother, he will be fine." Cerndrose chuckled forcibly. "For us however we still have much to do. We must quickly clean the animal the boy killed before nightfall if we are to return to the village by morn."

Angion shook his head vigorously. "No we must camp the night. I cannot say how, perhaps it is the spirits watching over us, but I feel that the belath waits out there for us to do such a thing. It is lying in wait for us to move so it may take us one at a time."

Cerndrose looked at Angion in shock, and a hint of it touched his voice. "Angion . . . I have known you for much time. I thought you better than such as that. That beast cannot be so wise as to plan that. Also if it wanted us dead we would be now, it could easily enter here and kill us all before we knew it was among us. If we sleep it surely will kill us, we must move in the dark for our cover."

Angion looked at Creashaw, the boy did not appear to be listening, but he pulled Cerndrose a bit further away, then whispered softly. "My friend you were not there that day. Remember I have faced these things before. Replore was killed right next to me. I battled the creature. These things do not think like an animal they think as you or I."

Cerndrose looked into Angion's eyes for a moment, and then nodded. "Yes . . . then we have more to do, we should not delay."

With that the men began setting up to spend the night in the plains. They stayed in a tight group for protection around a small fire hoping it would keep the belath back.

Skreal circled the two legs camp, somewhat put out that they did not move. They huddled around a small . . . "Fire" they called it, from what Skreal could read of them. Most of their minds he could reach, but there was one he could not touch at all. The small one somehow was immune to his probing.

Skreal watched them intently waiting for them to lay down to rest. He had plans for them. He was not going to let them rest well tonight. As their fire began to die Skreal saw that they began to fall to sleep. He smiled for he noticed that they had difficulty seeing beyond the light of their fire and with it dying he could get close without them knowing. As they fell to sleep Skreal crept up close then when he was close enough he roared loudly.

The hunters jumped up quickly grabbing their spears, looking around for what made the noise. Skreal ran around behind them and threw a body of one of the horned animals into the center of them. A few of the men stabbed the body before realizing it was a dead animal.

Skreal circled their camp several times then he saw an opportunity he could not resist. One of the hunters was slightly apart from the rest of the group and was looking directly at him, but the fool obviously could not see him for he was looking side to side blindly. Skreal crept up slowly, and quietly until he was within striking distance, then for an instant he let the man see him. The man barely had time to scream before Skreal snapped him up in his jaws. He then disappeared into the darkness before the others knew what had happened. He dropped the body a short distance outside their camp and decided he had tormented them enough for the time being, and he watched them for a while to learn more about them.

The hunters stayed on alert for some time after Skreal toyed with them. It took some time for them to feel comfortable enough to relax, but when an hour passed without an incident they began to settle back down to rest. Yet even then they kept up their guard in case the belath did decide to return.

Angion looked over at Creashaw in wonder. The boy had not moved the entire time even when the creature had roared at them. Cerndrose saw where Angion looked and shook his head. "He looks though he is speaking with the spirits."

Angion looked at him blankly. "He did not move from that place even when the belath was just beyond him. He must be more hurt by what he has seen than we thought."

Cerndrose frowned and looked at Creashaw. "I can go speak with the boy. He may speak with me and say what he did not to you."

Angion shook his head. "No let him be if by morn he does not move then I will break him from it."

Skreal moved away seeing the two men had finished speaking. He could not understand most of what they had said, but he was learning. The one thing he did know was that they spoke of the small two-leg that was somehow immune to his probing. The small one intrigued him. He decided he would have to investigate it before he killed it, and find its secrets. By this time the sun was soon to rise and Skreal felt he needed to rest for a time so he returned to the den.

As the sun rose it found Creashaw sitting aside waiting for Angion and the others to rise. There were a few men wandering around to alert the rest of any danger, but for the most part Creashaw was alone. He looked out over the plains and wondered how a creature like the belath could be allowed to live.

Angion awoke and looked over to see if Creashaw was well and found the boy looking at him. He smiled when he saw this. He was happy that the boy had come out of whatever had a hold upon him. "Did you rest any over the night?"

Creashaw shrugged his shoulders in answer. "Some yes, but I had much to think of. It was not an easy thing to do. I had many thoughts of going out into the night and facing the beast."

Angion shook his head vigorously. "That would have been unwise. The beast would have killed you in moments."

Creashaw smiled and nodded. "Yes I know. That is why I have been waiting for you. I was wondering, Angion would you teach me to be a great warrior like you? So I may defend our people against creatures like the belath."

Angion was taken aback by Creashaw's words. "Well that is not what I had expected." He smiled warmly, pleased with what he had heard. "I would be honored to teach the next defender of our people."

Cerndrose walked up just as Angion said the words and smiled himself. "As would I, if you would have it so."

Creashaw looked up Cerndrose and smiled back. "I will take all help that I can. I hope to be as The Great Slanoth someday, and I could use all the help I may get."

"That is a good goal to achieve Creashaw. I do hope that someday you will find your dream."

"Thank you Cerndrose. I was afraid people would laugh at my dream. I am glad at least some feel it is worthy."

Angion shook his head slightly angered. "Creashaw no dream is unworthy of achieving. I know that if you asked any man here he would say the same. Any man who would laugh at you would be a fool." Angion then stood and stretched. "Come now we have much to do before we can go. I hope that the beast is not out there so we may return to the village."

Creashaw shook his head "No Angion, the belath is gone. I could somehow hear it, it returned to its den to rest some time ago."

Cerndrose and Angion both looked at the boy then looked around at the other hunters to see if they had heard the boy. When they saw that no one appeared to have heard him, they sat down on either side of him.

Angion leaned in close and whispered to him. "Take care in saying such things. Some may think you bewitched."

Creashaw looked at him in shock, but Cerndrose nodded in agreement. "Yes Creashaw it is true. There was a man who passed through our village that had spoken of such things. He had warned of it, saying that one of our people would see the thoughts of others, and he would be the sign of many changes in our world. The man had long lost himself and was not of his mind, but some took his words as truth."

Creashaw looked at the two men, eyes wide with fear. They both nodded to him seeing he understood. Then without another word they stood and began preparing to leave.

The hunters built makeshift gurneys of tightly bound grass to carry the bodies of their fallen friends, and the meat from the jerusom. They dared not touch the ones that the belath had killed for fear of what it might do. Those they regrettably left behind.

When they were done the hunters looked over the place where it had happened, and all said a prayer to the spirits to cleanse the place of the evil that had invaded it. When they were done they all turned away and headed back to the village.

Chapter 11

The Village

As they arrived at the village, many people came to great them. But when the people saw their weary and defeated faces they stepped back. Then the people saw the bodies upon the gurneys and gasped in shock. The wives of the men noticed who was upon them and screamed in terror. They ran to the side of their men, and cried out uncontrollably. A few of the hunters who knew them well went to console the women.

Angion looked at this, and sighed. He looked at Creashaw, and told the boy to go home and tell his mother he had returned. Creashaw turned and began to run home, but when he noticed Angion did not follow, he stopped "Angion Are you not going to return with me and tell mother how I killed the jerusom?"

Angion shook his head sadly. "No Creashaw as the leader of the hunt I must speak to the elders of what has happened. They must know there are belath in the area."

"I will come with you then, Angion. I had seen all that had happened. I would be of much help."

Angion frowned not wanting to subject the boy to remember the events of the past day, but he was unsure how to not let Creashaw know this. He quickly came up with an idea. "No Creashaw you must tell your mother what has happened. It is important that she know. All warriors must inform their elders of what has happened in the field, and you would be doing a great service for me if you would inform her. Also tell her I will return home when the elders decide what to do with the belath."

"Yes Angion." Creashaw said in a sad voice, as he walked away head hanging down.

"You go speak with the elders, and I'll just go and tell mother that we are back. A true warrior would not have to go and tell his mother he was home. A real warrior would just go and tell the elders what had happened." Creashaw mumbled under his breath as he walked away.

Cerndrose walked over to Angion sighing. "This is not good for our people. The women will not leave their husbands' side . . ." He faded off when he saw Creashaw walking away. He pointed at the boy and looked at Angion. "What did you say to the boy?"

Angion shook his head and sighed. "I told him to go and tell his mother that he had returned safely. Why do you ask?"

Cerndrose nodded towards Creashaw. "Well you should do something about what you said. He does not seem to take it the way you had hoped."

Angion turned and looked at Creashaw walking away. He sighed and called out to the boy. "Creashaw could you come here a moment I have something to tell you."

Creashaw turned, and frowned wondering what was wrong. When he got close to the men he looked up and smiled sorrowfully. "Yes Angion."

Angion looked at the boy and smiled "Creashaw you were very brave out there. The last two days you have been a true warrior. I am proud of you, when most boys your age would have run you stayed as I had instructed."

Angion paused a moment to let his words to sink in, then after a moment he went on. "It takes a brave man to stay when everything within you is telling you to run. Also what I have asked you to do now will take much courage. You must face your mother's wrath. I myself only have to speak with the village elders."

Creashaw thought about Angion's words for a moment and smiled brightly. "Thank you Angion. You are right I will have to tell mother what had happened. It is likely she is worried sick about us." Creashaw then ran off towards home, dreaming of being a great warrior. He imagined himself fighting a belath like the great Slanoth.

Cerndrose looked at Angion and smiled. "You handled that well. The boy is much like his father was, is he not."

"Yes," Angion sighed. "Almost too much like him. He does not remember him but he cares for him."

Cerndrose patted Angion on the shoulder sympathetically. "You are going to tell him aren't you?"

Angion nodded. "Yes he has a right to the truth. I do owe him that much. The spirits know my father did not give me so much before he left us."

Cerndrose nodded and smiled sadly. "Yes well do it carefully the boy may get a bad idea of revenge." Then just at that moment Cerndrose's wife came running looking for him.

Angion pointed and smiled at him. "You had best go and reassure her you were unhurt."

Cerndrose smiled at him, and took his arm gripping tight. Angion squeezed in kind and the two nodded to each other.

"Thank you my friend." Angion said as he let go.

Cerndrose nodded and smiled. He then turned and joined his wife and went on home.

Angion sighed and turned to the elders' hut. He knew that there had to be something done about the belath, but he was unsure what the elders would decide. When he arrived at the hut, he paused a moment before entering.

As he stepped into the hut Porton the oldest of the men stood, and smiled at Angion. When he saw the dire look in Angion's eyes however he frowned. Porton spoke in a dry raspy voice. "Angion what has happened. Did the hunt not go well?"

Angion sighed and shook his head. "The boy Creashaw got his first kill, but I have dire news. We returned only with one jerusom."

Porton smiled and waved this off. "Worry not of this Angion we will send out another party in a few days to get more."

Angion shook his head and cut the elder off. "I mean no disrespect to you elder, but there is more and it is far worse."

He paused a moment as the elders muttered words among themselves. When they finished he continued. "We would have returned upon the day past, but we ran into some trouble. The boy and I were ready to take two jerusom when a young belath attacked them."

The elders stood and stared at Angion in shock at his words. They all began voicing their concerns about the situation. Porton, who alone remained seated, raised his hand, and told the others to calm themselves and to sit. When the others were all seated he looked at Angion and continued. "This is surely dire news, but tell me was it a single creature or was there others with it?"

"I am afraid it was not. There were two adults with it, and that is not the worst I fear. Jeddah, his brother, and Selanth were killed by one of the creatures. The beast appeared to be toying with us. I fear it may find the village before long."

The elders all began to talk amongst themselves. For a time the discussion became heated, then after a few moments they seemed to come to an agreement. Then once again Porton was the one to speak. "We will set hunters at the outskirts of the village to guard and give warning if the creature should attack."

Angion shook his head disagreeing with them. "That would not be wise. The beast will easily kill any who stand watch out there. We set camp the past eve and it was getting close without anyone seeing it. It stayed outside of the light of our fire but not far from that, Selanth was killed not five feet from the edge of the fire light."

The elders looked at one another and nodded agreeing on the action without a word. "We will then set large fires at the outskirts of the village to be sure the beast does not enter."

Angion sighed He knew they were the wisest men of the village but they only knew what they had heard of these creatures. Angion knew that if the creature wanted to get into the village it would, but he did not voice this to them. They needed some sense of security. "Yes I will get upon it at this moment." He said instead. "If that is all we will need you to give the fallen their final rights for burial."

The elders then moved in close once again talking softly. When they were done they looked almost fearful. "Angion It could be seen in your eyes that you think the fires will not be enough."

Angion nodded in reply.

Porton sighed and scratched his chin. "Yes . . . I was afraid of such myself. So we have decided."

At this moment another of the elders broke in and cut Porton off. "No . . . we cannot ask such of any man."

Porton frowned deeply at the other man. "What would you have us do then leave the village?"

At this point Angion spoke up "Leaving would do nothing, but give the creature more chances to kill us. We are safest here within the village"

"Yes as I had said." Porton said as he scowled at the man who had spoken up. "Now if there will be no more arguments I will continue." Porton then scowled at the rest of the men sitting there, and all moved back in fear.

Porton satisfied that there would be no more interruptions looked back to Angion. "Now as I was saying we have decided that since you know most about these creatures. You would be the best hunter to find the beasts' lair. We ask you to go and keep a watch over the creatures and be sure they do not come near the village. Also, you must find if there is any way that the creatures can be made to leave."

Angion nodded his agreement to the elders' wishes. He stood and bowed to them and began to leave. "In your wisdom I shall follow. I shall do all I can to fulfill what you ask of me."

The elders bowed their heads in acknowledgement. "May the spirits guide you in your journey, and we will be there shortly to give the men a burial."

As Angion began to leave he stopped and turned back. "Pardon elders I yet have something to ask."

"Yes Angion what is it we may do for you? We are here to share our wisdom with all who need it."

Angion sat back down and thought for a moment. "I was going to train Creashaw in the ways of being a warrior. I ask for you permission to take the boy on this journey. I could be alone with him and teach him to live in the wilds." Angion paused for a moment and sighed at a hard memory. "He could also learn much about his father's killer, he must know more about them. He now speaks of battling them to defend the village."

Porton frowned, and some of the others whispered amongst themselves. "Does the boy know his father was killed by a belath?"

Angion shook his head. "No we feared he would do something rash if he had known. We kept it from him for that reason, but now I think is the time he should know. He has seen what they are capable of. I think he now has great respect for their strength."

Porton looked around at the other men each nodded to him in turn. He looked at Angion and smiled. "We will grant your request and wish you luck for you must face a threat far worse than even the belath. You must go and speak with the boy's mother."

Angion cringed at the thought. "Yes I know. No doubt she is upset already, she will surely be unhappy when I ask to take the boy out again. She has a mighty temper and the aim to match."

The elders all nodded, and mumbled their agreement rubbing their heads. They all had faced her wrath at one point or another. "Ah we do wish you the best of luck Angion, and be sure you duck." Porton chuckled.

"I will try to remember, and I will find the way to turn the beasts away. I have more to fear for this time."

Porton smiled, he knew well what Angion spoke of. He had seen the way the man looked upon Sheminal. It was the way a man looked upon the woman he loved. "May the spirits be with you, and guide you in your journeys Angion."

"Thank you father," Angion said as he left the elders' hut. *"I pray the spirits watch over us all, for if that belath finds us we all will be in danger."*

Angion turned and headed home where he knew Sheminal awaited him, and he knew she would not be happy. Angion had taken Sheminal, and her son in when Replore had died. He had promised his dear friend, that he would take care of them, if anything were to happen to him.

There were times when Angion wondered how Replore could have been married to the woman. She was headstrong and opinionated. She also had the temper of a cornered badger. Yet even at the worst moments, all Angion would have to do was look at her, and he knew. Sheminal was the most beautiful creature Angion had ever seen.

Replore had been a lucky man to have her as his wife. She also had a softer side to her. Angion had never known another woman with so gentle a hand as Sheminal, or one that could make him yearn for her like she did. Angion however was always respectful of her, even when she teased him.

The day that Replore had died Angion went to Sheminal himself to tell her of her husband's fate. It had been the hardest thing he had ever done. He had told her all that had happened, and greatly stressed how brave her husband had been, trying to bring her some honor. The entire time he was telling her the story she merely stood there staring at him as though in shock. When he finished however she had broken down and wept beating his chest with her fists. Angion had pulled her close and held her as she cried. Creashaw being only a babe and not understanding why his mother cried had begun screaming as well.

Hearing both of them cry had torn Angion to pieces. He had prayed to the great spirits to never cause them such pain ever again, because he would not be able to handle seeing Sheminal in so much pain. He wanted to go back and change the fates and give himself up so Replore would live instead. Death would have been better than to see her in the pain she had felt.

A tear ran down Angion's cheek as he remembered the day. He had lost a dear friend and caused the woman he loved unbearable pain. When Sheminal had been able to collect herself again Angion had offered to take her in and provide for her, as Porton had done for his mother and himself after his father had abandoned them. Sheminal had accepted his gracious offer, but wanted to wait a day to mourn her loss. It had been at that point that she noticed the gash on Angion's chest. She had frowned at him and scolded him. "Angion you are bleeding to death upon my step, come inside so I may tend to your wounds."

When she had finished Angion tried to rise and return to his own home and she had glowered at him. "Angion you stay right there, if you try to move I will club you." She had warned him while shacking a large stick inches from his nose. Angion chuckled softly at this memory. It had been at that very moment that he realized how much he really loved her. Yet he had never said a word of it to her.

As Angion came out of his memories he noticed he had hardly gone one hundred paces. He laughed when he realized this. *"Look at me I have no troubles going to face the belath, yet here I am dreading the thought of facing the woman."* He shook his head in disgust then headed home. *"I do not believe what that woman does to me. She can make me so happy but when she is angry I fear facing her."*

Chapter 12

Sheminal

Angion stepped up to the door of his hut, and he could already tell Sheminal was upset. He could hear her yelling inside. Yet what was worse he could hear things hitting the wall. She was yelling at Creashaw as far as he could tell, because she was yelling about men being all muscle and no sense, or something of the sort.

Angion tentatively opened the door to the hut. The first thing that he saw was a clay bowl flying straight at him. He barely had enough time to duck it, and moments later he heard it shatter on the ground behind him. *"Yes she is quite upset."*

Creashaw noticed that Angion had arrived and ran out the door while his mother's attention was off of him. "Good luck Angion," he said as he ran by. Angion smiled and waved his thanks.

Angion did not take his eyes off of Sheminal, even when Creashaw ran by him. He wanted to be sure she did not find anything else to throw. Her fists were clenched so tightly her nails dug deeply into her hand. Angion could see her anger burning in those eyes, and he knew he was in more trouble than ever before.

"I know why you are upset, but I assure you we are quite alright. Much has happened and I do not know what Creashaw has told you but there is much we must speak of."

Sheminal stood there looking at Angion furious at him. He had put her son in great risk, and now he was acting as though nothing happened. When she heard his words, which was typical of a man, they only infuriated her more. She walked up to him and smacked him across the face before she even realized it. When she did she felt ashamed and began to cry.

Angion stood there and took her slap without flinching, but when she began to cry it crushed him. He tried to take her into his arms, and comfort her.

"No" Sheminal said as she pushed Angion away. "No you stay away from me. You nearly kill my son and then you want to hold me. Have you no idea how scared I have been, these past few days that you have been gone and when you return I only find that all my fears were real."

Sheminal then began pacing around the room to keep from hitting him again. Her fury had returned full force now. "Don't you remember what had happened the last time you came across these things? If not, I shall remind you, my husband was killed by it, and now my son almost was. How dare you come in here saying that everything is well?"

Sheminal then stopped in front of Angion, her head barely reached the top of his chest but somehow she seemed to tower over him. "I do not need another friend coming to me bearing bad news. Creashaw told me three men were killed yesterday. What if it had been you and my son, where would I be then?"

Angion nodded sorrowfully and looked down in shame. After a moment he looked up into her eyes a tear rolling down his face. "Yes I do remember when Replore died. Do you think I have not thought about it much the past few days? Seeing the beast only made it worse. I wish so that I could have taken his place, but . . ."

Sheminal cut him off by smacking him again. "I never want to hear you say such a thing again. Had it not been for you I would have been lost here. There was a reason why it happened as it did, we may not know what it would be yet, but there is." Sheminal then turned away from him and began to really cry. Angion could not help but to try and comfort her. He had caused her pain, and it hurt him more than he could handle. As he gently touched her she turned to him tears streaming down her face, and frowned.

Angion gently wiped away her tears with his hand and smiled at her. "I am so very sorry I have put you through this. I would not have taken Creashaw out there, had I known that the beasts would be there."

Sheminal looked up at him and shook her head sadly. "Do you not see I was not only afraid for my son but for you as well? If you were to die I would have no one to watch over us. You are as thick headed as one of those jerusom."

Angion smiled and shook his head vigorously. "I think not Sheminal. There is not a man in the village that would turn you away."

"Ha," she scoffed. "Who would wish to take me in. I have lost a husband and then there would be you. Also I have a son who is becoming more trouble than I can handle. No . . . no man would want me."

Angion gently took her hands in his, and looked deeply into her eyes. He saw a fire burning there and he smiled warmly. "I would always take you in Sheminal, nothing would change that."

Sheminal returned his smile and looked at his hands, they were hard and well-worked hands, but they could be so gentle. She looked up into his eyes and saw his love for her. She had known for some time that he loved her, but because of her son she did not allow herself to see it. She slowly pulled one of her hands from his and reached up and touched his cheek. Angion melted into her touch and she smiled at him.

Suddenly there was a loud noise outside their hut and Sheminal quickly pulled her hands away and called out. "Creashaw come in. Everything is well."

The door opened and Creashaw peeked in and looked around. He saw his mother and Angion both looking in a better mood. *"Good,"* he thought, *"It will make this so much simpler if she is not angry."*

Creashaw had made a decision and he was not going to let his mother interfere. He was now a man, and Angion had made him a promise, and he was going to hold Angion to it. He stepped into the hut with the confidence of one who had nothing to lose.

Sheminal looked at Creashaw and felt a different air about him. He had been gone for only a short time, but it seemed he had grown somehow.

Creashaw stepped up to his mother and looked her in the eyes, and worked hard not to flinch from the pain he saw there. He could not say why but he had the feeling she knew what he was going to say. He swallowed the lump in his throat and found his voice. "Mother . . . I"

His mother smiled at him sadly and it choked him up even more. "Yes Creashaw," she said in a subdued voice.

Creashaw nearly burst into tears at hearing the pain in her voice, but he choked them back and stood straight. He knew if he showed weakness now she would surely say no to him. "Mother Angion has promised to train me to be a warrior."

Sheminal stood there a moment then burst into tears and fell to her knees sobbing. Creashaw could tell the very moment when her heart was crushed, and it hurt him far more than seeing Jeddah be killed.

At this point Angion stepped up and shook his head. "I am sorry Creashaw, the time for that will have to wait for now. The elders have put it upon me to find the belath's lair and try to drive them out, and I have made a promise to your mother that I would not intentionally put you at risk against them. I will speak with Cerndrose and ask him to train you in my absence."

Creashaw shook his head angrily. "No . . . this is not right. Your promise to me came first."

Creashaw then ran out of the hut slamming the door behind him. Angion looked out after him and sighed, it had been one of the most difficult things he had to do. Angion turned to see how Sheminal fared. He was slightly startled to find her standing right behind him, her anger now replacing the tears in her eyes.

"You told my son you would train him to be a warrior. Do you have no knowledge of how I feel about that? I wanted more for him than that. I do not want him to end up like his father has, and what is this about you going and facing these beasts again? I will not have it. I will go and speak to these men who think they are so wise, and have my say to them." With that Sheminal began to storm out of the hut.

Angion gently caught her by the shoulder and shook his head. "No Sheminal, you must not dishonor me so. We may not always agree with the elders' decisions, but we must follow them. They only do what they feel is best for the village. So I must do what is asked of me."

Angion sighed and paused a moment, because what he was about to say was going to be difficult. "As for training Creashaw I did not only make him that promise, but I also made it to Replore before he died. He gave me his sword and told me to hide it away until his son was ready to use it."

Sheminal stood there in shock at his words. "You said to me that his sword was lost. You lied to me. How dare you, you speak to me of honor, but you lied to me."

Angion shook his head. "No Sheminal I did not lie to you. Replore's sword went to the spirit world, so yes it was lost to this world, until Creashaw was ready for it."

Sheminal shook her head and turned away refusing to hear this. "No he is still a boy he is not ready for this."

Angion sighed deeply knowing his words were going to hurt, but it was something that he knew she needed to hear. He gently grabbed her shoulders, and turned her to face him then looked into her eyes. "Sheminal . . . is it that he is not ready for it, or is it that you are not ready for it. The sword has been calling to him. I first saw it the eve past, but it is getting stronger. Did you not see it in his eyes earlier?"

"Yes," Sheminal said through another fit of tears. She buried her face against Angion's chest and began beating her fists against it. "Why Angion . . . why must you do this to me."

Angion flinched at her words, but stood there and let her get her fears out. "I am sorry Sheminal, but it is not of my doing. The spirits have chosen him for something though I know not what. You know that I cannot refuse you, any wish so if you would wish me not to train your son I will not."

Sheminal stopped crying almost instantly and pushed herself away from Angion. She threw her hands up into the air and walked away from him. "I give up, you will never change. You are like all the others."

Angion stood there confused not quite sure what had just happened. "Sheminal what are you speaking of? Why are you upset once again? As I told you if you do not wish me to train Creashaw I will not."

Sheminal turned back to him furious. "Ooh . . . that is what is wrong. You act like such a fool at times, like all men. I wish someday you would listen for once. If any one were to train Creashaw I would want it to be you, and since he seems to feel he needs to be a warrior then you will have to do it. What I do ask of you is that you do not go out there and face those beasts again."

Angion's heart dropped at Sheminal's request. He had given his word to the elders and now she asked him to break that. "Sheminal, I beg you please do not request this of me. You know I cannot go back on my word to the elders."

"Ha . . . you say you cannot refuse me anything and here you are refusing me moments later. I see how it is you care for me."

Sheminal's aim was true. She hit him in the one place where he had no defense. As she looked into his eyes she saw a coldness fill them. He bowed his head and walked away from her, and headed for the door. At that moment she regretted her words and wished she could take them back.

She called out to Angion, but he did not respond. He merely left her alone in the hut. Sheminal fell to her knees crying wishing she were dead.

When Skreal awoke from his rest he found Terial and Thrash playing in the sun. He yawned in boredom, and stood to stretch.

His mate seeing him up roared in pleasure then came over to him and tried to be affectionate. Skreal however in no mood for this snapped at her, and warned her away. She meant little to him. She was an inferior creature and he had no desire to mate with her.

Skreal tried mating with others like himself many times before, but all had been failures so he had killed the hatchlings and their mothers. When he found Terial, however she had shown more potential than any of the others. The wizard had performed experiments on her as he had on Skreal, and this made her stronger and more agile. Skreal also knew there was something more she was hiding from him but he did not care. She was stronger than the rest, and he had hoped she could make others more like himself.

Much to his pleasure he was correct. Their hatchling proved to possess much of his strengths. He had little use for Terial now, other than to raise Thrash when Skreal was unable to. He had decided long ago that when her usability was over he would kill her, like all inferior creatures.

Terial shied from him fearing his wrath, confident that she would leave him alone Skreal turned away from her, and focused on his hatchling. *"Come I will show you something more. We will find the two-legs' lair, and trouble them."*

Thrash roared in glee at Skreal's thoughts. He had gotten tired of staying at the den. The horned beasts had been a pleasure, but to face these things that Skreal spoke of seemed more interesting.

Skreal did not bother saying anything more, he merely turned away and headed for the last place where he had seen the two-legs. Thrash looked back at its mother roared a joyful farewell and followed.

When Skreal arrived at the place he had killed the two "men" he quickly found their trail away from the area. He let his offspring get the scent of the creatures and allowed him track them all the way to their gathering place.

As they got near to the village Skreal stopped Thrash, explaining to him that these two-legs had some intelligence unlike the horned ones. He knew they would set guards out to watch for danger, and they also appeared to have built large "fires," they called them, to keep him at bay. He laughed at this for he feared nothing. Yet he still decided to hold back and allow Thrash to watch the creatures' activities.

After a short time of watching the two-legs Thrash was anxious to run into the midst of the creatures and start killing as many as he could. Skreal smiled at the young one's enthusiasm, but he did not want the two-legs all dead yet. He did compromise however by letting Thrash attack one of the guards.

Thrash roared in glee at this. He moved in slowly until he spotted one of the two-legs close to one of the fires. He crouched down as far as he could, and watched its movements waiting for the right moment to attack. Then the two-leg turned away from him and he pounced. The man did not have a chance Thrash was upon him in a moment. He managed to let out a short scream before he was torn to pieces.

Skreal watching from the darkness smiled at what Thrash had done, but he was also somewhat put out by how quickly it happened. He decided he was going to have to teach the young one to toy with them more. He did like Thrash's enthusiasm however.

Suddenly Skreal heard more of the two-legs coming to help the other. He smiled and pondered letting Thrash kill them as well, but decided against it. Skreal called Trash back and congratulated him for a job well done. Then the two-legs appeared carrying fire on sticks trying to ward the two off. Skreal smiled at their feeble attempts of trying to drive him away.

Thrash already excited from the taste of blood wanted to kill them, but Skreal forbid it for the time. Instead the two roared at the two-legs making all but one of them step back in fear, the one who Skreal despised. Skreal may have let Thrash kill them had that one not been among them, but he had plans for that one. Then suddenly another two-leg joined the others and when it saw him it screamed in fear. Skreal relished the fear and told Thrash to smell it and enjoy it.

Skreal then decided that he had, had enough fun. He roared at the two-legs one last time and turned away calling Thrash to follow and the two returned to their den leaving the two-legs to their fears.

The light of first dawn peeked into the hut, and Sheminal arose to find Angion preparing his things to leave. She sighed deeply thoughts of asking him not to go raced through her mind. She had a difficult night, plagued with dreams that she could not remember. She knew though that if she asked him not to go it would hurt him.

Instead she walked over to him and hugged him tightly. She looked up into his eyes and saw the pain she had inflicted in them, she wanted to scream. "Angion please forgive my words to you last night. I was acting out of anger. I did not mean the words I had said to you."

Angion smiled at her and hugged her back. "I know this Sheminal, and I know that you do not wish me to go, but it is something that I must do. As for your son however I will keep my word to you. If you do not wish me to take him I will not."

Sheminal smiled warmly. "Thank you Angion for understanding. I would just not want to live if anything happened to him."

Angion nodded his assent, knowing that would be her answer. "Very well then, will you tell him, for I have a long venture to make and little time in which to prepare for it?"

Sheminal nodded sadly. She really hated to do this, but her fear of losing her son was far too much to overcome. "Yes of course Angion, I will tell Creashaw."

At just the moment Sheminal said the words Creashaw walked into the hut a large frown upon his face, and carrying two water skins. "Tell me what mother?"

Sheminal jumped at the sound of her son's voice. She turned to him and forced a smile. "We have decided that it would be best if you did not go with Angion at this time, at least as long as those monsters are still out there."

Anger flared up in Creashaw's eyes. All his life he had feared his mother's wrath, but now he thought nothing of it. "Was it the two of you who decided, or was it just you mother?"

Angion stepped up at this point, he was not going to stand by and let the boy disrespect his mother as such. "No Creashaw it was my decision not to take you along. Where I go will be no place to train you, it will be far too dangerous to do so. So I will not have you speaking to your mother in such a way."

Creashaw dropped the water skins right where he was standing. "Here then, I have brought you some water for your journey." With that Creashaw stormed out of the hut.

Sheminal looked after him with pained eyes, and a tear rolled down her face. "Angion what has happened to my son?"

Angion walked over picked up the water skins and sighed deeply. "He has become a man." He then gathered all of his things and hugged Sheminal once again saying goodbye.

Sheminal shook her head not wanting to hear that. "Safe journeys," she said instead.

Angion smiled and hugged her even more tightly then left the hut. He went out of town and quickly found the belath's trail. He followed their winding path for an entire day. He began to wonder why the creatures were traveling in a most erratic fashion. Then it came to him, they were trying to throw off anyone following them. He smiled at the intelligence of the creatures.

Sometime after dark Angion found the belath's lair. It was in a large stone that seemed to have been carved out to provide shelter from the hot sun during the day. Then Angion noticed something disturbing. There was only two of the belath resting there. The large male was nowhere to be found.

Angion reached back, and released his axe from its harness. Suddenly he heard a loud roar from his left side. He turned to face the creature and screamed in pain as one of its razor sharp claws severed his hand holding the axe. He looked at the stub where his hand had been for a moment in mute shock then turned to run, but the belath swung its tail around and caught his legs smashing them. Again Angion screamed and he tried to drag himself away.

The belath seemed to laugh at his feeble attempts of escaping, but Angion knew nothing else to do. He knew he was as good as dead, but his will to live did not give up. The belath then picked him up with one of its claws and carried him over to the others and dropped him before the young one. The young belath looked into his eyes and saw his fear and roared in glee. The last thing that Angion saw was the creature's large maw coming straight at him venom dripping from its long teeth. Before he died Angion managed to scream out one word. "SHEEEMIIINAAAL"

Sheminal awoke with a start, tears streaming down her face. "Angion no . . ." she screamed out.

Creashaw ran over to his mother very concerned for her wellbeing. "Mother what is wrong, are you well?"

Sheminal shook her head sorrowfully. "No Creashaw I am not, Angion is dead. The belath has killed him."

Creashaw shook his head not wanting to believe this. "No mother this cannot be. Angion would not fall so easily."

Sheminal looked up into her son's eyes with tears streaming down her face. The pain in her eyes was impossible to deny. Creashaw flinched at the sight of her crying so. He knew from the look in her eyes that she spoke the truth. "They killed him Creashaw. Porton and the other elders sent him to his death. They sent him out there alone knowing how dangerous these things are, and now he is dead."

Sheminal's face then changed from one of sorrow to one of fury. Creashaw stepped back in fear. He had never seen his mother so angry. Sheminal stood and went into the back storage room and brought out two javelins wrapped in cloth, and she headed for the door of the hut.

Creashaw looked at her in shock. He had heard her speak of his grandfather's weapons, but he had never seen her holding them, much less carrying them out. "Mother where are you going?" he called out fearfully.

Sheminal did not stop or even turn around to answer him. "I am going to set things right," and with that she walked out the door and headed for the elders' hut.

Creashaw fearful she may do something rash ran next door to Cerndrose's hut to get help. After a short time of Creashaw pounding on the door, Cerndrose threw it open and scowled. He was about to tear the boy apart for making such a racket at so late an hour, but when he saw the fear in the boy's eyes he called him in.

Creashaw shook his head to this. "There is not enough time. Please come with me I fear mother may kill someone."

Cerndrose looked at the boy in shock not quite sure he heard Creashaw right. "What . . . Creashaw slow down a moment did you just say?"

Creashaw nodded and waved Cerndrose on. "Yes I will explain on the way just please help me stop her."

Cerndrose nodded and ran after the boy. "Now Creashaw what is happening, and why did you say such of your mother?"

Creashaw looked back at Cerndrose as they ran. "The belath has killed Angion and mother blames the elders for it. She took grandfather's javelins and ran to the elders hut with fire in her eyes."

Cerndrose stumbled slightly when he heard that Angion was dead. He did not doubt the boy, but it was not easy to hear. When he heard Sheminal had the weapons however, he understood the boy's concern.

Sheminal stopped in front of the elders' hut, her father's weapons strapped to her back. She was determined that if they would not do anything about this she would. She pounded hard upon the door being sure she was heard, and was not ignored. After a short time Porton popped his head out. When he saw Sheminal's tear stricken angry face he opened the door wide. "By the spirits child what is wrong with you," he asked.

Sheminal frowned at him and forced her way past him so she could face all of the elders at once. When she found them all inside looking at her in shock, her frown hardened. "None of you feel it do you? You know nothing of what you have done, do you?"

The elders did not answer her. They simply stared at her in shock. The sight of her with the javelins pointing out over her shoulders was something to be beheld. She had never used them, but they seemed to belong there.

Sheminal shook her head at them. "You sent a man to his death, and you just stand there like you have no knowledge of it."

Porton was the first to recover, and he shook his head and walked up to her. "Child who do you speak of, everyone is fine."

Sheminal reached over her shoulder and in one fluid motion had one of the javelins out and stuck it deep into the floor of the hut before her. "Angion . . . You sent Angion out to find the belath and now it has killed him."

Porton stepped back in shock, as much from hearing the news as from the look in Sheminal's eyes. At just that moment Creashaw and Cerndrose burst through the door.

"Mother no . . . pleases stop don't do it." Creashaw shouted when he saw the weapon in the floor.

Sheminal looked at him anger burning in her eyes. "Go home Creashaw. You do not understand, and Cerndrose if you are not with me then you leave as well."

Porton then raised his hands for everyone to calm themselves. "Now Creashaw, Cerndrose stay your hands. We are all well, but Sheminal has a grievance let her have her words." Porton then turned to Sheminal and nodded to her.

Sheminal then looked back at Creashaw, and Cerndrose and scowled, she turned back to Porton and went on. "As I said the belath has killed Angion. So I tell you that I place his blood on your hands."

Cerndrose gasped in shock of the curse. "Sheminal no you must not do so. You do not understand what you are saying."

Porton waved Cerndrose to silence then turned to Sheminal. "Child what makes you think that Angion is dead?"

Sheminal pulled the javelin from the floor and held it out before her. "Here take this weapon and drive it through my heart. It will do no less damage than what has already been done by your hands." When Porton did not motion for the weapon she replaced it in its holster on her back.

Sheminal then took his hand in hers and placed it over her heart. "Can you feel that, it is my heart being torn apart every moment I stand here arguing with you? If you do not understand then I will go and find Angion myself." She then turned away from him and headed for the door.

Cerndrose stopped her just as she stepped past him. "Sheminal what are you doing?"

Sheminal looked up at him and smiled sadly. "Cerndrose, you Angion's best friend you should know in your heart the truth."

Cerndrose nodded sadly. "Yes Sheminal I feel it as well, but you must not do this. The elders did not know this would happen."

Sheminal frowned at him becoming angry again. "They sent him out there alone with no thought of what would happen." She shook her head and sighed. "Cerndrose, of all I thought you would understand." Sheminal then walked out the door.

Creashaw, who was in shock until this moment, shook his head and looked at Cerndrose. "We mustn't allow her to go out on her own. The belath will kill her."

Cerndrose nodded and the two ran out of the hut after Sheminal. She was at the outskirts of the village when they caught her. "Sheminal wait, if you are going after him let me gather a hunting party so we may have a better chance."

Sheminal stopped and turned to Cerndrose, her face covered with more tears. She nodded and smiled. "Thank you Cerndrose."

Creashaw walked over and hugged his mother, and she cried on his shoulder. Cerndrose went and gathered ten men. Each of them was more than willing to risk their lives for Angion, for he had done so for each of them on at least one occasion. Sheminal smiled when she saw all of them ready to die for him, it was a touching sight. Cerndrose nodded to her, and then called the men to surround her for protection and they headed out.

As they passed one of the large fires set to protect the village they heard a loud roar. The men stopped, and moved into a defensive position. They scanned the fading darkness, but could not see anything. A moment later they heard Porton calling out from the elders' hut asking what was happening. One of the men turned back and shouted back that there was a noise out ahead.

Suddenly from the darkness a large ball of green acidic venom flew past them, and as it passed the fire ignited it. The ball of fire hit the door of the elders' hut, and exploded igniting the entire building and those around it. The screams of the people inside could be heard loudly as they burned alive.

The hunters seeing this charged out into the darkness after the source. Cerndrose, Sheminal, and Creashaw stayed behind however, and they called for the others to stay but their words fell on deaf ears, and a few moments later the three heard the Screams of the men as they died. Then as quickly as they started the Screams stopped, and all was quiet but for the sound of the fires roaring around them. Sheminal looked at Cerndrose with fear in her eyes. "What is happening here Cerndrose?"

He looked at her and shook his head. "I am not sure, but I think the belath has decided to come to us."

Sheminal shook her head in dismay. "No, this cannot be happening! I must find Angion."

Then as though she had called him up into existence Angion's body landed before them. Sheminal began to scream at the sight of his tattered remains. One of his hands were missing cut off at the wrist, and two gaping holes that seemed to be burnt with some acid nearly cut him in half.

Sheminal then looked up and screamed even louder. Standing just within the light of the fires was the most horrifying creature she had ever seen. Its scaled skin seemed to shimmer and wave in the firelight. When it saw her looking at it with terror in her eyes, it seemed to smile at her. Sheminal stepped back at the sight of that wicked smile. It was insidious and pure evil. At this point Cerndrose and Creashaw looked up from their fallen friend's body and saw the beast.

Cerndrose infuriated beyond all reason charged at the beast. The belath moved like quicksilver and swung one of its claws at Cerndrose cutting him into many pieces. Blood and entrails splattered the ground as the portions of what had been Cerndrose fell.

Sheminal stared in shock at what she had just seen. She could not even move when the beast came charging at them. Creashaw tried to pull her away to safety, but she was paralyzed. Then the belath reached them and bit into Creashaw and lifted him up shaking him back and forth until the lower half of his body tore away and flew a few feet away.

It then dropped the remains and came after her. Sheminal stood there in mute shock as she looked up into the beast's large maw coming down at her. Then everything went black.

Chapter 13

Leaving Home

Sheminal opened her eyes and she saw a desolate wasteland. "Is this the spirit realm? I did not think it would be like this."

Sheminal then heard a familiar voice from behind her. "No my dear this is the realm in between. Many spirits become trapped here however."

Sheminal turned around and she saw her dead husband standing there. "Replore is it really you? Oh I have missed you for so long."

Replore nodded and smiled at her. "Yes my dear Sheminal it is me, and I have missed you as well. I fear this is not the time for a reunion though."

Sheminal shook her head not hearing him. "No Replore we are in the afterlife together, so let us move on to Destinta."

Replore shook his head sadly. "No Sheminal that is not possible. First you are not truly here, what you have seen was only a vision of what will happen if you do not allow Creashaw to go with Angion."

Sheminal stepped back in shock. "You mean what just happened never really happened? It was a dream?"

Replore nodded to her then waved and he was gone.

"Wait Replore please don't go. I need you . . . I need you." Sheminal then awoke with a gasping breath, and she was soaked in a cold sweat. She buried her face in her hands and began to cry. Suddenly from outside Sheminal heard a loud commotion. She pulled herself together, and got up. She went outside to see what was going on. When she got outside she noticed the noise was coming from the outskirts of the village. She ran over to the place where it was coming from and saw a group of men there. Then she saw it, the monster from her nightmare. Sheminal began to scream in terror. It had come for her again, she thought. She fell to her knees and screamed ever harder.

Angion turned at hearing the scream and saw Sheminal on her knees behind them. He called out for Creashaw and pointed to her. Creashaw nodded understanding what Angion wanted. He ran over to his mother and knelt down beside her.

Sheminal looked up at Creashaw not seeing him, she seemed to be elsewhere. Creashaw took her shoulders and lightly shook her. "Mother we must get away from here. It is not safe."

Sheminal then came out of her nightmare and stared in shock at Creashaw. "Creashaw you're here and you're alive. Is that . . . that the belath?"

Creashaw looked at her unsure how to answer her. "Yes mother of course I am here." He then looked back at the beast behind him and nodded. "Yes that is the belath the one who killed the men, and that is why we must go. It is too dangerous here."

Sheminal shook her head vigorously. "No it will not enter here. I wish to get a closer look at it."

Creashaw shook his head. "No mother it is too dangerous, if it decides to attack we will not be able to protect you."

Sheminal frowned at her son. She was not going to be denied the chance to see the beast that had killed her husband. She could not say how, but she knew it was the same one that had killed Replore. Sheminal stood, and against the protest of her son, and the hunters she stepped out in front of them and yelled out to the beast. "May you be damned by all those that you kill, and never find the peace of Destinta?" With that she spat at the beast and turned away uncaring if it killed her. It did not kill her however, instead it roared in defiance seeming to have understood her, and disappeared into the darkness.

When the creatures were gone Sheminal turned around and headed back to the hut. Angion and Creashaw tried to stop her but she did not listen. Instead she went home and returned to bed, and laid awake there for the remainder of the night.

Angion looked at Creashaw when she was gone. "What did she say to you? Have you any clue what is wrong with her?"

Creashaw shook his head in confusion. "When I spoke with her she seemed surprised that I was here. I tried to take her to safety, but she refused, and then she did that." Creashaw said as he pointed out to where the belath had gone.

Angion shrugged, and went over to the men, and sent them out in groups to keep watch over the village. He also gave them orders to call him if there was trouble.

When all the men were out scouting, Creashaw joined Angion and sighed. "Mother will never let me go with you now."

Angion looked back in the direction Sheminal had gone, and he sighed. "Well we will see won't we?" Angion then looked out where the belath had gone and shook his head. "They will not return this eve. Tomorrow is going to be a long day, it would be best to turn in now."

"Yes if mother agrees." Creashaw scoffed, but even in the mood he was, he agreed with Angion and they headed home. When they arrived they found Sheminal already in her room so they went to their places and slept as well as they could.

At dawn Angion awoke and found that Sheminal had already gotten up. He went outside the hut and found her working over the fire pit cooking more food than was needed for morning meal. When Sheminal saw him she smiled. "Angion good morn did you rest well?"

Angion slightly confused by this nodded. "As well that could be expected knowing that those beasts are out there."

Sheminal nodded and smiled all the more. "Does Creashaw still sleep?"

"Yes he is still inside asleep, but I can go and wake him if you would like."

Sheminal shook her head. "No he should get as much rest as he can for the journey. I also would like to speak with you alone for a short time."

Angion was slightly bewildered by this. "So you have decided to let Creashaw accompany me?"

Sheminal looked away dreamily then shook the nightmare away. "I did not have much choice in the matter unfortunately. Creashaw is becoming a man now. I can see how clearly he wishes to go and I do not think I could hold him back for much longer."

Angion was not surprised by her words. He had seen it in her eyes the day past, but he was surprised that she agreed so easily.

Sheminal walked over to Angion and looked up at him. "I just have a few things to ask of you. Come back to me safely. Do not do anything foolish, and watch over my son."

Angion nodded and smiled. "Of course Sheminal I will do the best that I can."

Sheminal walked a short distance away from Angion then turned back to him. With a troubled look upon her face she went on. "I have only one other thing to ask. Promise me that no harm will come to my son."

Angion frowned and shook his head "Sheminal You know as well as I, that I cannot make you that promise. There are a number of things that could happen you know that. Yet I do know that the village is no longer safe."

Sheminal sighed and nodded. "Yes of course you are right. I had just hoped, but I thank you for not making a hollow promise."

Creashaw awoke to an empty room and was disappointed to be alone. Fearing that Angion had already left, he quickly dressed. He ran out the door and found Angion and his mother talking by the fire. He also noticed there was more food on the fire than was needed for a morning meal.

When they saw him Angion and his mother stopped speaking. His mother smiled and came over to him and hugged him tightly. "I love you dearly my son, always remember that whatever happens."

Creashaw's heart sank at her words. She was not going to let him go. "I love you as well mother." He turned to the fire and looked back at her. "Are you making food for Angion's venture?"

Sheminal smiled sadly, yet proudly. She could hear disappointment in her son's voice. He thought she was not letting him go, but he said nothing of it. She could see clearly he had grown much of late. "Well of course it is. I could not send my two men out with nothing to eat now could I."

Creashaw's eyes went wide at her words. "Mother did you just say?"

Sheminal smiled warmly and nodded.

"Are you saying that I may go with Angion?"

Again Sheminal nodded. "Yes you may on one condition however. You must pay heed to everything that Angion tells you."

A large grin spread across Creashaw's face. "I will mother, thank you." Creashaw said, and he ran into the hut to gather his things. When he came back out he hugged his mother tightly and whispered into her ear. "Thank you . . . Oh thank you mother. I will make you proud I promise."

Sheminal reached out and touched his cheek, as a tear ran down her face. "You already have my son . . . you already have. Now it is time for you to follow your destiny wherever it may lead you." Sheminal then ran into the hut crying and shut the door behind her.

Creashaw looked after her, and began to head for the hut to try and calm her. Angion stopped him by placing a hand on the boy's shoulder. Creashaw looked up at him, and Angion shook his head. "Let her go Creashaw, your mother has just done the most difficult thing. If you go in there it will only make it harder on her. Give her time she will be fine."

Angion looked at the door of the hut and sighed. *"You know something don't you Sheminal? I wish I could see what it is that stirred your fears."* He looked at Creashaw and smiled warmly. "Well now are you ready to go? It may be some time before we return, so you must be sure."

Creashaw looked up at Angion beaming. "I have been waiting for this day all my life Angion. I have never been so sure ever before."

Angion nodded and looked around at everything. The village seamed peaceful and he breathed in deeply dedicating everything to memory, so he would remember if he never returned, as he did he smelled the delicious scent of Sheminal's cooking. He looked at Creashaw and pointed at the fire. "Well at least we will not go hungry. Your mother has made quite the meal for us."

Creashaw was looking at Angion wondering what he was doing as he stood there just looking around. When Angion finally spoke he mentioned the food. This puzzled Creashaw. "Angion what is wrong? Is there something out there in the village that I don't see?"

Angion smiled at the question and shook his head. "No Creashaw I only wish to remember the peace here. Being away for much time you can grow weary and need to return. So I try to remember as much as I can to keep me company on the long nights."

Creashaw more confused by the answer shook his head, and turned to the fire. "That does smell wonderful, and it would be a waste to leave it. I will miss mother's cooking." Creashaw said as he began putting the dried meat, and bread into a pouch.

Angion chuckled at this. He saw the confusion in the boy's eyes but he knew that Creashaw would understand soon enough.

When Creashaw had most of the food in his pack, leaving some for his mother he turned to Angion. "I am ready when you are."

Angion nodded. "Very well let us go then." Angion placed his pack on his hip and the axe in its harness and headed for the place where the belath had attacked the night before. When they reached the fire at the outskirts of the village Cerndrose was waiting there. When he saw them he smiled and headed over to them.

"Angion old friend, you be sure that you teach this boy right, or I will have to do it." The two men smiled at one another and gripped arms in friendship. "You take care out there I will be asking the spirits to watch over you."

Angion nodded. "Thank you friend, for some reason I think we will need it." Angion said as he looked at the boy.

Cerndrose turned to Creashaw and smiled even more brightly. "Now you watch out for this big lug, will you? Be sure he does not get himself into trouble and good luck in your quest to become like the mighty Slanoth."

Creashaw smiled back and laughed. "Thank you Cerndrose, and do not worry I will keep him from getting into too much trouble."

Cerndrose chuckled at this looked to both of them, and sighed. "You both return to us safely."

The two nodded and said they would do their best and headed out into the plains following the trail Skreal and Thrash had left.

The belath's trail was easy to follow. They trampled a large swath of grass, but Creashaw noticed that it was not straight, it seemed to move in all directions, and even at points they retraced back upon one another. Creashaw looked up at Angion and mentioned this.

Angion nodded, he seemed slightly rattled. "Yes this shows intelligence. You see they appear to know that their trail would be easy to find so by moving like this they try to throw off anyone who would follow. They do not wish to be found. Yet they do appear to be heading north likely to the mountains."

Creashaw looked up at Angion in amazement and wonder. "How do you know that from just this trail Angion? It seems to be going everywhere."

Angion stopped and smiled at Creashaw. "Look out there, find the smoke from the fires in the village, we have traveled for some time, but there should still be some smoke in the air."

Creashaw looked around out at the horizon and quickly found a small amount of smoke rising into the air. He pointed it out to Angion.

Angion nodded. Good now where is the first sun in the sky?"

Creashaw looked at him puzzled for a moment and pointed to the right. "It is there Angion, it has yet to hit mid-day so it is to the . . ." Creashaw looked at the sun then quickly looked where he had seen the smoke. He stared at Angion in shock. They were directly north of the village.

Angion saw that the boy understood. He smiled knowingly and turned to follow the trail. Creashaw stood there for a moment in shock staring at Angion's back. At that moment he realized how much he had to learn. He quickly followed Angion. After a time, Angion stopped at a point where the trail moved sharply to the right. He had a dark frown upon his face.

Creashaw looked up at him puzzled. "Angion what's wrong, you look as though something is bothering you?"

Angion looked at Creashaw and the boy stepped back from the fear he saw in those eyes. Angion pointed out in front of them. "Just a ways ahead of us there is the place where the belath killed the jerusom. A few days have passed now, and there likely would not be much left, but there should be enough to feed small scavengers. However I cannot hear any sounds from them. There is something wrong there."

Creashaw looked in the direction Angion pointed He did not know how Angion knew where the exact place was, but he did not doubt him. He held his breath and tried hard to listen for any sounds, but as Angion had said everything was quiet. Suddenly he had a strange sensation as though he were reaching out to the place of the kill. He jumped in fear of the sensation and it quickly vanished.

Angion looked at him concernedly, and placed his hand on the boys shoulder. Creashaw jumped at the touch, but when he saw it was Angion he sighed in relief.

"Are you well Creashaw? You appeared to be elsewhere for a moment there."

Creashaw nodded vigorously, his hands were shaking, but he smiled. "Yes Angion I am fine I was only trying to listen for any sounds out there. Now that you have pointed it out it is troubling that's all."

Angion could see in the boy's eyes that there was something more than that, but he decided that the situation before them was more important. "Yes I agree. We should go and find what the reason is for this." Angion then left the trail and headed for where he knew the kill had occurred. Creashaw glad that Angion did not pursue it any further followed.

A short time later Angion stopped suddenly, and Creashaw nearly ran into him. "Angion what is . . . ?" Creashaw began to say but when he looked where Angion stared he gasped in horror. Angion was right. It was the place where the belath had killed the jerusom. The scavengers however were there, many different types of them, but they were all dead. It was a gruesome sight. Creashaw instantly lost all the food in his stomach and more.

Angion stared out at the carnage. The jerusom were torn to pieces and the area was covered with blood, and the stench was nearly unbearable. It smelled of death, but it was more than that, there was a strange acrid smell to it.

Angion frowned and decided to investigate further. He walked over to one of the larger Scavengers lying near a jerusom and what he saw was disturbing. The animal's eyes were full of blood and its belly seemed to be burned out by something. It also appeared that some smaller scavengers tried to feed upon it, but they too were lying dead next to it. At this point Creashaw walked over and stared in shock. "Angion what did that to it. It looks like . . ."

"The belath's venom did this." Angion said almost as shocked as Creashaw was. "Somehow it appears to be deadly even after a few days. Look there those small animals fed upon this one and yet they still are dead. This is not good, if it can kill even twice removed there is no telling what theses beasts may be capable of."

Creashaw looked at Angion, fear burning brightly in his eyes. "Angion what are we to do. They know where the village is. We have got to find some way to stop them."

Angion looked at the boy and felt the fear pouring off of him. He smiled inwardly hoping that fear would help the boy hone his skills, and hopefully it would keep him from doing something rash when he learned the circumstances of his father's death. "We should go from here. We must find a place to make camp."

Creashaw looked at Angion in puzzlement. "I thought we were going to find the belath's lair."

"I have a good sense as to where they will be, and I know of a good place to make camp where we will be hidden from them. It will take most of the day to reach it so we must go now." Angion headed northwest, and Creashaw looked around one last time then followed.

Chapter 14
Master and Student

The second sun was just setting as they reached a large stone. Angion led Creashaw around to the backside of it, and there was a small cleft cut into it. It appeared to have been used many times before, for there were signs of many campfires upon the ceiling of the crevice.

Creashaw looked at Angion in shock. "I did not know this was out here it seems it is used often."

Angion smiled at him. "Yes indeed it is. Many travelers stop here to rest. It gives good protection from the weather. The mountains to the north block most storms from there and the rest the stone covers. There is another farther to the west but it is now cursed and is never used. That I am afraid, is where the belath are likely hiding"

Angion looked around the stone and smiled. "It has been some time since anyone has been here. If you head towards the mountains there, you will find a few trees. Go and collect some wood for the fire. Be sure you are back before dark. Many dangerous things lurk in the darkness of night. I am going to check the area to be sure the belath have not been around here. With that Angion left Creashaw to do as he was told.

"Ok Angion, I . . ." Creashaw began to say, but when he turned to where Angion had been, he was nowhere in sight. It seemed as though Angion had never been there. Creashaw could hardly believe his eyes. He could not understand how a man as large as Angion could just disappear.

Making a mental note to ask Angion how he did that, Creashaw headed towards the place Angion had pointed out. He quickly found the small forest, and gathered more than enough wood for a fire. Creashaw returned to the stone well before dark and found that Angion had not returned. He called out for Angion, but got no answer. He hoped that Angion had not found anything. For a moment he had a feeling of dread, that perhaps something had happened to Angion, but he shook it off. "Angion of all would know what he is doing." He chuckled.

Creashaw then began to get a fire going. When the fire was burning well he went over to his pack to get some of the meat and bread his mother had sent with them. He was rummaging through the pack looking for a piece of bread when suddenly he got the feeling there was someone behind him. His heart pounding Creashaw turned quickly, and jumped when he saw Angion standing right behind him. "Angion . . . I did not hear you come up. How long have you been there?"

Angion smiled warmly and chuckled placing a hand on the boy's shoulder. "I only just arrived a few moments ago. You have a good sense, but we must work on it. I will teach you to know when someone or something is near before it can be seen."

Creashaw smiled excitedly. "I would like that. Could you also teach me to vanish as you did earlier?"

Angion nodded, his smile growing brighter. "Yes of course that is all part of what I will teach you, but for now is there any more food in there?"

Creashaw smiled and nodded. "Yes of course Angion, just a moment." Creashaw then pulled out some meat and bread for Angion and the two sat down by the fire.

When they were finished eating Angion turned to Creashaw. "Now Creashaw I have a few things I must discuss with you." Creashaw sat up waiting intently for Angion to go on. He did not want to miss any wisdom Angion was going to share.

Angion smiled inwardly at this, the boy was going to be an enthusiastic student. He was glad, for it would make things much easier. "You have much potential and could become a great warrior, but you must remember one thing above all. Know your limits, and know when it is time to back away. It is not cowardly to avoid a battle when you can. Many times a disagreement can be resolved without a fight, yet there are the few times when it is unavoidable. At those times it is good to know all that you can about your foe, and if you know your abilities it will be easier to find a way to win."

Angion paused a moment to see if Creashaw understood. The boy nodded confirming that he did. Angion smiled at this, the boy certainly was sharp. *"Yes he will be great one day, if he is led correctly."* "You see I have brought you out here with the belath for that very reason. I want you to learn respect for the creatures, and also to learn as much as you can of their behaviors. I was not here when you arrived because I had gone to see if the beasts were nesting in the place I told you of."

Creashaw frowned. He was slightly upset that Angion would go without him. "Where they nesting there?"

Angion shook his head not liking the boy's tone. "Yes indeed they were, and do not worry you will have many opportunities to observe them. I wanted to get there quickly and unnoticed."

Creashaw nodded in understanding, he knew he would have slowed Angion down if he had gone along. Angion saw that he was not going to get any arguments from the boy and he was glad for that, for what he was about to tell him was not going to be easy? "You had asked me when it was that I had faced a belath before."

Creashaw nodded excitedly. "Oh yes. I would love to hear the story Angion."

Angion frowned sadly "Yes well you will not be so excited when you hear the truth of it."

Creashaw looked at him with a puzzled expression upon his face. "How could I not be excited about it Angion, You faced one of those things and you are still here. That alone is a feat of amazing skills."

"Ha . . . it was more a feat of blind luck than of skill. I did nothing to be proud of that day. Now if you are ready to listen without interrupting I will tell you."

Creashaw nodded excitedly.

"Good, then I will begin. It was several years ago. I was only a few years older than you are now. Your father and I were the best of friends and you were just a small boy. We were out here in a hunting party. The jerusom had moved through the area seeming to be in a hurry. The first sun had already set, and dark was approaching. The hunting party decided to make camp in the caves that the belath have now made their lair in. There was still some time before full dark when we had everything set so your father and I decided to see what we could find as to where the jerusom had gone."

"We came upon a strange trail that we had never seen before. We decided to follow it and see what it was. When we reached the end of the trail we found a scene much like the one we saw earlier today, yet the scavengers had not yet found the kill. Your father and I walked around the scene unbelieving. We had never seen anything like it, and we were at a loss to say what could have done such. We knew then that if the beast were allowed to continue to kill as it was the jerusom would be wiped out. We made a pact to never allow it to do so."

Angion sighed and paused a moment bowing his head. Creashaw could easily see that this was not an easy memory for Angion. Creashaw was about to ask Angion if he was well, but he lifted his head, and Creashaw jerked back in shock. Angion's face seemed haunted and there were tears rolling down his face. Creashaw had never seen Angion look so hurt.

Angion then continued. "We were going to try and find where the beast had gone, when suddenly we heard the most horrifying screams that you would ever hear, and they were coming from the camp. Those screams will haunt me to the day I am dead. Fearing the worst we ran back to the camp to try and help, but when we arrived we were already too late. The carnage was horrifying. Even the scene with the jerusom seemed pale to it. There was blood everywhere and most of the bodies were unrecognizable. The creature did not kill for food. It had killed for the sheer pleasure of it. We spent the rest of the night giving the dead a proper burial. That night we vowed that we would return the same upon the creature. We knew we would need our strength so we rested that night. At dawn we headed out to track the creature. Its trail was easy to follow, and had we been more experienced we would have known it was far too easy. Our anger and inexperience made us foolish however."

Angion sighed and shook his head. "We blindly walked right into the Creatures trap. It had doubled back on us and hid from sight waiting for us to pass by. When we passed it, the belath jumped out behind us, and bit into your father's shoulder and lifted him up. I could hear the bones cracking as its jaws clamped down on him. Your father screamed in pain as the venom rushed through his body. Moments later he went limp, and the creature tossed him to the side."

"I barely had enough time to jump out of the way as it tried to bite me. Rolling away I drew my axe and the beast seemed to enjoy this. It circled me watching my every movement. Then suddenly it attacked, moving like lightning with no warning. It slashed me with its claw. That is where I got that large scar upon my chest. When it saw that it had drawn blood it roared and pounced again. This time I moved away from its attack and swung the axe and cut its left arm. It screeched in pain and swung its tail and caught me in the side. I flew about fifty paces away before I hit the ground, and fell unconscious."

"When I awoke the creature was gone. I crawled to where your father lay to see if I could do anything. I was far too late however. He was long dead at that point. I looked over his wounds and I was shocked at what I saw. They were fused as though someone had taken hot embers from a fire and sealed them. I gave your father what burial I could, and prayed over him hoping he would find Destinta."

"I returned to the village to tell everyone what had happened. When I arrived I went straight to your mother's hut and fell unconscious at her feet. I later learned what it was that we had faced. The elders told me of it from my description, and they also told me all they knew of them. Until now I have never seen another, and the one I injured well it was never found. So ends my story. Now that you know the truth how do you feel about the belath?"

Creashaw wiped a tear from his eye. Angion could see anger burning behind those eyes. "So it was a belath that killed my father." Angion nodded in answer. He felt for the boy, and he could still remember the day that Sheminal told him his father was not going to return. Wiping away more tears Creashaw looked up. "One day I will find this belath and I will avenge my father's death."

Angion smiled at the boy's devotion. "Yes I knew you would do as much. Now do you understand why we have kept this from you, and why I have brought you here? We did not want you to go out and try to find it before you were ready. Now that they are here I want you to learn as much as you can of them. I am going to give you more than a fighting chance against them."

Creashaw smiled sadly. "Thank you Angion that means much to me." He broke into tears and turned away so Angion would not see.

Angion walked over and hugged the boy. "It takes a brave and strong man to cry when he learns something such as this. I am proud of you. I will leave you to speak with your father now. Call me when you are finished." Angion then walked off into the darkness to watch over the boy and give him time alone.

Creashaw sniffed and wiped away the tears. "Father," he shouted into the night. "Father what do I do? These creatures that killed you are so strong. I do not know how I will face them. Angion promises me that he will help me, and I will do whatever it takes, for one day father I will avenge your death. I do not know how as yet, but I will. I promise you the creature that took you from us will pay dearly. I will not allow your death go unchallenged father. You may rest now father for I will take over where you left, and father I love you."

Angion smiled. Creashaw had spoken well in his eyes. He could see much of his father in the boy. He knew that was part of Sheminal's trouble. Creashaw was the image of his father in most respects.

Angion sighed softly looking up at the sky. "Well old friend I have kept the first part of our agreement now I will complete my promise to you."

Angion turned and headed for the mountains. As he neared his destination he saw thick thorn bushes covering the area. Below the bushes were dozens of skeletons ranging from small animals, up to a couple of humanoid creatures, likely goblins. All of these things were victims of the blood thorns. The Thorns had sprung up when Angion had placed the item in its hiding place many years ago to protect it from any thieves. Now as he approached the thorns began to wither and die for they had served their purpose.

Angion walked up to the cave, and he paused a moment before entering. This was where he had released Replore's sword to the spirit realm several years ago. He closed his eyes feeling an old pain that would never fade away. In that moment he came to a realization, and prayed to the spirits. *"You knew this day would come, didn't you old friend. Even then before your death you knew. It is hard for me to think about it, but it is so."* Angion sighed at the memory of his friend and entered the cave.

The cave was pitch black and had a feel about it that spoke of its enormous size. Angion could see nothing beyond a few inches, except a soft light glowing in the back of the cave. He brought no source of light for he knew it would desecrate this holy place so he carefully walked towards the light. When he was close enough to see the source of the light he noticed it was directed upon a stone pedestal, and upon that pedestal was Replore's sword. Only it was no longer just a sword. It was far more than that. Angion gasped in disbelief at what he saw, he knew it to be the sword only because of the runes upon it, and otherwise it was no longer the sword he had placed upon the pedestal all those years ago. It was now a weapon he had never seen before. It had its own inner glow.

He had never seen one, but he instantly knew it for what it was. This was a spirit blade. He had heard legends of men who had carried them. They were said to hold the knowledge of many fallen heroes, and could impart the knowledge upon the wielder. Angion knew then the boy was receiving a most precious gift.

After a moment of shock Angion collected himself and lifted the weapon from the pedestal. Instantly the light shining upon the pedestal vanished and the weapon seemed to take on the glow. He could feel the power of something beyond anything he knew flowing through the weapon. He tried a few swings with it and found it to be of perfect balance and he was amazed at the deftness of the weapon. Angion knew in the right hands this would be a formidable weapon. He looked around for the scabbard for the weapon and found it on the pedestal as well. He grabbed it and headed for the exit.

As Angion walked away a misty glowing figure stepped out from the darkness. When Cargon saw Angion carrying the weapon he smiled warmly. "Teach the boy well. The fate of many things relies upon him."

As he walked away Angion suddenly felt a strange presence and he even thought he heard words being said, but as he turned to look all that greeted him was the pitch-blackness of the cave. He stood there staring into the darkness for a short time watching for any strange movements, but saw none and the feeling had quickly faded so he turned and left.

As Angion neared the camp he heard a birdcall and he smiled. He then answered the call with one of his own letting Creashaw know that he was around. A short time later he arrived at the camp sight, and Creashaw was fast asleep. He frowned and shook his head. "Ah the young and foolish, he decided I was nearby so he thinks it is safe to sleep."

Angion looked down at Creashaw slightly disappointed, but he decided to allow the boy to sleep. He walked over to his bed roll and laid down and rested in a state that left him alert to what was around him, but not quite awake. It was an old trick that many adventurers learned quickly, and those that didn't did not live long.

As morning broke Creashaw got up and stretched, he looked up at the first sun rising, and smiled. This was going to be the first day of his training, and he was excited.

"Ah you awake Denor. I hope that you have rested well."

Creashaw turned to the sound of Angion's voice. He smiled all the more hearing Angion call him apprentice. "Yes I did Angion."

Angion frowned at the boy. "From this date on you will call me Coronoth. You have much to learn about being a warrior. The first will be obedience. Now then you are going to run around this stone ten times before we eat."

Creashaw looked at Angion in disbelief. "But Angion . . ." He began to protest.

"Very well Denor twelve then. Do you wish to add more?"

"No Coronoth." Creashaw said as he began to run.

As Creashaw came around the Stone for the first time Angion frowned, and yelled out to him. "Denor what takes you such time? You should have been past here twice now. Move faster or I will need to add more times to make up for your speed."

Creashaw frowned at Angion, but he picked up his pace as he was instructed. This was not what he had expected would be his first day. The next time he came around Angion smiled, and nodded. "Much better Denor now you have only ten more keep it up."

After the ninth time around Creashaw began to get a stitch in his side, and he slowed down to try and regain his breath. Suddenly he heard Angion yelling out to him, telling him to pick up his pace. Creashaw sighed and glared back at Angion, but again he picked up his pace as he was ordered. As he came around for his final round Angion told him to walk his final one and slow himself down.

Creashaw nodded more than happy to get a chance to rest a little. He walked around the stone one last time breathing deeply, and trying to work out the stitch in his side. By the time he came around the face of the stone his heart had stopped racing and his breathing had calmed, but the memory of the pain in his side remained. He found Angion sitting to the side idly sharpening his axe. He frowned and walked over to Angion. "Why did you make me run around this stone like that? What purpose did it serve?"

Angion did not answer. He did not show any signs of even hearing Creashaw. He simply went on sharpening his axe. This frustrated Creashaw and he was about to say something, but Angion looked up at him. Creashaw stepped back shocked by the look in Angion's eyes, he saw something there that he had never seen before . . . anger.

"Everything that I do here Denor, I do for your own good. You must learn to take orders without question. I assure you this will not be the last time that you hate me. The run is to build up your strength and it was also a punishment for last night. You should never go to sleep when you are alone in the wilds. There is a trick you can do to rest, which I will teach you, but you must never go to full sleep when there is no one to watch your back. You will not live long that way."

"But Angion you were nearby, I made sure of that before I went to sleep. I knew that everything would be well since you were around."

Angion shook his head sadly. "Only a fool would think as such, and I know you are no fool. Think Creashaw, what if a viper or some such creature, were to come near and decide to bite you. You would be dead, and I would not hear a thing until it was too late."

Creashaw bowed his head in shame. He had not thought of that the night before. He knew Angion was right, and he could have kicked himself for being so naïve. "You are right Angion, I should have known better. It will not happen again."

Angion smiled at the boy and laughed slightly. "Ah it is well, so long that you learn from your mistake. Now eat I have something that I must give to you."

Angion stood and walked to the back of the cleft to retrieve the boy's weapon. Creashaw ravenously hungry from the run wasted no time before digging into breakfast. Angion Carried the weapon wrapped in oilcloth over to where Creashaw ate.

When Creashaw was finished eating Angion called to him. "Creashaw I have a gift for you that I have been holding for ten years past now. It has been hidden away here for all this time waiting for the day you were ready for it. I feel now that the time has finally come that you should have it."

Creashaw looked up at Angion with a puzzled look upon his face, not quite sure what to think. "What is it Angion?"

Angion smiled he had anticipated this moment for a long time. It is your father's sword."

Creashaw's mouth dropped open in shock. "But Angion my mother said it was lost. How could you have it?"

Angion laughed heartily at the boy's confusion. "Your mother was not wrong Creashaw. The sword was lost to this world. It was taken to the spirit world for a time, and there it remained until this day came. The day you were meant to wield it. I warn you though it looks nothing like what you have ever seen before. Being in the spirit world has changed it.

Angion unwrapped the weapon, and Creashaw stared at it in shock. Angion was right he had never seen anything like it before. It was indeed a sword but the blade curved slightly, and seemed to have an inner glow. The weapon seemed to have a presence about it as though it were alive. Creashaw reached out and touched the hilt, and the weapon began to hum. He quickly pulled his hand back in shock.

Angion saw this and smiled. "Do not fear it Creashaw. What you see here is called a spirit blade. The glow is merely a semblance of its power, and it proves that it belongs to you. It will only show its true nature to the one who is meant to wield it. When you hold it you will find knowledge coming from it."

Creashaw looked at the weapon in mute shock for a moment. Then he slowly reached out and took the weapon, and as Angion had said he could feel knowledge from his father being imparted upon him. A tear welled up into his eye for the memory of his father.

Angion nodded smiling warmly "Guard that with your life Creashaw and it will in turn guard you. Only those that are of your blood will see the weapon for what it is, all others will see it as a strange weapon. Remember also that all that wield it in that state will impart their knowledge upon it. So when you pass it on to your son he will gain the knowledge of your father and any that you gain. It was wrought from pure spirits so it can never be used to do anything that would be evil."

Creashaw looked at the weapon resting in his hands. It seemed light as a feather, and balanced perfectly, and almost as though it was ready to do battle at a moment's notice.

He looked up to Angion and frowned. "Angion if only blood of my blood may see the glow of the blade, why is it you can see it?"

Angion chuckled at the question. "The weapon chooses whom it deems to be blood line. Perhaps it is because your father saw me as his brother, and that I have taken care of you and your mother in his absence. Whatever the reason however, your father has honored me."

Creashaw nodded in agreement. "Well I could not think of any other person more deserving."

Angion waved this off modestly. "I have only done what is right, and what I had promised him. Now then, are you ready to continue your training?"

Creashaw nodded vigorously. "Yes of course. I have been waiting for this day for a long time." He strapped the weapon's harness onto his back and put it into place and stood there waiting for Angion to explain what they were to do.

Angion nodded satisfied the boy was ready. "Good then we will be going to the Belath's lair to see if the male has returned yet, but you must remember to do only what I tell you. You must also remain quiet for if it hears us we will be in grave danger."

Creashaw nodded and smiled in understanding, and excitement. He knew that this was going to be extremely dangerous, but that made it all the more exciting. This was the day he had waited for all his life. "I am ready to go. I have been waiting for this for a long time now."

Angion smiled and nodded at the boy. "Yes Denor I know." With that the two were off. As they approached the belath's lair Angion looked at Creashaw, and put a finger to his lips and pointed towards the lair. Creashaw nodded that he understood, and they quietly crept up to the lair.

When the lair finally came into view Angion was glad to see that all three creatures were there. They moved in a little closer, then Angion had Creashaw lay flat in the grass beside him. Angion noticed that like most creatures of the plains the belath rested more during the day. The two adults appeared to be sleeping while the young one was playing. Every now and then the young one would try to get one of the adults to join, but they seemed in no mood for it. The female however seemed more tolerant of this behavior than the male did. Angion made a mental note of this, and much more throughout the day. Mostly he watched how the young Creature played to see if he could find anything useful.

As the day wore on Angion decided there was nothing more to learn from watching the young creature. He looked at Creashaw and saw a look of shock on the boy's face. Angion tapped Creashaw on the shoulder and pressed a finger to his lips when the boy turned to him. Angion then pointed back the way they had come and motioned for Creashaw to get up, and they headed back to the camp.

Chapter 15
Plans Coming Together

Skreal returned from scouting around the lair. He had picked up the Scent of a two-legs and searched around for it, but found nothing. Now disappointed that the two-legs were not around he went to a shady spot in the lair and curled up for a mid-days' rest. Thrash was romping around and playing.

Skreal watched with one eye partially open. Thrash on occasion tried to get him to play as well, but Skreal was in no mood for it. Unlike his mate he disliked the hot burning orbs that sat up in the sky. He much more preferred the darkness.

After a short time of watching Thrash he grew tired and closed his eye and rested. Suddenly Skreal awoke from his sleep, he sensed something was out in the grass. He did not move his head yet he scanned the area for what could have disturbed him. Thrash was still romping around in mock battles, fighting things only he could see. Skreal allowed it only because it seemed to hone the young one's skills.

Skreal looked past Thrash to the grass line and quickly found what he was looking for. He smiled wickedly at the sight of the two men hiding in the grass. He yawned largely and looked right at them and smiled again. Skreal then stood and moved back farther into the shadows and laid down watching the two.

Thoughts of charging at them and killing them raced through his mind, but he dismissed them. He wanted to enjoy killing these two. He wanted to make their deaths memorable. A plan began to form in his mind, and he got great pleasure from those thoughts. The only thing that gave him more pleasure than thoughts of killing was the actual killing itself. He loved the scent of fear that would billow off his victims before they died. Skreal also enjoyed their screams of terror as he attacked them. He found also the more he toyed with them the more pleasurable the final kill was.

"MMM . . . yes these two, I will gain much pleasure in killing them. I will make them fear me like nothing they have ever known." Skreal smiled at his thoughts. He was truly going to enjoy killing them.

After a time he saw the two-legs begin to leave cautiously and he chuckled to himself. Had they only known their presence was allowed only because Skreal deemed them to be of no threat. He more so enjoyed watching them and planning their deaths than anything.

When the two-legs were gone Skreal called his mate over and mated with her to relieve himself of the pent up anticipation. She screamed with pain, and pleasure as they rolled around and attacked each other. When Skreal was done with her she walked away bleeding from the many wounds he inflicted upon her, but she was happy. Skreal having relieved himself went back to his rest.

When they arrived back at the camp, Creashaw looked up at Angion and frowned. "I think the large male knew we were there."

Angion looked back at Creashaw and shivered at the thought. "You put my fears to words Creashaw. If it knew we were there why did it not attack?"

"Perhaps it saw us as no threat Angion."

Angion frowned and scratched his chin. "Yes that would be the best of answers. It does not sit quite so well with my feelings however. I feel there is more to it than that."

Creashaw looked at his Coronoth in confusion over this. "If not such, what could it be then Angion."

Angion shook his head confused and frustrated. "I wish it, that I could say Creashaw."

A shiver ran down Creashaw's spine at the fear he heard in Angion's voice. If Angion was afraid there had to be much to worry about.

Angion went to his pack and took out some of the smoked meat and handed some to Creashaw. "Here we must not make a fire with the belath knowing we are here."

Creashaw frowned at the meat he did not much care for cold food. Angion chuckled slightly at this.

"You had best become accustomed to such meals. The road of adventure you look forward to will find you eating worse than this I do assure you. A hot meal is a rare thing on the road."

Creashaw nodded and took the meat. "I know, it's just that I miss mothers cooking. I know she made this, but it is not the same."

Angion nodded and smiled. "Yes she is quite the cook, is she not?"

"The best in the village." Creashaw said with a bright smile.

They sat there and ate for a time while discussing different things that Sheminal could do. When Angion was finished eating he stood up, and picked up Creashaw's weapon and handed it to the boy.

Creashaw looked up at him in confusion, not quite sure what Angion was doing.

"Take it, I will teach you to use it now."

Creashaw took the weapon and smiled brightly, quickly standing. Angion stepped away a few paces and turned back to Creashaw.

"Now come attack me."

Creashaw looked at Angion in total confusion at this point. "Angion I cannot attack you, you do not have your axe to defend with."

Angion frowned darkly. "I told you not to question me when I am training you. Now attack!"

Creashaw shrugged, and holding the weapon he charged with the blade over his head. Everything after the first moments seemed a blur, for the next thing Creashaw knew he was laying on the ground with his own weapon at his throat. Angion was standing over him looking very disappointed.

"You left yourself far too open for a counter attack. Had I had a weapon you would have been dead before you even hit the ground."

"I . . . I'm sorry Angion, I."

Angion cut Creashaw off shortly. "There are no apologies here. This was only your first mistake. You will make many more. The most important thing is that you learn from each one of them."

Angion then offered Creashaw a hand up, and Creashaw gladly took it. Suddenly Angion roughly pulled Creashaw up and again Creashaw found the point of his weapon at his throat. He gasped in disbelief.

"Angion bent his head down and whispered into the boy's ear." Never take your eyes off of your enemy. Always keep your eyes focused on his, his eyes will always tell you his intentions."

Creashaw nodded in mute shock at what just happened. He could not believe what Angion had just done.

Angion then let Creashaw go and handed him back his weapon. Seeing the shock upon the boy's face he frowned. "Why do you look so shocked? While I train you in this way you should see me as an enemy. I will teach you most of the different tricks men will try upon you, yet you must remember I cannot teach you everything. Most of your technique will come from your experience. So do not think what I say is written in stone."

Creashaw nodded. "I understand Angion I will do my best to remember that."

Angion chuckled at this. "Ah Creashaw you are so very eager to please. I do not want you to tell me what you think I wish to hear. I would rather you speak your heart."

Creashaw smiled brightly and nodded. The two then went on with the training, and did so well into the night.

When Creashaw awoke the next morning he found Angion practicing with his axe. For a few moments he sat there in shear amazement. Angion wielded the large weapon as though it was a part of himself. At times Creashaw had trouble seeing where his arm ended and the axe began.

After a short time Angion rested the axe on the ground, and leaned on the handle smiling at Creashaw. Creashaw clapped his hands not quite sure what else to do.

Plans Coming Together

Angion shook his head and chuckled at the praise. "What is that for? I did nothing needing such."

"Oh Angion, that was amazing. I have never seen anything like it. I looked like a wonderful dance."

Angion chuckled even harder at this. "I once heard a man call it the dance. He told me many men try hard to learn it. I found that it comes naturally to you. You cannot be taught it. When you are ready for it, the dance will come to you."

Creashaw frowned in slight disappointment. Angion smiled at him however and handed the boy his weapon.

"Come we have a long day before us. Let us not waste it here worrying over when you will be ready. It will come to you one day trust in that."

With that Angion harnessed his axe, and reached into his pack and tossed Creashaw some smoked meat and began walking out into the plains.

Creashaw sighed and put his weapon's harness on his back and put the blade in it, All the while chewing on the tough dry meat. He turned to get a skin to take along, and when he turned back Angion was nowhere to be seen.

He began to panic, he had only turned away a moment and Angion had disappeared. He wanted to call out, but he thought better of it. Instead he looked out over the plain scanning the area. After a short time of not seeing anything, but the waving grass he slowly walked in the direction he saw Angion last heading.

Creashaw walked about one hundred paces when suddenly everything inside him seemed to be screaming at him. He released the spirit blade from its harness and the feeling of foreboding grew stronger. He looked around slowly scanning the area.

When he still did not find anything, he took another step forward. Suddenly he found himself lying flat on his back being dragged by the rope around his feet. He thought about cutting the rope but he found he had dropped his weapon from the shock of the fall.

Suddenly he stopped and a moment later Angion was standing above him shaking his head, and the large blade of his axe resting a breaths distance from Creashaw's head. Creashaw looked up at Angion with part fear part shame, and much admiration. Creashaw sat up and loosened the rope around his ankles, and slipped out of it. He stood, and turned to Angion and found him still in the same position.

"I failed dangerously." Creashaw said hanging his head low.

Angion said nothing in response, he merely sighed shook his head and walked over to where Creashaw had lost his weapon and picked it up. Creashaw walked over and Angion handed the boy his weapon, then without another word he turned and began walking.

Creashaw looked after him not quite sure what to think. He harnessed the spirit blade and followed. Hundreds of thoughts and fears raced through his mind. He began to wish Angion would say something. The silence was murder. He began to rebuke himself for failing so miserably. He thought about all the things he had done wrong and soon he nearly forgot what had really happened. His thoughts began to get mixed with other memories, some he did not recognize as his own.

After about an hour of this he could not take it anymore. He stopped and called out to Angion. "Angion please say something. Tell me what did I do wrong?"

Angion turned around and smiled. "So you have finally finished. It took you some time. I began to wonder if you would ever get done."

Creashaw Looked at Angion in shock and puzzlement. "What, do you mean that you are not angry with me?"

Angion laughed heartily at this. "No I was never angry with you. I knew that if I said nothing you would punish yourself enough for me."

Creashaw's lower lip began to quiver in anger. "Angion do you tell me that had I said anything to you all this time you would have spoken to me."

Angion nodded, still chuckling under his breath.

"So I went through all that for naught? I went over and over that moment many times over for naught?"

Angion stopped chuckling and shook his head. "No, it was not all for naught. You know what you did wrong correct?"

"Yes I think, but . . ."

Angion cut Creashaw off by raising his hand. "Yes you know, I can see it in your eyes. As I have said before it was better that you see what you did wrong over me pointing them out to you. That way you learn from experience, not from me telling you, which as I have said before is a much better teacher."

Creashaw saw the wisdom behind Angion's words and nodded. "I understand Angion. So where does our adventures lead today?"

Angion smiled, he knew the boy was sharp. *"He may one day even outshine me."* Angion was proud of Creashaw on many levels.

"We are going to see what our friends are up to today. So far we have seen the young one at play, and the adults sleep. I want to see them doing what is normal for them outside of sleeping. Perhaps then we may find some way to drive them away."

Creashaw said nothing in reply. He was more than happy to be able to see what these things could do. He had witnessed it a few days ago but all of that seemed a blur now. He wanted to learn as much as he could about these beasts so when it came time for him to face the one that had killed his father he could.

As they approached the belath's lair Angion stopped suddenly. "They are not here."

Creashaw looked at Angion in puzzlement. "What, how do you know, I don't see any tracks at least not any new ones."

"I do not hear them breathing."

Creashaw's face went from puzzlement to shock. "You can hear them breathing?"

Angion pressed his finger to his lips. He scanned the area using all of his senses trying to find where the belath had gone. Suddenly he heard something. It sounded like a snort from the jerusom.

"They are after the heard. It would seem we are in luck, they are on the hunt once again."

Creashaw looked at Angion in complete bewilderment. "How do you know that Angion?"

"Something has got the jerusom stirred up. They have not been terrified yet, but they are on edge over something."

Creashaw frowned. Angion's answer helped little to stay his shock, but he knew where Angion was headed. "You mean something like the belath, right."

Angion smiled and nodded. "Yes exactly, the jerusom have likely gotten a hint of their scent, yet are unsure of it. From what I can hear they seem to be alerted but not yet bolting."

Creashaw shook his head in dismay. "A dangerous mistake, the belath will be upon them before they do run. Not much different from my mistake."

Angion smiled at Creashaw, proud of him. "Yes a very deadly mistake. If we are to see this we must hurry however, the belath will not take long to attack."

They quickly ran to where Angion had heard the sounds. They found the jerusom moments before the belath attacked the poor animals.

The large male and the young one quickly killed two apiece seemingly without thought. They seemed to kill out of sheer pleasure of it. The female however seemed slightly choosier about her kills. It appeared she was killing for food alone.

In a few moments the slaughter was over, and seven jerusom lay dead. The female and the young belath held off from eating for a moment until the male approached the largest jerusom, and stepped on it, then tore off a large piece of meat. The male swallowed the chunk bones and all. It looked up to the sky and roared. The roar was deafening.

Creashaw began to shake at the sound. It seemed to course its way right to his heart. He felt an overwhelming sense of dread. He turned to Angion and tried to get his attention but he seemed lost somewhere.

As Angion watched the beasts he noticed many things about their quirks in all of them, but his attention kept being directed towards the large male. There was something familiar about him. Then when he stood over the jerusom and roared it came to Angion, and he stared in shock. This was the same creature he had faced before.

Suddenly Angion became aware of Creashaw poking him in the side. Angion looked over at the boy and he looked terrified.

"Angion might we go now, that thing is more horrifying than I want to think about."

Angion shook his head. "Take a good look at that creature Creashaw, for that is the beast what killed your father."

Creashaw's eyes went wide, and his vision went dark. The shock of Angion's words and the sight of the Creature were almost more than he could bear. When he could think again he looked at the belath. *"No that is more than just the average belath."* Creashaw had heard all the stories of the creatures many times over, but none of them came close to describing the nightmare that stood before them. This thing whatever it was could not be a belath.

Creashaw looked at Angion, and shook his head fearfully. "Angion are you sure. You said it was a belath that killed him, but now that I see this thing like this, it is no belath. This is more horrifying than any of the stories describe."

Angion nodded regrettably. "Yes I agree it is. I do not know what has happened to it, but a belath it is and I have no doubt that it is the same one that killed your father. It moves much the same way that the one did all those years ago. What stands out most of all however are those eyes. I will never forget those eyes.

Creashaw shook his head in despair. "Angion if it is as you say then how, will I ever avenge my father's death? All of the stories I have heard say the belath were created as killers, and this one is even more deadly than any other."

Angion frowned darkly. "If that is what you truly believe then the belath have already won. Think of the great Slanoth, he completed tasks that others said never could be done. It is only impossible if you believe it to be."

Creashaw looked up at Angion in awe. Angion always had an answer for every problem. He knew if there was a way to defeat this thing Angion would find it. "Thank you Angion, I think you are right. Someday I will find the way to avenge my father's death."

Creashaw filled with hatred for the beast, and confidence of what Angion had just said stood tall, and yelled at the belath. "You there, belath."

The large male looked straight at Creashaw and seemed to smile at him. Creashaw looked into its cold dark eyes, and shivered. What he saw behind those eyes was pure and absolute evil.

Creashaw shook off the chills running up his spine, and raised his upper lip in a snarl. He pushed away the fear he felt and remembered his father. "In the name of my father, beast I will never fear you again, and one day I will face you and kill you. I promise you this."

The belath seemed to understand him, for it roared at him loudly as though in challenge. Then suddenly Creashaw felt a violent assault in his mind. The belath was trying to control him, but Creashaw was faster, he put up a wall around his mind to block the creature.

Creashaw suddenly heard laughing at the outskirts of the wall. *"Puny two-leg, you think this can stop Skreal. Your block is weak, but you have amused me. You dare challenge me. NOW YOU DIE!"*

Creashaw screamed from the pain in his head. His wall held but barely. Then suddenly he hit the ground hard and was shocked out of the trance, and found himself looking up at the sky. Seconds later he saw a large ball of green sludge flying over him. Angion had pulled him down just in time.

Angion looked at him angrily, but also with a questioning look. Creashaw knew he had an explanation to give, but suddenly he heard that same evil laugh. *"Lucky one, two-leg go now and I will spare the two of you."*

"My name is Creashaw. Remember that Skreal for my face will haunt you beyond your death."

Skreal smiled wickedly. *"Mmm . . . I will take much pleasure in killing you Creashaw, near as much as I will in killing that other with you. Then when I am done with the two of you I will kill the rest of the two-legs where you stayed."*

"Skreal if you dare harm anyone in the village I will hunt you down from beyond the spirit realm if I must."

Skreal laughed once again. *"You puny creature you can do nothing to me. Nothing can harm me. Now go if you wish to live any longer. I would rather get more pleasure from killing you, but if you want to die now I will gladly kill you where you are."*

Creashaw looked over at Angion and saw fear and concern on Angion's face. He had his axe out and was gripping it so tightly his knuckles were turning white. He was staring out at the belath ready to fight.

Creashaw smiled at Angion, even under the worst times Angion was guarding him. "Angion we must go."

"What has that beast done to you Creashaw? We cannot go. It will attack us the moment we turn away."

Creashaw shook his head. "No Angion that is not what it wants. If we remain here it will attack."

Angion looked at Creashaw, unsure he had heard correctly. When he looked into the boy's eyes however he saw that Creashaw truly believed this. "Very well then, stay low and move slowly." The two began to move away crouched down with Angion walking backwards to be sure the belath did not decide to attack.

Skreal then roared at them. *"NO! You stand, and walk away Creashaw, and do not look back or I will kill you now."*

Creashaw stood and turned to Skreal frowning angrily. *"How am I to trust that you will not kill us when our backs are turned?"*

Angion seeing Creashaw standing frowned darkly, and angrily motioned for him to get down. Creashaw only shook his head and looked back to Skreal.

Skreal laughed even harder this time. *"You cannot trust me Creashaw, but you may trust that I will not kill you when you are not facing me. I want you to see your death coming."*

"You will not find me to die as easily as you think Skreal." Creashaw looked down at Angion. "It says we are to walk away and not look back."

Angion stood and looked at Creashaw in puzzlement. "It said?"

Creashaw nodded "The belath. It said if we look back it would attack."

Angion looked at Creashaw in shock, but nodded and the two began to walk away. Angion bent down and whispered to Creashaw. "You have much to explain at camp."

Creashaw nodded. He knew before that he would have to explain everything to Angion. Suddenly he heard Skreal's evil voice again.

"Creashaw"

"Yes"

"I do so hope what you say is true. Your father died like a child weak and pathetic, he did not put up much of a fight. He was most disappointing."

Creashaw roared in anger, and instantly had his blade in his hands ready to attack the belath. When he turned around however the three creatures were gone. He could see the carcasses of the half eaten jerusom, but the belath were gone. Suddenly he heard that insidious laughter again.

"Skreal I swear I will kill you!" Creashaw shouted at the top of his lungs, and he heard a roar in reply.

At the moment Creashaw stopped Angion had his axe in hand, and was searching the area. When he heard Creashaw yell and then the reply he turned to the boy.

"All right Creashaw." he said sternly. "That is all. You will tell me what goes on here now."

Creashaw looked up at Angion tears pouring down his face. "He killed my father, and now he mocks him. He says that my father died like a child, and with no honor."

Angion shook his head. "Creashaw I know not how you hear this thing, but I will promise you upon my honor that your father died most honorably."

Creashaw wiped the tears from his eyes and tried to smile, but it was more of a mournful smirk. "I can hear the belath speaking in my head. It is hard to describe, but of late I have been able to do strange things."

Angion raised his hand, stopping Creashaw. "Say no more of this. It is dangerous to speak of such things, and I cannot help you in it. So now since this thing spoke to you what did it say to you?"

Creashaw looked up at Angion and frowned. "Angion I have never seen nor heard of anything so evil as this thing. All those stories you told me of them does not describe what this thing is."

Creashaw walked away for a moment to collect himself. When he turned back Angion flinched slightly at the haunted look in the boy's eyes.

"It said that its name was Skreal."

Angion flinched again at Creashaw's words. "It has a name?"

Creashaw nodded. "Yes and it spoke mostly of killing us and how much pleasure it was going to get from doing it. Oh yes and it knows you and hates you more than any other. It also spoke of killing everyone in the village."

Angion shook his head vigorously. "No this makes this much more difficult. If these things can speak as you say that means they are not only animals. So it does all of this for pleasure. That does not bode well. Come we must return to camp there is still more I wish to know."

When they arrived at the camp the second sun was falling on the horizon. Angion started a small fire and sat down. Creashaw brought over some of the dried meat. Angion told him to describe everything that had happened.

Skreal and the other two belath returned to the lair after the confrontation with the two-leg that called itself Creashaw. Skreal was pleased he had enjoyed the challenge. He was somewhat saddened however, because he knew that he did not have much more time before he had to kill the creatures. His plans were beginning to unfold and there was not much time left before he had to move on.

Thrash was somewhat upset. He had much wanted to kill the two-legs, but Skreal would not allow it. Skreal had almost hated to refuse the young ones requests, but he was not going to allow his plans to be ruined.

Terial however seemed to be acting somewhat strangely and Skreal was not happy about that. She did not get into the kill as normal, and she seemed distant. Skreal did not care about that one way or the other, but it was unlike her, and that he did not like. He dismissed her actions however so long as they did not hinder his plans he would let her be.

After the two bright orbs in the sky fell and the sky was dark Skreal decided to pay a visit to the two-legs. So he left Thrash and Terial behind and headed for the two-leg camp.

When Skreal was out of sight Terial slipped away from the den. She had a very pressing matter to attend to, and she could not take the chance that he would follow her. She slipped into the darkness keeping a watchful eye to be sure that he was not lying in wait for her. She knew there would be repercussions for her actions, but the importance of her quest greatly outweighed the pain and punishment she would have to endure.

She traveled slowly at first, doing her best not to make any sounds that he would hear. She had many of the same abilities Skreal possessed which made the two of them quite different from even their own kind. Yet he had changed even further than she had making him one of a kind, almost.

Terial knew his plans and knew what it would mean, but she did not have the strength to stop him. There was however one who just might. She was trying to ensure that fact. So when she was absolutely sure he did not follow her she broke out into a full run covering the miles in amazing time.

When she finally reached her destination she stopped and took a short rest, she had covered much ground but expended a lot of her energy. She searched the area for the place she had been shown and quickly found it. A massive cave opening scarred the side of the mountain there she knew the dragon awaited her.

Terial was leery about entering the cave however, for dragons were natural enemies of her kind, and this one was older and more powerful than most. Even Skreal would be hard pressed to defeat this dragon. Setting aside her revolutions however she set herself for whatever may come of this meeting and she climbed to the opening.

When she finally reached the cave she listened intently. She could hear the distant sound of claws scratching against stone. Then a deep yet feminine voice echoed out from the back of the cavern. "Come in Terial I had begun to wonder if you were going to make it here."

"So dragon is that the reason you are so far from the rest of your kind?" Terial said inclining her head towards the egg.

Instantly the dragon stood up towering over Terial. "You will not come near her. Her destiny is far too important for me to allow that. I know you or who you are. You and that monster you call a mate murdered the last female dragon of mating age, and her child. Those atrocities have been well noted among us. This one here is our last hope, and I will die before I allow you to get near her."

Terial stood up on her four back legs and inclined her head in a semblance of a bow, and she smiled as warmly as she could. "Fear not dragon, I have no intent to harm any of your kind. I like you are here for the sake of my child. My mate is as you would call him, is the one with the grudge against your kind, and stopping him is the other reason I have come. So here I bare myself to you, my defenses are down, kill me if you wish, but it was you who called me here."

The dragon sighed in relief then settled back down. "Yes you are right. I am sorry for my reaction, but as I said she is our last hope." There was a slight pause as the two sized each other up then the dragon continued. "So then onto why I called you here. As you likely know there is a change coming and our world will never be the same."

"Yes I have foreseen it as well. That is why I agreed to come." Terial said impatiently.

"Yes well have you also seen that our children's destiny is intertwined. They will depend upon one another one day. So I have a gift for your child, one that will benefit them both."

The dragon turned back and picked something up from behind her. When she turned back around she held what looked to be a small box between two long claws. She handed it to Terial who looked it over and noticed it was completely smooth with no seams or hinges. Terial looked up in confusion, for even her enhanced vision could not see any way to open it.

The dragon smiled at her, understanding her confusion. "It is a puzzle box, and can only be opened if all the conditions are met correctly. Within it there is a soul stone which carries the essence and strength of a certain being. The one you hold there carries that of my mate the oldest dragon who has lived in many millennia, and soon I will join him there. When the time is right and the box is opened the stone will give your child our strengths, abilities, and knowledge. There is only one other stone that holds more power, but it is guarded by a horrible beast that even I would avoid. So take care and give the box only to him and make sure he knows when the time is right."

Terial looked at the box in her claw with reverence, then looked back up at the dragon. "This is a gift beyond words. Are you sure you wish to give this to me?"

As I said, I do this this not just for your child, but for mine as well. So yes I am quite sure of what I am doing."

"I have something to ask of you then dragon. Open the box that I may leave a message for them."

The dragon smiled at her. " I have already prepared it for you. Simply tap the mark here on the top twice and speak to it. Then when the box is opened an illusion of you will appear above it to convey your message."

Terial nodded then placed the box in a pouch behind her jaws for safe keeping. "Again I thank you dragon. I must take my leave however, for if I am to long he will become suspicious."

"I understand. Much luck to you Terial, and may you receive all that you desire."

"To you as well dragon" Terial left the cave, and the dragon behind.

As Skreal approached the two-legs camp he could hear them clashing their weapons together. He smiled wickedly at this. They had to rely on things they carried to fight with. Skreal always found it humorous. He felt that made them truly inferior.

He crept up to their camp and watched as they played. The large one continually was knocking the one that called himself Creashaw on the ground. Skreal found this fact even more humorous. He quickly decided that this Creashaw was in no way worthy of battling him. He decided he would allow Thrash to kill the thing for him.

Skreal then focused his attention on watching the larger two-leg. He found it to be much more worthy of his attention. He found its skills to be far superior to any other two-leg he had ever faced before. That was an added plus to the fact that this was the one that had hurt him so long ago.

After watching them for a short time the larger two-leg suddenly stopped and stared straight at Skreal. Somewhat surprised Skreal stood up on his back legs. The two-leg followed his movement.

Skreal smiled at this *"So you can see me. Yes killing you will be quite pleasurable."*

The two-leg then began saying something to him in its strange language. He picked up bits of it, but not enough to understand it. Skreal found speaking with them in their minds so much easier, they tended to have pictures associated with the words which made them easy to discern. But this chattering the thing was doing seemed so crude to Skreal.

When he heard it pause seeming to want an answer Skreal gave it the only one he knew it would understand. He roared at it as loudly as he could, and then sent out a mental thought saying that its time to die was steadily approaching. Then with that Skreal left the two-legs to themselves.

When Skreal returned to the lair he found that Terial was gone. He was angered for a moment, but found it to fit into his plans. He had been looking forward to the day that he could kill her, for he no longer had any use for her. He decided that he would find her later and deal with her then. For now he had other more important plans like killing the two-legs. In fact the more he thought about it the happier he was she left. This way he did not have to explain to Thrash why he killed her

Skreal went to sleep smiling. Everything was turning out better than he could have hoped. Soon the two-legs would be dead then he would find Terial and feast on her flesh, and steal her soul as well.

When Creashaw was finished telling Angion what had happened, Angion was even more disturbed than he was when he did not know. He started to get pains in his head just thinking about the creature entering his mind.

"That is not something that I really needed to know. It only makes this more disturbing. It is too much like magic for my liking. I must say it is important, but I almost wish you had not told me."

Angion closed his eyes and rubbed his temples trying to stop the headache that was developing. Then a moment later he opened his eyes and looked at Creashaw.

"What say you should we practice for a time. Perhaps it will help us forget for a time."

Creashaw was only too happy to oblige. He had wanted to do so since he had gotten up on the morn.

After they had been practicing for a time, and both suns were well below the horizon Angion suddenly felt a presence. He stopped quickly motioning Creashaw to do as well then turned around to see what was out there. He quickly spotted two small glowing green eyes watching them.

He heard Creashaw behind him saying. "It's him. It's Skreal."

Angion ignored the boy he knew well who or what it was, and he had a good idea what it wanted. He saw the beast stand up on its back legs.

Angion readied his axe to defend against an attack, when none came he began to shout at the Creature. "Come creature, or Skreal as you call yourself. I am the one you want. You know me as well as I know you. We have met before, and I know you hate me for what I did to you that day long ago. So come let us finish this now. This time however, only one of us shall walk away. I am ready to meet my death are you?"

The belath roared at him, as though it were answering. It stood there for a few moments then turned and disappeared into the night.

Angion turned to Creashaw to see if he picked up anything the Creature might have said. Creashaw did not say anything at first, he just stared after the belath.

"Creashaw are you well? Did the creature say anything to you?"

Creashaw shook his head clearing it. He looked at Angion and frowned. "It did say something, but I think it was directed at you. I caught it as though it was reflected off of you. Skreal said that your time to die was quickly approaching."

Angion shook his head puzzled. "What do you mean it reflected off of me?"

Creashaw paused a moment to think of how to explain to Angion what had happened. "After the Belath roared at you. It sent out a crushing thought, one that could kill a weak-minded person. Somehow though when it reached you it was cut apart, as though it had hit the edge of your axe and passed right by you. I caught the end of it, and had I not blocked it I may not have come out unhurt. I do not understand how it happened."

Angion shook his head. "Worry not of it, we have a long night ahead. I do not believe the belath will return tonight, but I do not wish to be caught unawares. You can rest lightly I am going to prepare for an attack."

Creashaw nodded laid down, and quickly fell into a light sleep. Angion had taught him to rest while still being aware of his surroundings.

Sometime later Angion decided he also needed some rest. Happy with the snares he had set up around their camp, he too retired for the night.

Morning came to them without incident. They both got up still weary from the night before.

Creashaw looked into his pack and frowned. "I am weary of eating dried meat. We have it for all our meals now. We are going to be out here for some time yet could we not get some fresh meat. The jerusom herd cannot be too far off."

Angion smiled and nodded. "Yes I agree your mother can cook, but having dried meat day after day is too much. It will be a good training exercise. I have also had my fill of the belath for a time."

Creashaw nodded vigorously. "Yes a day without those things would be a relief. We can go on as though they were not around at least for a short time."

"Yes that would be good. Just be sure to keep an eye and ear open for any signs of trouble."

"That, I can do." Creashaw said with a bright smile.

Angion found it difficult to put the belath too far from his thoughts, but he did his best to think only of the hunt ahead. He was going to keep an extra sharp eye out, but only as though he knew there was a dangerous animal out in the field. He only hoped it would not be a mistake.

Skreal awoke at first light. He stood and stretched yawning largely. He smiled when he saw that Terial had not yet returned. *"Good my plans are beginning to fall into place."*

A few moments later Thrash awoke and looked around. *"Where is mother?"* he asked when he saw Terial was gone.

Skreal smiled darkly. *"Yes my plans are working better than I had hoped."* He then looked at Thrash with false anger. *"Terial has abandoned us. She said that we were horrible monsters, and she wanted nothing to do with us. Especially not you, she said had she not hatched you she would have killed you long ago. She did try, but I stopped her and drove her away."*

Thrash looked confused and saddened for a moment, but Skreal quickly averted his questions by asking Thrash if he would like to help him kill the two-legs.

Thrash roared in glee, and the two left the lair and headed for the two-leg's camp. When they arrived there the camp was empty, but Skreal quickly found the trail and they went after Creashaw and Angion.

Angion and Creashaw quickly found the jerusom herd, and they quickly put the belath to the back of their minds. They quickly found a young animal wandering a short distance away from the herd, and decided it would be their best chance. They slowly stalked the animal being sure to stay down-wind.

They slowly crept closer to the animal, each carrying two spears. Angion looked over at Creashaw and saw the boy grinning brightly. "This is your kill Creashaw. Be sure your aim is true and swift."

Creashaw looked up at Angion, his smile widening even more. Without saying a word he turned back to the jerusom, and began to move closer. He wanted to be sure that he could reach the animal.

Creashaw was about to attack when suddenly the herd all lifted their heads up, snorted then began to run away from them.

Creashaw watched them in shock, and confusion. He looked back at Angion for some kind of explanation, but Angion was looking back.

When the jerusom bolted Angion cursed himself for a fool. He looked back behind him but he could not yet see what he knew would be there. A moment later his fears were confirmed. He heard two of the belath roar in glee. Then suddenly the creatures were upon them.

Chapter 16

The Proposal

Shepard looked at Slanoth in disbelief. *"Bah . . . Come now Slanoth. I did think better o' ye than tha'."*

Lysandas unable to hold back his frustration, at not being told about anything having to do with his city voiced his concern. "What is this prophecy you speak of? If there is something that is threatening my city I must know about it."

Slanoth shook his head. "I am sorry Lysandas, but it was unclear what it meant. I happened across it just the other day. It was in a book Randor, and I had retrieved from a wizard many years ago. It was far too dangerous to leave around for anyone to find so we brought it back here, where we could keep it safe."

Cestator frowned and looked at Slanoth. "Did this book have strange runes, and two claws holding it closed?"

Slanoth could hear a hint of trouble in Cestator's voice, and it bothered him. "Yes Cestator it is in fact The Tome of Islangardious, if that is what you were thinking. We know that it is the first of many artifacts that were created in the time before The Dark Knights' rule."

Cestator shook his head. "This does not bode well Slanoth if my father learns that it is here he will stop at nothing to get it." He looked out over the water troubling thoughts of what may happen if Valclon learned of the books presence here. "He sent me on many quests to find that book. I killed thousands of innocents trying to find it. All those false trails I followed, and to think it was here the entire time."

Slanoth nodded. "It has been here for many years, though I do not think long enough to account for all your adventures. We knew that if it fell into the wrong hands it could be disastrous. But now I think this was not the best place to keep it particularly with that prophecy predicting what it has."

Cestator smirked. "You don't understand how right you are Slanoth, that book is evil to the core. It has only one purpose, and that purpose will lead to nothing good. Tell me could you read any of the other pages?"

Slanoth shook his head, but before he could answer Shepard cut him off. *"We can no be worry'n bout tha' right now. Those blasted things never done not but served themselves."* Shepard then pointed out over the water at the ships approaching. *"Don't ye be think'n we be need'n to think o' someth'n ta be do'n bout them?"*

Cestator turned to Shepard and frowned. "If that book is in the temple and my father learns this. Trust me those things out there will be the least of our concerns." He looked at Slanoth and William in turn. "No one must ever learn that the book is here."

Lysandas again frustrated by being left out of the loop spoke up angrily. "Enough of this, what is this book, and the prophecy you continue to speak of?"

Albrecht nodded his agreement. "If there is a threat to our city it is only right that we know of it."

Slanoth shook his head sadly. I had hoped it would never come to this. The Tome of Ages, as it is also called is a book that has but one purpose, to find the other artifacts that nearly destroyed our world in the time when the Dark Knights ruled. The prophecies contained within will all lead to this goal. This one we read mentioned something that may mean the fall of Cerdrine.

"I be know'n enough bout dis book, tha we can no be worry'n bout what it may soun' like. Me sentiments be to no worry 'bout tha right now. What we be need'n ta worry 'bout is, what are we go'n ta be do'n bout them out thar?" Shepard said, pointing at the ships.

Slanoth looked out at the ships and smiled. "I might have a way to slow them down at least. They will not make the passage through the rocks before nightfall so that should give us more time. They would be foolish to try to cross at night. Even the most experienced sailor would not sail that in the dark, and if they do . . . well the rocks will likely do our work for us."

Cestator looked out over the water and nodded in agreement. "I highly doubt they will try. They are experienced mariners and they are smart not suicidal. Everyone who has ever sailed the seas knows of the razor rocks in the port of Cerdrine."

Slanoth nodded. "Good, now we have a lot of work to do and very little time." Slanoth walked over to the stairs and called to two men standing at the base.

The two men ran up to him and saluted. Slanoth ignored this, and continued "Tell the heralds to get all the people in the city square."

The two men nodded and ran off to do as they were bid. When they were gone Albrect looked at Slanoth and asked. "What do you purpose we do about this? Surely you have devised some sort of plan if you have called the people to the square."

Slanoth nodded. "I have indeed. I will need all of my men to defend the gates against the undead army. So I will need you to bring at least half your men here to stop these things, and I must leave most of it to you. I have much work to do of my own. I am sorry."

Albrecht shook his head. Do not worry for it Slanoth. I think my men will be more at peace fighting monster such as that, the undead have a way of putting fear into the hearts of the bravest of men."

Cestator hearing this spoke up. "I will remain here to help in the efforts against the Spider-lords."

Slanoth frowned and shook his head. "No Cestator I need you at the gates. I will need every man I can get that does not fear the undead."

Cestator scowled deeply at being knocked down. "I am the only man here in this city that knows anything of these creatures."

Slanoth sighed deeply. He was growing weary of the battles with the man, and his pride. "Yes Cestator I do know this, but as I have said I need you more at the gates. It would help if you could tell the men what to expect, but until the undead are defeated I need you."

Cestator frowned, but nodded. "Very well Slanoth." He turned to Albrecht. "Gather your men as quickly as you can and meet me at the base of the stairs."

Albrecht nodded and smiled. "Thank you Cestator. I will meet you there in two hours' time."

Cestator nodded gruffly then walked away. William looked after him and sighed. He looked to Slanoth questioningly.

Slanoth understood what William was asking and nodded. William smiled slightly then followed Cestator.

"I that thar lad be need'n to be learn'n to follow orders better."

Slanoth shook his head sadly. "Yes I agree Shepard. He must learn that and so much more. He has made strides, but he still has trouble trusting others."

"Aye, but he do seem to trust William right well."

Slanoth smiled warmly. "Yes William seems to be one of the few people he does." Slanoth again looked out over the water and frowned. "Well there is nothing to be done about that now we have a bigger problem to attend to."

Slanoth went on explaining his plan. About half an hour passed and the messengers returned and saluted the three men. "Lord, the people await you in the square." Slanoth nodded. "Thank you my son. You may go now and return to your duties."

The men nodded, and walked away.

"Sadly even with this war, there are matters I must attend to, so I will leave the rest in your capable hands gentlemen. I do however expect you to keep me informed of any changes." Lysandas said befor leaving the wall.

Everyone bowed in respect, and bid the king farewell. When he was gone, Slanoth turned to Shepard and Albrecht. "Shall we go?" The two men nodded, and the three headed for the square. When they arrived there, they found William and Cestator waiting by a small quickly erected dais.

Slanoth smiled at the two. No matter the situation the two seemed to feel it necessary to be his guards. Slanoth stood atop the dais, and raised his hands for silence. The people quickly quieted down.

When he was sure he had the people's attention Slanoth shouted to them. "Good people of Cerdrine, I have need of your help. I am

The Proposal

sure by now you know of the army outside the city. Well I will not lie to you. The army is not the only thing we face. There is now a new threat at the north wall."

Shouts came up about how the wall could not be scaled and many other questions. Again Slanoth raised his hand for silence. A few moments later he again had silence and he went on. "I know that the wall has never before been threatened, and that is partly why Cerdrine has never fallen."

This time a loud cheer went up, and Slanoth waited for it to subside before continuing. "The north wall my never have been threatened before, but we have never before faced a threat such as this. An army of ships approaches carrying men who ride giant spiders into battle. They will then have the ability to scale the wall."

A loud gasp filled the air, and questions of what he expected. A few men even asked if he was asking them to help fight. Slanoth smiled warmly trying to ease the people. "We are not asking you to fight, but if you wish to, your help will be welcome, and General Albrecht will be glad to take care of you. However that is not why I am here, I am here to ask you for all the oil and grease you can gather. We must make the wall impossible for them to climb. Now go and hurry. Soldiers will be waiting for it at the base of the north wall."

Again a loud cheer went up and the people began to disperse. At this point Albrecht approached Slanoth. "I have much to do in preparation for this, as do you. Perhaps we will have the chance to speak again before this begins, though I do not believe so. So good luck and may Cargon smile upon you."

Slanoth smiled and nodded. "Thank you Albrecht; I pray for the same for you. I pray it for all of us."

Albrecht smiled in return, then turned and went to his duties. Slanoth watched him go and sighed. *"I so do hope that Cargon grants us mercy friend, for we will need it."*

When all the people were gone Slanoth stepped down. Cestator approached him frowning. Slanoth shook his head wondering when the man would ever show something different. "Slanoth you do know this plan of yours is not going to stop them? The spiders will still get over that wall."

Slanoth shook his head in disappointment. "My son do you not understand? I knew this would not stop them. It should delay them some. Though that was not the only purpose behind what I have done. You see before the people were panicked and ready to run. Yes I might have stopped them the first time, but they have been waiting in their homes growing more anxious all the while. I have given them a task and a purpose. Yes it may be only fetching oil but it is something."

Cestator shook his head. "A fool's errand if you ask me."

"Bah lad, don't ye know nothing 'bout this sort o' thing. Da people do start get'n upset when they be trapped in their homes and da city be under siege. All tha' Slanoth did be do'n is give'n them something to set their mind to."

Cestator scoffed at this but said nothing. Slanoth sighed and wondered if he would ever reach the man. He could see the good in Cestator, but it was buried so far it hardly showed.

Slanoth looked at the north wall for a moment, and closed his eyes. *"Cargon I pray that you protect us from these threats. We have never faced an enemy such as this."*

When Slanoth opened his eyes he saw Cestator staring at him intently. "What is it Cestator?"

Cestator shook his head dismissively. "Nothing, I was only wondering if perhaps you could show me the book."

Slanoth smiled and shook his head. "Must you not meet Albrecht at the north wall soon, and also there is much to do at the two gates. When all of this settles I will be more than glad to show you."

Slanoth then turned to William, his smile now gone. "William go, and tell Braggor to gather all those whose faith is strong, and have them meet me in the center court of the temple. I must speak with them."

William nodded. "Yes lord Slanoth." Then without a pause William ran toward the temple.

Slanoth looked over at Shepard and saw the man smiling and, this puzzled him slightly. When Shepard saw Slanoth's questioning look he pointed behind Slanoth.

Slanoth turned around and saw Cestator standing there fuming. Slanoth cupped his hand over his forehead and sighed. When he looked up Cestator seemed even angrier. "Cestator as I said there is not time for this."

"It will take no time for you to hand me the book. Did you forget what I told you the book was? There may be something within it that will destroy this army."

Slanoth shook his head sadly. Then looked deep into Cestator's eyes, and found he was wrong. The good in the man was not buried it was floating in a void of darkness. It almost seemed lost there. Slanoth knew then that it would take more than he had to fill that void.

"Yes Cestator I do remember what you said the book was, and that is the very reason I will not use it. If it is as you say nothing will come from it that we need use. Now as I said I have much to do. If you wish to join me you may, but in any case you will be within the temple as soon as you finish with Albrecht."

Then without giving Cestator a chance to say a word Slanoth turned to Shepard. "Are you joining me?"

Shepard nodded. *"Aye, I do be right behind ye."*

With that the two men headed for the temple leaving Cestator standing there burning with anger. He stood there for a few moments staring after the two men, wondering why he was bothering. He knew he could leave this city and get past the army without much trouble. He could leave all of this behind and go his own way.

Suddenly he was pulled from his thoughts by the feel of someone pulling on the end of his tunic. He frowned darkly when he saw a small blue-eyed boy, no more than six years old looking up at him.

"Sir . . . could you please help me." The boy said in a soft scared voice. "I . . . I lost my momma in the crowd and . . . and when everyone left I couldn't find my way home."

Cestator sighed and forgot what he was angry about and knelt down before the boy. "What is your name lad?"

"My name is Joshua sir." Then the boy's eyes went wide as he looked into Cestator's eyes. "You . . . you're him. You're really him aren't you?"

Cestator stepped back in confusion. "What are you talking about boy?"

"You're the one mother tells me stories about, the man she tells me will come for me if I am bad. Have you come to take me away?"

Cestator shook his head and smiled. "No lad I have not come to take you away. I am here to protect you."

The boy smiled brightly and wrapped his arms around Cestator's neck "Oh then I know everything will be alright. Thank you, sir."

Suddenly Cestator heard a woman's voice calling the boy's name. The boy let go of Cestator and smiled even more. "That is mother, oh thank you sir for helping me, bye now."

The boy turned and ran towards the sound of the woman's voice calling to her. Cestator looked after him and smiled lightly. "I hope you are right Joshua." Cestator turned and headed for the north wall.

When the two were gone a figure stepped out from behind a large tree a few feet away and spoke in a sad voice. "Ah, I do wish that I could change what is to happen my friends, but I fear it is beyond even my power. The days to come will not soon be forgotten I fear."

Cargon walked the empty courtyard admiring the beauty of the place. *"It is quite the shame what is about to happen here. I have always loved this place."* Cargon sighed sadly then disappeared.

Suddenly there was a glimmering in the air and a dark robed man stepped out. *"Even Cargon himself is unable to stand against us. What is this book that Cestator wishes so much to get his hands on I wonder. Perhaps I should speak to master Valclon."*

Gorloan then muttered a few words and waved his hand before him a doorway opened, and he stepped through.

Once again Cargon stepped out from behind the tree. This time he frowned as he stared at the spot where the wizard had stood. "I may not have the power to stop what is about to happen here, but I can keep you from getting that book. No . . . no evil will ever lay hands upon that book so long as I am. I will not allow that thing to fall into the hands of evil again." Cargon then disappeared in a great flash of light.

The Proposal

A few hours later Cestator walked past the same place, returning from helping Albrecht plan a strategy at the north wall. The suns had just fallen below the horizon and darkness began to fill the square. He walked right past the place where he had seen the young boy without a thought. He was headed for the temple.

When he arrived at the gate William was there waiting for him, with a big smile. "I knew you would return. Some had their doubts, but I knew. Come Cestator Slanoth awaits us atop the wall."

Cestator nodded and followed William. When the two climbed the stairs they found Slanoth at the edge looking out over at the gathering army. Cestator looked around, but could not find Shepard anywhere. He mentioned this to William, and before William could answer Slanoth turned around and smiled.

"So Cestator you decided to join us after all."

Cestator looked at Slanoth with a frown. "You speak as though I had a choice in this."

Slanoth's smile faded slightly, but remained. "You have always had a choice. You could have run and left all of us for dead, as you were thinking of doing."

Cestator smirked and shook his head. "So you knew. You are full of surprises."

Slanoth laughed at Cestator's words. "Oh, come now Cestator. I have been around for a long time. It was not hard to see it in your eyes. I only left you to your own destiny. As for Shepard he is at the south gate preparing that wall for the attack."

Slanoth then turned away and looked out over the wall. He had tried to guess many times how many fires burned out there but they were too many to count. He sighed and shook his head sadly. "Tell me Cestator can you feel the evil pouring off of this army? To me it is a physical entity. What is it like to you?"

Cestator frowned and looked over the sea of bonfires. "I can feel the intent of this army. They want the two of us dead."

Cestator then looked at Slanoth anger raging in his eyes. "They are besieging the city to kill two people."

Slanoth frowned and nodded. "Yes Cestator their first attempts to kill us have failed so they will kill every man in this city to get to us, and they likely will not stop there."

Fires raged in Cestator's eyes and he turned to the army again. "So long as I live they will not succeed. There has been enough of this."

Slanoth placed a hand on Cestator's shoulder. "Calm yourself Cestator raw anger only leads to darkness. You must learn to hone and control your anger, or one day it shall consume you."

Cestator sighed and released his anger, something in Slanoth's touch and his words relaxed him. He looked at Slanoth and smiled. "Thank you Slanoth this only reminds me of things I would rather forget."

Slanoth smiled sadly and nodded. "We all have things in our past that we would rather be forgotten Cestator. The important part of them is that we learn from them, and do all that we can not to repeat them."

Cestator nodded and turned towards the wall and looked out beyond the army to the horizon.

At this point William walked over and stood beside him and smiled. "You know Cestator for the longest time I carried hatred towards you. I would have done anything to get the chance to kill you. Then someone opened my eyes and let me see why, and I found it was slowly consuming me. I turned away from the hatred and now look at us. I would lay down my life for you my friend."

Cestator smiled warmly and looked at William, and he saw sincerity in the man's eyes. "And I would do the same for you my friend."

The two men then gripped arms in friendship. Slanoth standing aside watched and smiled. He looked up to the sky and nodded. "There is hope yet lord." When Slanoth looked back down he saw the two men were deep in conversation. He turned and headed for the stairs and left them to their conversation. He had some important matters to see to.

Slanoth returned to his quarters and began to study the prophecy once again to try and discern its true meaning. After many hours of studying and checking other books on prophecy he found the prophecy to be more disturbing than he had first thought.

Slanoth then spent the rest of the night writing a letter. As the sun began to rise he sealed the letter and imprinted his personal seal into the wax. He gingerly wrote Shepard's name on the front and left it on the center of his desk

A tear rolling down his cheek Slanoth stood and adorned his armor. He left his quarters, but as he stepped out the door he looked back and smiled sadly. He closed the door and locked it, but left the key in the lock and headed for the wall.

When Slanoth neared the wall he noticed there was a lot of activity. He frowned, knowing what this had to mean. He had not gotten any rest in some time, and it seemed he would not. He climbed the stairs to the top and saw that everyone was looking out over the wall. He knew the army had to be on the move. He quickly found William and Cestator at the center of the wall above the bridge.

Slanoth walked over to them and frowned at their backs. The two seeming to feel his Glare turned and looked at him. They looked about as worn, and tired as he felt.

Slanoth shook his head at them. "Did either of you get any rest the past eve?"

William shook his head. "No more than you have from what I can tell. Cestator and I have been working with Shepard and General Albrecht on a plan to defend all sides."

Slanoth sighed and shook his head. "Now tell me Cestator this was your idea was it not?"

Cestator smirked. "We needed to combine all of our defenses, if one falls we will all fall."

Slanoth smiled. "Yes I thought so. Now tell me, what is the army up to this morn?"

William's face went dark quickly. "It would appear that the leader of this army wishes to speak to you lord."

Slanoth looked at William in shock. "Are you quite sure? What reason would he have to speak to with me, should he not want to speak with General Albrecht?"

William shook his head. "No lord, he does not. We offered, but the beast would not listen he wants only to speak to you."

"Yes and I could tell you what it is that he wants." Cestator scoffed.

Slanoth walked over to the edge of the wall frowning. "Yes Cestator I know what, or rather who it is they want. I also know what the offer will be, but it makes no matter they shall not get it."

Slanoth looked out over at the mass of creatures upon the bridge. They covered all, but the final few feet before the gate. Slanoth smiled at this he was not going to be intimidated. He looked around to try and find the leader of the army, but at first he could not find anyone who fit the stature to lead such an army. After a few moments however he saw something that left him speechless. Slanoth then looked at Cestator in mute shock.

Cestator saw the look and nodded. "The ogre is leading the army. One of Valclon's own creations, he found that they have a high capacity for intelligence, with a bit of help. It also makes him very dangerous. There is a reason most are dumb as an ox."

Slanoth nodded more disturbed by this than the undead out in the field. "Yes if they were intelligent most races would have much to fear."

Slanoth looked back out over the wall and called out to the creature. "You there ogre, you wished to speak with me?"

The ogre looked up at Slanoth and smiled. "You the one called Slanoth?"

It took near all Slanoth's strength not to flinch at the ogres stare. Cestator was right there was intelligence behind those cold eyes. It was a chilling sight. "Yes I am the Slanoth that you seek."

The ogre chuckled deeply at Slanoth's words. "I did hear tell that you were more than a puny human. It make no matter though I do have a deal for you."

Slanoth shook his head angrily. "I know what you want, and I will make no deals with you."

The ogre smiled darkly and nodded. "I did hope you would say that. Now I can come in there and take what I want."

Suddenly at the other end of the bridge the creatures began to move to either side of the bridge and a lone rider rode up the center. There was no room for the creatures to move but the ones in the middle seemed so intent on getting away that some of the creatures at the edge were pushed off and fell to their deaths. When the rider got to the front with the ogre it stopped and nearly every man atop the wall gasped in disbelief.

"Cargon have mercy upon us. What in all of Trecerda is that thing?" William gasped.

Cestator shook his head and answered as he stared out. "That would be a wraith William. In life they are fanatical men that give themselves to Valclon for power in death."

When the wraith reached the front it looked up at Slanoth and all that could be seen in its dark hood was two red glowing eyes. The creature spoke in a harsh dry voice. "Slanoth you would be wise to reconsider your words."

"Lord Slanoth, look there." William called out and pointed to the other side of the bridge.

Slanoth looked out to where William pointed and saw a large log being passed up to the front.

"Lord they mean to batter down the gates should we drop it?"

Slanoth looked down at the bridge then out into the field. He paused a moment working things out in his mind. He looked at William and nodded.

William nodded in return, and ran to the back of the wall and called to a man standing at the base and gave him the message. The man saluted him, and ran off.

As William got back to the front of the wall the wraith called out again. "So Slanoth have you decided to hear our offer or must we use force?"

Slanoth frowned darkly. "I will never take an offer from a creature such as you, foul beast. I command you creature of darkness in Cargon's name be gone and return from whence you came."

The wraith began to laugh at this. "You fool your pitiful god has no power over me. Now you shall feel true power."

The wraith began to raise its arms when suddenly there was a loud grinding sound at the base the bridge inside the rock wall. The wraith looked up at Slanoth and Slanoth smiled warmly.

Suddenly there was a thunderous sound below the bridge and it began to shake violently. The creatures upon it began to panic and try to get off but they were packed on too densely to move far. Then as suddenly as it started, the bridge stopped shaking. The creatures began to calm slightly but then the ones in the center of the bridge began trying to push their way off the bridge but the mass would not move.

Cestator suddenly realized what was happening and laughed loudly. "Here is your answer wraith. Look behind you."

The wraith looked back just in time to see the army upon the bridge trying to flee before it fell. Then the bridge fell out below them, and thundered against the rock walls on each side. Hundreds of creatures fell to their deaths upon the rocks below, all but the wraith and the ogre in command who was holding the wraith's spectral steed.

Cestator chuckled wickedly at the two Creatures. "So did you enjoy that Manthral?"

At hearing its name the wraith looked up at Cestator, and its red eyes glowed in the darkness of its hood. It pulled back the hood and revealed its dry mummified face.

All but the most seasoned of men upon the wall gasped in horror at the sight. Cestator however paid no attention instead he turned to an archer standing close to him. You there pay no attention to the wraith. I have need of your skills."

The archer nodded more than happy to forget what he was seeing.

"Good, now there is a crest upon the face plate of the wraith's horse. Could you hit it from here?"

The man looked over the wall and saw the crest Cestator spoke of. The man looked back at Cestator and nodded. "Yes sir. It is small, but I can hit that mark."

Cestator smirked. "Good I will distract the wraith, and when his concentration is fully on me I want you to hit that mark. You must hit it dead center or this will not work, understand?"

"Yes sir, I can do it. May I ask what it will do?"

Again Cestator smirked. "It will make them fall." Without another word Cestator turned back to the wraith.

"So Manthral you have not answered me. Did you enjoy that? I found it quite amusing myself."

The wraith smiled evilly and began to laugh. "Ah so it is true. I had been told, but I would not have believed what I was told. You have turned from the darkness, and now you cower behind these walls with those weak men."

Cestator chuckled. "I could come down there and kill the lot of you if you would like."

The wraith laughed heartily at this. "Ah Cestator do you forget, you are no longer immortal? You would be quickly overwhelmed."

Cestator smirked and shook his head. "Perhaps I would be, but not before I took a good portion of you with me."

Manthral shook his head. "You are more than welcome to try Cestator, but why do so foolish of a thing. Join us now and together we will take Cerdrine once and for all. Perhaps your father will show mercy upon you for it."

"Ha . . . Valclon shows no one mercy. You know that." Cestator turned to the archer and nodded.

He turned back to the wraith and shook his head. "You for one should know how much mercy Valclon shows to his enemies."

Just as Cestator finished his sentence he heard a "Thwack of an arrow leaving a bow. Cestator watched the arrow in flight and smiled the man's aim was true as he had said, but just before the arrow reached its mark the ogre caught it.

Cestator then saw a glint of steel in the ogre's other hand and he yelled to the man to get down. The man however did not seem to hear. He appeared to be in shock and staring at the arrow in the ogre's hand. Cestator did not waste a moment. He jumped, and tackled the man to the ground. As they hit the ground Cestator heard a blade whistling through the air above them. He rolled off the man and shook his head. "Are you alright?"

The man looked at Cestator in shock then looked up at the blade buried to the hilt in the stone behind him, and shook his head. "I owe you my life. Had you not done this that blade would be buried in me."

Cestator shook his head and waved the man's words off. "You owe me nothing, we are all brother's here. Each looks out for the other."

The man smiled and nodded. "Yes that is true, yet still I thank you."

Cestator stood, and nodded offering the man a hand up. He turned back to the wall and looked out.

The wraith seeing him called out. "So Cestator shall I take that as your answer?"

Cestator looked at the other men standing upon the wall around him. He smirked at the wraith and shook his head. "Nay Manthral, you may take that as our answer. For I swear to you in the name of our lord Cargon every man here will fight you to his last breath, and we shall fight down to the last man."

At Cestator's words a loud cheer went up across the wall, and as Cestator's words spread to the ears of the other men around the city the cheer grew. Slanoth looked at Cestator and smiled he knew no matter what else the man was in the past, he was a true leader.

Hearing the cheers, the wraith snickered and turned its horse away and the three walked calmly to the other side and rejoined the army.

When they were gone Cestator turned to Slanoth. "We have dealt a blow to them, but they will recover quickly. This wall is now unapproachable we should move most of the men to the south wall."

Slanoth nodded in agreement. "Yes you are correct, but when do you think they will attack?"

Cestator looked out and shook his head. "I would think not before dawn tomorrow Manthral knows I have boosted the men some here today and he will want us to brood a bit more."

Slanoth frowned, and rubbed his cheek. "Yes you may be right. The longer we are trapped in here the worse things are going to get. We must end this quickly before moral begins to wane."

Chapter 17
The Undead Bane

Throughout the eve the men moved to the south wall. When Slanoth and Cestator arrived Shepard approached them.

"I did hear that you dropped the whole lot o' them in da drink." Shepard said with a chuckle.

Slanoth shook his head regrettably. "I had hoped I would not have to, but the mass that we face would be more than could be dealt with. We will be hard pressed as it is now to defeat this army of undead."

"Aye ye do be right thar. I even do hear tell thar be a wraith in thar control'n them, be tha' true?"

Slanoth nodded sadly, but it was Cestator who answered.

"Yes there is, and he is one of the strongest, his name was Manthral. You can be sure we will see displays of his power."

"Aye tha' do be some bad news, fer sure. So what do they be after here? Thar must be some kind o' reason they be attack'n us. No army in thar right wits do attack a Dwarvern built city without no reason."

Cestator smiled darkly. "Oh, they have a reason."

He did not get to finish what he was going to say before Slanoth cut him off. "Yes they have a reason, but they will not get what they want."

Shepard looked at Cestator and grinned brightly. *"They be want'n yawl, don't they."*

Cestator smirked and nodded. "Yes that is what they said, but that is not all they want. They want Cerdrine itself. This is a move to something far greater than just killing me. Isn't it Slanoth?"

Slanoth looked at Cestator in shock for a moment, unsure what the man knew.

Cestator still with his dark smirk that chilled the blood nodded. "Yes you know more than any of us here don't you. You are keeping something from us."

Slanoth frowned and shook his head. "The burdens I carry cannot be revealed. They will in their times, but I alone must carry them."

Shepard looked at Slanoth in shock. *"Slanoth I do have been yer frien' fer most o' yer life an ye be keep'n secrets from me?"*

Slanoth nodded sadly. "I am sorry Shepard I trust, and love you dearly old friend, but as I said, the burdens I carry are for me alone to carry. The fate of many things lies within my silence."

Shepard shook his head and sighed. *"I no like it Slanoth, but If you feel so strong as ye do 'bout it I will no argue you for it. Ye promise me though if it git too much fer ye then I be the first ye come to."*

Slanoth smiled and nodded. "Of course old friend I would go to no other."

"Right ye best not." Shepard snorted. *"Now we do have lots to be do'n here. I do have some ideas here. Ye know da places on da wall where the floors be wider an heavier?"*

Slanoth nodded. "Yes why?"

Shepard smiled darkly. *"Well they do be tha' way fer a reason. They be tha' way so they can hold a catapult or ballista."*

Slanoth's eyes opened wide at the possibilities. "We could wreak havoc upon them from here."

Shepard nodded. *"Aye, but da question be how quick can ye men get them up here. Thar do be the pulley system to get tha' parts up, but how fast can we build it."*

Slanoth smiled. "If we start now we can have all of them launching by the time the second moon reaches its peak in the sky."

"Well then wha' do we be waiting fer? Let's be move'n an build'n."

Several hours later when Slentros and Darnoth, the two moons shone brightly in the sky the catapults and ballista were finished. And an hour later they had them loaded with bullets covered in burning pitch.

The crews watched and waited for their signal, and Slanoth looked out over the camp of the army and shook his head. He turned to Shepard and nodded.

Shepard smiled and raised his arm as high as he could. *"Now ye blasted fools will be learn'n why ye no should be attack'n a Dwarvern city."* He dropped his arm and the catapults let loose their fiery bullets. All struck home hitting different points in the camp, and exploding in massive bursts of flame. Men and Creatures alike began running everywhere. Again Shepard dropped his hand and a loud cracking sound erupted as the ballista loosed their deadly spears. Screams of pain and terror erupted from the army camp below as they were impaled by the deadly volley.

A loud cheer went up from the wall as the men watched.

"Load them blasted things again Git them while they be hurt, an aim fer them siege machines they be have'n out thar." Shepard yelled out.

The teams quickly loaded and prepared to fire again. Shepard again dropped his hand, and the balls of flame flew out towards the camp. This time however they did not strike their target, instead they exploded a good distance above the camp on some invisible barrier.

"Blast . . . Wha' in all o da world done caused tha'?" Shepard cursed when he saw what happened.

Cestator turned to him and frowned. "This is Manthral's doing. We got lucky to get the first volley through."

"Well blast ye lad. Why did ye no tell us dis woul' happen? Ye could have saved us lot o' time here."

Cestator shrugged. "It sounded like a good Idea to me at the time. Besides he will not be able to keep up that spell forever. He must remain conscious of it so long as it remains, and it takes much concentration for him to maintain."

Shepard smiled and nodded. *"So if we do keep him busy keep'n it up, he can no cast any more spells. Is tha' wha' ye be say'n lad."*

Cestator smiled wickedly. "That is exactly what I am saying. So how many fire bombs do you have?"

"Ha . . . Lad thar do be enough o' those things in da store rooms to be launch'n one every few minute fer about three day now, an more can be made right easy. Will tha' thar thing be block'n our arrows though?"

Cestator shook his head. "I would guess it would not though I cannot be certain. In my experience however, many of these spells are quite specific. So to stop all missiles would take more energy and concentration than say one that stops just catapult missiles."

"Aye, tha' may be, but what if they do have other spell casters among them? Then wha' we gona do?"

Cestator smirked and started to chuckle, but Slanoth answered Shepard instead. "Come now Shepard you must know something about wraiths."

Shepard spit over the wall angrily. *"Bah . . . I do know 'bout as much o them as I care to. No good ever did come out o' them spell casters. Dwarves only use magic to help in build'n as Downorth did teach us."*

Slanoth smiled and shook his head. "Well Shepard no wizard would ever work beside a wraith. They despise the creatures."

Shepard looked out over the wall and chuckled. *"Well then tha' be what I do like to be hear'n."*

Shepard then noticed no firebombs had been fired in some time. He turned to the nearest catapult team and yelled. *"You thar, load up an fire another right quick."*

The team looked at him in confusion and he yelled all the louder. *"Fire tha' blasted thing now. We got's ta keep tha' blasted spell caster busy."*

The men nodded and quickly loaded and fired their weapon. This time the bomb got closer, but again it hit the invisible wall.

Cestator smiled. "He was beginning to let it go, he likely thought we were done."

"May hap, but he will no be find'n it a restful night tonight."

Shepard went to each of the teams and told them to continue firing in succession.

As Shepard was doing that, Slanoth called William over and pulled him aside. "William I need you to go over and see how General Albrecht fares, and inform him on how thing go here."

William nodded, and quickly ran to do as he was ordered. When William was gone Cestator walked over and shook his head. "Lord you look near to falling over. You should go and rest some. Things should remain somewhat quiet for now."

Slanoth shook his head. "I thank you for your concern Cestator, but I could not rest while this is going on out here."

Cestator scowled and moved forward glaring at Slanoth. "You have not rested in many days now. I will personally go and get you if anything at all happens. In the state you are now in you will be of no use to any of us."

"Aye, I do be agreeing wi't da lad thar Slanoth, ye be gitt'n yer arse inside an git yerself some rest."

Slanoth looked at Shepard and smiled. "Well it would seem I am far outweighed in this. Very well then I will do as you ask."

When Slanoth was gone Shepard looked at Cestator and nodded. *"Thank ye lad, I been try'n ta git him ta do tha' fer some time now."*

Cestator looked after Slanoth, and sighed. "Yes well we will need him tomorrow he inspires this entire city like nothing I have ever seen."

Shepard chuckled softly. *"Aye, tha' be da price o' glory. He done many things in his day an many a tale be told to him. Ya know even him looking so young as he do still no can hide wha' he be. Could ye see it in his eyes lad?"*

Cestator nodded sadly. "Yes he is more than physically tired. His spirit is tired as well, but yet he still fights on."

"Aye an tha' be why people love him so much, no matter wha' it cost him he always do wha' is right, an he no give up no matter wha'."

Cestator nodded. "Yes that man deserves every bit of respect. He believed in me when no other would. It may sound strange but he feels like a father to me, more so than Valclon does."

"Well lad thar be no shame in tha' most folk here would say much da same. He do be a good man."

Cestator shook his head and turned away. "Yes well there is much to do."

"Aye, ye be right."
With that the two men found other things to do.

Slanoth headed back to the temple and on his way he passed many people preparing for the battle ahead. All waved to him smiling warmly. Slanoth returned the gesture and walked on. A few minutes later he arrived at the temple. He headed for his private quarters. As he passed his office he glanced at the lock for a moment, but walked on. He went into his room and retired for two hours.

When he awoke there was still an hour till dawn, but he got up. He felt somewhat refreshed, but the weariness was still there. He shrugged this off and headed for the wall.

When he arrived there Shepard and Cestator were moving among the men giving orders. Then Slanoth noticed that William had returned, and he headed over to the man.

"William so what does Albrecht have to say."

William turned around and the man looked scared. "Lord . . . The general says that the ships made it through the rocks without trouble. They have not started the attack as of yet, but there are fifty ships awaiting below, and according to Cestator there is at least ten of the giant spiders in each."

"Hmm . . . so that would mean there will be five hundred of the beasts at least. This does not bode well."

"No Lord, and I fear that is not the worst. Through our efforts yesterday and throughout the night we have not done much to this army. All the creatures that died in the fall yesterday the wraith brought back as creatures of the undead."

Slanoth nodded solemnly. "Yes that is as I had expected, and has General Shepard kept the creature busy with its spell?"

"Yes lord he has. We found if we launch them at random the wraith keeps the spell active."

"Yes that is good, now has anything else happened while I was away?"

William nodded and pointed to a group of men with long cloaks. "They have come to lend their services."

The cloaked men seeing William point at them came over. The one who appeared to be the leader stepped up to Slanoth and bowed his head. "I presume you would be the lord Slanoth am I correct?"

Slanoth nodded his head in response. "Yes that would be I, and who would I have the pleasure of speaking to?"

The man pulled back his hood to revel an old and worn face. "I am Malketh leader of the wizard's guild.

Slanoth smiled and put out his hand. "I was hoping that I would hear from you. I welcome any assistance you may give."

Malketh took Slanoth's hand and shook it. "I have been told that there is a wraith in this army."

Slanoth frowned and nodded. "Yes I have near as much hatred for the creature as you."

Malketh frowned darkly. "Perhaps, but while you hate all creatures of the undead, to us the Wraith is an abomination. Any wizard willing to do such a thing has forfeited his life."

"Very well then I suppose you will be handling the wraith for us?"

Malketh nodded. "Yes you will have nothing to fear from the creature. In turn however I have something to ask of you."

"Of course if it is within my abilities it is yours."

"Yes I thank you for it is a simple thing I ask. You stand well with Lysandas, do you not?"

Slanoth smiled. "Yes of course. What is it you need of our king?"

"It is not the king that I want. It is his advisor Gorloan that I want. We have many questions for him but we have not been able to get to him."

Slanoth face went dark at the mention of the man's name. "Yes I have many questions for the man myself. It is my belief he knows a bit more of this than he tells."

"Yes he does. I believe he has somewhat to do with how they appeared here without being seen."

Slanoth frowned and shook his head. "I know not for that, yet I will speak with the king on allowing you entrance to the palace."

"Thank you Slanoth. You are as noble as they tell."

"I only do what is right by Cargon. How others view it is upon them."

Malketh bowed slightly. "Yes your modesty proves you are true to the tales. It has been a pleasure speaking with you Slanoth Paladin of Cargon." Then without another word Malketh covered his head with his hood and turned away.

Slanoth turned back to the wall just in time to see the army begin to advance. He turned to all of his men and shouted to them.

"Prepare yourselves. I know the army of undead creatures outside this wall is something that would make any man's blood run cold, but remember this, my friends. Cargon is with us and he would never let such creatures overtake one of his temples. They cannot stand before his glory."

Then as he was saying the words he got an idea. It would be difficult he knew, but he felt deep in his being it would work. He called for Braggor, Shepard, Cestator, William, and a few other men who he knew had strong faith. When he had them gathered around he told them his idea. "We must join together and gather the other men and combine our powers to form one massive strike."

Shepard shook his head in confusion. *"Wha' do ye be talking 'bout thar Slanoth? How we suppose ta be do'n tha'?"*

Slanoth smirked and chuckled slightly. We will combine our powers and cast one massive holy strike upon those undead creatures."

"Tha' can no be done Slanoth ye know tha'. Why the ability hath been lost long a time now. Heck most of da men here do no, know how to be cast'n da spell."

Again Slanoth smirked, this time it touched his eyes and it seemed out of place to all who saw it. "I know the spell, and all I need is for the men to focus on their faith in Cargon, and stand around me."

Shepard shook his head. *"Tha' do be too much power fer one man to handle Slanoth, do ye be sure ye can handle it? Haps I can help ye dar."*

"No Shepard, as you said it is much power, and unless done just right it could kill you. I'll not risk any other's life in this."

Cestator tired of being left in the dark as to what they were talking about spoke up. "Wait here what is this you two are going on about?"

Shepard looked at Cestator and frowned. *"Slanoth here be talk'n bout handle'n enough power ta be destroy'n all o' them undead beasts out thar."*

Cestator stood there in shock a moment. "That would take the power of . . ."

"A god, Aye, an now ye see why I no am like'n it."

Cestator turned to Slanoth and scowled. "You must not do this. If you misspeak one word you will be no more. We cannot afford to lose you."

Slanoth stood a few inches shorter than Cestator, but as he stepped up to the man he towered over him. "As I told Shepard I will not risk another man's life here. I know how to stop those damned creatures, and I will use every ability that I have to be sure of that."

For the first time in his life Cestator stepped back in submission. "Yes Lord, but I will do everything I can to be sure it works."

Slanoth smiled and let down his imposing posture. "Thank you Cestator, I had hoped you would."

Cestator turned away with the others, and gathered all the men they could find. When they were gone, Shepard turned to Slanoth. *"Do ye be sure 'bout this Slanoth. No one hath tried dis in near ten thousand year?"*

Slanoth shook his head and sighed. "To be quite honest old friend I am sure of only one thing. I will not allow those abominations to get within these walls, and I will do anything I can to be sure they do not."

Shepard nodded sadly. *"Aye tha' did be what I thought ye would be say'n. Well then we best git to it 'cause that thar army will no be wait'n fer us."*

Slanoth nodded and looked around and happened to catch a glance of Malketh and his wizards. They were watching him intently as though they knew what he was about to attempt. He even thought he saw them nod to him.

A moment later the men all surrounded him asking what they needed to do. Slanoth raised his hand for quiet and quickly got it. "Now there is not much you must do. I will need you to focus on your faith in Cargon, and concentrate it upon me. You must believe with all your hearts that Cargon has power over these creatures. Can you do this for me?"

A loud cry of, "Yes Lord," and "Cargon" went up, and Slanoth choked back a tear.

"Good, now begin." Slanoth shouted, before he began chanting the words to the complicated spell. He quickly felt the power from all the men around him, and was nearly overwhelmed by it, but his wisdom and determination kept him focused. After a few moments he completed the spell, and directed the energy towards the sky above the army.

Everyone atop the wall not involved in the spell stared in shock as the sky began to get brighter. Then seemingly out of the heavens came a blinding beam of pure light, and it struck the undead army with explosive force. When it hit it sent out thousands of smaller beams in every direction, and any undead creature hit was instantly turned to dust.

Moments later the light vanished and all of the undead creatures were gone. A loud cheer went up from the wall and the men, all but Slanoth, Cestator, Shepard, and William, ran over to see what had happened. Slanoth had collapsed from exhaustion and the others stayed to help.

"I'll be blasted Slanoth ye did it."

Cestator frowned "Yes he may have, but he cannot do anything more."

Slanoth waved them off. "Yes perhaps, but it did work, now just allow me to rest here for a time. The army should have to regroup after that. I am sure that was not something they expected."

"I no think tha' be a good idea Slanoth. It might be a bit hard to defend ye if'n they regroup down thar an find a way up here."

A dark figure then stepped up to them and spoke. "We will watch over him while you do what is needed."

Slanoth smiled and took a deep breath. "Thank you Malketh. See there Shepard you have nothing to worry about."

Shepard frowned darkly. *"Bah I'll not leave ye to a bunch o' spell casters."*

"He will be better off in our care than in any other. He has just channeled great power and we know of a few things to speed his recovery."

Cestator seeing sparks between the two men knew he had to do something before Slanoth decided to. He stepped between them and glared at both.

"I mean no disrespect to either of you, but stop bickering. We are all working for the same goal. Slanoth there needs help, and Shepard no matter how you feel about this man what he says is true."

Shepard scowled darkly at Cestator, but he did not even flinch. *"Alright then, but ye best be keeping him right safe now."* He scowled then stomped off.

Malketh nodded to Cestator then bent down and handed Slanoth some leaves to chew. Slanoth took them and did as he was told. He looked up at Cestator smiled, and nodded his thanks.

Cestator smiled and nodded in return. Then went back to the wall to see what was happening there. As he looked out he was not surprised at what he saw. The army below was in some disarray but it was reforming rather quickly.

William came over to him and shook his head. "Do you think we killed the wraith in that attack?"

Cestator shook his head. "I doubt we did, but I did notice while we were casting it that Malketh and the other wizards cast a bit of magic themselves. They also would not be using their power to help Slanoth if Manthral was out there."

"So you think that the wizards killed the creature?"

Cestator nodded. "It is likely; wizards despise wraiths for everything they are. They once were wizards at one point, but they give up their souls to serve the darkness."

William shook his head sadly. "I have heard that the darkness offers power readily and quickly, but the price is so great. No one in their right mind would go there."

Cestator sighed and placed a hand on his friends shoulder. "The road that we travel is hard and rough. There are many trials and tests along the way. Some see that and give up. That is when the lord of the dark whispers to them, and shows them any easy road where power comes quickly, but they cannot see the end of the road, that is cleverly concealed from them."

William looked into Cestator's eyes and frowned. "Cestator I have heard that many times before, yet it has never hit me quite like this. I would guess it is because you have come from that. However I still do not understand what happens to these people that would make them go to the dark. The road we travel may be hard, but the rewards are great, and I know what awaits me at the end."

Suddenly from behind them they heard Slanoth's voice. "Yes, but unfortunately it is not so apparent to everyone."

William turned quickly in shock and found Slanoth standing right behind them. "Lord I thought you were resting by the stairs."

Slanoth smiled warmly. "Yes William I was but Malketh gave me something to help. I will not be casting any spells for a time, but I do have some of my strength back."

Slanoth looked at Cestator who was still not facing him. "Cestator Do you truly believe what you have said there?"

Cestator turned and frowned. "That is what you teach, is it not?"

Slanoth shook his head. "That is not what I asked Cestator. Were you spouting those words for the sake of anyone listening, or do you truly believe it?"

Cestator turned and looked out over the wall again, and after a few moments he spoke softly. "I now have lived my life in both worlds. I have seen horrors that make this which we face like a child's bad dream. I have also seen wonders that would make you gasp. I have seen men who serve good, do things that would astound you. I have seen them defy the darkness to the last breath."

Cestator paused a moment to reflect on those memories. When he continued he sounded more confident. "That is what turned my heart you know. The shear defiance I saw even when there was no hope of anything but death, there was the defiance. I knew that if one child alone like that could have faith there had to be something to it. So to answer your question, yes I do believe that to be true."

Slanoth smiled, and placed his hand on Cestator's shoulder. "I had hoped you would say as much. So my faith in you is not wasted. I am glad, however would you promise me something?"

Cestator looked at Slanoth from the corner of his eye, unsure what Slanoth could possibly want. "Very well what is it you would ask of me?"

"Take the book. You are the only one that knows the true meaning of it. I fear there may be others that know of it. I will not be able to protect it forever, and I need someone that I may trust it with."

Cestator looked at Slanoth skeptically. "Do you truly understand what it is you're asking me to do here?"

Slanoth sighed deeply and nodded. "Yes I do know. It is a great weight that I am placing upon you, but if any man can do it I think you can. It cannot remain here, and I know you are not likely to stay long after your training is done."

Cestator turned away and shook his head. "I never thought in all my days that I would find the book, and be the one to hide it from Valclon. Having it will paint me as a target you know?"

Slanoth closed his eyes and took a deep breath. "Yes I know that is why I asked. I will not force it upon you, but I hope you will accept."

Cestator turned back and had a fire burning behind his eyes, and the right corner of his mouth curled up in his wicked smirk. "I'll do it." He said then turned and walked away.

Slanoth's blood ran cold and his heart skipped a beat at that half smile, and for a moment he almost regretted what he had just done. He looked to the heavens and softly said a prayer. "Dear Cargon I do hope I have done the right thing."

Suddenly Slanoth felt a hand on his shoulder and he jumped slightly. He looked back and saw Shepard smiling at him.

"Worry not fer tha' lad Slanoth he do be on da side o' da righteous he do be. 'Sides he do have William thar to watch over 'im."

Slanoth smiled sadly and shook his head. "I do hope you are right Shepard because I have just laid the fate of the world in his hands."

Chapter 18

Nightmares Among Them

As dawn broke of the third day of the siege the men on the north wall looked down to see the black ships below moving ever closer to the wall. When they got as close as the rocks would allow they stopped and giant webs shot out from the decks and connected to the wall making a bridge from each ship.

Albrecht moved back from the wall and called all his archers and crossbowmen. When all of them moved to the front he ordered them to ready their weapons.

He moved back to the wall and looked down. What he saw was like something out of a nightmare. Cestator had described the creatures to him, but what he saw was worse than he had imagined.

Albrecht shook off the chills running through him and turned to his men. "Do not think about what you see down there. We knew what was coming and we must do our job. If any of those things gets over this wall the city will be doomed. Remember they are still only bugs."

The men cheered, but it was slightly subdued. Albrecht sighed and shook his head, he needed to get the men's spirits up. He took up his bow and set an arrow, and drew it back and aimed at the lead spider, which was already beginning to climb the wall. He aimed for one of the creatures many eyes and released.

The arrow struck home and the Creature reared back, but held on. The men seeing this however became reassured, and they began to fire at the creature. The spider was quickly covered in arrows and fell back into the sea carrying its rider with it.

A cheer went up at this, Albrecht felt somewhat reassured by the men's newfound moral, but he knew if it was going to take so many arrows for each they would run out long before all the creatures were dead. He just wondered how the men would fare when it came to close combat.

He told the men to conserve the arrows and only to use them to deter the spiders. He knew he was going to have to find a better way to defeat them.

Moments later three more spiders began to climb the wall. The men fired arrows at them to no avail the creatures spun webs before them catching the arrows before they could reach them.

Albrecht ordered the men to stop firing. They did so reluctantly and he could tell that they had lost some of the moral they had gained. He quickly reassured them however. "Remember men the oil will stop them, and give us time."

Just as Albrecht spoke the words a screeching sound came from over the wall. Everyone looked down to see the three spiders falling.

Another cheer went up, but was cut short when the spiders stopped their fall by spinning webs like ropes connecting them to the wall. The spiders then began climbing back up undeterred. By this time even more of the Creatures began to climb.

Some of the men began to panic, but Albrecht quickly got them under control. Then the lead creatures stopped at the bottom edge of the oil and began chattering.

Albrecht and many of the men looked over the wall in anticipation at what the creatures would do. The last thing they saw was a massive amount of webbing heading straight for them. A few moved away in time, but many were quickly wrapped in cocoons of sticky filament. Albrecht was among those that were caught. Some of the men tried to cut them out but only got caught by the sticky fibers themselves.

The second in command tried to take control, but the men were in too much of a panic for him to take control. He grabbed one other man near him and told the man to fetch Shepard Slanoth or someone to help. The man all too glad to be away from the nightmare before him nodded and ran down the stairs to get help.

Slanoth was looking out over the wall watching as the ogre was trying to reform the army. Shepard however was taking advantage of the fact that the wraith was gone by bombarding them with firebombs, but the army seemed determined, or perhaps scared to fail. Either way the army refused to give in.

Suddenly Slanoth heard a commotion coming from behind him. He turned around and saw a haggard man coming towards him. When the man reached Slanoth he bowed down before him.

When he stood Slanoth saw shock and fear in the man's eyes. "What is the matter my son you look as though you have seen death itself?"

The man shook and at first could not find his words. When he spoke however his voice was shaky and subdued. "Near to Milord, the monsters found a way to get around all we do, and General Albrecht is dead Milord. The men are in chaos Sloan has tried to take command but the men are too frightened to listen. I fear the north wall is about to fall."

Suddenly Slanoth heard a harsh voice coming from just beyond them. Slanoth looked up and saw Cestator and William coming towards him.

"I can handle it Slanoth. Shepard has the army here under control, and as I had mentioned before I am the only man here that has dealt with these creatures before."

"Yes Cestator I think you are correct. Now hurry from the look of this man, things must be in quite a shambles there."

Cestator ran down the stairs without a moment's hesitation. William looked at Slanoth questioningly.

Slanoth smiled and waved his hand dismissively. "Go William help. Cestator will need someone else there who still has their wits about them."

William nodded and ran after Cestator. When the two men reached the north wall they could scarcely believe their eyes. Trained soldiers were acting like frightened women. Cestator quickly began grabbing men and pulling them aside. William quickly gathered himself and began to help.

When they had all of the men atop the wall gathered aside Cestator frowned at them, the men flinched slightly but Cestator could tell their focus was not on him. It remained on the cocoons behind him.

Cestator's frown darkened. "Pay no heed to them. There is nothing any of you can do for them. They are dead, now unless you wish to be like them you must do as I say."

Then just as Cestator finished saying this, a large web flew over the wall and connected itself to the floor. The men went wide-eyed in fear at the sight of it.

Cestator turned to look and shook his head. He turned to William. "Find a torch and light that web. It will burn quickly so watch yourself."

William nodded and went to do as Cestator instructed.

Cestator satisfied that the task would be done turned back to the frightened men. "Now fire is the one thing that these things fear most. They quickly catch fire for some reason. The men that ride them have found ways to not use it, for most obvious reasons. Now then . . ."

Suddenly, Cestator was cut off from what he was saying by William shouting behind him. "By the gods, you said it would light quickly, but I never thought."

Every man there then moved to the wall just in time to see the Giant spider burst into flames and fall into the sea below. They all cheered and began lifting their hand in triumph.

"We have not won yet, so calm yourselves." Cestator shouted over the roar.

Having new respect for Cestator, the men quickly quieted down and listened intently. Cestator seeing he had their full attention now, nodded to them. "Good now tell me did you use all of the oil on that wall there?"

The men shook their heads but only one man spoke up. "No Milord there was much left-over when we were finished."

Cestator smirked. "Good then take a few men with you and gather it quickly. We are going to give these things a surprise."

When the man left to do as he was ordered Cestator called over another man. The man stepped up and saluted him. Cestator ignored this and told the man to gather pitch arrows. The man nodded saluted again and ran off.

Cestator then looked around and quickly found what he was looking for. He walked over to one of the fire basins and smiled, it was filled with wood as he had hoped.

"You there," he called to another soldier standing aside. The man looked at him fearfully, but saluted him. Again Cestator ignored this and went on. "Get these fires burning and do it quickly we do not have much time."

The man nodded ran into a nearby door and grabbed a torch and began lighting the fires. By this time the men returned with the oil. When Cestator saw it he was slightly surprised how much they had accumulated.

Cestator ordered the men to bring it to the wall. When they got there a few of them looked over and shouted in fear. Cestator frowned and joined them at the edge and looked down. He saw thirty spiders working their way up the wall. "Let more come," he said wickedly. Stay back however unless you wish to join the others here that did not get out of the way quickly enough."

"Lord I have all the pitch arrows that could be found." The soldier said as he returned with ten quivers filled with arrows.

Cestator nodded to the man. "Now give each of the archers one of the arrows, and return to me when you are finished for more instructions.

"Yes sir," the man said without question, and went about his duties. He returned quickly with seven quivers still brimming with arrows.

Cestator looked at the remaining arrows and smiled. "Now I have an important question for you. Is there an open square anywhere nearby?"

"Yes sir it is a short distance down the main road there."

"Good, then I want you to take half of the men here down into the city. Get every able bodied person out of their homes and fortifying the road. I want the spiders to have no choice but to go the way we will be leading them. The rest of us will lead them into the square where I want everyone in hiding waiting for my signal to attack."

Suddenly Cestator saw a black spindly leg reaching over the wall. "Damn," he shouted. "Go now and hurry we will hold them off as long as we can but you need to hurry."

The man saluted and called out to several men, and they all ran down to the city to prepare it for the battle to come.

Not even taking time to pay attention to the man's salute Cestator turned to the archers. He pointed at one and shouted, "lite your arrow, and kill that thing quickly."

The man quickly turned to lite his arrow, and just as he turned back around and drew it back the head of the giant creature peeked up over the wall. He froze for a moment at the sight of the hideous creature. It was black as the darkest night, covered in short course hairs and shaped unlike any other spider any of the men had ever seen. The beast almost seemed malformed, and its mandibles measured nearly two feet long and were dripping with venom. Its eyes were dark orbs showing nothing but malice and death. The thing on the spiders back was cause for the archers pause however, for it did not look like any man. It was impossible to tell if they were wearing armor but if it was the armor was made to match the creature it rode. Nothing of the riders appearance could be seen for the armor covered them completely and so seamlessly it appeared to be part of its body, even where the eyes would be the helm had eyes upon it like the spider it rode.

"Fire now, kill that damn thing." Cestator shouted.

That was just enough to break through to the man. He quickly took aim and fired the arrow striking the spider in one of its several eyes. Instantly the giant spider burst into flames and fell back over the wall. Everyone on the wall held their breath for a moment hoping to get some reassurance that it was indeed a man on the creatures back, but they heard nothing as the two burned and plummeted to their death.

Everyone look to Cestator but he was already on to his next orders and ignored the questioning looks. Now everyone grab some of that oil, but leave three buckets and dump it over the wall onto our friends down there. It is time we show them how we treat invading armies here in Cerdrine. A loud cheer went up and the men ran to the edge of the wall dumped their oil over and ran back. A few of the men were a bit too slow to get away however and they were pulled over the side by webs, and into the waiting mandibles of the spiders below.

When everyone was clear Cestator shouted to the archers to light their arrows and fire down on the oil covered creatures below. Without question they did as he ordered, and instantly a huge roar of flames engulfed the entire wall. Yet still the men could hear no screaming coming from over the wall. A few of them became disheartened. "How is it these me can be dyeing and not utter a single sound? Do they not feel pain or are the not men at all?" One of the soldiers said voicing everyone's concern.

William moved over to Cestator and leaned in close. "They need some reassurance from you I think my friend. I feel much like they do but I do trust in you. You need to prove to them they can trust you will lead them out of this safely."

Cestator frowned slightly not being used to lead men in this way, but he understood where William was coming from. He raised his hand for silence, and slowly the men quieted down. "I have faced these creatures before and I assure you they are just like you, and I. They feel pain, and can die just as easily. They have just learned to conceal these things in battle. For they know their greatest weapon is that of the fear they impose upon others. Do not fall into that trap. We are the warriors of Cerdrine, and the last thing these bugs will see is the bottom of Cerdrine's boot."

The men began to cheer, "Cerdrine" over and over. It quickly grew into "Cestator the boot of Cerdrine."

Slanoth was looking out over the wall at the army regrouping out of the catapults range when he heard the chanting begin. When he made out what was being said he smiled. "Cargon has blessed you Cestator." He whispered to the wind.

"Well I do hope he has blessed us all."

Slanoth turned at the strange voice and saw Malketh standing behind him.

"Yes I do think he has Malketh."

The wizard then stepped up beside Slanoth and looked out with him. After a moment of silence he spoke. "That was a dangerous spell you conjured earlier."

"Not more than what you did my friend. I forgot to thank you for what you did."

Malketh looked at Slanoth with mute shock. "What I did?"

"Yes you destroyed the wraith. And for that I am grateful."

"Well yes . . . but it could not have been done if you had not cast such a spell making him have to concentrate on protecting himself from it. By the time he realized we were attacking as well it was too late. So I would say we owe nothing to each other."

Slanoth nodded. "I agree, but I still thank you for offering your help."

Malketh bowed deeply before Slanoth. "It was an honor to work beside the renowned Slanoth. Now if you please we shall take our leave. Our work is finished here."

"It has been an honor working beside you as well Malketh. May Cargon smile upon you."

Malketh smiled and turned. "He has done so already." Slanoth heard the man say as he walked away.

Just as Slanoth was going to turn back to the wall Shepard walked up. *"Aye, it do sound like da lad do have them rally'n behind 'im over thar."*

"Yes it does. I am glad that he is with us."

"Aye me too he do be one o' da best students I ever did have."

Slanoth smiled and looked out at the field before him and the army beyond. "Yes I must agree. There is not much more I can teach him however. What he needs to learn now he must do on his own."

"Tha' he do. Tha' he do . . ."

When the flames began to subside from the lack of fuel the men began to approach the wall to see what had been done. What they saw made them gasp.

Far below they could see many dead spiders upon the rocks below. But even still more of the creatures were climbing up the wall for the moment the flames were keeping them at bay, but with the dwindling fuel that would not last much longer.

A few of the men turned to Cestator asking him what they were to do without enough oil to stop them any longer.

Cestator knew this was going to happen and he was prepared for it. He raised his hands for silence and the men quickly quieted down.

"This situation was inevitable. Yes we may have killed several of the creatures with the oil, but that was because they did not expect it. I will not lie to you, some of us will die here." He paused momentarily to be sure all understood, when the men's faces did not change he went on. "If you listen to what I tell you our chances for survival will be much higher, and I promise you we will defeat them. Now are you with me?"

The men shouted as loudly as they could, that they would follow him to the end. Cestator nodded pleased with the result of his speech.

"Good then this is what we must do. Gather enough large shields to make a wall so we may hide behind. This is why we saved the buckets of oil. I want you to coat the shields with it. That will be the best defense against their webs. Behind the wall I want the three best archers. The rest of you and those who do not have a large shield, I need you need you to help fortify the street and the square. The rest of us who are left up here will be relying on you to get it done quickly, so it is ready when we lead the spiders down. Be sure to take the pitch arrows with you, but leave three behind. Use the rest to keep the creatures on the street when we lead them down. I want none of them to get off that road."

Cestator then turned to William who was standing at his side. "William I need you to lead the efforts down in the square. You will need to make haste my friend, for it will not be long before we can no longer hold them here."

One of the men spoke up before the rest could go. "Sorry to interrupt sir but if you let them take all the pitch arrows we will run out of arrows trying to bring those creatures down before they are all dead."

Cestator scowled slightly but he understood their concern. "That would be true unless you know where to aim. You see there is one place where they are quite susceptible to arrows. It is small, but I know where it is. Unlike the spiders you are used to seeing spinning webs to catch their prey. These creatures have a small gland just below their fangs where the webbing comes from. You must wait until they are about to shoot it they will raise their front legs up, and even then the place is small and you will not have much time. If you archers can hit that spot it will bring the creatures down instantly, and all that will have to be dealt with are the riders. That is where I will come in."

The men began to protest this but Cestator cut them short. "The rest of you will be busy enough fending off the spiders themselves. Very few have ever even seen these things and lived to tell the tale. Why do you think it is you have never heard of them? No do not fear for me I am more than able to handle the riders, but as I said I will need you to take down the spiders. Remember also we need only to delay them long enough that the square can be fortified. We will keep moving back slowly leading them into the trap."

The men seemed somewhat reluctant, but they agreed then did as Cestator had ordered. Before he left William put a hand on Cestator's shoulder. "Good luck my friend. May Cargon shine his guiding light upon us and get us through this."

Cestator nodded and clasped arms with his friend. "See you soon and be sure you are ready for a fight."

The two separated, and William led the group down into the city to take charge of the efforts there.

Cestator turned back to the waiting men and noticed there was still some oil left. He took this and spread it out over the top of the wall, leaving a clear path for their escape down the stairs. By the time he finished the men were set in their positions, and as they watched the smoke floating over the wall slowly diminished.

Cestator looked at them and frowned. "Be prepared it will not be long now." Then as though conjured up by his words two black spindly legs rose up over the wall.

Cestator quickly moved aside out of harm's way, hoping the men would not freeze again when face to face with the creatures. Moments later the first Spider was over the wall and staring right at the shields. The rider made some motions and said a few words in their strange tongue and the spider lifted its front legs.

"Now," Cestator shouted, "Shoot now!"

Just as he finished his words three arrows hit their mark and the spider dropped. The rider seeing its mount down jumped off and ran at the men, but Cestator was faster, he was upon the rider before it took three steps. As he knew would be the case this rider was skilled in the dance but still was no match for a Blade Master. Cestator easily blocked the riders first swing and brought his dark blade around low and sliced clean through his opponent's left leg the blade did not even pause as it struck armor or bone. The rider instantly fell to its remaining knee and Cestator beheaded his opponent. As he was about to move away he heard the men shouting at him.

Cestator quickly jumped away from the sticky web that was heading straight at him. But instead of moving away he ran straight for the spider, and avoiding its front legs he cut the fangs off. The moment he was clear the spider went down. The archers had found their mark again.

This time however the rider went for Cestator seeing him as the threat. This rider was just as skilled as the last, but Cestator was far beyond a match for his opponent, and he quickly dispatched this one as well. This time he pulled the helm off of the rider. The men behind him all gasped in shock. The rider was a woman. Cestator turned to them. "See here they are like us the only difference is they believe like their mounts the females are the stronger of them. Do not let this deter you from killing them because they will not think twice about killing you or your entire families." With that he threw the helm aside. That was the moment when matters got out of control. Seven of the spiders crested the wall and headed straight for him. Cestator now knew it was time to move. "Go now down the stairs to the streets, we cannot hold them here any longer."

As he said it more spiders began cresting the wall. He quickly dove to the side and a thick thread of web flew by where he had been standing and struck the shield wall. Because of the oily surface it did not stick however. Seeing its attack missed its mark the creature was about to try again, but before it could three arrows found their mark once again, and the spider fell hard. The rider quickly jumped off her dead mount, and one of the soldiers dispatched her before she could regain her balance.

"Go get out of here all of you, get down to the street." Cestator yelled as he was preparing to fight off another of the spiders that was rearing up to bite him. Once again however one of the soldiers jumped in the way, and raised his shield to block the attack. It did no good however for the spider's fangs punched right through the shield and pierced the man's arm. He screamed as the venom sent fiery pain rushing through his veins. "I'm sorry," Cestator said before stabbing the man through the heart saving him the misery of a slow agonizing death.

Suddenly Cestator had a ring of men around him. "I told all of you to get down to the street." He shouted at them angrily.

"We will not leave you here to face them yourself. You need to survive, for without you all will be lost." One of the men said in answer.

"Very well then move back, we cannot fight all of them up here. Do the archers still have the pitch arrows?"

"Yes sir." The same man answered. "They are waiting for us at the base of the stairs with their arrows lit. They are ready to set this wall a fire as soon as we are clear."

Cestator smirked, "good of you to anticipate my plans."

"It only made sense sir with how well it worked the first time." The man said as they began backing up towards the stairs.

At this point seeing their targets trying to escape the spiders tried firing their webs at the men. The soldiers held their shields up and foiled the attacks however. As they stared down the stairs Cestator called down to the archers. "Light those bastards on fire."

Instantly the men on the stairs saw three flaming arrows flying overhead and they landed on top of the wall. Suddenly there was a loud *Whoosh* as the top of the wall was engulfed in flames.

"Move, get down there quickly. That fire will not last long there was not much oil left, and I only meant for it to give us enough time to regroup at the base of the wall."

Without question the men ran down the stairs and turned back to what was happening up on the wall. Cestator however looked around and surveyed the fortitude of the streets and was pleased with what he saw. They had built up large piles of wood against the wall on either side of the road. A man stood behind them with a torch. Along the road as far as he could see they had made makeshift spikes with whatever could be found and even had overturned carts blocking the side passages. Behind these were crowds of people with pitchforks spears or any other object that they could find that made a serviceable weapon. Cestator was surprised at the number of people behind the walls. It appeared to him that the frightened mob had found their courage.

"Sir the flames are dying out." One of the men called out.

Cestator turned back to the wall. "Prepare yourselves they will be coming over soon. As want any of them to make it off the street. Archers I want you to stay your arrows unless you have an absolute kill shot. Don't waste your arrows on trying to drive them."

"Yes sir." The three men said and move a short distance down the road, but staying well within range.

Suddenly a shout went up. "There they are." Cestator looked up at the wall and saw the spiders starting to come over. "Get ready men. We need to lead them to the square and the others are ready for us." He then looked to the men at the wood piles and ordered them to lite them.

The men did as they were told and backed away, and stood by several water buckets incase the fires got out of control. The roaring fires worked perfectly the creatures shied away from the flames, and came down the wide street. The people on the sides began throwing stones and rotten food or anything they could pick up. This caused the spiders to become distracted and they began moving towards the people.

Frustrated by this Cestator was about to yell at the people but suddenly he noticed the archers on the roofs. He looked up at one of them that was facing him and pointed at his eye. The man nodded and spread the word.

The archers took aim on the lead spider and let loose their volley. A majority of the arrows hit their mark and effectively blinded the spider. The creature went crazy and began flailing around. Cestator wasted no time taking advantage of this. He ran over and cut off all of its legs on the left side. The spider fell to the ground throwing its rider off. Cestator paid no heed to the rider however for the soldiers quickly surrounded her. Cestator instead drove his blade into the creature's abdomen and sliced it open. A green foul smelling fluid poured out of the gaping wound and the spider went still.

Cestator jumped aside as another spider attacked. He easily avoided the attack but the road was now slick with the fluid from the first and he lost his footing for just a split second. But in that time he knew he would not be able to avoid another attack. Three arrows struck the creature but because of his proximity to the creature they missed their mark. He brought his sword around in a futile attempt to stop the fangs even though he knew it was over.

Suddenly he heard someone shout. "Cestator look out." A second later someone tackled him knocking him out of the way. When they hit the ground Cestator looked at his assailant, it was one of the men with him. The man smiled at him, but that smile turned into a look of pain and horror as the spiders fangs sank into his leg.

Cestator was instantly on his feet. He cut off the spider's fangs, then its two front legs. With all his strength he drove his sword down through the creatures head when it fell forward, and the tip buried itself into the road. The rider jabbed her sword at Cestator intending to exact her revenge upon him. Cestator was faster however. Abandoning his sword he knocked the sword aside with one hand, and pulled out his dagger with the other. He buried it hilt deep up into the riders head.

A moment later another spider fell beside him with two arrows protruding from its gland, and the rider one in her throat. Cestator pulled his weapons out and fended off another attack, the archers on the rooftops turned the creature into a pincushion dropping the creature.

Cestator dropped to the ground, and a shot of webbing flew over him. He rolled to his right avoiding one of the spider's legs that nearly impaled him. Suddenly the creature burst into flames.

Cestator Scrambled to his feet, to avoid being crushed under the burning spider. Suddenly he heard a woman scream. He turned to look and found one of the creatures had breached the defenses and was attacking the people. Then he saw that the monster was feeding on a young man, and what had to be his mother was attacking the Spider with what appeared to be a kitchen knife. Twenty men and women lay dead or dying around the creature, and Cestator had to watch helplessly as the woman died on the rider's blade.

There was no way to get to them however for the spider had created its own blockade of webbing stopping men and arrows alike. Just as Cestator was about to curse himself for a fool he saw two flaming arrows fly past him and headed for the monster. The fiery projectiles burned through the shield and struck their target instantly igniting the spider and everything around it.

Black smoke billowed up into the sky and the stench of burning flesh filled the air. "Get that fire under control." Cestator shouted at the people standing around watching the scene in mute horror. His words spurred them into action, and the people quickly got the fire under control.

Cestator ran over to the man who had saved him but he was already dead. He frowned, and cursed himself for a fool to make these people suffer like this. Knowing he could do nothing for the man except for not let his sacrifice be in vain, Cestator rejoined the rest of his group.

"What shall we do now sir? Are we to remain here and try to hold them any longer?" One of the men asked.

"No we need to fall back and head to square. We cannot continue this here or more innocent people will die. We need to keep these things moving. Right now we are the biggest threat to them so they will follow us. I just hope William and the others are prepared for us."

The men started backing up battling an occasional spider as they led them into the trap. The archers on the rooftops and side streets help control any that tried to veer off and flank them, but those were few and far between. As Cestator had said the men in front of them retreating were their biggest threats, and they were focused on eliminating them.

When they finally reached the square it was a massive open space surrounded by large buildings, and all the streets out were blocked. It seemed almost deserted for nothing stirred. The air itself was still as though the entire city was holding its breath. Cestator and his small band backed up as far as they could from the entrance, with the archers' backs against the wall of one of the buildings.

The spiders filed in after them, and seeing they had the group cornered the first wave pressed forward. The men continued to take down the lead spider, but in the open space they were quickly getting surrounded. "Where are the others?" One man called out. "We cannot keep them at bay for long. We are going to be overrun here soon."

Suddenly one of the men misjudged a web shot, and it went over the top of his shield and struck him in the face. Instantly he was pulled into the writhing horde of spiders. The creatures began fighting amongst themselves over the body.

Cestator noticed this and called out to one of his archers. "Aim for one of the riders. I have an idea."

"Are you sure sir? We are about to be overrun here." The man questioned.

"If I am wrong it will change nothing." Cestator said with a scowl. "But if I am right it may buy us some time."

The man nodded not questioning him any further. He took aim and fired. The arrow found its mark slipping between the rider's helm and armor piercing her throat. Suddenly the spiders went wild and pounced on the body of the fallen rider.

"Just as I had expected," Cestator chuckled. "These things are ravenously hungry from the trip over the sea, and the smell of blood is driving them mad."

By this time all of the spiders had clambered into the square, and they nearly filled the immense space. The ones that the riders could keep under control continued pressing down on the small group of men, despite the feeding frenzy that was going on near them.

"Damn William where are you?" Cestator cursed.

Suddenly a door opened beside them and William peeked out. "Right here my friend." He said with a grin. Then at that moment the square became alive with activity outside of the milling spiders. People appeared in every window, and every street surrounding the square. "Come in here take a moments rest." William called to the small group, and he moved aside. Of the twenty men that had stayed behind with Cestator only twelve remained. They all filed into the building Cestator taking up the rear.

"Take down the riders and it will cause a feeding frenzy. Those things are barely under control." Cestator told William after he closed the door behind him.

"Yes we saw that." William answered. "We lost eight men in that flight here and several innocents died as well."

"We could not spring the trap until they were all within the square. Otherwise there would have been more casualties." William answered sadly. "But now it is time you and your men rest. You just may have saved us all."

"Pardon my interruption Sir William." One of the men following Cestator said. "But, I owe those bastards out there. The men they killed were my friends, and I'll not hide away while they are still out there."

Cestator looked at the men around him, and saw the weariness in their eyes. "Is this how the rest of you feel as well?" He asked, and got a resounding, "Yes sir." He let a slight smile touch his lips hearing the conviction in their voices. "Well then let us get out there and show them that we will never be beaten." The men let out a loud cheer, and burst the door open, and charged out into the square. "Are you coming?" Cestator asked as he headed out the door.

"Of course I wouldn't want to miss out on all the fun." William answered. Before following Cestator out he turned to two men that were still inside awaiting his orders. "Go and inform Lord Slanoth what is happening here. Tell him that the city is safe from this side."

"Yes Sir." They said and ran out the back door of the building.

With that done William followed Cestator out the door into the square. By this time there was absolute chaos between the spiders. The riders had lost all control of them and they were attacking each other. This made it easy for the archers to pick them off, and any time one was wounded and could not protect itself those around it swarmed the unfortunate creature and its rider.

Cestator's party cut their way through the creatures taking full advantage of their chaotic state. The spiders being cannibalistic by nature had found a greater source of food, and so they paid no heed to the men walking through them.

An hour later the last two spiders fell to the archers arrows. A loud cheer went up, and the twelve men looked to Cestator, and they all shouted. "Cestator Spider slayer!" then the crowd outside the square took up the chant. "Spider slayer, spider slayer!" the sound resonated throughout the entire city and shook the walls.

The makeshift walls came down, and a horde of people clambered over the bodies of the spiders to get close to Cestator. The twelve men surrounded Cestator and William to keep the crowd at bay. William looked around them in shock. "What did you do?" he shouted so he could be heard over the noise.

"Only what I said I would," Cestator answered. "But I have an idea." He raised his hand up for silence, and a short time later the noise quieted down. Climbing up onto a large pile of spiders so he could be seen by all, he called out. "People of Cerdrine hear me."

Again a loud cheer of, "Spider slayer!" went up. Once more Cestator raised his hands for silence, and when it was relatively quiet he went on. "I say we have won a great battle here today, but the war still rages outside our gates." A low grumble of disappointment began to brew, but Cestator stopped it quickly. "Hold I say, for the army outside those walls is made up of only hired men. These men were depending on the undead, who Lord Slanoth has destroyed, and their allies here which we have defeated." Cestator bent down removed the head of the spider he was standing on, and lifted it over his head. "So I say we show those men what we do to those who dare attack Cerdrine."

A cheer went up louder than ever before, and everyone who was able took a spider's head, and waved it in the air chanting, "Cerdrine." Cestator took a moment to take it all in how with a few choice words he could rally these people behind him. He jumped down, and with his now appointed guards he headed for the west gate with all the people in tow.

Chapter 19

The Light Falls

Slanoth stepped out of the guard house after conferring with the two men that William had sent. He had debriefed them in great detail trying to learn as much as he could as to what had transpired on the other side of the city. *"What horrific creatures."* He thought to himself, as he walked over to Shepard.

The fire bombs and ballista missiles constant bombardment seemed to have quite an effect on the army outside. *"They are waiting for their spider friends to come through and open the gates."* They were sure to stay just out of range of the weapons the burning bodies piled up just inside the weapons range gave testament to the teams accuracy with the mighty weapons.

Suddenly Slanoth heard a loud chant coming from the center of the city. At first he could not discern what was being said, but after a short time he was able to puzzle it out. The people were chanting "Spider Slayer"

"So do ye be think'n tha' be mean'n tha' they done beat them critters back thar?" Shepard asked as Slanoth walked up to him.

"I truly do hope so old friend. That would surely be a tide turning event here. Right now it is obvious the only thing keeping these men here is fear of their master, and the hope that the spiders will do most of the work for them."

Suddenly another loud cheer could be heard throughout the city, this time it did not last quite as long however. *"Blast I would Sher like ta be know'n wha' be go'n on out thar"*

"I agree old friend. Those people are certainly rallying behind someone. Do you think it may be Cestator?"

"Would tha' no be a turn o' events. Anyway from da soun' o' thins I would be bet'n tha them spiders be done fer."

Then the third wave of chanting came, only this time it was different, and it was louder than ever before. It started getting closer and was not stopping. Shepard looked out at the army in the distance wondering if they could hear the noise, and if it was affecting them in any way. He was not surprised to see a bit more movement between the tents than usual.

Slanoth came over and nodded towards the army. "It would appear that they are getting a bit agitated."

"Aye, they can no be like'n da soun' o' da cheer'n go'n on here. I would be guess'n they did be expect'n screams o' horror by now."

The chant continued to grow louder as the people approached the wall. Then just as they reached the outskirts of the buildings they stopped. A moment later a soldier came running up the stairs. "Lord Slanoth, General Shepard pardon my interruption but your presence is requested at the stairs."

"Is it Cestator, my son?" Slanoth asked.

The man nodded. "Cestator is among them, yes my lord." The look in the man's eyes as he spoke showed disbelief and amazement.

"Among them, wha' do ye be mean'n by tha'?"

"He is surrounded by the people general."

"What people are we talking about here my son? Is it the soldiers or someone else?" Slanoth asked even more curious than ever.

"There are many soldiers among them yes. But I would venture to guess he has every man, woman, and child in the city out there with him. But that is not all they seem to be carrying." The man paused a moment trying to think how best to describe what he had seen. "No I think it would be best if you just go and see for yourself."

Their curiosity piqued Slanoth, and Shepard followed the man to the stairs. When they looked down they were amazed by what they saw. The man had not been joking it appeared that everyone was behind William and Cestator.

When he saw them Cestator called out to Shepard and Slanoth. "Lord, General I present to you the enemy that threatened the people." He then lifted the spider head up into the air. Everyone behind him followed suit and began to cheer. "Hail to Cestator, spider slayer. Hail Cestator savior of the people."

The two stared at the scene in shock. they had never expected anything like this. Cestator had rallied all the people behind him, and they were praising him. Shepard was the first to recover from his shock. *Aye lad job well done, were it no' fer da lot o' ya, we would likely be finished. Now, what say you? Should we send that army out thar a message?"*

Cestator looked back behind him and smirked, when he turned back around his smirk was still there and it made some of the men that were watching him take a step back. "That is just what we had in mind."

"Aye, well load dem things in da catapults an' let's give 'em to 'um!" Shepard said with a chuckle.

Cestator and William climbed the stairs up to the top of the wall with twelve men behind them. They began handing the heads over to the men working the catapults. The rest of the men on top of the wall started a line to the others and started handing heads down the line.

Slanoth walked over to Cestator questioningly "You look exhausted go inside and rest a bit."

Cestator shook his head "I will rest when I am sure all is well, and all of my men are safe."

Slanoth looked at the men standing behind Cestator, and he raised an eyebrow. "I assume it is all of you he speaks of?"

"Yes sir," they answered. "Cestator brought us through the battle. He risked his life for us so we shall serve him until the end."

"Did I jar's hear wha' I be think'n I did hear?" Shepard asked as he walked up to the group.

"Yes you certainly did Shepard, and I am just as curious as you are." Slanoth answered, and the two of them looked at Cestator for an explination.

"I will tell you when I am sure all of my men's wounds are attended to." Cestator said matter-of-factly, then he walked away heading for the guard house. The twelve men followed just a step behind him.

Shepard frowned, he did not like being left in the dark. He could not argue Cestator's loyalty however, nor the loyalty the men, were showing him in return. He found himself grinning like a happy dog.

Slanoth on the other hand simply looked at William. "You were there. Tell us what happened."

William shook his head. "I do not know all that happened, but Cestator knew those things would get over the wall so he sent a majority of us into the city to fortify it. He kept only twenty men with him, and those twelve are all that are left of them. Those men led the spiders to the city square where we had laid a trap for them. I am not sure what happened on that rute but I heard those men saved a great many lives. Then even when they were given the chance to hide out and rest, they followed Cestator out into a writhing pit of spiders that were attacking anything that moved. When it was all over everyone in the city praised him as their savior.

"Pardon the interruption." A soldier said as he approached the three. "General you asked to be informed when those things were fired."

"Ah yes thank ye lad." Shepard said with a big grin, and he looked back at Slanoth. *"Shall we see wha' them bastards do thik o' our message?"*

"Lead the way," Slanoth answered. The three walked over to the edge of the wall and looked out. The scene below them was horrible. The ground had been curned up from hundreds of boots treading over it. Scattered around were craters where the fireballs had struck, and the ground around them was chared black. In a majority of them were what remained of burnt bodies. The dead and dying littered the field. The men out there did not stand a chance without the undead or the spiders. At the farthest reaches of the field masses of black heads were scattered around. This was where everyone's focus was for they did not want to think about the rest of it.

After a short time a small party rode out from the distant camp, and headed for the black mass. Everyone on the wall watched in anticipation as they approached the spider heads. One man got off of his horse, and picked up a head then jumped back up on his horse and the group rode back into the camp. A short time later they could hear shouting coming from deep within the tents.

A cheer went up on the wall when the sound reached them. *"Ah they can no be too happy 'bout tha' one. Now if'n they wan' in they gonna have ta be do'n it they 'selves. I be wonder'n wha' they be plan'n ta be do'n."*

Slanoth shook his head. "I don't know Shepard, but I am sure that we just hurt the plans that they did have. It will likely take them some time before they do anything. Meanwhile I am going to check on Cestator. William come with me please I have some other questions I need to ask you."

"Yes Lord Slanoth." William said as he followed.

As Cestator walked up to the door he turned to his men and smiled. "Come let us take that well deserved rest everyone spoke of. I want you men to care to the wounds you have and take a few moments to rest." They entered the guard house and found it to be a spacious room with a table and a few chairs. Several beds were set along the wall where the men that stayed there could rest. The light came in from several arrow slits set in the circumference of the walls. They found some bandages and began attending to each other while they sat, and rested.

Cestator looked over his rag-tag group of men and was happy to see that none were too hurt, but they were certainly weary from the battle they had fought. "I want to thank all of you. You stood in the face of something that would have frightened most men and you fought gallantly. If my word can pull any weight here I am going to recommend all of you to be honored as heroes."

The men all began to protest, but Cestator stopped them. "No do not argue, I do not make such claims lightly. So please take it as it is intended. I did what was expected of me, and I have faced those things before. But all of you put your faith in a man you knew nothing about except the stories you have heard, and none of those were good I am sure. Again I say you did that and faced creatures from most men's nightmares without flinching."

"We did what we had to sir." One man said. "Yes and it was you who gave us the courage to do it," piped in another.

Suddenly the door opened, and Slanoth and William entered. "From what I am told you men have performed admirably." Slanoth said with a smile. "Tales will be told of the bravery all of you have shown this day. But I fear this is not yet over. There is still an army outside these walls. We have a need for such men as you."

Cestator smirked, "you know that I will do all that I can."

"As will I," William added.

"You may count on us as well lord Slanoth." The other men said as they stood.

"So all of you look weary and on the brink of collapse yet you still are willing to lay down your lives for this cause?" Slanoth asked somewhat surprised.

"Yes lord," they said in unison.

Slanoth's smile broadened, "well I stand corrected. It will not be tales, but legends. Very well then, for now I want you men to rest you have more than earned that. General Shepard or myself will return for you when you are needed." Without another word Slanoth left the room.

Cestator looked around the room. "Well you heard him, bunk down and get some rest we have more work to do soon enough"

"Yes sir," the men said saluting him. Cestator retuned the gesture, and all the men found a cot to rest on.

"What do you make of this?" William asked in all the commotion.

"I am unsure," Cestator replied. "What I can say is, whatever they have planned for us we will be at the front of the action."

"Yes well whatever it is I wish I knew exactly what they were planning." William said with a frown. He quickly decided that it was not a good idea to worry over it and joined the other men.

Cestator watched William walk away and smiled. *"Soon you will be ready my friend, it is going to strike you very soon."*

Slanoth returned to where Shepard waited for him, and he sighed. "The time has nearly come my friend. William is going to be the next."

"Aye ye could see it in he eye couldn't ye? Dis will no be easy fer 'im ta except ye know."

"I think you are right there old friend. We will have to pray for him in hopes that he does not take it badly. So tell me have you figured out what they are doing out there?"

"Aye they look ta be build'n a battering ram, an a few siege towers. I'd be say'n they will no be try'n anything till morn'."

"That makes little sense, they should know we would destroy them before they reach the wall. There has to be more to their plan than that." Slanoth said somewhat fearful.

"Aye ye would think so, but it do seem tha' ogre no be too smart. This should be over right quick. Why don't ye go an git yerslef some rest? Thar will be noth'n go'n on till morn'. Me I is gonna go an see to da gates, an be sure they be ready in case tha thing do make it here." Shepard said with a wink.

Slanoth caught the subtle expression and nodded. "Well I trust your judgment old friend. I will see in the morning then." Slanoth left heading for a distant set of stairs in the general direction of the temple.

Twilight began to settle on the city when Slanoth made it back to the gates. Shepard was there waiting for him. "How long has the spy been here?" He asked when he was close enough not to be overheard.

"I did notice 'im earlier today. He be good fer I did no see 'im, but out da corner o' me eye, an when I did look he were gone. Thar no be many what can escape me notice, but he done it"

"Assassin you're thinking then?"

"Aye thar be no doubt he be into da black arts. Da question be, why he be here. Tha' army hath all but lost, so wha' be their plan?"

"My guess would be that he is here to be sure they make it to the wall. But why send an assassin, unless they want to kill a few key people?"

"Aye that be my thought also. So I did make sure those men guarding the catapults an ballista got away from them fer a time. We no need ta loose good men fer them. So we will be need'n ta come up wit a plan stop dis army from get'n here."

"Yes the army itself we should be able rout them quickly enough. We now outnumber them, but with an assassin inside, and the siege towers they may just make it inside."

"Not if we be meet'n them on da field, then we will be on even ground 'cept them towers which I do know how ta be deal'n wit'"

"Yes, but Shepard there will certainly be reinforcements waiting for the gates to be opened. They will have to be dealt with."

"Aye an tha' be where Cestator an his ban o' men do come in. Da reinforcements will sure be some of da best they do have. So wha' better way ta be rid o' them than ta send our best. They will no even know wha' hit them. When dis be over."

The two then spent the next few hours hashing out a plan, going over every detail, and covering every possible situation that could arise. They knew that if they missed anything it could be disastrous. So they even tried to come up with the most unlikely circumstances.

Dersloan surveyed the situation, He cared little for what Shepard was doing. The dwarf was intelligent, but like most dwarves he was as silent, and subtle as a bolder rolling down a hill. He waited patiently for the guards to slack, giving him a chance to do his deed. He smiled darkly when he saw his opportunity. As he knew would happen the men grew weary of watching the weapons and began playing a game of dice.

He quietly took out his blowgun, and gently pulled out one of his glass darts then filled it with acid. He was sure to measure out only enough to disable the weapon. Too much and the damage would be noticed beforehand, but too little and it would not have the desired effect. The darts range was limited but it was the best way to accomplish his goal, for he knew dead or missing guards always raised suspicion, and that was the last thing he wanted.

Like a shadow Dersloan crept in closer until he was within range to hit two of the weapons. He waited patiently for the men to cheer for a good roll, and he fired two darts. The projectiles hit their mark perfectly, and the men's cheering covered the sound of the fragile glass breaking. He went around and repeated the process until all of the weapons were damaged.

When his task was done he moved to a secluded spot on the wall and tied a message onto an arrow and shot it out towards the waiting messenger. He then slipped out into the city to avoid being noticed.

An hour before dawn Cestator, William and their men were awakened by Shepard's gruff voice. *"Come on thar lads, Da time fer action be here. I be know'n ye no wana be miss'n out o' da fight."*

Cestator looked up at Shepard and wiped the sleep from his eyes. "The army is on the move then?"

"Aye that they do be, they hast been working through da night. Course it still won't be do'n them no good. I did just be think'n you two would be want'n ta help finish dis."

William jumped up quickly, but nearly fell back down. He caught himself however and chimed up strongly. "Yes Sir we surely do wish to."

"Woe lad no so fast thar. I be want'n da two o' you and yer men ta be in da extra group. Sides ye no be ready ta fight yet, ye still have no found yer feet."

William did not like the sound of what he had just heard he wanted to face the enemy not be a standby. Cestator however who was watching Shepard's every move even those of his eyes read exactly what Shepard was saying and smiled.

"I mean no offense General," William sputtered, "but I do not wish to be put on some reserve group. Cestator and I are two of the best swordsmen here, not to use that would be a waste."

Shepard chuckled heartily and shook his head. *"Aye Lad I do be know'n that, an I will be using da two of you as much as I can. Ya see, you two an a few other choice men will be my little surprise fer them out thar. Ya see they more an like know I will be hold'n back some men they'll be expecting tha' fer sure. Wha' they won't be expect'n though is a third group come round to hit their extra men. I did pick some o' da best men ta make a quick strike and wipe out their reinforcements. So when ye be ready meet da other men at base o' da wall. Thar be some secret entrances that ye can sneak out behind them. Be that understood?"*

William quickly spoke up. "Yes sir, thank you General for having faith in me."

Shepard chuckled and shook his head. *"Lad if what I hear bout you from a dozen men, Slanoth being one o' them thar be no question you be thar."* He then looked at Cestator questioningly. *"An wha' about ye do ye be up ta it?"*

Cestator smirked wickedly. "You could save some of your men and send William and myself and consider it done."

Shepard and William both looked at Cestator in shock. William was stunned into silence. Shepard however was not.

"Ye has lots o' faith in this lad's abilities don't ye. We be talk'n 'bout a hundred or more men. I would no send jus' two men out thar."

One of the men with them spoke up as well at that moment. "Sir you cannot leave us behind either."

Cestator frowned and shook his head. "I would not send many more. Too many men will be easier to spot. I say send the two of us because we can hit them quickly, and be gone before they know we are there." He looked at William and nodded. "Besides William here is one of the best swordsmen I have ever seen. He learned the dance quickly and adapted to it faster than any I have seen, so as I said before send the two of us and the job will be done. Also I appreciate what you men did, but this is a task that will require stealth. We will have to move quickly, and be done. Your best place would be helping at the front line."

Shepard looked at the two men and scratched his chin pacing back and forth, and finally he stopped in front of William and looked deep into his eyes and nodded. *"So lad wha' does ya think o' what Cestator thar be say'n bout ya?"*

William shook his head vigorously. "Cestator thinks too much of me. I am still learning. I agree I could best most of the men in the temple, only because I know their limits, but to do what you are asking."

Shepard quickly silenced William by turning away. He looked at Cestator and looked into his eyes and saw confidence there. He smiled and nodded. *"So be it then the two of you will be on your own. Remember though the rest o' us are count'n on ye."*

Shepard then handed Cestator a rolled up parchment. *"Here dis be a map o' da secret passages you'll be need'n it."* Shepard left them saying, *"good luck lads I be count'n on ye. Da res o' ye meet me out at da gate soon as ye ready I has another task fer ya."*

When Shepard was gone William turned to Cestator. "I thank you for the bode of confidence, but are you sure we can do this?"

Cestator smiled at his friend and put a hand on his shoulder. "Everything I told Shepard was true. I do not make false claims. He saw it in you as well as I could from the first time I met you."

"What are talking about, what did he see?"

Cestator pointed at William's chest. "You have the spirit. You have all you need inside of you. You only have to find it. It is hard to explain, but you will know when it comes to you. Your time is near I can sense it, and I think this will be the turning point for you."

William shook his head. "I hope you are right Cestator because I do not feel any different than I have in the past."

Cestator smiled and slapped William on the shoulder. "Don't worry if I am wrong you should still be more than a match for those men out there. Besides we will have the advantage."

William frowned and shook his head. "I almost hate to ask, but what would that be."

Cestator gave William his half smile and chuckled. "They will never expect two men to attack them. They might be watching for a large group so we can likely get between them easily."

William shook his head and sighed. "I knew I would not like your answer."

The two men gathered their things and headed for the entrance to the passage.

When Shepard arrived at the gates where the Slanoth was gathering the army he approached his friend with a bright smile. *"Ye be right Slanoth tha' boy be bust'n wit it. Me I thought he might burst out right thar."*

"So old friend, everything went as planned I would guess." Slanoth answered.

"Aye that it did, they did jus' as we had thought. Ye know it be quite a rare thing ta see. I only had ever seen tha' in someone eyes once before in all my year. An it be so close to another."

Slanoth chuckled, he knew who Shepard was referring to as the first, but he would never boast of it. "Yes unfortunately it would seem to be a symbol of the times."

Shepard nodded. *"Aye tha' do be true. I only wish I could be thar to see it happen."*

"I know my friend, but you know as well as I do, it will only come out beside someone he truly trusts. Besides you were there the first time."

"Aye tha' I were an so were Randor. Tha' were quite the sight ta see. We was cornered an bout done fer an ye just snapped. I think it did scare us much as it did them ogres."

Slanoth chuckled softly at this. "You were scared by it. No one was more surprised than I. It happened so quickly and none of us knew at the time what it was. William however has others around who know his secret."

"Aye ye be right thar. Though I no think it will make much difference to him when it happens."

Suddenly Shepard was interrupted by a guard calling down from atop the wall. "General the army is on the move. They are carrying two large rams."

Shepard smiled brightly. *"Ah it be time."* He looked around at the men behind him and his grin widened. *"Be ye ready ta finish dis."*

A loud shout of approval went up from the men waiting. Shepard nodded he had been waiting for this moment for some time. *"Good then soon as da gates open charge them and be quick. We won't get but a moment 'fore da surprise be gone."*

Shepard then called up to the men working the winches for the gates to open them. Then a moment later he heard the two levers being pulled and the rumbling of the chains as they fell, and suddenly the gates were open wide.

The army on the other side of the wall looked slightly shocked at the speed the gates had opened and for a moment they stood there dumbfounded. Shepard's men however reacted instantly, and they were upon the army in moments.

Cestator and William were just at the outskirts of the armies reinforcements when the battle began. "It's begun," William whispered softly.

Cestator nodded in agreement. "Yes we must strike now. Remember your training it will help you, but also look deep into yourself you have great abilities waiting there."

William shook his head in confusion. "I know nothing about what you think I am, but I hope you are right."

Cestator waved him off, and pointed at the army and began counting down fingers when he had a closed fist he charged at the army and William followed.

The two quickly dispatched a few of the men, and as the soldiers realized what was going on, they were shocked by what they saw which cost them dearly. Between the two Cestator and William killed thirty men before they even got their swords clear. Then someone began shouting orders and the men became more organized.

William was shocked at how much ground they were gaining. He had expected these men to be more organized. Then William's fears became reality, the army regrouped and the men were more prepared. He found himself taking more time fending off attacks from all sides, which made it harder for him to defeat each opponent before him. He took a quick glance over at Cestator and saw the man was cutting a swath through the army, no one could touch him.

Suddenly William felt a glancing blow on his right shoulder. He turned back just in time to block another blow, and quickly found himself on the defense. He quickly realized this man was the leader, and likely the one who rallied the men. The man knew how to use his weapon well, he was not a blade master, but was not far from it. William knew he was going to be in trouble if he did not end it quickly, but the man seemed to know his every move and countered it.

Suddenly William had a sinking feeling in the pit of his stomach, and it seemed someone was screaming at him inside his head. He wasted no time pondering this instead he quickly dropped to one knee and ducked down. Seconds later a large battle-axe cut through the air above him.

The two men looked down at him in shock, not quite understanding how he was still alive. In that moment something snapped inside of William's mind and he suddenly had a boundless amount of knowledge. He suddenly knew things that he could have never known.

A wicked grin spread across William's face, and he slowly stood up. The two men seeing the sudden change in him right before their eyes turned to run, but William cut them down before they took a single step. He began walking through the army cutting down anyone who got near him. After a short time the army began to scatter and flee from the two. No one wanted to face them, and soon Cestator and William were standing alone in a field of bodies.

William looked around at the carnage they had caused and shook his head. When Cestator walked up to him he frowned. "Is this, what happened to the orcs? Is this what the kings men found?"

Cestator only nodded in reply.

William shook his head. "I know what these men intended to do. I know they would have killed us and anyone that got in their way, but that makes this no easier. We slaughtered them like cattle. As an aspiring paladin this feels wrong. Perhaps if they had been orcs I might have felt differently, but they were men."

Cestator shook his head sadly. "It is no different whether it be a man, orc, or even a goblin, the emptiness is always the same. That is the curse to the gift. You wondered why I turned . . . you now have your answer. I felt that perhaps if I had a reason it would keep me from going mad. The best advice I can give is always remember what it is you fight for that alone will get you through."

William shook his head and fell to his knees. "If this is the price of all this knowledge I have, then I don't want it. Make it go away please Cargon take it from me."

Cestator walked over and place his hand on William's shoulder. "It will get better my friend I promise, and I am sorry but there is nothing anyone can do when it chooses you that is the way it is."

Suddenly their conversation was interrupted by a blaring horn. A smile spread across Cestator's face. "It sounds as though the army is in need of reinforcements. I think that we should not disappoint them now should we?"

William looked up at Cestator, and shook his head. "Absolutely not . . . Slanoth and Shepard are depending on us."

Cestator's smile brightened and he gave William a hand up. "Now that is the spirit of a paladin." Then with that the two ran towards the city to help in the battle.

Slanoth quickly cut down any man that dared stand against him in his search for the leader. He knew if he could kill the ogre the men would quickly scatter without someone bullying them.

Suddenly he heard a horn blaring, and he quickly prayed that William and Cestator had accomplished their task. He looked in the direction he had heard the sound and easily found the ogre looming over the men swinging its giant sword cutting down anyone in its path whether friend or foe. Seeing this Slanoth became even more determined.

Slanoth called out to the creature, and pointed his sword at it in a challenge. Somehow the creature heard him over the noise of the war going on around them. The ogre looked at Slanoth smiled, and headed straight for him. It paid no heed to anyone in its way any who did not move were knocked over and crushed under its large feet. Slanoth calmly stood his ground waiting for his opponent.

All the men in the field began to realize what was about to happen and a circle began to form around Slanoth with an opening for the ogre to get through. The sky began to cloud over and had anyone dared to look up they would have seen two figures watching from above.

When the ogre finally made it into the circle it laughed darkly and charged at Slanoth. Slanoth easily blocked its swing, but when the two swords clashed a loud crack of thunder roared through the air, and everyone was stunned for a moment.

Then the battle continued the two trading blow for blow neither one gaining any ground. It was easy to see these two were evenly matched. The battle raged on with each side of the field shouting and chanting for their leader and for a time there was a kind of peace.

After a short time of battling the ogre, Slanoth realized he would tire long before this creature would, so he knew he was going to have to finish this soon. His opponent however seemed to know every trick he tried. This was one of the most dangerous opponents he had ever faced. It had the size and strength of an ogre but the intelligence of a well learned and well trained man.

Slanoth continued to move in and out striking and fleeing. He knew if he went head to head with the creature it would overpower him. Then suddenly as he was moving he caught a glimpse of two figures watching from above, and he knew the battle would soon be over, and he felt at peace.

As Cestator and William broke through the tree line they found a huge circle of men surrounding Slanoth and the leader of the army. The two were locked in a heated battle and it seemed to be a stalemate at the moment.

"By the gods Cestator, have you ever seen the likes of that?"

Cestator nodded solemnly. "Yes once before, but that is a sight not often seen." Then Cestator stopped short when he caught a glint of light from the city wall. Then he saw just a hint of movement and another shimmer. An icy chill suddenly ran down his spine and a feeling of dread overcame him. Without saying a word Cestator drew his sword and ran towards the city. William not sure what was happening followed suit.

When Cestator got near to the circle where he knew he could be heard over the crowd he yelled at the top of his lungs. "Slanoth get out! Move out of the way!"

Slanoth hearing Cestator's voice glanced around quickly and when he spotted Cestator their eyes locked and for a moment they both knew. Then suddenly Slanoth felt a sharp pain in the middle of his back. His eyes opened wide in shock and he fell to his knees, the fletching of an arrow protruding from his back.

The ogre seeing his opponent was down stood above him, sword raised over its head ready to finish the job. It never got the chance however for at that moment there was a loud roar and somehow Cestator was suddenly inside the circle his sword slicing through flesh and bone. The ogre's large sword fell harmlessly to the ground as his cold dead eyes stared at Slanoth. Then ever so slowly the head slid off the neck and fell to the ground and the body followed suit.

Slanoth seeing this let out a final wheezing cough and fell onto his side. When Cestator saw Slanoth fall over an intense roaring fire burned behind his eyes. He ran into the circle of men killing every man in the attacking army that he came face to face with. It did not take long before they began to run screaming about a raging fire demon killing everyone.

When the rest of the army was either dead or gone Cestator returned to Slanoth's side. Those who were tending him moved aside when Cestator knelt down. He looked at them questioningly, but all shook their heads sadly.

Shepard on the other side of Slanoth shook his head tears rolling down his cheeks. *"It do no look good lad. He be worse off than ye were when I did find ya, an he were da only one that could fix ya up."*

When Cestator touched Slanoth's face his eyes opened, and Cestator could see the pain behind them and he wanted to scream.

Seeing Cestator's pain Slanoth tried to speak but instead he coughed weakly, and blood spattered everywhere. Cestator shook his head in dismay. "No Slanoth save your strength I will find someone to heal you."

Slanoth shook his head and motioned Cestator to come closer. When Cestator was nearly on top of him Slanoth lifted his head slightly and spoke softly into his ear. "My time is here yours has just begun grieve not for me I lived my life, and I am ready to join Cargon. Before I go however I wanted you to know that I am proud."

With that Slanoth's head fell to the ground and his body went limp. Cestator looked down at Slanoth and screamed, "NO!" He looked up to the heavens and shouted. "Why . . . why bring me here? Just for this, why does death follow me everywhere?"

William, who was standing just behind Cestator fell to his knees in sorrow, and begged Cargon to take Slanoth to him and let him find peace. Then suddenly he heard someone calling his name he stood and the man came running over. "William its Ciara she is hurt badly and she is asking for you."

"What . . . what has happened to her?"

The man shook his head sadly as though he had something to do with it. "The man who shot that arrow was fleeing from us, and I do not know why she was there but Ciara was atop the wall and happened to get in his way. He stabbed her in the belly three times then left her for dead."

William looked back at Slanoth and frowned. "I'm going to her. Can you handle this without me?"

Shepard nodded. *"Aye lad, me I only be wonder'n why ye still be here. Thar be noth'n ye can be do'n fer Slanoth."*

William did not waste another moment. He turned to the man and nodded. "Take me to her, and be quick about it."

A few moments later William was at Ciara's side. She reached up with a shaking hand to wipe a tear from his cheek. William smiled at her and took her hand. He could see she had lost a lot of blood and was near death, but he looked at her and told her she would be fine.

Ciara smiled weakly. "William you are a terrible liar I can see in your eyes. I am dying I know that as well as you. I just wanted to see your face one more time before I die."

William shook his head in denial. "No Ciara I won't let you go. I will do anything not to lose you. I love you. I wanted you to be my wife."

Ciara was racked with a fit of coughing then tried to smile reassuringly, but the blood at the corners of her mouth defeated the purpose. "I would have loved to have been your wife William. You are the man I have been looking for my entire life, but now another will have a chance. And don't worry for me it no longer hurts the pain is gone . . ."

William sat there holding her hand as he watched the life slip from her eyes. He wailed in grief as he lifted her body up to his chest. "NO . . . Ciara, no don't leave me. Oh dear lord Cargon please help me. Please do not take her from me. I would give anything for her life."

Suddenly William heard a strong voice just above him. "William, what can I do for you?"

William looked up and saw a shimmering figure and the other men all bowing down around him. "Lord Cargon?" Was all he managed to say.

The figure nodded and knelt down beside William. "Yes my son I have come to grant you a wish so long as it is within my power. You have been faithful to me, and you showed your worst enemy kindness when no other would. That is the way of a true Paladin."

William wiped tears from his face and tried to smile, but it was too hard so he looked down at Ciara. "I have only one wish. I would have Ciara back I love her more than life itself. She is everything to me without her I would rather be dead."

Cargon nodded and sighed. "I thought as much. I can do it, but there is a price."

William nodded vigorously. "Yes whatever it is I will pay it."

Cargon smiled and shook his head. "I know you would William, but the price is not only yours it is hers as well. Think on it before you answer, you must be sure she will be ready to pay the price."

William nodded his consent. "I will Lord, name the price please.

Cargon looked at Ciara then back at William and sighed again. "Well first of all I must tell you that I cannot save both of them."

William looked at Cargon questioningly, "both of them?"

Cargon nodded sadly. "Yes she was carrying your child. She was looking for you to tell you when this happened. I am sorry William." Cargon paused a moment before continuing. "Now remember think hard about what this price will mean if you accept. If I am to bring Ciara back she will not be able to bear you another child, she will be barren."

William thought about it for a moment then nodded. "Yes please bring her back I will love her no matter what, but I swear I will find this man and bring him to justice.

"Are you sure of this William once it is done it is done and I cannot change it."

William nodded. "Yes I could not live another moment without her. I cannot stand seeing her this way."

Cargon nodded and smiled. "Very well then it is done," and with that Cargon disappeared into thin air.

William looked down at Ciara and her eyes fluttered open. William seeing this hugged her close and kissed her head. "Glory to Cargon Ciara you are alive. Oh how I died when I had lost you."

Ciara looked up at William and smiled warmly. "What are talking about William you never lost me. I have been here all this time."

William kissed her passionately and shook his head. "No my dear Ciara, you had been dead moments ago, but Cargon restored you. Sadly though, he could not save our child."

Ciara flinched slightly at William's words. "Do you mean my child is gone?"

William nodded sadly, but said nothing more.

Ciara said nothing for a short time and the pained look in her eyes was killing William, and when she finally did speak her voice trembled and cracked.

"I weep for the one I have lost, but there will be others and I would want them to be yours William."

Her words crushed William's heart, for he dreaded what he had to tell her next. "Ciara . . . my dearest love I am afraid we shall never have another child. The price for returning you was that you could never bear another child."

Ciara jumped up and slapped William's face. "How dare you. You selfish bastard I would rather have died. To have felt that amazing feeling, of a life growing within me then lose it, and now never to have it again. You have cursed me William. How could you do this to me? I hate you, get out of my sight."

William stood slowly looking deep into Ciara's eyes, and the tears he saw pouring down her face crushed him. He tried pleading with her one last time, but she only slapped him again then ran off.

William watched her go the pain in his heart overpowering the sting in his cheek. When she was gone from sight William slowly turned away and began walking. The other men in the hall just stood aside as he passed and did not say a word to him.

Chapter 20

The Labyrinth

After William left, Shepard looked over at Cestator and sighed deeply, and the pain in his voice was strongly apparent. *"Be ye alright lad? Ye did take dis really hard from da look o' what ye did out thar."*

Cestator said nothing at first he only lifted Slanoth's body and pulled the arrow from his back. He studied the fletching intently and memorized the pattern. When he looked up at Shepard the fire burned behind his eyes once again. "This arrow is from one of my father's elite assassins. Each of them has a specific pattern, and when I find the owner of this arrow he will pay dearly."

Shepard shook his head sadly. *"Lad I do be know'n wha' ye be feel'n, but it will be near impossible to find someone like tha'. No doubt he be long gone by now he will no hang 'round here. 'Sides ye know what Slanoth would be have'n ta say 'bout ye do'n such o' that."*

Cestator frowned and looked up at the wall. "Yes I know all of that, but there is no one, nor is there anything that will stop me from bringing justice to this."

Shepard sighed and nodded. *"Lad I knew ye would say as much, an I would be wit ya, but I did make Slanoth a promise ta take care o' things 'round here when he were gone. Course I did expect it ta be a long time from now, but he did make me promise."*

Cestator shook his head and looked deep into Shepard's eyes. "I would not take you with me. I'll not get any one else involved in this."

"Ha . . . if I were want'n ta go ye woul' no be able ta stop me lad, 'sides I do think thar be at least one other who would go wit ya no matter what."

"William . . . yes I know. I would hate to taint him with this. This will be a dirty job and I may have to deal with some unpleasant people."

"Aye that may be, but let's worry fer tha' later. Fer now let's get Slanoth inside."

Cestator nodded in agreement and lifted Slanoth's body as he stood. The two walked side by side and headed for the temple. As they passed, every man woman and child knelt down out of respect for the fallen hero.

When they reached the temple Cestator headed straight for The Hall of Legends. Standing before the great doors he sighed, and pushed them open. After a moment's pause he entered with a long procession following. Cestator walked past all the statues, and headed for the end of the hall, and as he passed each statue bowed its head slightly and drops of water trickled from their eyes.

When Cestator finally reached the end of the hall he laid Slanoth down at the feet of Cargon. He looked up tears pouring down his face. "Cargon give this man a place here beside you. If there ever was a man ever deserving the right to be here it is Slanoth. He deserves every honor you can give. He was a true paladin." Cestator knelt before the statue and said nothing more. He designated himself as Slanoth's honor guard.

Many people came to pay their respects to Slanoth, and each tried to say some words of comfort to Cestator, but he never acknowledged if he had even heard them. Then on the third and final day William came to see Slanoth. Cestator could not help, but notice the pained look on his friend's face. At first he thought it was because of the loss of their mentor, but somehow that did not quite fit.

William walked up to where Slanoth lay without saying a word to Cestator. He then said a prayer to Cargon to bless Slanoth. When he was finished he knelt down beside Cestator and began weeping.

Cestator looked at his friend out of the corner of his eye and frowned, but did not say a word. He knew there had to be something more to his friend's sorrow, but he was not one to know how to comfort someone. Instead he only stayed in the same position and did not move knowing if his friend needed to talk he would.

The two remained there for a few hours without saying a word. Then as the day began to fall towards night William finally spoke. "She left me and wants nothing of me. She will not even speak to me."

For the first time in three days Cestator moved his head, "Ciara?"

William nodded sadly. "Yes when Cargon brought her back from death he could not save our child, and she became barren. She blames it on me. She told me I should have let her die. I tried to save myself from the pain of losing her, but this is worse. I see her often, but it is as though I am seeing a ghost for she will not acknowledge me."

Cestator shook his head. "The mind and feelings of a woman, they can be the hardest things to learn how they work. There is something, but first tell me what would you do for a chance to get her back?"

"I would do anything Cestator you know that. Without her I am lost in a sea of sorrow."

"Yes I know, but are you willing to risk everything even your own life to save her from what has been done."

"Cestator if you know a way to reverse the curse I have placed upon her I would gladly give my life for her."

Cestator nodded. "Good because the suggestion that I have may very well kill us both."

William shook his head and stood. "No Cestator I will not ask you to risk your life for this. It is my fight not yours."

Cestator stood, and placed a hand on his friend's shoulder. "I'll not let you go alone my friend. You put faith in me when no other would and I owe you a debt and I mean to repay that, besides without me you will never find it."

Once again tears welled up in William's eyes and he gripped Cestator's forearm. "Thank you my friend I could never ask for more than what you give me."

They were softly interrupted by footsteps coming towards them. When they turned to see who approached William fell to his knees in a bow, Cestator however only bowed his head slightly.

Lysandas smiled walked up to William, and tapped his shoulder. "Rise William you need not kneel before me here. We are in the presence of one who is greater than us all."

William stood slowly somewhat unsure of himself. "Your Majesty what brings you here this day?"

"I have come here to honor an old friend, and to honor two heroes." Lysandas walked past the two and stood before Slanoth. "My family owes you a great debt of gratitude old friend. I only hope what I do now will begin to repay that."

Lysandas bent down and gripped Justice, and Slanoth's hands seemed to release it to him. "Thank you Slanoth and fare well my friend."

As Lysandas lifted the sword a wind blew through the hall and Slanoth's body turned to dust and blew away. Cestator and William both watched this in shock, but said nothing.

Lysandas turned to the two and nodded. "Now my two heroes take a knee."

The two men did not say a word and did as the king had bid them. Lysandas smiled down at them and laid Justice upon each of their shoulders in turn. "For services rendered above and beyond what was called upon, and by the power vested in me by my father and our lord Cargon I dub thee Cestator and William knights of the kingdom. Now rise and receive your just rewards."

The two stood, and Lysandas first stood before Cestator and held out justice. "I was told by Cargon himself that you are to carry this, may it serve you well. Cestator nodded and took the sword then strapped it to his back.

Lysandas smiled and nodded, and then he walked behind the two and picked up Slanoth's armor that was lying there. He stepped in front of William and handed over the armor. "Once again I was told by Cargon that you are to wear this. Wear it with pride Sir William."

With a tear in his eye William nodded. "I will Your Majesty, and thank you."

Lysandas stopped William short by raising his hand. "Wait I have not finished. I have been told you have become a blade master and that sword you wear will befit one of your mastery." Lysandas turned and called for a servant.

A man came running down the hall carrying a sword wrapped in oil cloth. When the man reached them Lysandas took the sword and dismissed him. He turned to William smiling brightly. "The dwarves gave my great grandfather this blade many years ago, now I pass it to you."

Lysandas unwrapped, the sword, and William gasped at the workmanship of the blade. It seemed to have an inner glow about it. Lysandas saw the shock on William's face, and his smile brightened. "It is called The Sword of Light. It was made thousands of years ago, and I believe your companion here carries its opposite."

Cestator nodded and pulled his sword and the two began to hum. Lysandas nodded and turned back to William. "Yes you see the two know when the other is near, now William take the sword."

William did as he was bid and strapped the sword to his back. Lysandas nodded. "Good now there is one last honor that I have to bestow upon the two of you. Please follow me." With that he turned and began walking away.

William and Cestator looked at each other, shrugged their shoulders and followed the king out of the hall. When they got outside there was a large group of people standing around, and they began to cheer when they saw the two men. The two were even more confused by this.

As they began walking down the road Shepard and Braggor stepped up beside the two, and Shepard shouted above the noise of the crowd. *"Congratulations lads da two o' ye done deserved dis here honor."*

William looked over a Shepard even more confused every moment. "What honor are you speaking of General?"

Shepard laughed at the question, but it was Braggor who answered. "Why the two of you are to face the trials of the Labyrinth."

William and Cestator both stopped dead in their tracks. When he realized the two had stopped Shepard looked back and frowned. *"What be wrong wit' ye lads, don't yer legs work."*

The two replied in shocked unison. "Did Braggor just say . . . ?"

"Aye lads he did. Da two o' you are ta face da trials o' da Labyrinth, now come on we be loose'n Lysandas."

Cestator and William looked at each other shrugged their shoulders then walked on. Shepard chuckled softy, and followed the others. As they moved on more and more people gathered to see the two off, and by the time they reached the lower beach there was a line all the way back to the city gates.

Lysandas stopped before a small boat with the royal crest upon it. He turned and smiled at William and Cestator. "Now this is as far as I may go the trip across to the isle is for the two of you alone. It has been a great honor to send you off, but you must make this journey alone. Good luck to you and remember to keep your faith."

William and Cestator both nodded, and Lysandas moved aside. The two got into the small boat, and dozens of people came down to cast them off, each wishing them good luck and offering kind words.

When they were out on the water the two began to row towards the isle where the Labyrinth resided. William looked at the darkness that seemed to loom over the place and shivered.

He turned to Cestator and shook his head. "I have heard many a stories of this place Cestator, and none of them were pleasant. What do you know of it?"

"Not more than what Braggor had told me when I had first arrived. All that I know is that it is where men go to be tested to become paladins."

"Yes that is why we go there, but inside we will face some of the most difficult tests. It will test our strength, and faith and much more. From the tales I have heard I almost fear going there."

Cestator frowned and shook his head. "There should be nothing to fear. I have faced many trials before nothing could be worse than what I faced getting out of my father's land."

"No Cestator you don't understand these trials are far more than physical ones. What I have heard is that we will face our deepest darkest thoughts and fears, those things that are better left forgotten. We will face the horrible truths of them and see how they would play out. Many good and strong men have run away screaming, gone mad from what they had seen."

Cestator listened intently to his friend and nodded when he was finished. "If what you say is true then we must work together here. This is not going to be easy if it works like that."

"Yes I agree Cestator I think we will need each other's help in there. This will be a great challenge."

William was suddenly cut short as the small boat stopped suddenly, as though it had hit something. He frowned at Cestator slightly annoyed. "You could have warned me that we were."

Cestator shrugged his shoulders and pointed behind William. "What was I to warn you of? We are surrounded by darkness and I cannot see past the side of this boat."

William looked around in shock. He could see nothing, but darkness all around him. He quickly looked back at Cestator, and was relieved that his friend was still there. "What is happening here, are we inside the Labyrinth or are we still at sea?"

Cestator shook his head frowning darkly. "I do not know you know more of this place than I. I cannot be sure of what we are sitting upon right now. The boat has vanished as well."

William looked down and stared in shock he could feel the hard ground at his feet, but all that he saw was the same pitch blackness that surrounded them.

He looked up at Cestator and shook his head. "I was never told of anything such as this, but be weary my friend somehow we are inside the Labyrinth."

The two awoke with a start. A sound had broken through their sleep. It was a sound that warranted much fear, one that Cestator knew all too well.

Then the sound came again and William jumped to his feet sword drawn and at the ready. He looked to Cestator for the answer to the question he dared not ask.

Cestator stood and drew his sword as well. "Hell hounds," was all that he said, as he looked around at the desolate wasteland.

William looked at him in shock. "Hellhounds how is that possible? There has not been a hellhound on Trecerda since the Trial Wars." Cestator stretched his arms out to the sides and pointed.

"Look around you William we are no longer on Trecerda. We have found ourselves in Drathmourn."

William shook his head vigorously. "No, that is not possible how did we get here?"

"I do not know we must have passed through a portal somehow though it is not one that I am familiar with."

Hearing this William looked around and quickly spotted an archway that shimmered inside. "There it is," he said as he pointed towards the archway. "Let us get out of here while we still can."

"No William it's a trap, that was not there a moment ago. If you run for it, it will be like you are chasing your own shadow it will forever remain just out of reach. Meanwhile those hounds will chase you down. The only way we are going to get out of here is to face those things and whatever might be following them."

William looked at Cestator in mute shock for a moment, and he wiped his brow from the sweat pouring down his face. "What do you mean following them?"

Cestator shook his head. "Let us not worry for that at this time, we must concentrate on the hounds first."

"Agreed, but I must say that sound the hounds are making is driving me mad. It seems to be burrowing into my mind."

"It will, if you allow it to, try to block it out. Think of something else, and remember they will come in fast and hard. Do not hesitate for if you do you will be finished."

The two men stood side by side watching as the dust cloud approached, and the sound grew louder and harder to block out. Then suddenly the hounds were upon them.

William was amazed at the speed and ferocity of the creatures, but he had no time to think about it, he was far too wrapped up in the battle for that. The battle however was over quickly the hounds being no match for the two blade masters.

The two had very little time though to catch their breaths, for just as the last hound went down two large hulking beasts with dark red skin stepped into view. One held a massive battle-axe and the other what seemed to be an uprooted tree covered with spikes."

"What in the name of Cargon are those things?" William asked in fear of the answer.

"Those are greal, and do not be fooled by their size they are fast, nearly as fast as the hounds were. Our best advantage is that they are not very intelligent, so try to outwit them."

William looked at the two Creatures as they approached, and shivered. He had heard many tales of the legendary monsters and had hoped to never face one, yet there they were.

He looked up to the heavens and prayed. "Oh Cargon my lord if you can hear your humble servant, lend me your strength"

"That will not work here William. Cargon has very little power here in Drathmourn. I am sorry William, but we are on our own."

William cut his prayer short and sighed. "Are you sure of that?"

Cestator nodded sadly. "Yes he could barely help me the first time I was trying to get out of here . . ."

Cestator stopped short there, and took a better look at the greal that approached. Most of the creatures looked alike to him, but when he looked into their eyes he saw something.

"William we are in the Labyrinth. I killed these two greal before. This is a test." He shouted when he realized the truth.

William did not have a chance to reply before the greal were upon them. He found what Cestator had said about their speed to be true. He also found it better to dodge their attacks rather than to try and block them. He managed to land a few blows but they did nothing, but bounce off the creature's thick skin.

"Cestator how are we to kill these things my sword does nothing to them."

"With these blades we cannot. If we had our swords we would be able to finish them, but as it stands now we do not have a chance."

William shook his head in denial of Cestator's words. "No I do not believe that Cargon would put us into this without some means of escape."

"Ha . . ." Cestator snickered. "Look around you William there is nothing here to help us."

It took William a few moments to get a chance to respond, but when he did he was slightly angered. "Cestator have you so quickly forgotten what Slanoth was trying to teach you? You must put your faith in Cargon and he will show you the way. He will guide your hand, but you must trust in him."

William began to pray as he dodged the greal's blows. "Lord Cargon your humble servant beseeches you. Show me the light and guide my hand so that I may defeat this creature."

Suddenly William's sword was engulfed in a bright light. He quickly swung it at the greal who tried to block the blow, but the sword simply passed through the club and cut the greal in half. The creature then disappeared as did William's sword.

Cestator saw this and smirked. *"That is all it takes, well that is simple enough."* Cestator then glanced up to the sky and prayed. "Alright Cargon I am asking for your help now, as you wanted me to."

Cestator frowned darkly when nothing happened. The greal seeing his frustration cackled in glee, and moved in more aggressively.

Cestator then cast a glance over at William, who seemed to want to help, but somehow seemed restrained. "William how did you do that? I ask for Cargon's help and nothing happens."

"Cestator you must believe in Cargon for it to work."

Cestator's frown deepened and it took him a moment to get a chance to answer back, but when he did his voice was harsh and filled with sarcasm. "I do believe in him I would not be here at this time had I not believed in him."

William ignored the sarcasm, but was slightly saddened by his friend's tone. "That is not what I am saying Cestator. You must believe with everything that you are that he is there with you helping you. You must have absolute faith in him that he will see you through this."

Cestator sighed helplessly. He knew William's words to be true. He could feel the truth of them deep in his soul, but to put his faith into something other than his own abilities was foreign to him. Doing so made him more than uncomfortable. The greal seeing his uncertainty cackled even louder and stepped up its attack again, which put Cestator completely on the defensive, and left him no time to speak.

Cestator knew he had to do something quickly but still the thought of doing as William suggested left him nervous. As he was dodging the greal's attacks Cestator managed to catch a glimpse of William, and noticed he was praying. He was slightly surprised by this, yet at the same time he was intrigued that William would put that much faith in Cargon. Then Cestator remembered the day Slanoth had first brought him to The Hall of Heroes, and he remembered what he had heard there. He remembered the paladins of the past whispering to him sharing their wisdom.

Cestator cleared his mind of all thoughts, and listened to the wind. Once again he could hear the paladins whispering to him telling him to trust in Cargon. He closed his eyes and took a deep breath and whispered to the wind. "I trust in you Cargon, guide my hand and show me the way"

William watched in amazement at what he saw. He was unable to move in to help his friend. When Cestator closed his eyes the greal became more excited. William tried to yell to him, but found his throat was closed up. What he saw next shocked him, even with his eyes closed Cestator was blocking every blow the greal threw.

Moments later Cestator's blade came ablaze in a light as bright as a thousand suns. The greal reeled back in shock of the blinding light, and Cestator cut it down before it could recover.

When it was over William found that he could move once again. He walked over to his friend smiling. "That was amazing Cestator. How did you do it?"

Cestator opened his eyes and looked at William. "I did as you said, I remembered the day that Slanoth blindfolded me, and brought me to the hall of heroes. I swear those statues spoke to me and told me many things over the course of those days I spent there. When I closed my eyes there I could hear them again, and they reminded me why I was here. After that it was simple to find what I needed."

Cestator looked towards the place where William had seen the portal and found that it was still there. "What say you should we make our way out of here?"

William nodded in agreement. "Yes that sounds good to me. Let us leave this place. I am soaked from this ungodly heat already, wherever we go next cannot be as bad as this."

The two trotted over to the portal, when they reached it they nodded to each other then stepped through. The moment they stepped through the portal, the temperature did not drop it only rose higher. William looked around and found himself inside a burning house, but Cestator was nowhere to be found.

"Well now I have found myself in the fire instead of in the oven, and I must say the oven was better." William called out to Cestator but got no answer. He began to walk out of the room to find his friend when suddenly he felt a presence behind him.

William turned around quickly to see who was there, with his hand on the hilt of his sword ready for a fight. He did not find a foe behind him, but the figure standing there made his heart drop farther than the thought of fighting the greal had.

The man behind him was his father. William was overjoyed yet quite shaken at the sight of his father. The man William had always remembered to be kind and loving now looked angered, and was scowling darkly at William. He knelt down out of respect for his father.

Then his father spoke and William's heart sank at the harshness of his words. "You have betrayed your family William. You find the man who murdered us, and befriend him. You made a vow to me that you would extract vengeance upon him, but instead you travel with him. How could you disgrace us in this manner?"

William stood hurt, and angered by his father's words. "No father you are wrong . . ."

William was cut off short by his father's angry words. "You are not to call me that. You are no son of mine. My son would not have betrayed his family, by letting such a monster live. Can you not see he is only trying to get close to you so he can kill you at his leisure, and he will do it with no remorse?"

Family was everything to William, and his father's dagger hit its mark. William staggered back for a moment, but he was not going to let his father's words go unchallenged. "No father you are wrong about Cestator. He is not the same man he was all those years ago. He now serves Cargon as I do."

"Ha . . . do you really believe that, if you do then you surely are a fool. Go look there in the other room and see how your friend serves Cargon."

William turned and went where his father directed him. As William walked through the doorway he was shocked at the scene he beheld. There were bodies strewn across the room and Cestator stood among them the blade of his sword dripping with blood.

From another doorway across from William another figure stepped out. This figure was a woman, and when William caught a glimpse of her face he reeled back in shock. It was Ciara, his one true love.

Ciara did not seem to notice the bodies littering the floor, for she merely walked right past them straight to Cestator. The two then embraced and shared a passionate kiss. William's heart shattered and he felt betrayed.

Suddenly Ciara's eyes opened wide in shock. William thought at first sight that it was because she finally noticed him standing there, but then he noticed the blood trickling from the corner of her mouth. William watched her lips speak her final words. *"Why Cestator?"* Her body went limp, as she slid off of Cestator's blade and fell in a heap on the floor among the other bodies.

Cestator seemed not to notice, for he did not move from the spot. He did not even look down at her. He only stared ahead of him with his back to William.

William heard his father's voice from behind him. "What do you think of your so called friend now William. He killed all of those people and he also killed your love for the second time."

William turned to his father his anger flaring brightly now. "No father, Cestator could not have done this. He never killed Ciara I was there with him when she was killed."

"Foolish boy are you so blind that you cannot see the obvious. He did not kill her in the flesh, but his hand was in it. He ordered her death as he did Slanoth's. Why do you think that army besieged Cerdrine? He is after the book. Valclon knew it was there and he sent Cestator there to get it. Now is your chance, go kill him before he can hurt any more people, and get his hands on the book. It would be the just thing to do. He must be made accountable for all the lives he has taken."

William shook his head vigorously. "No father that cannot be true. Why would Cestator do something like that? If he knew the book was there why go through all the trouble, why not just take it?"

"Ah William do you not understand anything. The book was sealed away and the only way to get to it would be to get rid of Slanoth. Valclon would do anything to get his hands on that book, and he sent Cestator because he knew that Cestator would get it done. Valclon also sent Cestator to kill the next potential. Why do you think he befriended you so quickly? He knew you would be the next to take Slanoth's place, he was getting close to you so he could kill you at his leisure."

"How . . . no I do not believe it. Why would he train me just to kill me, why not just kill me right away, and how did he pass the last test if he is not a believer?"

"Think William he began to train you so he would know your abilities, and he also wanted something of a challenge. As far as the last test, remember he is the son of a god. He merely waited for you to show him what he needed to do then he copied you. Now do the right thing, and kill him before he can get the book."

William looked over at Cestator who had not moved, and wondered what to do. *"Is my father right? There have been times when it seemed he was not working for Cargon. Oh dear Lord please help me see what is right and just."*

William then heard Slanoth's voice only it was not actually Slanoth. It was a memory of Slanoth telling him when he was unsure of something to follow his heart, for it would never lead him wrong.

William looked inside of himself and suddenly realized something he had been blinded from, by seeing his father again. A dark scowl spread across his face as he turned back to the figure that was his father.

"Every word that has crossed your lips has been a lie, except one thing. You are not my father. My fear and love for him clouded my mind, but now I can see clearly what you are. You are a demon that looks like my father, but you are not him."

The figure smiled evilly at William. "So now you know, but you shall not live long enough to enjoy that knowledge."

The Creature charged at William bearing long sharp claws. William however did not hesitate. In one fluid motion he had his sword out and he separated the creatures head from the body.

William fell to his knees sobbing from what he had just done. Even though it was not really his father it felt as though he had lost him once again.

Suddenly William heard a loving and gentle voice coming from behind him. "You did very well William I am proud of you my son."

William jumped up turning quickly. "Father is that truly you?"

The shimmering figure standing there smiled and nodded. "Yes William it is truly I. Cargon allowed me a few moments to speak with you. I wanted you to know that we are all proud of you William. You have grown to be a great man."

Tears flowed freely down William's face. "Thank you father I was so afraid that you would be disappointed in me."

"Never William, now I do not have much time, but there is one more thing I must tell you before I go. There is one last Chance for Ciara and yourself to have a child. It will not be easy for you there is much that has to be done, but I believe you can accomplish it."

William's eyes brightened at the chance. "Truly father, how am I to do this then?"

"Follow your heart William, it will lead you. You have a long journey ahead of you. I fear that is all I am allowed to say so goodbye my son, and remember I will always love you."

"I love you as well father, and thank you."

William's father waved to him then was gone. William stood there a moment pondering his father's words wondering what was in store for him. He turned, and headed for Cestator to see how his friend fared.

The moment Cestator stepped through the portal he found himself inside of a burning building. He looked around for William, but could not find him. He thought that odd for a moment, but for only a moment for seconds after he stepped through he saw a group of orcs charging at him.

Cestator smiled wickedly. *"Is that all you have for me? This test will be simpler than the last."*

The orcs charged at Cestator fire burning in their eyes, but as most orcs Cestator found they had little to no skills. He quickly grew tired of killing them, but they seemed to not stop coming. Then when his arm was tired from swinging his sword the orcs suddenly stopped.

Cestator sighed, and wiped his sweat soaked hair from his eyes. He happened to catch a quick glimpse at the bodies at his feet. What he saw made him stagger back in shock, for the bodies on the floor were not orcs, but men and women. Some were even holding dead children. The frightened and horrified looks upon their faces cut him like a dull sword.

"No what kind of trick is this. These were orcs a moment ago. This cannot be." Cestator then looked at the sword in his hand it was covered in blood. He looked back at the bodies and shook his head. *"No, this cannot be true this is no longer who I am. If I must pay for my past wrongs then I am willing, but to force my hand like this . . .*

Suddenly Cestator heard a frightened squeak from the room behind him. He turned at the sound, and there she was, the small girl he had spared so many years ago. She was hiding under a table scared to death.

Cestator looked around at the burning house and knew there was not much time left, and he was not going to let her die in the fire. "You there come out of there, we have not much time."

The little girl shook her head vigorously never taking her eyes from Cestator. She wrapped her arms around one of the legs of the table.

Cestator sighed in frustration. He had little patience as it was, and the heat of the fire did not help matters. "Come now child if you stay there you will surely burn alive."

Again the small girl shook her head, but this time she spoke, and her voice sounded like the chiming of bells touched by fear. "No if I go out there you will just kill me like you did everyone else."

Cestator frowned looked at his sword then threw it away from him and held his arms out for her to see. "I swear to you upon my honor, no harm will come to you if you come with me. Do it quickly though we have not much time this fire will devour us soon."

The girl stared into his eyes and seemed to see right through him. Then slowly never taking her eyes from his she let go of the table leg and crawled out. She stood and began walking towards him, and with each step she grew a little older. By the time she stood before him she was a stunningly beautiful woman that took his breath away.

The woman smiled at him and his heart raced. She gently touched his face, and it sent a tingle through his entire body. She moved in closer and began kissing him passionately, and Cestator melted into the kiss.

Suddenly the woman's eyes opened wide in shock, and Cestator felt a strange yet familiar weight in his hand. He moved back away from her and looked down. His eyes opened wide when he saw his hand buried deep in her chest.

When he looked back up into her eyes they were filled with tears. "Why . . . you gave me your word. I thought you loved me?"

Cestator tried to respond, but as he began to speak he saw the life slip from her eyes and her body fell off his sword. Cestator looked at her body in mute shock. *"Why do you show me this? Is this what is to come? If that is so then I am finished, you have won."*

Cestator stood there not moving waiting for the fire to come and consume him, for he would rather have died than to have seen what he just did. There was a deep ache inside him which he had never felt before and he wanted it to end.

A short time later William came walking up to him, and put a hand on his shoulder. Cestator did not even turn to look at his friend. "Go on without me William I can see you have past your test so go. I am going to remain here. There is no reason for me to continue on."

"No Cestator I'll not go on without you. You are my friend, and even if you were not I would not leave you here to die."

Cestator turned and looked at him, and William took a step back the pain in Cestator's eyes was staggering. Cestator pointed at the woman at his feet. "Look at her William, she is dead. She is dead because of me. I killed her. I killed the one reason that I am here. So you see there is no reason for me to go on."

"Cestator this is not real remember, we are in the labyrinth. So this woman whoever she is, you did not kill her. It is only a shadow of her."

"Perhaps that is true William, but what if it is a vision of things to come. You see I could not bear that. So if I remain here it will never happen."

"Cestator that is foolish you cannot give up on all you have worked to become because of a trick. You must believe me this test is a trick. A very painful and harsh one, but it is only a trick."

"And why do you say this William?" Cestator looked deep into William's eyes and saw the pain there. "Ah I see you saw something that you did not care to. So now I know what Braggor meant, that no man who enters is ever the same."

Cestator looked back down at the woman and sighed. "Very well William I will go with you. You must promise me something however."

"Yes of course Cestator I would do anything you ask."

Cestator turned to William and pointed to the woman on the ground. "If this ever comes to pass kill me."

William was taken aback by his friend's request, but he thought of how he felt when Ciara was killed, and being a man of his word he agreed.

Satisfied that William would keep his word Cestator nodded. "Good, now let us leave this place."

"Yes I agree I only hope wherever we go is cooler this time. I do not think I could stand the heat any longer."

The two headed for the door to the outside, and as they steeped through they found themselves in a frigid land covered with ice. A freezing wind whipped past them, and sent a chill up William's spine.

"Now I asked for cooler, but this is not what I had thought would come." William said as his teeth began to chatter. He looked at Cestator and was surprised. Cestator was looking around as though the cold did not touch him. "Cestator are you not cold. I fear I may freeze here soon if we do not find some shelter."

"I have learned to ignore such things as heat and cold." Cestator replied, but he continued to scan the horizon as he spoke searching for something.

"Is there something out there Cestator? All that I can see is ice and snow."

Cestator nodded solemnly, "I know this place I have been here before. This is the land across the seas where the bone spiders live."

William looked at Cestator in confusion. "You mean something lives in this place, how is that possible?"

"Yes I have never found anything more here but they seem to thrive in this wasteland. This is where the spider lords found their mounts."

As the two were speaking there suddenly arose a faint sound like something walking across the ice. Cestator looked in the direction of the sound, and saw what he had feared would be there. He quickly turned to William and told him to run. Without hesitation he did so himself.

William followed suit, but before he did he looked back and saw a massive black spot moving over the snow covered horizon. "Would that be them," he asked when he caught up.

"Yes and they are quite deadly if you are wondering. I lost nearly one thousand men to them the last time I was here."

The two ran on as hard as they could, but the sound of the spiders continued to get ever closer. Then just as William felt he could run no longer the two reached a giant wall of ice with an opening large enough for them to get through. William looked at it then at Cestator. "I think we are meant to go in."

Cestator nodded in agreement and the two stepped through and the two found themselves in a large cavern of ice, and on the other side was a shimmering exit. Between them and the exit however was an indescribable monster. It was as though all of their nightmares had come to life in one creature.

"What in all the heavens is that thing?" William cursed under his breath.

Cestator shook his head in confusion. "In all my travels never have I seen anything like it.

The two turned around to go back the way they came but they were blocked. The spiders had created a giant web covering the entrance. William stepped back away from the entrance, but was quickly stopped by Cestator's hand on his back.

"Do not move any further, that thing whatever it is, does not like it."

William turned back around and found the creature staring at him intently, seeming almost ready to attack. William instinctively reached for his sword but found it was not there. "My sword, it is gone is yours?"

"Yes, but what good do you think they would do against that. The damned thing does not even have a solid form."

William shook his head. "There must be some way to get past that beast the exit is just on the other side."

Cestator did not answer for a few moments. Instead he was staring intently at the creature. When he turned to William he had a questioning look about him. "Tell me William when you look at that thing what do you see."

"What are you saying Cestator? I see nothing, but a monster with no true form. I cannot make anything out of it."

"Look again William and watch each change they are quite specific. That thing is, for lack of better words all of our past demons."

William did as Cestator bid him and stared intently at the creature and gasped. "By the gods all of my past wrongs, everything that weighs heavy upon me is in that thing."

Cestator nodded. "Nothing like being faced with your past, no wonder men go mad here. Facing that would break even the strongest of us."

Suddenly something dawned on William. "Dear me Cestator that thing must be absolutely horrifying to you, taking who you were."

Cestator smirked and forced a chuckle. "I have seen more in that thing in the last few moments that I would rather forget than I think any man ever has, but I am not going to give up now. I am going to beat this thing."

"Yes, I am sure but how are we to do that? How are we to get past it when it is all the wrongs we have done in our lives?"

"Think about this William. What could be the purpose of showing us everything we have ever done wrong?"

William thought for a moment. Then when the answer hit him he realized it was so simple he felt foolish. "Ah of course we are being shown this so we may face them and learn from them."

William noticed Cestator kneeling down and staring intently at the Creature. He seemed to be completely captured by its gaze. He looked into its eyes as Cestator had and out of respect knelt before it as well. Then William was faced with his child hood and the first wrong he had committed. It was a simple thing and he dealt with it quickly then the next came. As he dealt with each he faced them in turn each one worse than the last, and each harder to handle.

When he finally finished the last Instead of a frightening monster before him, there was a kindly old man smiling. "You may pass William. You have completed your tests." The old man said to him in a soft voice.

William stood and smiled back at the man. "Thank you lord, blessed is he who walks in the light of truth."

The old man smiled and nodded stretching his hand out behind him as he turned aside so William could pass.

Beyond the man William could see something shimmering. After a few steps he saw what it was. It was a single pendant made of red platinum formed in the shape of the mighty phoenix.

William turned to the man questioningly. "I see only one pendant there where is the one for Cestator?"

At this the man sighed. "Alas, I see that his path follows a different road. Now go, you have proven yourself worthy."

William took one last look back at Cestator, and wondered what the man had meant, but he realized that if he was meat to know he would have. He sighed turned back and headed for the exit.

Cestator watched as William stood and headed for the exit. He saw William pause and look back at him with a troubled look about him. *"Go William I will be there with you soon."*

Cestator smiled when he saw William turn back and head for the exit. Cestator could not see beyond the Creature, but he knew what was there. He knew this was the final challenge and he was proud for William.

Cestator watched as William reached the exit, and noticed something change in the Creature's behavior. It seemed to forget Cestator was there. Then as William reached for the pendant it roared loudly and charged at William.

"William run, get out of there! It is coming for you!"

William turned when he heard Cestator's voice and Saw the monster coming for him, only this time it was more horrifying than before. He saw things in it that made his heart nearly stop, and he was petrified with fear.

Cestator seeing that William was frozen in place realized he had to do something. He could think of only one thing and he knew what the outcome of that would be, but he did not give the consequences a second thought.

Cestator jumped to his feet and charged at the Creature, then realized as he ran he had a flaming sword in his hand. The creature sensing his approach turned to him. "William, go now I will deal with this."

"No Cestator get back it will kill you." William shouted back, but it was too late, moments later the two collided with explosive force that threw William out the exit and clear of the destruction.

Shepard sat in Slanoth's office staring at the letter lying on the desk before him. It lay there unopened haunting him. *"Ah Slanoth ye knew dis would be happen'n didn't ye. Blast ya why did ye be do'n dis ta me. Ye knew well I can no be do'n dis me self. Why didn't ye say something ta me?"*

Shepard stood and looked out the window, he shivered at the sight. Down below he saw the bay and in it was the Labyrinth. *"Ah that damn place do give me da chills an I never been in it. I know not how ye went thar. Cestator went in ye know, I do hope da lad do make it out fine."*

Shepard began to turn away from the window when suddenly there was a large explosion that rocked the city. Shepard turned back to the window and saw a roaring fire where the Labyrinth had been.

"By all that be mighty, what in all da heavens happened thar?"

Suddenly the door behind Shepard burst open and Braggor ran into the room. "General what happened I was just in the hall and I heard the rumble? Are we under attack?"

"No,' less they be targeting da Labyrinth. Tha' be what done blew up."

"Did William and Cestator make it out?"

Shepard shook his head sadly *"I do no be sure. Da only thing tha' I did see were da blaze tha' be thar now."*

When William awoke he hurt all over. The pain however reminded him of what had happened. He looked back and saw a roaring fire where the labyrinth had been, and everything was reduced to ashes.

"Cestator are you there, can you hear me?" William shouted into the roaring flames, even though he knew no one could survive the blaze. He began to stand, and as he did he felt a strange weight on his neck. He looked down and realized the pendant was hanging there. *"Am I truly deserving of this. This symbol has blood upon it. Cestator gave his life to you so I could escape. He is more deserving of it than I."*

William was torn from his thoughts when the flames were suddenly drawn inward upon themselves. When they reached the center they seemed to be drawn into the ground. William stared in shock at this. He had never seen anything like it, his entire life.

Just as William was getting over his shock the ground below him began to rumble and shake. Then from the place that had consumed the fire, the ground erupted with searing flames, but what he saw next shocked him more than anything else. A large fiery bird about the size of a man burst from the top of the flames and flew straight up so high it nearly disappeared. The bird then dived back to the ground and disappeared leaving no trace of its presence, but a bit of smoldering ash floating in the air.

When the ash settled William was again shocked when he saw a figure standing there. The man was covered in soot, and he could not see his face from the distance, but he knew it had to be Cestator. He noticed that Cestator's clothes were now rags and they hung limply off of him. Cestator appeared to notice this as well for he tore his shirt off, and started walking towards William.

When the figure got closer, and William saw that it indeed was Cestator he took the pendant off and held it out to Cestator. "Here my friend you are more deserving of this than I"

Cestator smiled and shook his head. "No William I did not complete my trials. That pendant was meant for you. You are a true paladin where I am not. Were it not for you I would have never passed any of those tests."

"No Cestator had it not been for you that creature would have killed me. You sacrificed yourself . . ."

Cestator raised his brow questioningly at William's words.

William shook his head in confusion. "No, this makes no sense back there where you came from was a roaring inferno just moments ago." As William said this Cestator turned around to see what was back behind him. "By Cargon, Cestator your back . . ." William stuttered as he stared in shock.

Cestator turned back around quickly wondering what William was talking about. "What is wrong William?"

"Your back it is covered in a tattoo of the phoenix." Was all William managed to say.

Shepard and Braggor watched as the flames collapsed in upon themselves, then they saw the phoenix burst up from the ash. *"By all that be mighty,"* Shepard exclaimed. *"That blasted book o' Slanoth's did be true."* He walked over to the desk and opened the letter Slanoth had written, and as he read the words Shepard fell back into the chair behind him.

Dear Shepard;

By the time that you are reading this I will be resting with our lord Cargon. I have been looking over the prophecy in the strange book, and I have learned something, our interpretation of it was incorrect. It is not Trecerda that is going to fall. I am sorry that I am not able to share this knowledge with you.

I ask you however, not to mourn for me my dear friend. My time has long been coming. It is time for a new generation of paladins to protect the world. It is time we step aside and finally get our long deserved rest.

Now I must get on to other more important matters. I know that you will be anxious to be relieved of the duties you have found yourself in, so I have sent for one who will take my place as head acolyte. He is a very able and trustworthy paladin and Cargon has blessed my decision.

So with that said, there are still some things that I need to ask of you my dear friend. What I am to ask you will be difficult, but please trust in me that they are important and I would not ask them otherwise.

First you must get William and Cestator to leave the temple. It is not safe here for them. Tell William that there is a way that Ciara may bear another child for him again. I have seen this in the book, though I do hate what it stands for. It has shown me this. Tell them they must head to the south toward the Dragon Spine Mountains and there they will find their first clue. Then as for the book it must go with Cestator. He is the only one who knows its true meaning and what it could do in the wrong hands.

Then lastly I must ask you to do something I know it will be quite difficult. I do hate to ask this of you but it must be done and you are the only man that I know who can. You must return to your people and convince them to come out of seclusion. We are once again on the verge of a great war, and we will need their help. I know that the dwarves do not take a request such as this lightly and frown on it greatly, but unless all the races act together we will not win. Something terrible is going to be released and unless all the races of the world work together we all will fall.

I am sorry my dear friend for putting such a great weight upon your shoulders but if there ever was one who could carry it you would be he. I will see you in the Promised Land my friend.

Forever grateful to you, your pupil

Slanoth

When he finished reading the letter Shepard laid it down on the desk and stared at it in shock. *"By da Gods Slanoth ye be ask'n fer more than be possible."*

"General the boat is returning from the labyrinth and there are two men in it." Braggor said as he turned away from the window. When he saw the haunted look on Shepard's face he stopped short. "What is wrong General you look as though you have seen your own death?"

Shepard did not say a word he just held Slanoth's letter out for Braggor to read. Braggor took the letter and read it to himself. When he finished Braggor dropped the letter back on the desk. "How did he know, and what is he speaking of? There is no war going on."

Shepard shook his head sadly. *"Lad, we did jus' see da firs' part o' da war here. Ye can be sure tha' Valclon no be finished yet. Ya see, them two down thar be our new hope fer win'n dis war."*

Braggor looked back out the window at the small boat that was now more than halfway back. "You mean to tell me our fate lies in their hands? Did that damn book tell you that?"

Shepard shook his head. *"No, Cargon told Slanoth dis some time ago. All tha' we found in da book was a prophecy foretelling his death, and da return o' da phoenix. Well no more o' tha' da walls be have'n ears round here, we should go an greet da lads back 'fore we send them off."*

Shepard stood and headed for the door stuffing the letter in his coat pocket. When the two left the room Shepard locked the door behind them. As they walked the streets towards the bay they noticed a large crowd gathering, but when the people saw the two well armored men they moved aside to let them through.

When Shepard and Braggor reached the docks William and Cestator were just rowing up to a dock. The people began to cheer as the two stepped out of the boat. Meanwhile Shepard and Braggor walked down the long dock to greet the two men.

William seeing the crowd on the docks took off his coat and handed it to Cestator. "Here my friend I think it would be best if those people did not see your back. It may cause quite an uproar."

Cestator Agreeing with William's thoughts adorned the coat. As the two got out of the boat a loud cheer went up from the crowd. "What are those fools cheering for?"

"Why, they be welcome'n their heroes back home o' course."

Cestator shook his head in disgust, but he could not keep a smile from his lips at the gruff sound of Shepard's voice. "If they think us that, then they certainly are fools."

Shepard stopped inches from Cestator then looked back at the crowd on the docks. *"Aye fools they may be, but I is no go'n ta discourage it, 'cause it give them something ta look up to since we lost Slanoth. Now I be sure da two o' ya mus' be downright exhausted."*

William stepped forward cutting off any more of Cestator's comments. "Yes general we both are quite famished."

"Aye I did be think'n so." Shepard and Braggor turned around and led the two back towards the temple. As they passed through the crowd the cheers only got louder, and many people reached out in hopes they could touch the two heroes.

When they were finally in the peace and safety of the temple, Shepard led them to the main dining hall where all the men awaited them. As the four walked into the hall, an applause went up, along with words of congratulations.

When they reached the end of the main table, the room quieted down. Shepard nodded and sat at the head. After Shepard was seated, the rest of the men sat and began eating, and talking as though nothing had happened.

"Braggor then looked at Cestator and William slightly confused. "Now you must tell us what happened there. We saw the entire place burst into flames, and yet the two of you look to have come out no worse for the wear save for Cestator's rags."

"Aye an, why it be tha' ye have a pendant thar William, yet Cestator no have one? What gone on in thar?"

Cestator shook his head and shrugged his shoulders. "The last I remember before the fire was a creature going after William as he reached for his pendant, and I decided to help him. When my sword struck the beast it burst into flames. I woke up and my clothes were as you see them, and I was in what remained of the Labyrinth."

Shepard and Braggor then turned to William questioningly. *"An, what do ye remember lad?"*

"Well I remember reaching for the pendant then I heard Cestator yelling. I turned and the most horrifying Creature I had ever seen was charging at me, and I could not move. When Cestator and the creature collided there was a great explosion. I was thrown to the ground, but when I looked up I was outside the Labyrinth and the entire thing was ablaze in a roaring fire and I found this around my neck. Suddenly the flames seemed to be consumed by the ground, and a few moments later I saw the phoenix fly up into the air. It dived, and disappeared just as it reached the ground."

William paused a moment and took a drink of wine. As it poured over his parched lips, and wet his dry throat he tried to find the words to continue. "That is not the oddest thing however." Once again William paused taking a swig of wine finishing what was left in his goblet, and he realized he was quite thirsty. He closed his eyes and sighed then put his goblet back on the table. He looked at Cestator for permission to continue.

When Cestator nodded William sighed and absently picked up his goblet once more, but when he realized it was empty he placed it back on the table, and looked at Shepard and Braggor each in turn. "A few moments after the phoenix disappeared Cestator stood in the exact place it had vanished. When he came over to me, I noticed he had a tattoo on his back."

"A tattoo of what William," Braggor asked when William said nothing more.

William looked at Cestator and shook his head. "I think it would be better for you to show them, than it would be for me to tell them."

Cestator nodded, and stood up turning his back to the men at the table. He took off the coat William had given him.

"BY ALL THAT BE MIGHTY!" Shepard shouted at the top of his voice.

This caught the attention of all the men in the room and they began to look. When they saw Cestator's back they fell to their knees in awe.

"The Phoenix has returned" Braggor managed to stammer. "But how is it?"

Cestator shook his head unsure himself. He put William's coat back on and sat down. "I don't know myself, but that is why William gave me this coat."

"Aye that did be a smart thing ta do at tha'. I know not wha' 'dis do mean, but it do reaffirm what Slanoth did be want'n me ta do."

Cestator and William looked at Shepard in shock. "What did you just say?" They both managed to ask in unison.

Shepard smiled, and chuckled loudly. *"Aye lads ye did hear me right. Slanoth done left a letter fer me 'fore he did pass on, an he had specific instructions about ye two. His letter did say thar be a way tha' Ciara can be bear'n ye another young'n lad."*

William stared at Shepard in shock. "How is that possible Ciara died after Slanoth, how could he have known about that?"

"He did read 'bout it in da Book O' Ages."

"Cestator didn't you say you knew of a way also? William asked, "Yes you did and Cargon mentioned something about it as well."

Cestator nodded and smirked. "Yes, and you can be sure that if The Tome mentioned it, the way will be nearly impossible."

William looked at Cestator with tears in his eyes. "Be that as it may Cestator, I will do anything to help Ciara even if it costs me my life."

"Very well my friend. You can count on me to be at your side."

William smiled and nodded. "Thank you Cestator I had hoped you would be willing to join me." William turned back to Shepard. "What are we to do to find this cure General?"

Shepard shook head sadly. *"Slanoth's instructions were no to specific thar other than say'n ye need ta head for Da Dragon Spine Mountains. He did say ye would find da firs' clue thar. Tha' no be all fer da two o' ye though I be afraid yer quest is gonna git a bit more hairy than tha'. Cestator ye be need'n ta take da book wit' ya. Slanoth done charged ye as its protector.*

Cestator nodded sadly. "Yes he mentioned it to me some time ago. I would guess he knew then what his fate would be. He knew I was the only person that knew the true power it holds, and the only person alive that has any chance to be sure, Valclon shall never have it."

"Aye tha' be what Slanoth were hope'n fer. Now eat up 'cause ye will be need'n yer rest ye got a long day ahead o' ya tomorrow."

The two nodded in agreement, and the conversations went on as normal, as though nothing had happened.

Chapter 21

Attacked

Cestator awoke to the sound of someone pounding on his chamber door. He got up quickly, and opened the door to find William standing there with a large grin upon his face. Cestator looked over at the window and saw that dawn was still some time away. He turned and headed back in the room to get his things. "Does anyone ever sleep here?"

William chuckled as he walked into the room. "Everyone is too busy to sleep Cestator. The new Lord of the temple has arrived this morning. We must prepare to leave by dawn, and Shepard will also be leaving today so as I said there is much to do."

Cestator looked at William in shock. "Shepard is leaving as well? When did this happen?"

William shrugged his shoulders. "Apparently Slanoth asked him to do something as well. He will not say what it is, but he is adamant about starting out as soon as possible, and he wants to see us off."

Cestator nodded and dressed quickly, he placed Justice in its harness on his back, and The Sword of Shadows in its scabbard on his belt. He grabbed his pack and looked in it to be sure the book was there. When he saw the book nestled in its place he nodded, and slung his pack over his shoulder. He turned to William and nodded. "Let us be off then." Cestator opened the door and they left the room.

William followed, and the two headed down to the main courtyard where many men were waiting for them. When they arrived they saw Shepard and Braggor standing before the men standing in formation.

Shepard walked up to the two smiling. *"Ah so now it be time. Every man here be in awe o' ye, but me well I jus' be right proud o' the two o' ye. Take a good look at dis place lads it may hap be da last time ye see it fer a long time. Ye be have'n ta promise me though tha' one day we all will be see'n one another here again someday."*

William and Cestator both nodded their agreement. Shepard smiled, and turned. The three then headed for the gate, and as they passed between the two rows of men each saluted to them by placing his right fist over his heart. As the three men stepped outside the gate a loud cheer went up from the City walls. Cestator looked up to see what appeared to be the entire city up there.

"They are wishing their heroes safe travels."

Cestator turned at the words, and was surprised to see King Lysandas standing before him. He bowed his head out of respect and saw that William was down on one knee. "I have done nothing for them to praise in such a manor."

Lysandas smiled as though not hearing the sarcasm touching Cestator's voice. "Oh, but you have. You and Sir William here have saved our fair city. Why, were it not for the two of you those monstrous spiders would have been walking all through it, then you two defeated the armies reinforcements yourselves. I would call those acts of heroism. Now I did not come out here to discuss this with you. I came out here to give you my best wishes, and this." He placed a large belt pouch in Cestator's hand. Cestator opened it and his eyes opened in shock. There was a small fortune of gold in the pouch. Cestator looked up at the king questioningly. It is my reward to you for saving my city, and I will not allow you to refuse it."

Cestator nodded and tied it to his belt. "Thank you your majesty. I am sure we will have use of it on our travels."

"Yes, I am sure. Now go find glory and honor, but I hope that you will always remember who you are and not forget your people here."

"Never your majesty, your people have showed me more kindness than I could have ever expected. I apologize if I seem harsh and brutal, that has been how I lived my life until I came here."

"Think not of it Cestator You shall always be welcome in my city. Now go while I am still allowing you to."

Cestator turned around and found William still on one knee. "William You can stand now it is time to go."

William stood slowly tears flowing freely from his eyes. "Yes of course Cestator. I am sorry I was only thinking of my father and wishing he were here."

Lysandas hearing this smiled, and walked over to William and placed a hand on his shoulder. "Sir William, Braggor has told me your story, and I must say that your father would be quite proud of you."

William smiled. "Thank you your majesty, you have done so much for Cestator and myself that we could never repay you."

"No William it is I who owe you a debt of gratitude. Now go you have many adventures ahead of you"

William nodded, and turned to Cestator. The two shared a knowing glance, and walked away. They could hear the people cheering long after the city had faded into the distance. When the sound finally stopped William looked at Cestator and smiled. "So begins our adventures. I wonder what the world has in store for us."

Cestator shook his head suspiciously. "I don't know, but to me it seemed we were somehow forced into this course of action."

"Forced or no I care not Cestator. If there is a way that I can heal Ciara I will do anything required."

Cestator smirked. "Would you do it still if it did not change the fact she curses your name."

William stumbled slightly from Cestator's words, but he quickly recovered. "Even if it cost me to my life, and I was cursed to damnation."

Cestator put his hand on William's shoulder. "Then it is worth whatever we face, and you can count on me to be by your side."

William smiled warmly and he swallowed his heart. "Thank you Cestator, that means much coming from you, and I swear to you, you will always be able to count on me." The two stopped for a moment and gripped arms looking deep into each other's eyes, and they felt a strange energy pass between them. After a moment the two shook off the strange feeling and walked on.

They traveled for many days without incident, even through the goblin infested Breakers Pass. The saw many skirting the rocks around them, but the creatures stayed away. The two figured that two well-armed men were deterrent enough.

After eight days of traveling the two finally reached the outskirts of the foothills, and found themselves at the outskirts of vast plains. The two stopped and looked out over the waving grass. William shook his head unsure what to do. "I am not so sure about this Cestator. There could be any number of things hiding out there. Is there no other way around?"

"None that would be reasonable, these plains stretch across nearly all of Trecerda. It would take months to get around them." Cestator answered

"I still do not like it. It is as though the ground itself moves here. A lion or something as such could easily catch us off guard the way this grass moves."

"Yes I know William. I remember once my father sent me here to convince these plains people to join his army. They are little more than barbarians, but they are fierce warriors, and they know how to use the grass to vanish into thin air. I went in with two thousand men, and left with less than two hundred. Everyone swore we were vastly outnumbered, but I counted little more than a dozen warriors."

"Ah blast Cestator. Did you have to tell me that? I like this little enough as it is. How do you suppose we cross this then?"

Cestator smirked and slapped William on the shoulder. "Well merchant trains pass through here all the time don't they? Perhaps these people will not bother with two men passing through."

William shook his head. "Merchant trains usually have guards and they take roads, we however will be walking straight through this grass. I hope you are right, that these people will not bother us."

The two decided to make camp for the night however, for sunset was quickly approaching. They got little sleep however because of the strange sounds they heard from within the sea of grass. Yet morning found them wide awake and ready to go, and they quickly gathered their things, and headed out.

They traveled for little more than an hour when suddenly they heard a loud horrifying roar. "What in the nine hells was that?" Cestator asked somewhat surprised by the sound.

William shook his head. "I don't know I was hoping you could tell me."

They suddenly heard two people yelling, then the clash of steel, as though a mighty battle were raging on.

"I don't know what that first sound was, but that sounds to me like someone is in trouble"

Cestator nodded. "Yes I think you are right especially if it has anything to do with whatever made that roar. Should we see if we can help?"

William did not waste any time answering Cestator's statement before running off in the direction of the sounds. Cestator smiled and quickly followed.

When the two got within sight of the battle they saw two large beasts that were hard to describe. A large barbarian and a young boy were squared off in battle against the creatures. The large barbarian seemed to be holding his own, but the boy was clearly in trouble.

Cestator and William looked at each other, and nodded. They drew their swords and ran to help the boy, but moments before they reached him the creature bit deep into his leg. The boy went down instantly and limply as though he were dead.

"Do what you can for the boy I will handle the Creature." Cestator managed to shout as they ran.

William did not waste any time replying. He quickly ran to the boy to see what he could do.

As Cestator approached, the creature which was the smaller of the two turned to him and roared at him. Cestator smirked wickedly and readied himself for the attack holding his sword over his left shoulder. The thing moved faster than anything Cestator had ever seen before, but he was ready for it.

The beast came at him on all six of its legs, and it swayed back and forth, moving like a snake as it came. As it approached, Cestator looked into its eyes and knew he had already won. He could see overconfidence in this creature's eyes. Somehow he could see that this thing thought he was going to be easy prey. Cestator also notice that the creature put most of its weight on its front legs, as it ran.

Cestator quickly devised a plan, and by this point the creature was nearly upon him, but even then Cestator did not move. This seemed to excite the creature for it began to move even faster. Moments later it was upon him, and it tried snapping him up in its large mouth. Cestator proved to be quicker however. He moved out of the way and brought his dark sword around, and cut off the creature's right front leg. With the momentum and the amount of weight the creature possessed it crashed to the ground from the missing leg. Cestator acted quickly and caught the creature while it was still down. He raised his sword up over his head the dark steel glinted in the creature's eye and it seemed to know its fate, but it was already too late. Cestator swung with all his might aiming for the base of the creatures head. The blade cut through flesh and bones, and did not stop until it hit the ground. The creature's head rolled away.

Cestator had barely time to take a breath before he heard a loud roar from somewhere behind him. He turned and saw another of the creatures charging at him. This one however was larger than the last, but again not nearly as large as the frightening monstrosity the barbarian faced. Cestator had very little time to ready himself before the creature was upon him.

The second creature also proved to be much more intelligent than the smaller one. As soon as it was within striking distance, instead of lunging at him it stood on its four back legs, and used its front claws to attack. The creature attacked with its claws and spiked tail all at once, and its speed was astounding.

Cestator was hard pressed to fend off its blows. The few times that he managed to strike a blow upon the creature, his sword simply bounced off its hard scales doing no harm to the beast.

When William reached the boy, he jumped back in shock. The wounds on the boy's leg were horrifying. He was also unconscious which William decided was a good thing. He saw that he was still breathing, but barely. He checked the wounds to see if there was anything he could do, and that was when he noticed the green streaks coming from the wound and running up his leg. *"Poison, why is it that I am not surprised by this?"*

He yelled up to Cestator as he looked the boy over. "Cestator watch the creature's bite it has venom in it. The boy here is not faring well. He appears to be nearly dead. I am going to need your help to heal him."

"Well you are going to have to do what you can without me, for I am a bit detained at the moment." Cestator shouted back.

William frowned in confusion. He knew from seeing Cestator in action before, that it could not have taken him very long to dispatch the creature. "What, have you not finished that . . ." William did not finish his sentence, because as he looked up he saw that indeed Cestator had killed the smaller creature, but now he face a larger and fiercer one. "By the gods, hold out for a bit more Cestator I am coming."

"No William, do what you can for the boy. Your weapon will be useless, even mine just bounces off this creature."

William hated to, but he conceded. He looked over to see how the barbarian fared and saw that the man was holding his own. William caught the man's eye, and he seemed to be saying the same thing Cestator was.

William sighed in frustration. He hated to be standing aside while battles were raging around him. Thinking of the boy's welfare however overpowered his frustration, and he quickly laid his hands on him, and began to pray.

After telling William to get back to the boy, Cestator decided he needed to stop playing this cat and mouse game, and find a way to kill this beast. He knew that his sword was all but useless against its hard scales.

Cestator studied how the creature fought, and he noticed something strange in its patterns. He noticed that the creature attacked only with its tail and claws. He began to wonder why it did not try to bite him, especially if William was right and it had venom.

Cestator decided to try and get the creature to bite, but try as he may it seemed reluctant to. He quickly formulated a plan, and when the creature used its tail once again Cestator let it hit him, running with the blow to minimize the damage. Yet even then the wind was knocked out of him, and it threw him several feet away. He hit the ground and rolled away gasping to catch his breath. He stopped and lay on his back not moving, hoping the creature would think him unconscious.

The creature seeing him down roared, and charged at him. As Cestator had hoped it opened its mouth to bite him. Just as the creature was about to bite down Cestator drove his sword up into the creature's maw, and into its brain killing it instantly. Using his sword as a lever he pushed the head aside as it fell.

Cestator stood and tried to free his weapon, but it would not move. The movement of pushing the creature's head aside lodged his sword into its skull. "Damn," he cursed, and tried once more to remove his sword, but it would not budge.

He decided to let the sword rest for the moment, he did not want to be caught off guard by the third creature should it decide to attack him. He drew Justice, and looked over to see how the barbarian fared, and was just in time to see the man get hit by the beast's tail, and be tossed one hundred feet away.

The monster looked in the direction of where William was helping the boy and seemed to frown. Then it saw the smaller creature and let out an ear splitting roar that made the blood run cold. It looked back at William, and Cestator could see it was going to attack.

Cestator knew he had to do something quickly to divert the monsters attention. William was in no state to handle this thing. He was not sure if he was either, but he could not allow it to go after William.

Cestator did the only thing he could think of, he yelled at it. "You there whatever you are I am the one you want." The creature turned and looked at him, it focused on his sword then back at him. Cestator smirked at the creature. "I am the one who did this. You ugly excuse for a snake"

Then seeming to understand his words, the Creature roared at him. When it finished their eyes locked and everything went black, and was replaced by a large burning room. Cestator recognized this room all too well he had been in here only days ago in the Labyrinth. This was the place where he saw the girl, and suddenly he realized there was another mind with him. It was the mind of the creature and it was pure evil.

Cestator did not understand what was happening, but this memory was refusing to die. He looked around and everyone was dead already, and the creature seemed to delight in this. Then as he looked around a bit more he locked eyes with the girl. She was shivering in fear, and he could feel the sword in his hand.

The creature seemed to feed off the girl's fear and grow stronger. "Kill her," it said in a raspy voice.

Cestator refused to listen however. He shook his head and threw the sword to the floor. "Be gone monster I will have nothing more of you."

The moment Cestator spoke the words the burning room disappeared and was replaced with a large laboratory. He now seemed to be the one along for the ride and the Creature seemed to be in control.

Cestator found himself looking down and he saw a crazed wizard, and what seemed to be a very young version of the creatures. The wizard was casting a spell upon the creature, and when he was finished Cestator found himself looking out of the creature's eyes.

Seconds later the scene faded and the two were back in the plains facing one another. They both shook the fuzziness from their heads and looked straight into each other's eyes. Cestator hated to think of what the vision he had just seen meant, and the Creature seemed to feel the same way because it roared at him and ran off leaving him alone.

Cestator placed Justice back in its harness on his back, and went to retrieve his other sword. When he pulled it the sword came out easily. He thought this somewhat strange, but he gave it no more thought than that. He had other concerns. First he went over to William to see how the boy fared.

William looked up when Cestator approached and shook his head. "He needs more help than I can give. I have healed the wounds, but the poison is beyond me I have never seen its like.

There seems to be something protecting the boy, but what it might be I cannot say."

Cestator frowned and shook his head. "I cannot say now, but the question is will he live."

William nodded reluctantly. "For a time, but if the poison is not removed I cannot say how long."

"Good, then we must see to the other man. I believe he is wounded as well. The large beast hit him with its tail."

William flinched at the thought, from what he had seen of the creature its tail was covered in spikes. "That does not bode well for our friend there. He could quite possibly be dead by now."

"Yes I know, but it is our duty to make sure he is not."

William nodded in agreement and stood. The two ran over to where the large man laid. When they arrived William reeled back in shock. The man was indeed alive if just barely, he was bleeding his life on the ground from a gaping hole in his side. William did not waste a moment more. He quickly knelt down and began to heal the man.

As William was healing him the man looked up at Cestator, and uttered a single word "Creashaw."

"If it is the boy you speak of, he will live for now, but he is in need of more help than we may give."

The man nodded in understanding and smiled. Then as he looked out at the field his eyes opened wide with fear. "The male, where," he asked panic touching his voice.

Cestator frowned and pointed in the direction the creature had run. "The one you battled ran off in that direction."

"My village," the man said as he tried to stand.

William pushed him down shaking his head. "You'll do them no good in your condition even if you made it there, Cestator will go . . ." William did not have the chance to finish what he was saying before Cestator was gone in the direction of the village.

Skreal ran off unsure of what had just happened. Something about that man made him feel something he did not understand. All he knew was that it infuriated him and he swore vengeance upon that one. He decided however for now he would kill all the others in their village.

He ran until he reached the outskirts of it, and took in the scents all around him. They seemed nervous for some reason. Even here they were carrying their weapons. Skreal smiled at this. "Good that will make it all the more enjoyable to kill them. I cannot wait to taste their fear."

Skreal circled the village deciding where he would attack first then he found it, a building that most of the men seemed to be watching. He flicked his tongue out tasting the air, and his smile grew there was a touch of fear here.

Skreal wasted no time after that. He roared loudly and charged into the village, and as he had hoped all the men around came charging at him. Skreal killed everyone who came near him. He tore the people to pieces tasting their blood and finding shear bliss in it. When he came to a hut, he burst inside killing all within. He let no one escape his wrath.

Sheminal came out of her vision with a start. *"We must flee."* She thought as she ran out of the hut, but when she got out she realized it was too late. She could hear screams from the other side of the village. As she stood there she saw Cerndrose, and she called out to him.

Cerndrose looked back at her and shouted to her. "Sheminal get yourself out of here the belath is attacking the village." He ran off in the direction of the screams carrying his bow.

"Cerndrose no, you mustn't you will die . . ." She cried out to him but he did not hear her words. Sheminal broke out into tears and sat there waiting for her fate.

After a moment Sheminal heard a vice speaking to her. "My dear wife your fate does not lie here you must go and look after our son he is in need of your help. Now leave the village and return when the beast is gone. A stranger will lead you to Creashaw."

Sheminal cried all the more, but she stood and ran out of the village. Everything within her screamed out of fear and anguish, but she ran on.

After leaving Sheminal Cerndrose ran for where he heard the screams. He knew it would likely mean his own death, but he had to try and stop this beast. On his back he carried his long bow. It was his favorite weapon, which his father had taught him to use. A weapon he had used since he was a young boy which gave him the strength to pull his large weapon.

Suddenly he found the creature. He drew his bow, and followed it until he could get clear shot. As he followed he noticed it was getting ever closer to his home and he prayed to the spirits that Kiara got out before this began.

Then suddenly his worst fears came to pass. Kiara stepped out of their hut with their son in her arms. He tried to shout to her to run, but the moment she stepped out she saw the belath and started screaming. This seemed to get the beasts attention for it turned straight for her, and snapped her up in its jaws. It shook her body side to side before tossing her to the ground and moving on.

Cerndrose stared at his wife and child for a moment. The rage began to well up within him, and he swore that he would have his vengeance upon the beast. When the red haze cleared from his eyes he walked over to his family and kissed the two upon their heads and went after the belath.

When he found the creature it was happily killing a group of hunters trying to give the women and children time to escape. Cerndrose knelt down on one knee and slowly pulled an arrow from the quiver on his back, never taking his eyes off of the beast.

The creature quickly killed the hunters, and proceeded to kill the women and children as well. Cerndrose however did not take notice of this, his focus was completely on killing this monster, and he was not going to be disturbed.

He notched his arrow, and pulled it back to his cheek. He quickly found his target, the creature's eye even though it was two hundred feet away.

The belath noticed him, and seemed to smile wickedly. It faced him directly and roared a challenge at him. Cerndrose did not falter in his aim however. He was in the place his father had taught him to go that let him focus no matter his surroundings.

He paused but a moment before he released the arrow as memories of his dear beloved crossed his mind. When he released the arrow it hummed as it cut the air and headed straight for its target.

Cerndrose watched the flight of the arrow speeding directly at the creature's eye. Then he watched as the beast turned its head at the last possible moment, and stared in shock as the arrow shattered on its hard scales.

Suddenly he felt a sharp pain in his right leg. He looked down to see blood flowing freely from a wound caused by a shard of the broken arrow buried deep in his leg. Still in shock Cerndrose looked back up at the belath just in time to see a large flaming ball headed straight for him, and he did not even have time to scream before he died.

Skreal quickly grew bored with killing these men after killing the one with the ranged weapon. There were a few more who tried to fight him, but most ran at the sight of him. These he quickly caught and killed before they could escape, and soon there was nothing left alive.

He looked over what he had done and smiled. Killing all of these men gave him a sense of power and he enjoyed it. Yet he did not feel satisfied he began to yearn for more, and even more challenging.

He knew there were many places out there where these men lived, and he decided he was going to purge the world of them, so he might become the Supreme Being. The more Skreal thought about this the more he liked it, and he decided he would continue to mate, to create more like himself so they would help him in his quest.

Skreal smiled wickedly, and roared up to the heavens challenging any to stop him. When he heard no answer to his challenge he laughed and traveled on to find the next slaughter.

The sound of a dark challenge echoed into Mother's lair. The ancient dragon lifted her head from her constant vigil over her egg to listen closely. The sound was quite disturbing to her for she knew the true meaning behind it. She looked up to where the exit to her cave was, and sighed. *"So it has begun, I hope the world is ready."*

Mother looked down at her egg and smiled. "You are our last hope my child. Soon will be your time to arrive."

She looked back up at the entrance to the cave and sighed. She knew that the time for action was coming soon, but she had other concerns for now, so she left the challenge unanswered. She laid back down and continued her vigil upon her egg.

When Cestator heard the final roar of the Creature he knew that he was too late, and all he could hope to do was perhaps find a survivor. He had little hope for that however for in some strange way he knew that it would not leave a survivor.

When he reached the village he was not surprised at what he saw. Blood covered everything and there was not a single body that was not torn to pieces. It did not only kill these people he defiled them. Cestator said a short prayer for the tormented souls as he walked by.

He did not find a single building left standing. The beast was thorough in its work. Cestator looked around and was appalled by what he saw, and he had been at the front of many wars. He had also witnessed the aftermath of them, but this was worse. The creature seemed to have been toying with these people.

Suddenly Cestator heard a woman scream from somewhere to the right of him. He turned, and ran in that direction. When he found the woman she was rummaging through some rubble of one of the huts. He approached her slowly, and in an unthreatening manner.

When he was within a few feet of her, she looked up at him with tears streaming down her face. Cestator noticed she was a lovely woman if a bit haggard, but being through what she had likely just been he was not surprised.

"My son, is he well?" She asked.

Cestator looked around the village and frowned. "I am afraid if he were here then I must say no. You are the only survivor I have found."

The woman wiped the tears from her eyes and shook her head. "No my son was out in the plains with a large man. They were supposed to be watching those things."

Cestator flinched as though struck by her words, and he paused a moment unsure how to tell her what had happened. "Your son . . . He is alive, if only just. He was bitten by one of those things and its venom is killing him slowly."

The woman put her head in her hands weeping, but after a few moments she stood holding two javelins. "Take me to him," she said as she strapped the javelins on her back.

Cestator was somewhat surprised by the woman's bluntness but, he took no offense to it. He nodded to her and led her to the place where he left William and the other two.

When they arrived back at the clearing William had carried the boy over to the large barbarian, and was speaking with the man. When William saw the two approaching, he stood and bowed to the woman. "Cestator who is this intriguing lady you have in your presence."

Cestator shook his head and looked at her, but the woman was too preoccupied with the boy. She quickly ran over to him and took him up in her arms.

When the barbarian saw her he seemed to be in shock, but he quickly shook it off, and reached out to her. "Sheminal are you well?"

She looked up at him and glared. "Look what you have done to my son, and our people that beast killed all of them. It was horrible, I escaped before it found me, but I could hear the screams Angion. It was horrible." She burst into tears holding her son close to her.

Cestator and William walked over to them, and Cestator knelt down before the barbarian. "I am sorry I could not make it to your village in time, but William and I would gladly help you, find some help for the boy. It would be the least we could do for you."

The barbarian nodded smiling sadly. "I thank you stranger for all that you have done, but I think we should not detain you any longer. I know of a place that may help Creashaw."

The woman looked up and shook her head vigorously. "No Angion we must travel with them. I have seen this in a vision, and that was very clear."

Angion looked at Sheminal in surprise, but he nodded in understanding. He turned to Cestator and extended his hand out to him. "Well friend I am grateful for your help. My name is Angion, the boy is Creashaw, and this is his mother Sheminal."

Cestator took Angion's arm in the sign of friendship smiling. "Well met Angion. I am Cestator, and my friend here is William."

Angion was surprised by the strength he could see in Cestator's eyes. He knew this man was going to be a powerful ally.

He extended his arm to William, and when the man took it he noticed the medallion around his neck. "I see you wear the symbol of Cargon. The spirits have blessed us by sending a paladin to us."

William smiled at the mention of his lord. "Yes I am a paladin, if only just. You see I got this only days ago. I am glad that we could be of some assistance, but my heart screams that we could not save your people."

Angion shook his head sadly. "It is the will of the spirits, though we may not understand it."

Sheminal spoke up angrily. "No . . . the spirits would never put our people through that kind of torture. That thing was sent by, The Nameless One himself."

Cestator shook his head. "I do not know what that thing was, but I can assure the both of you no one sent it. That monster is acting on its own."

Angion began to stand and William tried to restrain him. "No my friend you must rest. The healing takes much out of you."

Angion nodded smiling. "Yes but we cannot remain here the blood covering this place will attract other not so pleasant animals."

"Yes," Sheminal said. "You should listen to Angion. There are many things that hide in the grass, and he is the best warrior in our village."

Cestator looked around and shook his head. "I agree, but what are we going to put the boy upon? We will not be able to carry him across these plains."

Angion pulled up some of the long grass and braided it. "We can make a skid out of grass bound together. We use this many times when we kill a large animal, and have more meat than we can carry. There is some rope back at our camp I can carry Creashaw that far, and we can rest there for the night."

Cestator nodded. "Very well that will do, but I will carry the boy. Trust me you will hardly have the strength to walk on your own." He bent down and lifted Creashaw into his arms under the watchful eye of Sheminal.

As Cestator lifted the boy he felt something strange. There seemed to be a force surrounding the boy. Cestator knew instantly what it was, though he had not seen anything of its like in some time.

When everyone was ready Angion led them to his camp, and showed them how to make the skid. As evening came around they finished their work and started a small fire, and sat around talking like they were old friends.

As the night wore on and the fire began to die Cestator looked at the others. "Get some rest I will watch out for you."

Sheminal shook her head vigorously. "I don't think I could sleep knowing that monster is out there."

Cestator smirked and laughed slightly, he placed his right hand over his heart. "I swear to you Sheminal, so long as I am here nothing will approach us without my knowledge."

Sheminal almost began to laugh, and comment on his words, but when she looked into Cestator's eyes she realized he was quite serious, and something told her that he was quite capable of holding to that promise. She knew at that moment this man was dangerous. He was perhaps even more dangerous than the belath itself, yet she felt completely at ease around him. "I cannot say why, but I think I could not be safer anywhere else. Thank you Cestator you have eased my heart for now."

"That is my duty Sheminal." Cestator said with a smile. He then disappeared into the darkness.

Angion shook his head and looked at William. "That is dangerous company you keep my friend."

William nodded and smiled. "Yes he is, but I would trust him with my life, and perhaps one day you will learn his story. I wish that I could tell you it but that is not my place."

Angion nodded. "I do understand, we all have a past and to share that is up to each of us."

William shook his head and looked out into the darkness. "Thank you for understanding Angion. It would be too hard for me to tell his story. There is too much pain there, for both of us." He shook off the fog in his mind and looked back at Angion. "You should rest now the healing takes much out of you, and you will need your strength tomorrow."

Angion nodded and looked over at Sheminal, but she was already sleeping with her arms around her son holding him close. He smiled, and laid down and quickly fell to sleep, exhausted from the hard day and the healing.

William watched this and sighed. He knew that helping these people was the right thing to do, but this was going to throw them off of their quest for a time.

Suddenly Cestator appeared out of the darkness and William jumped. "By the gods Cestator, please warn me next time would you?"

Cestator did not reply. He only sat down next to William and did not speak for a moment, but when he did he whispered. "When you were healing the boy did you notice something strange, as though there was something protecting him?"

William nodded slightly, and whispered back. "Yes to be truthful, when I first laid my hands on him I felt a presence there for a moment. It seemed to be keeping him alive."

Cestator nodded. "Yes, that is just as I had thought. The boy is carrying a soul blade."

William looked at Cestator in shock. "A soul blade, are you sure? There has not been such a weapon in existence since before The Trial Wars."

"I am quite sure I destroyed one ages ago. That man had the same feel about him, and the blade protected him to the end."

Cestator stood up stopping any more questions, though he knew William had many. "You should get some rest William it is going to be a long day tomorrow."

"What of you Cestator should you not rest yourself?" William asked as he settled down for the night.

Cestator smirked and shook his head. "I have trained myself to go on very little sleep. It is quite dangerous to sleep when there are many who want you dead." He once again disappeared into the darkness.

William shook his head and sighed. *"Cestator you have seen more trouble in your life than any man should. I hope Cargon smiles upon you, and makes you prosper."*

From above Cargon looked down at the small group resting among the rock. He smiled when he heard William's prayer. "William is a true paladin isn't he?"

Slanoth smiled and nodded. "He is true to the cause, even at the expense of himself. I think he will be one of the greatest, and it was a pleasure to have known him."

"I do believe you are right Slanoth. Oh but what a surprise it is. I tried for so long to touch his heart, but he kept it closed with his hatred."

"Yes I must agree, for many years I could see the potential in him, but he held his hatred for Cestator too tightly to reach him. Who would have known that being confronted with his chance for revenge that he would do the right thing?"

Cargon chuckled and looked Slanoth in the eyes. "You did, as well as me. You knew him better than he knew himself. Why, you were just the same when Shepard found you."

"Those are days long past Lord. Many things shaped my life, and made me the man I had become."

"Yes and you put William on the right path, and he has followed your teachings, and most of all he has followed his heart."

Slanoth nodded, but sighed regrettably. "Yes I know, but I hate that I have burdened them with that cursed book. It will bring them many troubles."

Cargon looked down at Cestator's pack leaning against a stone and shook his head. "It was not you who burdened them with it. Such was Cestator's destiny, Valclon knew this as well as I, and that is why he sent him looking for it. Little did either of us know how it would come to him? You see the book is his, it belongs to him. It is a part of who he is. It was only a matter of time before it found him."

Slanoth took all of this in, not quite sure what to say. He was completely taken aback by this, so he said nothing.

Cargon turned and began to return to his realm. "Come Slanoth there is much still to be done." Slanoth stood and followed Cargon, and the two faded into the air.

As dawn approached William, Angion, and Sheminal awoke and found Cestator watching over them. Sheminal placed her hand on Creashaw's chest to see if he was still breathing.

"The boy is alive, though I do not know for how long. If we are to save him we should go immediately." Cestator said as he walked over to Sheminal.

Everyone agreed with Cestator and they quickly headed out. Angion led the way with Cestator behind carrying the skid with Creashaw upon it and Sheminal and William following beside the skid.

Chapter 22

Finding help

She sat on the steps of the temple, enjoying the warm sun of a beautiful spring day. There were very few clouds in the sky, and a soft breeze danced through her long dark hair. The flowers planted nearby set a light perfume in the air.

Keriana smiled warmly, she loved the spring it was her favorite time of the year. She was leaning her head back when suddenly she heard a soft rustling sound from the bottom of the steps. She looked down and saw a small chipmunk scurrying around looking for food.

Keriana laughed softly as she watched the little animal scurry around. She reached down and tore off a small piece of the bread she was eating and held it out towards the chipmunk. "Hear you are little one," she said with a smile.

The chipmunk hearing her looked up, and saw the bread. He slowly scurried up the stairs until he reached the bread. When he was close enough he sniffed it, then took it from her hand and ran back down the stairs. At the bottom he sat up on his hind legs and ate his prize. When he was done he looked up at her as though saying thank you and then ran off.

Keriana chuckled merrily at this, and waved to the little fellow. *"Oh how I do love this place. I have learned so much here. I don't know how I could have been happy in the city."*

Keriana was suddenly torn from her thoughts by a gruff voice in the back of her mind. "Are you feeding those rodents again Keriana? I don't know why you bother."

"How many times do I have to tell you not to do that Heroth?" Keriana said with a stern look upon her face as she turned around, but the moment she saw her dear friend she began to laugh again.

"Do not blame it on me that you cannot hear me approach. You can be sure that I know whenever there is someone nearby."

Keriana frowned at Heroth and looked out into the forest. "I can hear a mouse scurrying through the leaves on the ground, but somehow you make even less sound, how is that?"

Heroth shook his head and yawned sleepily. "It is in my blood, it is what I am. You know I have no sure answer for you."

Heroth laid down next to Keriana, and placed his head in her lap. She smiled and ran her fingers through his thick hair. "You know for being such a big tough boy, you certainly are just a little pussy cat."

Heroth yawned again and shook his head. "Yes well I will never admit it to anyone."

Keriana laughed heartily, and kissed Heroth on the head. "Well don't worry your secret is safe with me."

"Why doesn't that make me feel any better?"

Keriana laughed even harder at this and jumped to her feet. "Well I'll tell you what. If you can catch me I promise I won't tell a soul."

Keriana ran into the temple and Heroth jumped up and went after her. When he finally caught up with her she was already in her quarters gathering her things to go on a hunt.

"What took you? I thought you were a great hunter." Keriana said as she slung her bow over her shoulder.

Heroth shook his head. "You went in a direction you knew I could not. I had to backtrack."

"Oh that is just an excuse Heroth. You knew very well where I was going, and you could have come straight here, and beat me. You just want everyone to know you're a big pushover."

"Only for you Keriana," Heroth said as he yawned once more. "Why do you use that thing?" He asked as he stared at her bow. "I use only what was given me on the day I was born."

Keriana scoffed at the remark, she knew it was in retort of her comment earlier. "You know very well that the bow is part of my heritage. It is in my blood you might say. Besides, I am not made of three hundred pounds of muscle."

Heroth stretched and smiled at her. "Well I guess we all cannot be perfect."

Keriana turned quickly with a dark scowl upon her face. "Oh I am going to make you pay for that one you big galute."

Heroth smiled. "You will have to catch me first," he said as he ran out the door and down the hall.

Keriana quickly grabbed her cloak and threw it over her shoulders, then ran after Heroth. She found him a short time later waiting for her at the top of the stairs outside. She did not stop however. Instead she ran past him and smacked him on the back as she ran by.

Heroth gave her a hurt look then stood and ran after her. He quickly caught up with her at the outskirts of the forest, and looked up at her happily. "I was hoping we would be hunting, I am simply famished."

Keriana chuckled lightly. "You are always hungry Heroth. I must say you eat more than anyone I have ever seen."

"Yes well I am also much bigger than anyone else you have ever known. It takes much food to keep me strong."

"Yes, well you still eat more that anyone I have ever known, even considering your size."

Heroth decided not to ague the fact any longer. He had learned long ago that it got him nowhere. Instead the two went on with their hunt quietly.

Drean led the two men up to the large doors to their master's quarters. He felt slightly more confident this time for it was not he who would bear the news of the defeat. Just as he reached up to knock he heard Valclon call for them to enter. Drean looked back at the two men behind him and the seemed slightly unnerved by this.

Drean opened the massive doors and entered the great hall, and the two men followed. Valclon was sitting at his desk, and he did not look pleased, Drean truly was happy he was not the one to bear the news.

"Lord Valclon, these men bring you news of the siege upon Cerdrine."

Valclon waved Drean off. "Yes, thank you Drean. Leave us now I will call for you when you are needed."

Drean bowed deeply happy to have been dismissed. "Yes Lord, as you wish." Drean left the hall smiling.

Valclon looked down at the two men over the top of his desk, and frowned darkly. One of the men was sweating, and seemed quite agitated, while the other stood his ground and waited patiently. Valclon smiled at this and turned to the agitated man. Valclon frowned more than anything he hated cowards, and this man looked as though he were about to lose control over his bodily functions.

"Tell me what happened at Cerdrine. There was, more than enough forces to overtake that city, where is The Book of Islangardious, and the traitor Cestator?" Valclon asked the agitated man.

The man looked as though he wanted to run, but his legs would not move. "Lord Valclon . . . I am afraid the army was routed. We nearly had them when suddenly a monster of indescribable might suddenly began killing everything in its path and the army fled."

Valclon's frown darkened even more. The one thing he hated more than cowardice was incompetence, and this man showed both. He looked up and smiled evilly "Ah Terial my pet your dinner has just arrived." He said as he pointed at the man.

The agitated man turned and looked behind him, and screamed when he saw a massive creature charging at him. The last thing he saw before he died was the creature opening its giant maw, and seeing its razor sharp teeth penetrate his flesh.

The other man did not even flinch as the creature lifted the body of his compatriot into the air, and tore it to shreds. Valclon smiled at this. This man was very intelligent for if he had moved he would have met the same fate.

Valclon nodded to the other man. "Now tell me what you know of the events I had mentioned before."

The man bowed deeply, and when he stood he smiled. "It would be my honor Lord. First of all for the undead, Slanoth cast a massive spell, and destroyed them all."

Valclon frowned and slammed a fist down on the desk. "Damn that cursed paladin, he has foiled me more times than any."

The man waited for Valclon to finish, but smiled all the more. "The spider lords were defeated by the traitor Cestator. Then the final attack was ordered and the army charged the gate. Again Slanoth charged out and eventually became locked in one on one combat with your general, and I put an arrow in his back and the ogre finished him."

Valclon laughed loudly when he heard this. "Ah very good, I commend you. You have removed a very large thorn in my side. Now go on."

The man nodded. "As for the monster that fool spoke of, it was Cestator in an awful rage over Slanoth's death. The army was disheartened and they fled in every direction. I however remained for a time and I learned that Slanoth had entrusted Cestator with The Book of Islangardious."

Valclon jumped to his feet at the man's words. He stared down at him fire burning in his eyes. "Are you sure of this? If I find you are lying to me you will wish you shared that man's fate."

The man nodded his head and smiled. "I am quite sure My Lord, I saw the tome myself. It is now in Cestator's possession. Though the opportunity for me to take it did not arise, and I knew you would want to be informed of this."

Valclon sat back down smiling. "You have done well, yet your use to me has not ended."

The assassin bowed down before Valclon. "I am at your command My Lord."

Valclon's smile darkened and he stared the man in the eyes. "Good, but first you shall have your reward." Valclon waved his hand out before him, and the assassin fell to the ground screaming.

When the man finally stood he was no longer a man. He was now a shade. Valclon nodded and smiled at his handy work. "There I have made you stronger, you are now my most dangerous assassin, for I have not only made you a shade, but you are also a man. You may change from one to the other as you will."

The shade bowed down before Valclon. "Thank you Lord. How may I be of service to you?"

Valclon nodded, very pleased with the man. "I want you to find what remains of the army, and kill them for their cowardice. Then return here and I will inform you on what task I need of you."

"As you wish Lord Valclon, it will be done not a single man will survive." The shade said as he disappeared.

Valclon sat back in his chair and laughed, pleased with what he heard. *"Ah brother your champion has fallen, and soon I shall have The Tome of Islangardious in my possession, and then I will be unstoppable."*

Three days after the small group of newfound friends set out to find help for Creashaw, they came upon a great expanse of mountains. "The temple is a day's walk through these mountains in a small valley. There is little danger here, if everyone is up to it we could make it there by morn." Angion said as he looked around at his companions. William and Cestator both nodded, but when he looked at Sheminal she scoffed and walked right past him without a word.

William chuckled slightly at this. "Well I believe you have your answer Angion."

Angion looked back at Sheminal and sighed. "I will never know what is right for me to say around her."

William chuckled harder and walked up to Angion. "No man will ever know my friend. Women are by far the strangest creatures."

Angion chuckled and nodded his agreement, and the two men followed after Sheminal.

Cestator looked at the two in puzzlement, not understanding how they could allow a woman to affect them in such a manor. He was determined that he would never let one of the weaker sex to control his actions or his thoughts, and he scoffed any who did for fools. Shaking his head in disappointment he lifted the end of the skid and followed the others.

As the first sun began to rise the temple came into view. William and Sheminal stopped and stared in awe of what they saw. The light shimmered off the white walls almost as though it were dancing across them. The two golden towers rose up from either side, reaching for the heavens.

Angion looked at the two and chuckled softly, remembering the first time he had laid eyes upon the wondrous place. Cestator looked at William and scoffed. "What is wrong with you? It is only a building."

William looked at Cestator in shock. "Have you no idea what this place stands for. This place is not only a temple to the almighty, but it was built by all of the races together. It stands for the unity of all nations. It was built at the beginning of recorded history. It is also the oldest building known of to have ever been built, and none have ever come close to matching the craftsmanship."

"No matter, it is still only a building to me, no matter who built it or who it was dedicated to."

Angion looked at Cestator in shock. "Come, now Cestator. Have you no sense of culture. Even my people who lived upon the plains know of this place."

Cestator gave Angion his half smile and shook his head. "Sorry friend, but where I come from culture is not something easily found. It is not safe to worry about such things."

Angion looked at Cestator questioningly not quite sure what to make of his last statement. Before he could enquire further however William spoke up. "Enough of this we must get Creashaw to the temple to get help, before it is too late, and standing here discussing this is not helping."

Sheminal shook off her daze and nodded. "Yes let us go now," and with that she headed off towards the temple. Angion looked towards the temple then back at Cestator, and almost asked the question on his mind, but thought better of it and followed Sheminal. Cestator and William shared a knowing glance and nodded to one another then followed.

When the group of friends finally reached the base of the temple stairs there was a wizened old man waiting for them there. He wore a warm smile that almost seemed to wrinkle his entire face, but his eyes seemed sad. Sheminal was the first to run up to him "Kind sir we have come a long way in hopes . . ."

The old man's smile then faded and he placed his right hand on Sheminal's shoulder cutting her off short. "I know why you have come, my dear. I know why all of you are here. I have been told of your blight, and I mourn for you. I fear however I can do nothing for your son. The venom that courses through his veins is beyond our abilities to remove."

Sheminal fell to her knees crying, and through her sobs she looked up at the man. "Is there no one who can save my son? I cannot let him die. Please help me there must be some way."

The old man sighed, and leaned heavily on his staff. "There is one who may be of help to you, but I fear the road is long, and dangerous."

"We will face any dangers there may be, to help the boy." Angion said as he stepped up.

The man smiled again. "Very well there is a wizard who lives in the mountains just north of here. The trail there is tricky and known only by a few, and there is one who resides here that knows the way. Unfortunately she has left this morning to do a bit of hunting, but she should return by evening."

There suddenly was a sound that interrupted the man's words. It was almost like a wolf baying, but the sound was not natural. Cestator and William instantly looked at one another. They both recognized that sound, and knew what it meant.

Cestator looked at the old man, a look of danger burning in his eyes. "Tell me old man. Is this person you speak of out there?" He said as he pointed towards the forest behind him.

The old man nodded still smiling. "Yes of course, but do not fear for her she can handle herself quite well, and she knows how to handle a few wolves"

William stepped up, and bowed before the man. "I beg your pardon Sir, but the sound you have just heard is no wolf. That was a Hellhound and if what you say is true then the lady is in grave danger."

Cestator nodded. "I agree. William you and I shall try and find her before it is too late." He looked to Angion and frowned. "I hate to do this, but we need someone to stay here in case the hounds try to attack the temple."

Angion pulled the axe from the harness on his back and set the head down on the ground leaning on the handle. "Nothing shall get past me. I swear this upon my honor."

Cestator smiled and nodded. "Good, I had hoped you would say that."

The old man's voice chimed in, this time with a touch of anger in it. "I say put that thing away. This is the Valley of the Almighty; no evil may enter this sacred place."

Cestator scowled and looked at the old man. "Be as it may, times are strange and I will not risk anything for blind faith old man." He turned and ran for the forest, and William followed.

Keriana quickly found the trail of a large deer, and she smiled. She called to Heroth and pointed it out to him. "Look here there should be enough meat on this one for both of us to feed."

Heroth smiled. "It's about time you noticed him. I picked up that trail some time ago."

Keriana scowled at him. "Then why didn't you say something, you overgrown hairball?"

"I didn't want you to feel inferior."

"Ooh, you are going to get it for that one I swear. When I am done with you . . .

Keriana was suddenly cut off by a loud baying sound. She looked back and frowned. "That was no wolf. Have you ever heard anything like it before Heroth?"

Heroth shook his head. "No, but everything within me is telling me we don't want to know."

"I agree, and something tells me we should get back to the temple to be sure everyone there is safe."

The two began to run back towards the temple. They did not get far before a stampede of animals came running towards them, and they had to jump to either side to keep from being trampled.

When the animals passed Keriana looked after them in awe. "What in all, the world could make the animals act that way?"

As if on cue there suddenly was another loud baying only it seemed to be right behind her, and as Keriana turned around she heard Heroth say. "They would."

What Keriana saw next nearly made her heart stop. The creatures before her were like dogs only bigger, and they had no fur, only what seemed to be seared flesh, and in places some bone could be seen. Small licks of fire burned where their eyes would have been, and a greenish drool dripped from their mouths that hissed when it hit the ground.

Keriana quickly notched an arrow in her bow, drew and fired. Her aim was true and the arrow struck the ground inches from the creature's foremost paw, but it did not seem to notice. The beastly thing simply growled at her, and suddenly the growling grew louder and seemed to come from all sides.

"Keriana we're surrounded, I don't think that we will scare these things away so easily."

Keriana nodded in agreement with Heroth's words, and as she did she fired another arrow and it struck the creature where Keriana knew its heart should have been. Once again however the creature did not seem to notice.

"What are these things?" she called out to Heroth.

"I don't know I have never seen anything like them before, but I do know one thing. We are in trouble."

Cestator and William quickly picked up the trail of the hounds, and what seemed to be every animal in the forest. They wasted no time pondering this however for they knew they had to move quickly to be of any help. It was not long however before they heard a low rumbling growl, and Cestator instantly had his sword in his hand.

The two men turned a corner in the road and nearly ran into the back of one of the hounds. Cestator acted quickly and cut down the creature before it realized he was there. William instantly drew his sword and turned to the right and dispatched another. The two men became like whirling blades, once one creature was down they moved to the next, and in moments all of the hounds were dead.

The two men stood together facing off against a very large white tiger. The creature was growling threateningly and standing between them and the woman.

Finding Help

The woman frowned darkly and pulled on the scruff of the tiger's neck and yelled at him. "Heroth stop it." She looked at the two men and scowled. "Put those things away."

Cestator scowled back at her. "I'll not sheath my sword until I know the treat is gone."

"If you don't put that thing away, I will give you a reason to feel threatened. It is bad enough you just out right killed those animals, no matter what they looked like."

Cestator exploded at the woman's words. "Listen here woman I do not take kindly to threats, so if you are going to make one against me you had best be ready to back it."

Cestator instantly found an arrow pointed at his throat with the woman smiling at him. He smiled back at her, and nodded. She looked down to find his sword at her throat. Cestator suddenly heard a loud rumbling sound. He looked down to find the white tiger moving threateningly towards him.

William standing to the side quickly had enough. "Stop this all of you. You are acting like children."

Keriana and Cestator both lowered their weapons simultaneously, and William stepped between them. He bowed before Keriana smiling as he came back up. "My Lady, I am William Paladin of Cargon. My friend here and I have come to ask for your help, and as for the monstrosities we killed there, they were hellhounds and are not of this world. There was no other way to deal with them I am afraid, for they would not have stopped until you were dead."

Keriana smiled and nodded to William. "Then I thank you William. I am Keriana, and my large friend here is Heroth. As a paladin of Cargon however especially one looking for help I would think you might keep better company than that."

This truly infuriated Cestator and he stepped forward an angry fire burning in his eyes. "I will have you know woman . . ."

William cut Cestator off short by putting a hand on his shoulder holding him back, and shaking his head. When he was sure Cestator would say no more William turned back. "You will have to excuse my friend, My Lady. He is much like me in that he has a burning hatred for all things of evil, yet his temper is quick to fire and slow to cool I am afraid."

"Well I hope he learns to keep it under control, before I decide not to even hear your request."

"Ah yes well I would ask you to hold your decision until you meet our other companions, whom I shall leave to make the request."

Keriana smiled and shook her head. "Why William you are just full of surprises, and please stop calling me lady. My name is Keriana call me that."

William smiled brightly and bowed again, "as you wish Keriana."

Keriana smile back. She found William to be quite a handsome man, and he had a warm and inviting smile, but most of all she thought he had the most intriguing blue eyes for a human. She gave William a warm and inviting smile, then turned ignoring Cestator's frown, and headed for the temple With Heroth close by her side.

When she was out of earshot William leaned in close to Cestator, and whispered to him. "It's her, the girl from the labyrinth. You never said she was an elf. If that happened when she was a young girl it must have been at least . . ."

"It was nearly two hundred years ago. That is of your time here on this world. We slaughtered every last one of her people."

Keriana looked back at the two and frowned. "It is quite impolite to whisper secrets behind someone's back. I would think better of a Paladin of Cargon."

William bowed deeply. "I beg your pardon my lady. We were discussing our trials in the Labyrinth, and that is not something that anyone likes to discuss openly."

Keriana frowned, and walked up to Cestator, and reached for the front of his shirt, but he grabbed her wrist in a painful grip before she got near to it. The pain from his hold nearly brought tears to her eyes, but she refused to show him any weakness, and refused to even flinch. He looked into her eyes and she saw more than a lifetime of pain mistrust and hatred. This time she did flinch, she knew not what this man had been through, but his bitterness was well rooted. She turned away unable to hold his stare any longer and tried to pull her hand away, but his grip was like iron.

"Release me now." She shouted at him.

Cestator frowned at Keriana, and then dropped her wrist. "If you do not want me to do that again, I would suggest you keep your hands to yourself woman."

Keriana quickly forgot the pain in her wrist, and her anger flared up hotly. This man angered her like no other, she could not explain what it was exactly about him, perhaps it was everything, but she could not stand being near him. "What kind of paladin are you? I thought Cargon taught his disciples more respect than that."

Cestator gave her a half smile, and it bothered her even more than his eyes had. The smile was dark and confident, almost too confident, but she could see he was not a man to push too far. When he spoke his voice was cold, and sharp. "You assume much woman. That is your first mistake. I am not a paladin. I took the trials yes, but it was never said that I completed them."

Keriana was slightly shocked, but more so she was intrigued by Cestator's words. All the tales she had heard of the brutal way men subjected themselves to the trials of the labyrinth said, that any man unable to complete the tests never returned.

Keriana smiled at Cestator and nodded. "Well then Cestator, you are an enigma, and I shall have to travel with you until I find your secret." She turned and left the two men standing there, wondering what had just happened.

After a moment William and Cestator followed after her, and they continued their conversation. "So if what you say is true she must be the last of the Slenstrati elves."

"Yes that is correct William. The elves were all at war with one another, and my father got word that the tome was spotted among them, but when I went there to find it they resisted. I ordered the place to be destroyed, and not one of them to be left alive. That was the first and last time I have ever gone back on my word."

"You know my father had told me the tale of how General Shepard found Slenstrati in ruins. He told me that many of the men who went there refused to even enter the gates."

"Yes well if Shepard entered that place, it says much about that old dwarf's mantle."

Keriana suddenly stopped and turned staring straight at Cestator. "Did you just say something about Sheparlandrious?"

Cestator smirked and nodded. "Yes, why do you know the old dwarf?"

"Perhaps, but it is none of your concern. All I want to know from you is when you last saw him."

Cestator cocked his head to the side smiling wickedly. "Well now perhaps that is none of your concern."

Keriana's eyes darkened, she was truly growing weary of this man's cross words. She clenched her fists ready to hit him, when suddenly she heard Heroth's voice in the back of her mind. "I don't think that would be wise Keriana. I think he knows something of your past. I don't know what, but they were whispering and looking at you, and if you do that you may never learn what he knows."

Keriana released her fists and patted Heroth on the head. "Thank you my friend, I don't know what came over me. I have never been so angry at anyone before."

"I know I can feel your anger, and it is scaring me."

Keriana smiled and bent down and hugged Heroth. "Thank you my friend," she whispered to him. She stood and looked at Cestator. "Very well Shepard as you call him is an old friend, and I wondered how he faired."

Cestator nodded. "We left him at Cerdrine little more than a week ago, and when we left the old dwarf was as solid and rude as ever."

Keriana chuckled slightly at Cestator's comment. "Thank you, it warms my heart to know he is well. Now we should really return to the temple before your friends begin to worry for you." Without another word said the three resumed their trek back to the temple.

Angion stood waiting for either his companions return, or the creatures which had made that horrifying sound, when he suddenly had a feeling something was about to break the tree line. He gripped his axe tightly not wanting to be caught by surprise even though he had not heard the sound for some time.

What emerged from the tree line however made him pause more than any beast could have. He saw a woman of such beauty his eyes opened wide. She wore leather armor yet it seemed to accentuate her more than take away from her beauty. She was slim yet muscular, and looked to know how to use the bow upon her back. Her face was that of a goddess, and her almond shaped green eyes seemed to pierce the soul, while her light auburn hair fell behind her pointed ears, and Angion knew instantly she was an elf.

Angion suddenly felt a sharp stinging pain on the back of his head. He turned around rubbing it, to find Sheminal standing there scowling at him. "Damn woman . . . why for did you do that?"

Sheminal's scowl darkened. "Well you were staring so hard, and your eyes were bulging so. I wondered that perhaps if I hit you hard enough they might fall out. It would seem I did not do it hard enough." Sheminal turned around and walked away without saying another word to him.

Keriana watched as all of this transpired, and she chuckled to herself at Sheminal's words. She knew instantly that, this woman was someone she could befriend. Then as she walked by Angion, she gave him a warm smile and shook her head, and approached the woman.

William and Cestator were close behind the elven woman, and they seemed to find humor in what they had seen. When they reached Angion, William shook his head. "There is nothing more dangerous than a scorned woman is there Angion?"

Angion scratched the back of his head and looked at Sheminal. "I tell you, I do not know where I stand with her. There are times I think she would not care if I were gone, and others she makes it very clear that she has claim over me."

Cestator shook his head and scoffed. "If you want the woman, then take her, and do not play these foolish games. Women are like anything else they need to be conquered, and put in their place."

Angion looked at Cestator and laughed strongly. "You have not yet found the one who turns your heart, have you my friend. Trust me when I tell you. When you meet the one you will do anything to please her."

"Bah . . . I shall never let any woman get the better of me. The feelings you speak of only make you weak." With that Cestator walked away before Angion could reply.

Angion turned to William and shook his head. William smiled and nodded, knowing well what Angion was thinking. He called Cestator to wait a moment.

Cestator sighed in frustration, but he turned and looked back. William and Angion were shaking their heads and calling him to wait. When they reached him Angion pointed at the two women. "It would not be wise to get between the two of them my friend. If they are to have at it, it would be best for you not to be between them. Two women can be worse than two large cats in a fight."

"Very well then, I will stand back, and watch the show." Cestator said with a grin hoping to see a bit of action.

Keriana walked up to Sheminal, and offered her hand. Sheminal looked at the hand, then up at the smiling elven woman. For an instant her jealousy burned, but only for an instant. When she looked into the woman's eyes she saw something unexpected. The woman had a gift, what it was she could not tell, but she could see the spark of it deep in her soul.

Sheminal then took the hand in hers and the woman's smile widened. "Hello I am Keriana. I am told you are in need of my assistance."

Sheminal smiled in return. "Well met Keriana, I am Sheminal of the Karlishion people. We were told you could lead us to someone who can heal my son."

Keriana was slightly shocked by Sheminal's words and it touched her voice slightly. "They can do nothing for him here?"

Sheminal shook her head sadly and nearly burst into tears, but she fought hard to contain herself. "He was bitten by a belath, and they fear anything they try may kill him. I cannot lose him to these things as well. No one has ever survived from a bite before. It is my fault he is like this. I should have never let him go . . . even knowing what the spirits showed me."

Keriana was bewildered by Sheminal's words. The woman spoke of things that Keriana could not understand, but when she found a break she quickly stopped Sheminal. "Now wait this thing, you called it a bela . . ."

"A belath, yes I am sorry I know not what to call it in your language." Sheminal said sadly. "They are large horrifying beasts, as something out of your worst dreams. Few who have ever seen one, live to tell of them, and fewer still have ever been known to kill one. The tales tell that the great Slanoth and Randor were the only two known to do so, that is until now of course. Angion tells me Cestator killed two including the one that bit my son. Although the spirits tell me, that in doing so, he has made a powerful enemy."

Keriana stopped Sheminal, more in shock than even before. "Wait just a moment there. I am sorry, but did you just say that bastard back there killed two of these things you are talking about?"

Sheminal nodded. "Yes, I saw the two creatures myself, and that is when Angion told me of how it happened."

"I see so if he killed the one that injured your son, how is it he made an enemy?" Keriana asked wanting to be sure she understood what was happening.

Sheminal suddenly burst into tears unable to control them any longer. Keriana began to apologize, but Sheminal waved her off and wiped away her tears.

When Sheminal finally collected herself again she tried to smile, but it felt forced and she was sure it looked so as well so she continued her tale instead. "I must apologize the telling of this brings up many memories. You see there was another of the creatures, one unlike any other. It killed my husband many years ago and now just a few days past my entire village. It is evil beyond anything ever known to this land, and somehow Cestator's destiny is tied to it. The spirits tell me that the beast will not rest until Cestator is dead."

"Hmm . . . I cannot see as I blame it. He has a certain air about him that makes me want to . . ." Keriana stopped short closed her eyes and prayed for forgiveness of her thoughts.

When Keriana opened her eyes again they opened wide in surprise of what she saw. Heroth had approached Sheminal, and she was kneeling beside him, petting him and scratching him behind the ears.

"Heroth," Keriana said questioningly, but he did not answer.

Sheminal looked up and smiled. "This is a fine friend you have here. I have never seen one of his color before."

Keriana now over her initial shock smiled back. "Yes, He has been loyal since the day we met, until now." With her final words Keriana's smile turned to a scowl.

This time Heroth looked up at Keriana, and when he saw her face he whined and lied down. *"I am sorry Keriana. She was in need of a bit of comforting so I thought."* He began to say in a meek tone.

Keriana began laughing at this. *"You really are a just a big soft lover boy aren't you?"*

Sheminal stood and laughed lightly when she saw this. "You can speak to him . . . Yes?"

Keriana was torn from her thoughts by this. "Yes, but how did you . . . ?"

Sheminal's smile widened. "I have a gift as well. At times I know things, and the spirits speak to me." She looked down at Heroth. "What did he tell you?"

"He said you looked sad so he wanted to comfort you. I told him he was in love." Keriana said chuckling.

Sheminal laughed heartily at this. "Well could you tell him I am flattered, and thank you?"

Keriana shook her head. "There is no need he can understand your words."

"Well then, thank you my great savior. You have made me feel better." As she looked back up at Keriana her smile instantly faded. "So Keriana will you aid us?" she said slightly louder so there would be no doubt the men coming up behind Keriana would hear.

Keriana quickly caught on to what was happening, and she played along. "Yes of course Sheminal. I could never refuse when a child's life is on the line. Shall we see how your son fares?"

A light smile touched Sheminal's eyes for a moment, but the mention of her son brought back her sadness, and she nodded. The two women walked into the temple, and Heroth stayed close to Sheminal's side.

Cestator watched and waited for the women to fight, but when he saw the two laughing he groaned, and began walking towards them. Angion and William more relieved than anything followed suit. As the men got nearly close enough to hear the women's conversation Sheminal looked up and saw them. The two spoke loudly enough to be heard then walked into the temple.

"What was that about? The last part I am sure we were meant to hear, but why these games?" Cestator said gruffly.

Angion chuckled and shook his head. "Those are women my friend, and one is Sheminal I learned some time ago it is best not to ask."

"I must concur, Cestator Angion is quite right. In all my dealings with women I have learned that women have secrets and it is best to let them keep them."

"Bah . . . as I said before thinking like that will get you nowhere. Knowledge is power, and if you let them keep things from you, they are one step ahead. You must not allow that."

William and Angion both shook their heads at Cestator but said nothing, which suited Cestator just fine. The three then continued following the women.

When Sheminal and Keriana arrived at the room where they put Creashaw Sheminal paused before opening the door. She looked at Keriana tears welling up in her eyes. "I am sorry. It is hard for me to see him even now. I cannot help, but to think it is my fault he is dying."

Keriana shook her head frowning. "You must not think that. You could have done nothing to change this. Somehow, and for some reason this was in his destiny, nothing you could have done would have changed that."

Sheminal smiled sadly and nodded. She turned back to the door, and opened it. The moment she looked in the room however she screamed and backed away.

Keriana looked into the room and her eyes went wide. She had never seen anything like what she was seeing at the moment. There was a boy lying upon the bed, with two large puncture wounds on his leg that looked to be from an enormous snake, and a green fluid oozed out, and it filled the room with a nauseating smell. That however was not what caused her to real back in fear. On the floor next to the bed, there were three priests, all dead and grotesquely deformed. Their bodies were twisted in horrible positions as though they died a horribly painful death. "May the almighty have mercy on their souls," she said as she backed away.

Hearing Sheminal's scream Cestator, William, and Angion drew their weapons and ran to the women's side. Cestator was the first to reach them, and he looked into the room. When he saw what had happened he scoffed and threw his sword back into its scabbard. He waved the other two down. "Stay your weapons there is no danger here, save entering that room."

Confused by Cestator's words the other two did as he advised, but looked into the room themselves. Angion sighed and shook his head. "I feared something like this. The venom kills even days later, but this . . ."

William however, reeled back at the stench. "By the gods what happened in there, and what is that awful stench."

Cestator shook his head. "It would seem that is the reason they told us there was nothing they could do."

At that moment the old man who first greeted the group walked around a corner seeming quite flustered. "What is amiss here?" He asked when he saw the group standing before the door.

Keriana turned, face haggard she answered him. "They are dead father."

The old man frowned, and motioned for Angion to step aside. Angion did as he was bid, and the man stepped up, and when he saw what had happened he scowled. "I warned them not to try this. There is an evil here that has never been seen before."

He began to walk into the room, but Cestator stopped him by placing a hand on his shoulder. The man looked at the hand and glared at Cestator. "Release me this instant," he said angrily.

"Do you wish to suffer the same fate those fools did, because if you enter that room you surely will old man."

The man's scowl darkened. "I told you once before, that no evil may harm us here.

"Well then if that is so what happened to those fools?" Cestator asked sarcastically.

"They were warned. They chose to ignore those warnings, and they embraced the evil. Now release me!"

"As you wish, but it is your fate." Cestator said as he raised his hands and backed away.

The old man sighed and shook his head. "That is why your friend there wears the pendant and you do not. His faith is pure and absolute and yours is not, and until you find it you will be cursed to carry that wicked weapon."

Cestator dropped his hands and stared into the man's eyes. "How did you know . . . tell me old man."

The man ignored Cestator, and he turned to Keriana. "Do you know why I am sending you on this journey my dear?"

Keriana nodded. "Yes father, they are in need of a guide and I know the way better than any other."

"Yes, but that is only partially correct. You must be a guide in more ways than that. There is much you need to do, and the time for you to begin has come." The old man looked at the rest of the group. "Now I am afraid it is time that you must begin your journey, the longer you delay the worse the boy's condition will become."

The man walked into the room, cleaned Creashaw's wounds and bandaged them. When he was finished he walked up to Sheminal and handed her more bandages. "I assume you know what to do with these, my dear."

Sheminal nodded solemnly, but said nothing.

"Good be sure you clean the wounds daily, but take care not to get the venom on your skin it can kill even now."

Again Sheminal merely nodded.

Satisfied his instructions would be followed he turned to the rest of the group. "Unless you wish to share the fate of those men, none of you try to heal this boy. The magic required to do so, requires more knowledge of the venom than any of you have. Is that understood?"

"Yes sir," William piped in. "I will be sure no one tries to heal him."

The man smiled and nodded. "Thank you young paladin, the lives of your friends and that young boy are in your hands."

William put his right hand over his heart, and stood tall and proud. "I shall not fail them, this I swear."

Cestator chuckled to himself, and shook his head slightly.

The old man caught the subtle movement however, and he sighed. *"Keriana has much work to do indeed."* He pointed to Cestator. "You there, get the boy. It is time for all of you to go." He said with a hint of anger touching his voice.

Cestator did not give the man a reply, he merely walked into the room picked up Creashaw and carried him out of the room.

The old man nodded when Cestator exited the room. "Good, now follow me I will give you a mule to help carry the boy."

Cestator frowned and shook his head, but before he could speak Angion broke in. "Thank you sir for the offer. I mean you no disrespect, but the animal will only slow us, and attract the attention of some animals we would rather avoid. Most would ignore us but the scent of the animal will attract them, and then if they catch a scent of the boy they would surely attack."

"I must concur with Angion." William piped in. "The animal would do us more harm than good in this situation."

The old man sighed and nodded solemnly. "Very well if you feel so strongly on this I will concede. I was only trying to lessen the burden upon you."

This time Cestator spoke up before anyone could stop him, and much to everyone's surprise he was polite. "Your concerns are much appreciated, but as Angion and William have pointed out the animal would be more of a burden. However if you could supply us with a small hand cart that would be more helpful to us."

The old man smiled warmly and nodded. "It would give me great pleasure to help. I am sure that we have something that would suit your needs, come follow me. He walked past Cestator, and down the hall to the courtyard, and Cestator followed carrying Creashaw, leaving the rest of the group behind.

Everyone looked at William questioningly, but he shrugged his shoulders, just as unsure of what he had just seen as the others. He followed Cestator and the old man, and the rest of the group unsure of Cestator's sudden change of disposition followed closely behind.

William quickly caught up with Cestator, and when he did he could not hold back the question burning in his mind. "What happened back there Cestator, every one of us was sure you were about to explode?"

Cestator gave William a half smile. "Of course you did. That was my intent, so in using diplomacy I kept control over the situation. Don't you know that at times it is better to win a battle through compromise than through force, besides a cart will make carrying the boy much easier?"

William nodded in agreement. "Yes I agree, but when have you ever not resorted to force?"

Cestator smiled, and shook his head. "This was the first." Cestator left it at that and continued on. A few moments later they found a cart that suited their needs and the party went upon their way.

Chapter 23
New Beginnings

Skreal stared intently at his next target, what the humans called a city. One of their grandest he had learned. He found the more of these pathetic creatures he killed the more he learned of them, and in turn the more he despised them. They were little more than the parasites that found their way beneath his scales and irritated him.

He was going to enjoy this however. He had slaughtered many villages along the way yet most put up little resistance. This would be the first full city he attacked, and he looked forward to see what they would do.

He could see many men patrolling the walls. He knew however they could not see him with his ability to shift. He stared at the large gates closed now to keep creatures of the night out. He could not help but laugh at this, the gates would be no trouble for him his only problem was how to keep the humans from escaping through them when he entered.

To find his answer Skreal reached out with his mind and searched the minds of some of the guards. He quickly found his answer and he smiled at the thought of the slaughter ahead. Before he attacked however he decided to try something he had learned just recently. He forced his will upon the guard that gave him his answer, and crushed his mind.

From within the wall came a horrified scream of pain, then a loud commotion. Skreal smiled at this, he had done this once before and watched it with glee. He knew that by now blood would be pouring from the man's nose and eyes. He strengthened his grip, and the screaming intensified. Skreal continued this for a few moments until he grew bored with it and dealt the killing blow.

When he was finished with the man he focused his attention upon the gates, and he decided now would be the best time to act. He quickly ran up to the gates and struck them with his tail, creating large cracks in them.

The noise caught the attention of the men atop the wall. They looked down, and began firing arrows at him. Skreal stood up on his four back legs and looked at the men as their arrows shattered on his scales. The foolish creatures did not seem to notice that their attempts were futile however for they continued to fire their arrows at him.

Skreal smiled at their foolishness, this seemed to frighten a few of them, and they turned to run, but they were too late. He opened his mouth and sprayed all the men with venom. They died screaming as their flesh was burned away. Moments later their skeletal remains fell to the ground, and Skreal's smile widened at the sight of his handy work.

He turned his attention back to the gates, which by now the men were trying to brace shut with large pieces of wood. Skreal laughed at their futile attempts to keep him out. He walked up to the gates punched his front claws through them, and pulled ripping them from their hinges.

The men on the other side of the gate stared in mute shock as he threw the gates aside. They turned to run, but Skreal killed them before they could take a single step.

With that finished Skreal turned to his next target, a door leading into the wall where the chains for the portcullis were hidden.

He dropped down on all six legs, put his head down and smashed his way through the stone wall. Inside the wall he found two guards, but not wanting to waste time with them he merely stepped on them on his way by.

He quickly found the chains, and just as he was about to cut them, he heard a group of horses galloping for the gate. He hissed angrily and cut the chains with a single swipe of his claws. Moments later he heard the satisfying sound of screams as horses and their riders were crushed under the falling portcullis.

Skreal ran out the hole he had made entering the room. He climbed up the wall, looked out into the field and saw that five men had escaped. He reached out with his mind and dominated one of them, and forced the man to kill his companions. He put a command into the man's mind and released him to warn others of Skreal's coming.

When he was finished Skreal turned back to the city behind him. He smiled wickedly when he saw the large group of men clad in their armor brandishing all sorts of weapons. This was better than he could have ever hoped for. He could smell fear pouring off of them but the fools did not run. They lined themselves up for the slaughter, and they were willing to try and fight.

Then suddenly something caught his eye. There was a large man standing off to the side, and not far behind him there was a small boy. The man had a large sword and appeared to know how to use it, much like the one that had killed Thrash. What caught his attention however was the fact the man was not afraid.

Skreal quickly probed his mind to see his motives, and found the man knew he faced his death, but he did not fear it. The man was almost welcoming it. Skreal was slightly intrigued by this. Every other human he had ever faced feared death, but this man seemed to be at peace with it. He decided he would have to learn what made this man different from the others.

It was now three months since Slanoth's death Serlawn had arrived to take his place, and Braggor finally had time to tend to things he had been too busy to take care of. On his way to his office he stopped a servant and asked him to find Bernard, for him.

The man nodded, "I know his whereabouts sir."

"Good send him to my office right away."

"Yes sir," the man said, and ran to find Bernard.

Braggor went to his office and began attending to some of the many things he had neglected in the past few weeks. A short time later there was a knock on his door. "Come in Bernard," Braggor called out as he shuffled through some papers.

Bernard opened the door stepped in and bowed slightly. "You asked for me milord?"

"Yes Bernard, I wanted to inquire on how young Jonah fared."

Bernard's face lit up at the mention of the boy. "Ah yes the young lad you sent to me a time ago. He is doing quite well milord. He is eager and quick to learn."

Braggor smiled and nodded. "Good I am glad to hear that. I am sorry that I have left him to your care for so long, but as you know it has been hard for me to even find time to rest.

"Oh it is no trouble at all milord, it has in fact been quite a pleasure and somewhat of a relief having the boy around. He is quite a warm and friendly lad, when he opens up. There is however sadness behind his eyes, and when I asked him about what troubled him he withdrew, so I left it be."

Braggor nodded solemnly. "Yes I saw as much when I first met him. That was part of the reason I sent him here. Again I am thankful to you for looking after him for me, but it is time that I take him."

Bernard nodded sadly. "Yes milord, I shall go fetch him immediately." He turned and began opening the door.

"Bernard, before you go I must thank you again. You have done me a great service here."

Bernard bowed and smiled warmly. "I am here to serve milord, and as I had said it was quite a pleasure to have the boy around. I can say he will be missed by many who are used to seeing him every day." He left the room, and a short time later there was a soft knock on the door.

"Enter," Braggor called out.

The door opened slightly and a small head peaked in. "You summoned me, Master Braggor?" Jonah asked in a soft voice.

"Yes Jonah, come in and sit down."

Jonah then slowly crept into the room, and sat in a chair before Braggor's desk. The entire time the boy would not look up at Braggor, he merely stared at the ground.

When the Jonah was seated Braggor leaned over his desk, and lifted the boy's chin so he could look into his eyes. "First of all

Jonah, there is nothing on the floor that should interest you. I am up here, not there on the floor. When you speak with someone always look into their eyes. If you look down they may think you have something to hide, or it is even possible that they could have a knife, and are ready to kill you. With you looking at the floor you would never know until it was too late. Now you are not hiding something from me, are you lad?"

"Oh no master Braggor I would never, hide anything from you." Jonah said shaking his head vigorously.

"Good," Braggor said as he leaned back in his chair. "Tell me Jonah do you know what Cargon stands for?"

The boy was slightly puzzled by the question, but he nodded. "Yes sir, Cargon is the lord of justice, and he stands for honor, and the things that a true warrior strives for."

"Very good Jonah, now tell me do you believe in Cargon and all that he stands for?"

Jonah nodded vigorously at this. "Oh yes Master Braggor. With all that I am. I have dreamed of serving Cargon for as long as I can remember."

Braggor smiled. "Good, that is a noble desire, and one worth pursuing." Braggor paused a moment before he continued. "Now Jonah, I have one more question for you. Why do you think it is that I have brought you here?"

The boy shook his head sadly. "I do not know sir. I asked Master Bernard, but he said I would have to learn that on my own."

Braggor nodded. "Bernard was correct, but I will give you a hint. Think about the questions I have asked you, and think about your answers. The answer to why I have brought you here lies within that."

Jonah sat back and thought for a moment, then suddenly his eyes opened wide, and a smile spread across his face. "Are you saying you are going to train me to be a paladin Master Braggor?"

"Yes Jonah, that is correct. You have the spirit and the eagerness required for it, and I think you would make a fine Paladin one day."

Jonah's smile widened at the praise, but faded away suddenly, and he hung his head. "I thank you Master Braggor, for this chance, but I am not worthy of it."

Braggor frowned when he heard this. He had known that something was troubling the boy, and now was his opportunity to find out what it was. "Why is that Jonah?" He asked with a puzzled look upon his face.

At first the boy did not say anything. He merely squirmed in his chair. Braggor's stare however left no room for escape. "It was my fault," Jonah said in a soft voice as he tried to get away from Braggor's intense gaze.

Braggor was not about to let the boy get away so easily however. "What was your fault?" He asked firmly.

A tear ran down Jonah's cheek as he began to speak, and his voice was broken with sobs. "Mother is dead because of me." The boy burst into a full fit of crying.

Braggor was slightly shocked by this. He knew it would be something big, but he did not expect what he had just heard. It made no difference however. Braggor intended to get to the bottom of this. He could feel Cargon guiding his words. He knew this feeling well, it usually meant there was a deeper truth behind the story. "Alright Jonah tell me exactly what happened the day that your mother died, and do not lie or leave anything out. Cargon will show me if you do. Then when you are finished, with the wisdom of Cargon I will decide who is at fault."

The boy seemed unsure of himself, but he stopped crying and looked up at Braggor and nodded. "Mother and I were out searching the forest for some spices she needed, and I found a patch of mulberries. Mother loved mulberries she always said they reminded her of when she was just a girl. So I decided I would pick some for her as a surprise, but just as I had started she called for me, and said we needed to get back home."

Jonah paused a moment and sobbed, at the memory of his mother, and when he began to speak again his voice had a hint of shame touching it. "I called back to her, and I told her I had found something and I would be there in a moment. I started picking, and I must have lost time, because mother called again more anxious the second time. So I stopped picking and ran back to her. She was so happy when I showed her the mulberries, but she never got to taste them. She thanked me for being sweet and thinking of her, but she said we needed to get home so she could fix dinner for father."

Jonah's face turned dark when he mentioned his father. Braggor took note of this, but he urged the boy to continue.

"Well when we got home father was already there, and he was angry. He started yelling at mother saying she was going to pay, and many other bad things. I stepped up and told him it was my fault we were late. He stopped yelling at mother, and came for me, but mother stepped in his way and father hit her for it. She fell to the floor and hit her head. I ran to her side, but she would not wake. When father saw her he pushed me aside and knelt down beside her and checked her. He looked at me and said she was dead, and that it was because of me. He said that he was going to call the city watchmen, and tell them what I had done. Then he said that if I was lucky they would throw me in the dungeon, but they would probably just feed me to the sharks."

Braggor could see the stark fear in the boy's eyes as he spoke of the sharks. He could tell the boy believed every word of what he was saying.

"I begged father not to call the guards. He told me then, that if I went to my room to think about what I had done, and not come out until he came for me he would consider not calling them. So I went to my room. I was there for five days with no food, but the mulberries I had picked for mother. I don't like them anymore. Then after five days father came for me and brought me to Master Higgins."

Braggor listened intently to Jonah's story to see if he could find any hint that the boy was lying, but he seemed too frightened to have made it up. Braggor was not surprised by the story however. He had heard many similar cases before, and he wondered how these people thought they could get away with it. Cargon always found a way to bring it to light.

When Jonah finished his story he looked at Braggor with stark fear in his eyes, and asked in a trembling voice. "Are you going to feed me to the sharks now?"

Had the boy not been so frightened, and serious Braggor would have burst out laughing. He held it back as best he could however. Yet even then a hint of amusement touched his voice as he answered. "No Jonah I am not going to feed you to the sharks. We do not do such things as that. Your father told you that to scare you into silence. You see, your mother's death was not your fault. Your father killed her then blamed you for it, and told you that so you would keep silent about it. When he was finished removing your mother's body he sent you away, likely so it would be assumed that she left him and took you with her. It was a brave thing you did telling me all of that. Cargon smiles upon such courage."

Jonah beamed at the praise. "Do you really think that Cargon is proud of me for telling you that?"

Braggor nodded smiling. "I know he is Jonah because I am proud of you. You see the one thing that your father did not count on was you meeting me. You see that is how Cargon works he brings such wrong doings into the light. That is why he is the lord of justice. Now for the difficult part however we must deal with your father."

Jonah jumped out of his seat when he heard this. "You are not going to tell him that I told you all of this, are you?"

Braggor nodded solemnly. "I am afraid that I must, and you must come with me. You must face him now or you will be running from him for the rest of your life."

Jonah's eyes got wide as Braggor told him this, and he shook his head vigorously. "No I cannot go see him. He told me to never come back."

"I understand Jonah, but you still have to face him. Remember none of this is your fault and without you justice cannot be served. Now do you believe me when I tell you this?"

Jonah continued to stare wide eyed at Braggor, in fear of the thought of facing his father. "If I go back there he will hit me again. Please Master Braggor I cannot go back there."

Braggor gave the boy a reassuring smile and shook his head. "Fear not Jonah I'll not let any harm come to you. This I promise to you."

Jonah nodded solemnly, and hung his head. "Alright Master Braggor I will do it for you." The boy looked up quickly fear once again touching his eyes. "Are you going to kill my father?"

Braggor shook his head. "No lad, I am not going to kill him, unless he leaves me no other choice. That is the way of a paladin we do not draw our weapon unless there is absolutely no other answer, and even then we do not use it unless forced to, for our own protection or the protection of others. That is your first lesson Jonah and it is one of the most important ones you will ever learn so never forget that."

Jonah smiled and nodded. "Yes Master Braggor, I will never forget it."

"Good, now let us get this done with. We have much to do today."

Jonah's smile quickly faded and the fear returned, but Braggor quickly stood and corralled him to the door giving him no time to argue. When they got to the city street Braggor told the boy to lead him to his father's home.

Jonah did as he was instructed, if a little reluctantly. Braggor was not surprised as the boy led him to the slums. Where most of the lawless people lived, that and those who could hardly afford to eat. The stench in the streets was that of rotting meat and waste. He saw people huddled in doorways wearing little more than rags. He hated to think that even in a grand city such as Cerdrine there were people that had to live this way.

After a time Jonah stopped before a dark and dingy alley that seemed to somehow reek worse than the rest of the slums. "Father's house is down there."

Braggor nodded and placed a hand on the boy's shoulder. "All will be well come show me which one it is."

Jonah looked up into Braggor's eyes his lower lip quivering in fear, but when he saw no fear in Braggor's eyes he pulled himself together, trying to show Braggor he was not afraid. He nodded and turned and headed down the alley, but his first few steps his legs felt weak and he nearly fell. He turned back to see if Braggor noticed, but the man only smiled and nodded as though he had not seen anything. Jonah was glad for this because he did not want to show weakness to his master.

When they finally stood before the door, Jonah began to shake in fear. Braggor saw this and knelt down beside him. "Take a hold of yourself lad. Do not show him your fear. Put your faith in Cargon, he will give you the strength to do what is right. If you show your father fear then he will know that he can intimidate you, and he will have won. I will warn you however if he is as I suspect he will do everything he can to break you. Pay it no mind as I told you I will not let any harm come to you, and remember his words are nothing more than words. You must however stay strong under the pressure. Now if you are ready knock on the door."

Jonah sighed and turned towards the door. He paused a moment to gather his strength then pounded on the door as hard as he could.

Moments later the door swung open and a large angry man stood in the doorway. "Who in the blazes is pounding on my door? You better have a damn good reason for it." He looked down and saw Jonah standing there, and his scowl darkened. "You . . . you little bastard, what are you doing here? Did you fail at that too you little bastard? I swear you're not worth spit."

Braggor cut the man off quickly before he could rattle the boy. "I would advise you to hold your tongue sir."

The man turned his fury upon Braggor. "Who in the nine hells do you think you are, telling me how to talk to my son."

Braggor frowned darkly he despised dealing with men such as this, but justice had to be served. "I would be Braggor, paladin of Cargon, and if you choose not to hold your tongue I will have to force you."

At the mention of Cargon the man's eyes went wide with anger, and he turned his attention back to Jonah. "What did you tell him you little lying bastard. I am going to . . ."

The man stopped instantly when he felt the tip of Braggor's sword at his throat. "I will not tell you again sir. Hold your tongue or my blade will taste your blood." The man nodded slightly, and Braggor replaced his sword in its scabbard. "Now then, Jonah told me . . ."

Braggor stopped short when he heard a small voice speak up. "Master Braggor I would like to tell him myself."

Braggor looked down and smiled. "Are you sure lad?"

Jonah nodded in response.

Braggor's smile widened and he nodded slightly. "Very well then I will be right here."

Jonah looked at his father defiantly. "I told him the truth about how you killed mother. Then about how you made me believe it was my fault, but it wasn't. You scared me into believing it, but you don't scare me anymore. I'll never be afraid of you ever again. I am going to become a paladin, and there is nothing you can do about it.

Master Braggor showed me the truth, and he taught me how to be brave."

The man's eyes darkened, and his mouth curled up in a snarl. "I'll teach you what bravery gets you, you little bastard." He said as he pulled a dagger from his belt and lunged for Jonah. Before he reached the boy however he fell to his knees clutching his bloodied wrist, and his hand fell to the ground before him.

Braggor held his bloodied sword at his side as he spoke calmly. "I warned you sir. You now have one good hand I would advise you not to raise it against the boy."

The man's rage turned back to Braggor, and with his good hand he pulled another dagger from his boot and lunged at him.

Braggor did not hesitate for a moment. He quickly spun away from the attack, and readied his sword in case the man was foolish enough to try it again. "I do not wish to harm you sir, but if you try that again you will leave me no choice."

"Die you bastard of Cargon." The man snarled as he lunged again.

Again Braggor did not hesitate, and in one fluid motion he spun around took the man's other hand off then ran him through. The man looked at his missing hand then down at the sword in his stomach. He tried to scream, but blood gurgled out of his mouth instead.

Braggor pulled his sword from the body and it fell to the ground in a heap, and in that moment Braggor recognized the stench he had smelled earlier. It was the smell of death. Despite this Braggor knelt down by the dead man and prayed to Cargon, asking him to have mercy upon his soul.

Jonah looked at Braggor in shock when he heard this. "Master Braggor, please pardon my interruption, but he just tried to kill both of us. Why do you pray for him?"

Braggor looked at the boy and smiled. "Because Jonah, Cargon teaches us to forgive even our worst enemy in hopes that perhaps one day they will see the light and be saved Even if it is in death. When you forgive someone who has wronged you, it makes you stronger because the gods smile upon such things, and they bless those who can forgive. Hatred is a terrible thing, for all that it can do is destroy, while forgiveness heals all wounds."

Jonah looked at his father and shook his head. "I don't know Master Braggor that monster killed my mother, and made me think I did it."

Braggor sighed and nodded. "I expected you would say as much, so let me tell you a story. This story began many years ago, but finished only recently. You see many years ago an army under the direction of a man called Cestator attacked a far off city. They destroyed it, killing nearly everyone. You see Cestator rarely ever left a survivor, unless he wanted them to suffer before they died. So in this city Cestator personally killed the noble family. In this family there was only one survivor, a boy near to your age. His name was William, and William loved his mother and father, and William was forced to watch as Cestator tortured and killed his father. Then he had to watch his mother be raped by the men in the army. When they were done with her Cestator placed a dagger in the boy's hand and made him slit his mother's throat, and to make the boy's suffering worse he fed their bodies to the orcs while he watched. When they were finished Cestator left William in a pit with no food or water, only the dagger he had killed his mother with. Well, down in that pit William swore he would learn to fight one day, find Cestator and avenge his parent's death."

"I was traveling with the king's army, and we were going to stop at the city for some rest and to get some much needed supplies, but of course we found it in ruins. We searched it for any survivors, and that was when I found William he was near to death, but he survived. When he told us the tale of what he had seen I decided I needed to return with him to the temple. He trained harder than any man. He learned anything that anyone was willing to teach him. He got the name The Tiger for his ferocity. He had very few friends, and even those that he did have kept their distance from him because of the anger and hatred he carried around. He trained for years, and became one of the best swordsmen at the temple."

"Then one day not long ago, Cestator came to the temple severely wounded, and William learned this. His rage and fury burned like a wild fire. Everyone there held some grudge with Cestator, but none as fierce as William's. He waited however for he wanted to face Cestator when he was in good health. Well the next morning Cestator entered the main dining hall, and was very disrespectful. That was more than most of us was willing to take from him, and we surrounded him with swords, and William was at the front of it. Thankfully however Slanoth kept his head about him, and he stopped us from doing anything. Yet it was not until later that day that I saw something that amazed me. Cestator returned from tangling with a group of orcs, and was covered in blood. When William saw him he approached Cestator, but he did not draw his sword. Instead he offered Cestator his hand in friendship. Now the two are the closest of friends, and are willing to die for each other. Cestator taught William the dance of blades, and William is now a master swordsman, and a paladin. The two were also knighted by king Lysandas, and are now upon a great quest. So you see, the gods reward those who have forgiveness in their hearts

"So William forgave Cestator for all of the horrible things he did to him, just like that?" Jonah asked in a unbelieving voice.

Braggor nodded. "Yes when William faced Cestator he felt all of his hatred and anger rushing out, and in the end he felt ashamed. So later when he faced Cestator again he asked for forgiveness for the way he reacted towards him."

Jonah shook his head solemnly. "I am sorry Master Braggor, that was an amazing story, but I am not sure that I am ready to forgive my father just yet. I feel terrible about it, but the memory of what happened is too fresh in my mind."

Braggor sighed, but nodded in understanding. "I understand lad, but remember this. You can never become a true paladin until you learn to forgive him, and the longer it takes the more difficult it will become."

"Jonah smiled and nodded, "I will work hard on it, but right now I just want to go and never come back here."

"Very well then lad we will go, but before we return to the temple however, we must inform the city guards of what has happened here. The guard house at the south gate is closest to us so let us go."

With that the two walked away leaving the body lying in the doorway. After a few steps Jonah looked back confused. "Are we going to leave him there like that?"

"Yes," Braggor said solemnly. "But do not worry about it he will be taken care of. There are those who take care of such things. Well that is unless you know of anyone who would take care of him?"

Jonah shook his head sadly. "No there is no one, but me."

"That is as I had thought, so worry not of it he will be taken care of and you will not need anything from there. You are now under my care and you will have all that you need."

The two continued on without another word. When they reached the guard house however they stared in shock. Before them five guards lay dead and a group of heavily armed guards stood there ready for a fight. When Braggor looked up at what the guards were looking at he pushed Jonah back, telling him to get away, and he drew his sword preparing for a fight.

Dersloan stepped into the Standing water, and curled his nose at the smell of sour ale mixed with blood. The place was dark and dingy, and was filled with what looked like every second rate thief or thug in the city. Rickety tables were scattered throughout the room, many looked to have been repaired more than once. Across the room stood the bar, and it did not look much better.

"Just the kind of place to find Boroth." He snickered. He scanned the smoke filled room and quickly found who he was looking for. The man was sitting at a table in the far corner where the light was weakest. It amused Dersloan that the man appeared to be the most menacing character in the room.

Dersloan wasted no more time. He walked directly towards Boroth, and when someone got in his way he scowled and the man quickly scurried away. Just before he reached the table however, another man sat down and began talking to Boroth.

Dersloan's top lip curled up into a snarl. He twisted his wrist slightly, and a small dart fell into his hand. He flicked his hand out, and moments later the man clutched at his throat then fell to the floor dead.

Boroth looked down at the man in slight confusion, but when he looked up and saw Dersloan approaching he shook his head chuckling. "I should have bloody well known it'd be you. Damn

Dersloan I thought you were dead. After the army retreated I didn't see ya, at the caves. I thought mayhap they caught ya or something. Course I should have known better than that."

Dersloan sat down across Boroth where the stranger had sat moments before. "Who was this fool?" He asked coldly.

Boroth shrugged. "Damn if I know, but he said he'd come from the lords land, and he had some urgent news."

Dersloan sneered at this. "He lied. I went before the master, and he was not there."

Boroth's Eyes opened wide in shock. "You mean to tell me that you went before the master, and you're still alive enough to come back here and find me. Damn you got more guts than anyone I ever seen, and damn lucky too. So did he have any orders for us?"

Dersloan nodded. "Yes, but first tell me is the army together?"

"Aye to the man, not that it is saying much, there is perhaps two hundred men left. They are hiding in the caves south of here. Arthur and I came up here to wait for orders."

Dersloan stood and smile wickedly. "So Arthur is here as well. Where is he?"

Boroth pointed at the staircase. "Upstairs in the room with a whore, it's the third door to the right.

"Thank you," Dersloan said as he headed for the stairs."

"Dersloan Hold on. You said you had orders for us." Boroth called out.

Faster than a snakes strike Dersloan drew his sword swung and replaced it in its scabbard. Boroth's eyes went wide with shock, and then a line of blood formed on his neck. He fell to the floor and his head rolled across the floor.

Dersloan then turned back to the stairs, but before he could take more than a few steps he heard the barkeep yelling at him. "Hey you there, what do you think you're doing? You just spilled blood all over all over the floor there. You're going to clean that up or I'll . . .

The barkeep did not get the chance to finish his sentence, for he was clutching at the arrow in his windpipe. Dersloan put his bow back on his back and scanned the room to see if any other fools wished to challenge him. The room however was deathly quiet, and everyone was staring intently at their drinks in front of them.

Satisfied that he would not be challenged again Dersloan headed for the stairs. When he reached the door to the room he could hear a man and a woman moaning on the other side. He snickered at this and changed to shadow form. He slipped silently under the door. On the other side he changed back to normal, and stepped up behind Arthur, and drew his sword.

The woman's eyes opened wide in fright when she saw this, and she tried to scream, but it came out only as a gurgling of blood. Dersloan drove his blade through both of them twisted it then pulled down. When the blade was free of the bodies he wiped it off on the sheets and put it back in its scabbard.

He slipped out the window and headed for the city gates. When he got there however the gates were closed and they were not allowing anyone through. "Curse it, what is going on here." He said under his breath.

A man standing in front of him looked back and whispered to him. There have been murders in town. Word is it is the work of the Viper. They are trying to keep him from escaping the city."

"Damn fools," Dersloan cursed. "I don't have time for this. Though I wonder how it is that they learned of it so quickly."

Dersloan pushed his way to the front of the crowd, and anyone who refused to move he killed and walked over the body. When he got to the front of the crowd he found the answer to his question. A man dressed in a long red cloak with a golden eye insignia upon it was talking to the guards. *"A seer, they've got a bloody seer."*

Just as he finished his thought the robed man turned to him and pointed. "Captain there is the man you seek. He is the vii . . ."

The man fell to the ground dead before he could finish his sentence. Dersloan drew his sword and stepped forward. The people who had gathered at the gates now ran for their lives.

The guards quickly gathered themselves, and Dersloan frowned. The last thing he wanted to do was to have to deal with the guards. Killing guards made things more troublesome, but he could see no way around it this time.

The captain stepped forward. "You there drop your weapon. In the name of his majesty I am placing you under arrest."

Dersloan smiled at the man and dropped his sword. "I give up. You have me at a bit of a disadvantage." He said with a sneer.

The captain ordered two men to apprehend Dersloan. The two approached cautiously keeping their swords at the ready, but Dersloan only stood there with his hands out in front of him. When the two reached him one put his sword to Dersloan's throat while the other stepped behind him to put him in chains.

When the second man was behind him Dersloan twisted away from the sword at his throat, and in the blink of an eye he had a dagger in each hand. He turned around and going down on one knee he stabbed the two guards simultaneously. Then as he stood, he threw two darts killing the other two guards leaving only the captain. The man stood there in mute shock at what he had just seen.

Dersloan picked up his sword and started walking towards the man. The captain pointed his sword towards Dersloan, and ordered him to stop. Dersloan paid the man no heed however, and when he got near, the man swung wildly. Dersloan easily blocked the swing and with a dagger in his other hand he slit the man's throat, without missing a step.

He headed for the gate and found it locked. He cursed the fools that had done so. He looked back at the captain lying on the ground, but realized he would not have time to find the keys, because he could hear a group of armed guards headed his way. He quickly decided to scale the wall.

When he was about half way up the wall he heard someone calling up to him. "You there, come down or the archers will fire."

Dersloan looked down at them and smiled. "Then shoot if you are so bold."

The man gave the order and the archers let loose a volley of arrows. Dersloan changed to shadow form, and laughed as the arrows harmlessly passed through him.Without a second thought he slipped over the wall and disappeared.

Skreal jumped down off the wall and landed in front of the group of armed men. When he hit the ground it shook slightly, and for a brief moment the men lost their balance. That moment was all that Skreal needed however, before they could ready their weapons

Skreal was among them. He tore in to them and before they even had a chance to scream they were all dead.

Skreal turned his attention to the lone man with the boy. When the small boy saw that Skreal's attention was on them he tried to run, but before he could get more than a few feet Skreal snatched him up. His long teeth pierced the body all the way through. Skreal smiled at the man so he could see the boy's legs dangling in the air. He dropped the body on the ground and stepped on it blood poured out from under his foot and he laughed mockingly.

This seemed to infuriate the man and it made Skreal laugh all the harder, but he stopped short when the man spoke to him. "You will pay for this Beast, and for every other life that you take."

Skreal smiled wickedly at the man's words, and for the first time he tried to speak the language of these humans. At first he could not form the words because the movements required felt foreign to him. When he finally did get them out however his voice was raspy and he had a hiss as though it were a serpent speaking. "And who is it that you think will make me pay. Certainly not a puny little creature like you, I am unstoppable, and I cannot die."

The man shook his head. "You are wrong Creature," he said after his initial shock was gone. "The gods will stop you. I know where it is that I will go when I die. Cargon has a place for all his paladins by his side. You however will spend eternity in the seven hells being tormented."

Skreal laughed wickedly at the man's words. "Your pitiful gods cannot harm me. I am too powerful and I grow stronger each passing day. When the time comes, and they try to stop me I will kill them, and as for you, well you will never see them."

"You are deluding yourself monster, but your day will come you can be sure of that." The man stopped talking and swung his sword at Skreal.

Skreal easily avoided the attack, and he gave the man a large wound across his back for the attempt. Yet the man did not seem to notice for he came back with another swing, and this time Skreal let the blade hit him. The man's eyes opened wide with shock when his large two-handed sword did not even scratch Skreal's scales. Skreal swung his tail around and swept the man's legs out from under him, breaking both of them.

The man screamed in pain as he fell to the ground. Skreal stepped over him and looked him in the eyes yet still the man showed no fear. Instead he tried to stab Skreal in the chest, but before he could raise his sword Skreal pinned his arms to the ground.

Skreal put his face mere inches from the man, and as he began to speak some venom dripped from his mouth and landed on the man's chest burning through his armor, and on to his skin. "Now it is time for you to die. And the final thing you will see is me and nothing else." Skreal punctured the man with his claws driving them fully through and into the ground below the man, and he watched as the life faded from the man's eyes. Then just before he was gone stark fear touched his eyes as he realized Skreal was taking his soul, and that look was then frozen upon his face and Skreal laughed heartily.

Skreal decided to leave the body as it was, so all could see what he had done. By this time however word had spread about his attack and people tried to hide in their homes, and what he enjoyed most was that men kept throwing themselves at him trying to stop him. It was more than he had ever hoped for. The men he killed as they came at him. Some he toyed with and let them think they might have a chance only to tear them apart, and those that hid, he simply burst his way into every household and shop he came across and killed everyone inside. Those he did not enjoy quite as much because they would only cower in fear and occasionally run, but they rarely put up a fight. Soon the streets were painted with blood.

Skreal was thoroughly enjoying himself when suddenly something struck him on the back of the neck with enough force to drive his head forward. He roared in anger, and turned to see what had struck him. What he saw amused him greatly. A group of men with their horses had snuck up behind him with two giant crossbows, ballista they called them. They had fired one of the massive projectiles at him, and the force of the blow had bent the head and splintered the shaft.

The men seemed slightly surprised that it had done nothing to Skreal, but they recovered quickly. Skreal smiled at them and roared a challenge for them to fire the second ballista. The men wasted no time answering his challenge, they fired the massive weapon and their aim was true.

The projectile screamed through the air straight at his bared chest. Skreal did not move until it was inches from him. Then just before it struck he moved like a flash, and twisted his body away, and grabbed the giant arrow in his large jaws plucking it out of the air.

Skreal then turned and looked at men standing by the ballista, with the two ends of the arrow sticking out of either side of his mouth. The men stared in shock as he bore down on the arrow and snapped it in two. He smiled wickedly and dropped the two pieces. The men turned to run, but Skreal charged at them, and before they could get away he slaughtered them all and destroyed the ballista.

Skreal continued his rampage, and when the soldiers stopped coming and he had gone through every building save one, he stood before it. The building was massive compared to any of the others and it had towers and looked to house many people. He had saved it for last for he had gotten from many of the humans that the people that lived here were of great importance to them. He wanted to savor their deaths, and be sure to take their souls.

He was just about to hit the gates on the wall surrounding the building when he heard someone talking to him. "Creature stop, your rampage ends here and now."

Skreal looked up and laughed when he saw five robed men standing on a large balcony on the second floor of the building. The man who spoke to him looked old and weak certainly no match for his power. So, not wanting to waste any time with them he sprayed venom at them and broke down the gates. Much to his surprise however his attack never reached them, it seemed to have hit an invisible wall. Intrigued by this Skreal stopped, and smiled. He had never seen anything like it before.

"As I told you beast, your reign of terror ends here." The man said when the venom was gone.

Again Skreal laughed. "And who might you be, that you think you can stop me, human?"

The man frowned at Skreal's remark. "I am Malketh leader of the wizard's guild, and as you can see your attacks are useless against us."

Again Skreal merely laughed at the man. This enraged Malketh and he waved his hands and spoke a few arcane words that Skreal could not understand. When he finished he pointed at Skreal and a massive fireball roared directly at him. Skreal's smile widened and he did not move to avoid the fireball. It struck him square in the chest and exploded on impact. The blast leveled every building within one hundred yards of him, and filled the air with dust and smoke.

When the dust settled and the smoke cleared the wizards were shocked to see Skreal standing there laughing at them. "You will have to do better than that, you pathetic creatures. I cannot be killed."

Malketh scowled darkly, and turned to his companions. "It would seem we will have to combine our efforts."

The other wizards nodded their agreement, and they all began chanting the words of another spell. When they finished, large bolts of lightning screamed from their hands. The bolts then joined together to create one enormous bolt that caused a deafening crack of thunder that shook the ground.

Again Skreal did not move, and the bolt struck him square in the chest. This time however the blast threw him backwards, and into a pile of rubble stirring up another pile of dust. When the dust settled the wizards smiled, and nodded in relief. Skreal was still lying there in the rubble and a small tendril of smoke floated up from where the bolt had struck him.

The wizards watched intently to see any signs of life from Skreal. After a few minutes that felt like an eternity with not even the rise and fall of the creature's chest they decided that their work was finished that the creature was indeed dead. Their victory was a sad one however. When they scanned the city for any signs of life they found none.

"This will be a day sadly remembered. Many lost their lives here, and for what purpose?"

Malketh shook his head sadly. "I do not know. Who can say what the beast wanted." He looked back at the palace and sighed. "We at least saved the family, though how many others we could not. What I wish to know is why we did not see this before. It could have been prevented."

"There are strange forces at work here. I have not seen the likes of such things since the Trial Wars."

Malketh nodded his agreement. "Yes strange and powerful forces." He looked out at the desolation around the city and sighed. "Come there is nothing more we can do here, we must go to the temple nearby to have the priests give these people the services they deserve."

With that the wizards turned around, and were just about to leave when they heard an insidious laughter that sent shivers up their spines. They turned back around and realized their mistake. Somehow the creature had slowed down its bodies functions to the point where it appeared to be dead even under the scrutiny of their magic.

The wizards stared in shock as Skreal got to his feet, and smiled at them. He had waited patiently for them to drop their guard, and now they were finished. "I told you pitiful humans, I cannot die. So here is a taste of what you have just given me."

Suddenly, much to the wizards' horror bolts of electricity jumped back and forth on Skreal's tail spikes. He opened his mouth and a bolt ten times the size they had cast roared straight for them.

Malketh quickly put up a ward but the force of the bolt staggered him, and he knew he could not hold it back for long. His companions added their strength, but it was futile. Skreal's strength was too great for them.

The bolt easily burst through their defense, and struck them with explosive force that destroyed most of the palace around them, throwing debris across the entire city. With that finished Skreal turned back to the city behind him, and flicked out his tongue tasting the air to see if there was any more life left. When he found nothing he roared another challenge as he did every time, to any who dared challenge him.

When no challengers came he yawned stretching his jaws. He went over to the remains of the palace, and curled up on top of it. When the rubble settled under his weight he fell fast asleep.

Again she heard the challenge from the monstrosity. A low rumbling roar escaped her lips. She knew well what he was doing, but there was nothing she could do about it. There was another who needed her attention.

She knew the time was nearly here and she could not leave yet. She laid her head back down and sighed out of sadness for those that were suffering. She closed her eyes again and went back to her vigilance waiting for the one to come.

Chapter 24

Being Followed

Three days after leaving the temple the companions found themselves deep in the Darlmoure Mountains. Keriana proved to be an excellent if prudent guide. She tolerated little from the men especially Cestator, the two butted heads many times over the trek. The others tried to keep them separated, but it did not help. The two could not even look at one another without glaring.

After one heated argument William took Cestator aside to calm him down. "Cestator calm yourself. Fighting amongst ourselves is not going to solve anything. Try to remember she is the reason you are here."

Cestator snarled and slammed his fist into a large boulder rocking it slightly, and when he pulled his hand away it was bloodied. He smiled as the pain flashed across his knuckles, it was an old friend and it was comforting. Then as the pain faded so did his smile. "I remember, and I also remember what Cargon showed me in the labyrinth. If we continue traveling with that woman it may well come true, and I may just be happy about it."

William stared at him in shock. "Cestator you cannot possibly mean that. Cargon would never allow that to happen. Besides can you not remember how you felt when you saw that?"

"Yes I remember, but that damn woman will not listen to reason. I tell you she tries her hardest to find a way to spite me."

William shook his head sadly. "I do not think that is so. I know what the problem between the two of you is, if you want to know. You both are so much alike yet you are absolutely different."

Cestator gave William a bewildered look. "What kind of nonsense are you babbling William?"

"It is not nonsense Cestator. Think about this for a moment. Both of you are dead set in your ways, and are absolutely unyielding almost to the point of coming to blows to keep them. That could be a good thing in some cases, but the two of you have values so different they are like day and night. It is inevitable that the two of you will fight until you learn to compromise."

Cestator turned from William angrily and stared at Keriana. "I'll not compromise anything for that woman." He said as he walked back to the fire.

"And that is why you do not wear a medallion my friend." William sighed as he watched Cestator walk away. He looked up to the heavens and prayed. *"Cargon, help them. I ask you please bring something about to change both of their minds."*

When he was finished William joined the others. The conversation at the fire was suppressed, and most of it was between the two women. The two had grown close in the short time they had known each other. Meanwhile Angion and Cestator sat across the fire wondering what the women were up to.

William shook his head and went over and checked on Creashaw. The boy's condition continued to deteriorate. Whatever was keeping him alive was slowly losing the battle against the venom. He knew the wizard would be the boy's last chance. If the wizard could do nothing then Creashaw was as good as dead, and William had been preparing himself to do what was needed to release the boy from his agony. It was not something he wanted to do, but if it came down to it he was going to be sure Creashaw felt nothing.

When William approached the boy he could just barely hear his raspy breath. This worried William and he knelt down beside Creashaw and felt the side of his neck, to check for the boy's heartbeat. He found one, but it was weak and his skin felt hot to the touch.

Worriedly William approached Keriana and bent down close to her ear, and asked her to step with him. Keriana frowned, but did as William asked. When they were out of earshot William spoke in a subdued voice. "How long, until we reach the wizard's castle?"

Keriana looked at him quizzically "Two days at least, why?"

William frowned at the news. "Let us hope you are wrong about that, because I am not sure the boy will make it through even the night. He has a deadly fever and his breathing is weak."

William suddenly caught movement out of the corner of his eye, and when he turned to look Sheminal was standing there with tear filled eyes and shock on her face. He cursed himself for a fool, and began to apologize to her.

Sheminal cut him off with a glare. "Is there nothing you can do?" She asked with a hint of anger touching her voice.

William shook his head sadly. "I do not dare. Anything I do may make matters worse. This venom is unnatural there is no telling what it will do if I try my magic on it. I know the first time I tried it only made things worse. You saw what it did to those priests at the temple."

Sheminal closed her eyes and bowed her head, and whispered sad words that William could not make out. When she lifted her head however there was a fire behind her eyes. "Watch him closely. I will return shortly." She said determinedly.

"Where are you going Sheminal?" Keriana asked a touch of concern in her voice.

I am going to get some herbs. I saw what I need, a short distance back the way we came."

Keriana picked up her bow and strung it. "Alright, but I'll come with you. This pass is not the safest of places to wander around alone."

"Thank you Keriana," Sheminal said with a smile. She turned to William and her face became serious. "If he gets any worse do whatever you can to keep him alive until we return."

"I will Sheminal, no matter what the cost, your son will survive. I swear this upon my honor."

Sheminal smiled again at William's devotion. "Thank you, but let's hope that it does not come to that." She turned to Keriana. "Let's hurry." The two jogged back down the trail they had come.

Confused and slightly worried Angion walked over to William. "What is the trouble? First you take Keriana aside, then her and Sheminal run off into the darkness alone."

Creashaw has taken a turn for the worse, and Sheminal went out to find some herbs to try and help him."

Angion smiled knowingly. "If she finds what she needs he will be well."

"You have that much faith in her abilities?"

Angion nodded. "Sheminal is what your people call a healer, but she is also more than that. She can speak with the spirits, and at times they show her things. She was very determined when she left, Creashaw will be well."

Without another word Angion turned, and joined Cestator by the fire. William walked over to Creashaw to check his condition, but nothing had changed, so he sat down beside the boy pondering Angion's words. *This is an interesting group we have. I wonder what plans you have for us Cargon."* When he did not get an answer he shook his head chuckling. *"What am I thinking? I am a paladin it is my place to help others in need."*

A short time later Sheminal and Keriana returned. "Any change?" Sheminal asked hopefully.

William shook his head sadly. Sheminal nodded, and went right to work brewing the herbs into a tea.

Out beyond the light of the fire two ghostly figures watched the companions. Cargon smiled at William's words, and then turned to his companion. "William truly is a sharp one isn't he?"

The other figure nodded in agreement. "Yes, he is one of the best I have ever seen. He is nearly Cestator's match in the dance."

Cargon chuckled at this. "Yes and nearly your match in his devotion."

"Yes I think you may be right. You made a good choice in him."

Again Cargon chuckled, and his companion looked at him in confusion. "You did choose him did you not?"

"No I did not. William was a bit of a surprise even to me."

"So that would mean . . ."

"Yes my friend, there are greater forces at work here. There is no telling what will happen before this is over. Unfortunately we are little more than watchers. Yet there are some small favors that I can grant them."

Cargon then put a small blessing upon the herbal tea that Sheminal was preparing. When he finished he turned to his companion. "Come our work here is done." With that the two figures disappeared.

Sheminal walked over to her son with a small bowl full of hot tea. "Lift his head," she said to William.

William did as she asked and he could feel the heat coming off of Creashaw. *"By Cargon I hope this works,"* he thought to himself. "How quickly will this work?" He asked Sheminal with a little concern touching his voice.

Sheminal shook her head. "It should not take much time. Though I am not sure, this herb is rarely found on the plains so I have not used it, but once before."

"I see, well I pray to Cargon that you are right because if this fever does not break soon he may not survive the night."

Sheminal did not reply. Instead she opened Creashaw's mouth slightly and slowly poured some of the tea in, and he reflexively swallowed. Instantly his breathing became more regular, and William could feel his fever dissipating.

"Praise Cargon," William shouted. "His fever has broken. You truly are a miracle worker Sheminal. I will never question your herbs again." He laid Creashaw back down and stood. "Alright I will now leave you to tend to him. If you need anything you have only to ask."

Sheminal smiled wearily. "Thank you William, for all you have done."

"There is no need for thanks Sheminal. It is my duty to serve." A warm smile touched his face as he spoke. "Besides we are all friends here, and friends help one another in times of trouble." With that William left Sheminal alone before she could say anything.

A short time before dawn Keriana awoke to Heroth growling angrily. The horizon was aglow, and it looked like a mighty fire roared behind the mountains. "What's wrong Heroth?" She asked aloud.

It was Cestator who answered her question however. "There are orcs nearby."

At the mention of the creatures Angion and William were suddenly alert, and a fire burned behind Sheminal's eyes.

Keriana shook her head in disbelief. "That is not possible orcs dare not enter these mountains."

"Cestator is right Keriana." Heroth said cutting her off.

"From what I can tell there is a rather large group of them as well." Cestator said, in a cold and strangely calm voice. "And it would seem that they are following us."

"Can we outrun them?" Keriana asked.

Cestator picked up his sword in answer. "No and I would never try to."

Keriana frowned at this. "Put that thing away. There is no need to kill them."

"Try and stop me woman. Those orcs won't have second thought about killing all of us. They have picked up our trail, and you can be sure they are not going to stop until either they are dead or we are."

"Well I will have nothing to do with this slaughter." Keriana said angrily. She turned to William. "Surely as a paladin you agree with me, do you not?"

"Yes lady, I know what it is you are saying, and if it were that a paladin was all that I am I would agree. It however is more difficult for me than that however, for I am also a knight of the crown. As such I have sworn an oath to my king that I would defend this land from such creatures as that. So you see if I were to do nothing I would be breaking my word to my king."

Keriana sighed in frustration and turned to Angion, but he was closely inspecting the edge on his axe. "Men," she said under her breath, and turned to Sheminal. Much to her surprise however Sheminal was strapping her javelins to her back. "Sheminal surely you are not going to take part in this?"

"I am sorry Keriana. I have no love for them, and they are threatening my son. I will not allow that, and since you have set your mind to stay here I thought you could watch over Creashaw, so I might get some of this anger out."

Keriana shook her head sadly. You humans are always so quick to kill anything that you think may be a threat. You care nothing for the lives of the creatures around you. Well I am going to stand firm on this. I will have nothing to do with the murder of any creature even if it is an orc."

"Suit yourself." Cestator said coldly. "But you had better keep an arrow at the ready in case any escape."

Keriana frowned at Cestator's tone, and words. "Don't you worry about me; I can take care of myself. You had better just worry about your own neck."

"Ha . . . I am more than able to take on the entire group of them alone." Without waiting for a reply Cestator turned away and headed back down the trail they had come the day before, and the rest of the companions followed.

When Keriana saw Heroth joining them she frowned. *"Heroth if you go with them to be any part of that I will not speak to you again."*

"But Keriana . . ." He began to complain to her, but she blocked him out of her mind before he could finish. Heroth whined like a big baby, but he crawled back to Keriana's side with his head hanging low, and he laid down at her side. Keriana looked down at him and her frown darkened. She walked over to Creashaw's side and glared at Heroth.

The companions easily found the orc encampment. It was a short distance back the way they had come. Cestator looked out from a large boulder they used as cover, and the stench from the creatures hit him. His nose flared in disgust, but he noticed there was something more to the smell than just the orcs.

He looked across the camp and found the source of the smell. Over a fire turning on a spit was a man. It appeared as though they had just put him on a short time ago, which told Cestator that they were traveling by night. He knew then that they were indeed following the companions, but why they were following and why they had not attacked eluded him. Someone had to be directing the creatures, and this troubled him. He decided it did not matter however for soon they would be dead.

As he pondered this, Sheminal crept around to see. "What is that awful smell?" She asked, and when she saw what was roasting over the fire, she reeled backwards.

Cestator covered her mouth quickly before she could scream. He put a finger to his lips telling her to keep quiet. Sheminal nodded eyes wide with horror. When Cestator took his hand away she whispered to him. "Are they going to . . . ?"

"Yes that is intended to be their dinner." Cestator said before she could finish her question.

Overhearing the exchange William and Angion came over wondering what was happening. "They are roasting a man over the fire." Sheminal said in answer to their unasked question.

This infuriated William. "I had my qualms about killing them before, but no longer. Those monsters will pay for this outrage. Cargon guide my hand and make their punishment swift."

Angion nodded his agreement. "Yes they will pay for this. My axe has waited long to taste blood and they will know fear this day."

Cestator laughed inwardly, he could not understand their devotion. He himself was here for one reason and one reason alone, his pure hatred for the foul creatures. He looked at Sheminal and she still seemed to be in a state of shock. He nodded to her javelins. "Those are magic, are they not?"

Sheminal jumped as though awoken from a dream. "Yes . . . yes they belonged to my father."

"What can they do?"

Sheminal looked at him quizzically then said, "They return after being thrown."

"Good, then you should remain at a distance."

Sheminal's face darkened with anger. She was about to let him know what she thought about his idea when he raised his hand.

"Stay your words until I have finished. You said they were your father's, and I know you are a healer. So I assume you have not had much practice with them."

Sheminal shook her head. "When I was a girl, but it has been some time."

"I thought so. Orcs are not something for a novice to face up close. They are fierce fighters, and are stronger than most men. So if you stay at a distance, and take them down that way, you would do the most good."

"Yes Sheminal Cestator is right if you got into the middle of them you would quickly find yourself in trouble." Angion piped in for support.

Cestator nodded. "Yes and also if you could do it on the run they will become confused. You see they may be brutal fighters, but they are not very smart."

Sheminal did not want to agree with him, but she could clearly see the wisdom in his words. After a few moments she hesitantly agreed.

"Alright then, when this is over I will help you train with them."

"You know how to use javelins?" She asked in surprise of his statement. "That is strange they are not used by many."

"I have mastered most weapons. It is a bit of a hobby of mine. Now however is no time to discuss it."

Sheminal nodded though she wanted to know more. *"What kind of hobby is that? There is something strange about him that he is not telling anyone."* Sheminal put her thoughts aside as the men neared the orc camp. She waited until the men made their move then sent a volley of javelins into the orcs, quickly moved and continued to throw volleys into the camp.

Keriana sat by Creashaw very frustrated with the acts of men. What they were doing was against everything she believed in. Elves were well known to be the protectors of the forests, and all of its inhabitants, but she was more so than most.

She knew orcs were vile creatures, but to slaughter them only for the reason that they exists was horrifying to her. Sitting around and waiting was only frustrating her all the more. When she could take it no longer Keriana stood deciding she was going to do something to stop this. She looked at Heroth with her piercing eyes. He lifted his head expectantly. *"Wait here and watch over Creashaw. I am going to try and stop this massacre."*

Heroth whined sadly. *"But Keriana . . ."*

"No buts Heroth. Creashaw cannot defend himself, someone has to protect him and I cannot allow this to go on."

Heroth whined again, but he laid back down by Creashaw's side alert to everything around him. Satisfied that Heroth would not follow her, Keriana headed back down the trail. She easily found the orc camp, and was put out to find that she was already too late. The others had already attacked.

Keriana was horrified by the scene, but yet somewhat intrigued by each of their fighting styles. Angion like most barbarians used his size and brute strength to overpower his enemies. She could tell that William was a blade master, though she could see in his technique that he had trained at the temple of Cargon. Sheminal stayed outside the camp throwing her javelins with deadly accuracy, and she kept on the move seeming to confuse the orcs. Though with her sharp eyes Keriana could follow Sheminal's every step.

The one that amazed most however was Cestator. She had been skeptical when he had said he could take the entire group of orcs alone, but that skepticism vanished instantly. It seemed as though the man was born with a sword in his hand. He had a style like none she had ever seen. The man was death incarnate.

Suddenly Keriana noticed an orc was moving up behind Cestator and for some unknown reason he did not seem to notice this. "Turn around you fool." She cursed at him, though over the distance and the noise of battle raging around him she knew he could not hear her, and his back was turned towards her so he could see her. She looked for the others but they were far too busy to take notice, and Sheminal was in the wrong position.

By the time she turned back the orc was directly behind Cestator, axe raised above its head ready to split his skull. "Damn you for making me do this." She cursed at him as she notched an arrow. Keriana quickly took aim and released.

Cestator battled fiercely. Any orc that dared stand against him was quickly cut down. When he pulled his sword from the throat of one exceptionally strong orc, three of the creatures stepped in front of him cackling madly as though they shared some humorous joke. Two of the creatures carried crude spears while the third wielded a long sword.

The orc in the center was the first to attack with its long sword it swung crudely at Cestator, but he easily parried the blow. When he moved in to counter however the other two orcs jabbed at him with their spears. Cestator parried one while dodging the other. The third thinking it had him at a disadvantage moved in swinging at him.

Cestator however had anticipated the move, and he kicked the creature's knee out breaking it. The orc fell to the ground roaring in pain, and clutching its ruined knee. Seeing their tactic fail did not seem to deter the other two however. They instead attacked all the more fiercely, and Cestator had all that he could do just dodging and parrying the attacks. He quickly grew weary of the confrontation.

Then suddenly Cestator found an opportunity to end the fight. One of the creatures over extended its attack and slightly lost its balance. Cestator grabbed the shaft of the spear behind the head and pulled the orc towards him, and drove his sword deep into the creatures gut. Abandoning his sword for a moment he took the spear and threw it at the second orc piercing its throat. The orc fell to its knees trying to breath past the gurgling blood.

Cestator did not waste any time watching the creature fall. He pulled his sword from the first orc, and walked up to the third, which was still roaring in pain. Cestator gave the creature a mocking half smile then put it out of its misery.

Suddenly just as he pulled his sword out he heard the howl of another orc directly behind him. He cursed himself for a fool, and turned around just in time to realize it was too late. He tried to raise his sword in defense, but he knew it was futile.

Just as Cestator accepted his fate the head of an arrow appeared in the center of the orc's forehead directly between its eyes, and they went blank. When the arrow struck the axe paused for a moment, then resumed its fall, but without the same force behind it. That moment was all that Cestator needed to get his sword up and deflect the blow. The orc fell onto its face the shaft of the arrow still quivering from the impact.

Cestator looked up to see who had fired the arrow, and he was not surprised to see Keriana in the distance her bow still in hand. He nodded his thanks to her, and he was unsure, but he thought he saw her frown, and curse him. Cestator did not dwell on it however, he knew there were still more orcs to deal with, so he went back to what he knew best.

Keriana returned to their campsite feeling soiled and dirty. *"Why him?"* She thought to herself. *"Anyone else would have been fine. He is a blade master so how didn't he know?"*

Heroth seeing her anguish broke into her thoughts. *"What is wrong Keriana?"*

She looked at him with pain and anger in her eyes. *"I killed one of them."*

Heroth turned his head in curiosity. *"I thought you were against killing for no reason."*

Keriana nodded sadly. *"I am, but it would have killed him. This is why I have lived in the sanctuary of the temple to stay away from things like this."*

"Well it was for a good reason that you did it, so don't take it so hard."

Keriana glared at him. *"I would not have, had it not been Cestator."*

Heroth cringed at the thought. He himself was not bothered by the man, but he knew how much Keriana disliked him. *"Oh,"* was all he said in reply.

"Oh is right, you have no idea what it was like. I have despised all forms of violence since I was just a girl."

Their conversation was cut short when the others walked into the camp. The men were covered in blood, and they smelled horrible. Keriana waved her hand in front of her face trying to dispel the stench to no avail. She pointed to the left of the trail. "There is a shallow river that way. I would suggest the three of you go bathe, because I am not traveling anywhere with you smelling like that."

Angion and William chuckled and went where she directed. Cestator remained behind however. "Great now he is going to gloat." Keriana said under her breath.

Cestator walked up to her, but he had a somber look on his face not the half smile she expected. When he spoke his voice seemed sad and subdued. "I am sorry you had to do that. I know what it is like to do something against everything you believe in. I also know I am the last person you would ever want to do that for, so I will only say thank you." With that he followed after William and Angion.

Keriana stared after him in shock. When he was gone from sight she turned to Sheminal. "Did he just apologize?"

Sheminal smiled. "Yes I believe he did. You gave him a great gift, and he knew that. He in turn gave you the greatest gift he had to give. It would seem that fate has taken hold of you. Your spirits are tied together somehow. The two of you were destined to meet. I do not know what for, but you cannot deny it."

Keriana shook her head in disbelief. "I am Sheminal, but I cannot believe that. I would not be here, save for my compassion for you and your son. When this is over I have every intention of parting ways with him."

Sheminal smiled warmly. "It is best that you do not fight it. He himself has accepted it some time ago."

Keriana looked at her in shock. "What, how long ago could it be? We have only known each other for a short time."

"I do not know I cannot see it. It is somehow clouded to me, as though it were so far in the past, that it is lost in the distance. I do not understand how it could be, but it seems to have happened many years ago."

"Perhaps he had his future told to him by a seer when he was young."

Sheminal shook her head in confusion. "No, that is not possible this was more than one hundred years past."

Keriana was taken aback by this. "What, how is that possible. He cannot be much older than you. He certainly is no elf, you must be mistaken somehow."

"No Keriana, I do not understand how it could be, but the spirits make it clear. It has been that and more."

Heroth laid there lazily listening to their conversation. He laughed softly to himself, humans, elves, and even the dwarves always thought too much, and usually found the wrong answers. He knew Cestator's secret. He had known the moment he had caught his scent. Cestator had asked Heroth to trust him, and he told Heroth his story. His words were sincere so Heroth had given him a chance. From that point on Cestator had proven to be a trustworthy friend.

Heroth Yawned lazily, then suddenly his keen ears caught the sound of boots walking over gravel. *"The men approach,"* he warned Keriana.

Keriana thanked him then looked to Sheminal. "Heroth says the men are on their way back."

Well we should prepare to leave. There is still some day left we should not waste it."

Keriana nodded, and the two gathered all of their belongings and doused the fire. When they finished the men still had not arrived. *"I thought you said they were on their way."* Keriana said as she glared at Heroth.

Heroth Yawned again then he stood and stretched out his front legs. He walked over to Keriana's side then answered her. *"I did, but you did not ask how far they were from here."*

Keriana glared at him again, and was about to give him a few choice words when she suddenly heard Angion's deep voice.

Chapter 25

The Wizard

When the men arrived back at the camp and found their gear ready and waiting they were slightly surprised, but no one said anything. They just looked at the women in mute shock.

"Shall we go?" Sheminal said after a moment. Then Keriana and Sheminal started down the trail. Angion grabbed the cart holding Creashaw and followed. William grabbed his gear and followed the procession.

Cestator stood there a moment looking down the trail where the orcs had been. He was sure they had been following them, but the reason why he could not understand. He shrugged his shoulders deciding he would find the answer sooner or later.

Cestator lifted his pack and it seemed awkwardly heavy, and then it hit him. The tome was in his pack. He had nearly forgotten about the ancient book. At that moment he instantly knew why the orcs were following them. They were after the book, and the fact that they found him said that Valclon knew where he was and that he had it.

He quickly shouldered his pack and caught up with William. "I know why they were following." He said quietly.

"Why," William asked in surprise.

"They were after the tome."

William's eyes went wide and he stopped in his tracks. "That would mean . . ."

"Yes it means that he knows I have it, and he knows where we are."

By this time the others had stopped and looked back at the two. "Who knows where we are?" Angion asked. "And what is it that he searches for?"

Cestator sighed regrettably. "I have made a powerful enemy, and I carry something he is willing to do anything to get his hands on, and it does not matter who gets in his way. So for the safety of all of you when Creashaw has been healed we must part ways."

"No," Angion said strongly. "I fear no man, and you helped us without a second thought when we were in danger. It is only right that we help you in your time of trouble."

"Well Angion it is not that simple I am afraid." William piped in. He turned to Cestator and nodded. "Cestator I think it is time that you showed them."

Cestator frowned, and paused a moment considering the repercussions of showing them the book. He decided that they had trusted him not knowing anything of who he was so he would have to put the same faith in them. He placed his pack on the ground and took the book out.

"A book, is that what this man is after?" Angion scoffed.

Cestator shook his head. "This is no ordinary book my friend. This is the tome of Islangardious."

Angion looked confused by this, but Keriana's eyes opened wide and her lip turned up in a snarl. "How did you come in possession of that thing?" She asked fearfully.

Seeing Keriana's reaction only confused Angion more, and Sheminal was strangely silent. Angion turned to Keriana in his confusion. "You know of this book?"

"Yes there are tales among the elves of it. It is said to be a thing of evil."

Angion scoffed at the idea. I must see this thing for myself."

Cestator placed the book down on a nearby stone, due to his distaste for the thing. Angion walked over and was shocked by what he saw. The book was large, more so than any he had ever seen. It appeared to contain only a few pages then in the next moment it contained many hundreds of pages. The cover seemed to be made of leather, wood and steel all at the same time. It was black as the darkest night, and had gold runes upon it that shifted and changed constantly. Holding it closed were two silver clasps formed in the shape of claws from some strange beast, and the tips seemed to be embedded into the cover.

"Magic, the blasted thing is cursed." Angion said angrily. "I'll rid you of the damned thing." Without another thought Angion pulled his axe from its harness, and despite the others' protests he swung it at the book. Inches from the cover the axe struck an invisible barrier showering Angion with sparks, and knocked him back to the ground.

"I tried to warn you." Cestator said as he helped Angion up. "The book protects itself from attacks."

Angion shook his head clearing it. "I do not understand what happened. When I saw that book the rage overtook me and I could not stop . . ." Angion cut his words short and opened his eyes wide in shock.

Confused slightly Cestator turned around to see what Angion was looking at, and to his surprise the metal clasps on the book had released and the book sat open. A strong breeze picked up blowing across the pass, blowing dust and sand around, but the pages of the book did not move.

Cestator walked over to the book, and his eyes opened wide with shock when he saw the words on the page. He read them aloud so all could hear.

"So it shall begin. The War of Ages will be more than any have ever witnessed. Eleven companions shall gather to face the fiercest evil the world has ever known. Before that however they will face their own differences which may tear them apart, but the fate of all depends on their survival. So beware ye who read this the end is near, for the evil that is unleashed is more deadly than any army, or even any plague, and there will be no stopping it. Know this, the only chance lies with the companions, but even they will find enemies among themselves. Know this unless they resolve their differences the world is doomed."

The moment Cestator finished reading the final word a bright flash of light came from the book and blinded them all. When their vision cleared the book was closed and sealed, and looking around they found themselves in a completely different place. Everything was different around them, but they all focused on one thing. Up at the end of one road was a massive castle. The horrific thing looked like a claw reaching up to the sky and they all stared in awe of it.

After a few moments however Heroth's voice broke into Keriana's thoughts. *"Keriana, Creashaw is gone."*

Keriana turned, and looked in the cart where Creashaw had laid and found that indeed he was gone. Sheminal noticing Keriana's concern looked as well, and ran to the cart screaming. "Where is Creashaw, where is my son."

The others turned to see what was happening, and they gasped in shock when they saw that Creashaw was indeed gone. Angion drew his axe and scanned the area for any tracks. "This is some kind of evil magic I tell you."

Suddenly the companions were torn from their shock by a deep gravelly voice that sounded much like two stones being rubbed together. "Follow, the master awaits your arrival."

Everyone turned around quickly to see what had spoken and they found a large creature made completely out of stone. Without a second thought Angion began to swing his mighty axe at the stone creature.

"Angion stop," Cestator called out. "That is a stone golem. Your axe will have no effect on it."

Angion stopped his swing short and glared at the golem. "Where is Creashaw," he asked the creature angrily.

"Yes where is my son?" Sheminal screamed as she pounded on the creature's chest.

Seeming to not notice Sheminal the golem looked at Angion. "The boy is with the master. Follow, the master awaits your arrival." Then without another word the golem turned and headed for the castle.

The companions looked to one another unsure what had happened, but they knew they had no choice but to follow. So abandoning the cart they followed the golem to the castle.

When they reached the massive doors to the castle everyone stared in shock at the sheer size of the castle. It put the palace in Cerdrine to shame making it seem to be a hut. Cestator instantly recognized the runes upon the doors, they were much like those upon his father's chambers, and he knew this place was more than it seemed to be.

The golem opened the doors to a massive entry room that seemed too large even for what they had seen outside. There were doors around the room and at the back a large staircase leading up into the darkness above.

When the doors closed behind them they heard a loud yet raspy voice echo through the room. "Welcome friends I hope that Gareth did not frighten you. Please make yourselves at home I have laid out a grand meal for you. Gareth will show you the way to my dining room."

Sheminal shook her head angrily, and looked around for the source of the voice but could not find one. "Who are you and where is my son? What have you done with him?"

"Ah so you are the boy's mother. Come follow the light I have questions to ask you."

Suddenly a small ball of light appeared before Sheminal, and it floated towards the back of the room to the stairs. Slightly unsure yet unwilling to abandon her son, Sheminal did as the voice directed and followed the light. Angion tried to follow, but after two steps he hit what seemed to be an invisible wall. He cursed under his breath and pounded on the wall with his fists to no avail. Then he took a few steps back and charged at it slamming his shoulder into it. A shockwave reverberated through the room and threw Angion back.

"I would not try that again Barbarian. The wall pushes back double the force that you put against it. Fear not I shall not harm her."

"Let me through wizard or I will . . ."

"You will do nothing, barbarian. I told you no harm will come to any here, now go follow Gareth and we will join you when we can."

This infuriated Angion, and he went into a rage and grabbed his axe, and was about to attack the wall. Seeing this Sheminal walked up to him and gently touched his cheek and smiled. Instantly the rage left him and he calmed down.

"Go with the others Angion. I will be fine." She said with a sparkle in her eyes.

Angion melted into her touch and sighed at her beauty. "I was only . . ."

"I know Angion, it is alright. I can take care of myself. Now go eat, I will join you as soon as I can."

Angion nodded to her, but when she turned to follow the light he shouted up the stair case. "If you harm one hair upon her wizard I will . . ."

The wizard either did not hear or did not care, because no response came. Frustrated Angion turned back to the others. The stone golem seeing everyone together said in its gravelly voice. "Follow," then headed for a pair of doors on the right.

Sheminal followed the ball of light for what seemed like forever until it came to a strange door struck it and disappeared. She was about to knock when the door opened and a raspy voice invited her in.

Sheminal cautiously entered. What she saw inside amazed her, again the room looked too large to exist in the towers they had seen from the outside. It was lined with shelves, and tables all containing books potions and any number of exotic items. Many she could not even name. There was a strange smell to the place like many different herbs mixed together, yet it was not unpleasant.

Sheminal found the wizard at the back of the room standing over Creashaw chanting and waving his hands. He was a tall man nearly as tall as Angion, and he wore a long grey cloak that covered him completely. She slowly and quietly approached, not wanting to disturb him out of fear that she may ruin the spell and do more harm.

When he finished the wizard turned towards Sheminal. The large hood of his cloak shadowed his face, and all she could see were two green glowing eyes. Sheminal stepped back in shock forgetting herself.

This seemed to amuse the wizard, because from within the hood came a soft chuckle. "I am sorry my child I have not had guests here in much time. I forget how people react at the sight of my eyes, but I assure you I will not harm you."

Sheminal shook her head. "No, I am sorry, I just did not expect . . . Please could you remove the hood however, I find it hard to speak to you like this. That is if you do not mind."

"I can, but I must warn you my child, I was once a man, but I am now far from it. You may find me disturbing."

"It can be no more unsettling than seeing only your eyes." Sheminal said apprehensively.

The wizard nodded and pulled back his hood. Sheminal was shocked by what she saw, but she controlled herself. The man's face was like that of a reptile, and his hands she saw had long claws.

"I am Gonslen. "What might your name be my child, and how did your son come to be in this state?"

"I am Sheminal. My son and Angion, the large brute with me, were attacked by a creature called a belath."

"Sheminal, are you of the plains people?"

"Yes why how did you know?"

A smile touched Gonslen's lips. "Yes I thought you looked familiar. You are just as lovely as your mother was, if not more. My child, please tell me how does your family, and the rest of your people fare."

Sheminal frowned darkly. "First, stop calling me child. Secondly you did not answer my question, how do you know all of this."

"I am sorry Sheminal. I know because I lived among your people for many years before this was done to me. I knew your mother and father well. They were dear friends to me. Now please tell me how do they fare?"

A tear fell from Sheminal's eye as she sadly said, "They are dead."

Sadness seemed to touch Gonslen's face. "I am sorry, they will be missed, and what of the rest of your people."

This time a roaring fire touched Sheminal's eyes. "Dead, all of them killed by the monster that did that to my son, we three are the last."

This time it was Gonslen's turn to be shocked. "What, this cannot be. I had many questions to ask you, but this only adds to them."

"Wait before you start. Tell me, how is my son?"

"Yes of course I am sorry. Your son will live, though I was not able to remove all of the venom in his body. I do not know what this will do, but he will certainly live. This in turn, leads me to my first question. What happened to him and how did he survive?"

Sheminal shook her head. "If you wish to ask questions like that it would be best if you ask them of Angion."

"I see well never the less your son is somewhat of a surprise to me. You see the creature that bit him never leaves anyone alive. The venom itself takes no more than moments to kill, and what your son had in him was mutated somehow."

Sheminal gave Gonslen a puzzled look, not quite understanding his words. He saw this and smiled. "Pardon me again, I forget myself. The creature that bit your son was unlike any other of its kind. The venom had changed somehow. So yes I would like to speak with Angion."

"What of Creashaw?" Sheminal asked with a touch of concern in her voice.

"He needs to rest for a time. I will have Gareth take him to a room, now come we must join your friends before they begin to worry for you. Come take hold of my robe and I can take us to them instantly."

Sheminal looked at Creashaw, reluctant to leave him behind. For some reason however she trusted Gonslen even despite his appearance. She sighed and decided that she was famished after all and Angion was likely quite worried, so she did as he said. He spoke a few words that she could not understand, and the room melted away before her eyes.

When the companions stepped through the doors to the dining hall they found a long table with many chairs, and a feast fit for a king upon it. Angion's eyes opened wide in shock. "By the great spirits, I have never seen such a feast."

"We have quite the gracious host it would seem." William said in response.

"Yes, but why would he be so to a group of strangers. There is something amiss here."

Keriana frowned at Cestator. "Do you always think that everyone has some hidden agenda?"

"It is the only thing that has kept me alive." Cestator said coldly.

William stepped between the two and glared at both. "Come now, let us forget our differences for a time and enjoy the graciousness of our host. Look, there is even food for Heroth, and he has no qualms about it."

Keriana smiled nodded to William and walked over to the table, and joined Angion who was already enjoying himself. Cestator looked back at the doors behind him then back to William. "I do not like this."

"Oh come now Cestator why would this wizard bring us here then help Creashaw if he wanted to do us any harm?"

Cestator shook his head. "That's not it, the wizard is no threat. What I do not like is how we got here in the first place. The tome brought us here, for what reason I do not know, but you can be sure there is a reason."

"Well then we should pray to Cargon that it is a good one. For now though, let us enjoy the hospitality. You know as well as I that we will not find it often on our travels."

Cestator nodded and the two joined the others at the table. At first no one spoke, but when the mood settled down and everyone was relaxed conversation began.

Angion was the first to break the silence. "Tell me has any of you noticed, that this place could not exist? Why the inside is even larger than the outside. This is some kind of evil magic I tell you."

Cestator chuckled. "It is no magic my friend. You see there are many different planes of existence. This castle must sit in more than one somehow. I myself have been to a few some are very strange while others are much like ours here. The spirits you speak of they exist upon another plane themselves."

Cestator was cut short when suddenly Sheminal and what looked to be a lizard man dressed in a cloak appeared in the room. Angion and William jumped to their feet in shock while Keriana merely watched in amusement. Heroth barely twitched an ear towards the new arrivals, and Cestator only nodded.

"Your friend there is correct barbarian. This place is on a nexus of planes. I hope that you are enjoying yourself."

"By the great spirits wizard, do not do such as that before me again. Else you may find my axe splitting your skull."

"Come now my barbarian friend. I have kept my word to you, Sheminal here is unharmed and the boy is well. Now please sit and eat."

Angion frowned. "I am Angion, and you would be wise to call me by that wizard."

"Yes very well then, and I am Gonslen, and who might be your companions Angion."

Angion pointed to each of his companions and named them off. When he got to Cestator Gonslen's eyes stared for a moment longer as though he saw something. No one but Cestator noticed this, and he frowned at the extra attention.

When Angion finished Gonslen nodded and smiled. "Welcome all to my home. I hope that you are all comfortable. If you do not mind I would ask a few questions about how you came to be here."

Cestator's frown darkened, but William was the first to speak. "We will answer any of your questions as best we can."

"Thank you, William. First of all I would like to know what happened to the boy, Creashaw was it."

"He was bitten by a young belath. I do not know what you call them, but that is what our people call them." Angion answered.

Gonslen nodded. "Hmm . . . Bringer of death, a most appropriate name for them Angion, but did you say that this was from a young one."

"Yes there was a large male, like no other I have ever seen before, a female and a young one. Cestator here killed the female and the young one, but the male escaped."

"If what you say is true it does not bode well for any. You see the large male was unlike any other you have ever seen because it is almost entirely a different creature. You are lucky to be alive the one you faced is not only the bringer of death it is much like death itself."

"What kind of nonsense are you speaking of wizard?" Cestator said coldly.

"Let me show you my dark friend."

Suddenly almost out of nowhere a belath climbed up upon the table only it was no more than the size of a large cat. The companions jumped to their feet drawing their weapons, and Heroth growled deeply.

"Come now relax all of you he will do you no harm." When everyone replaced their weapons and settled back down Gonslen continued. "You see this is what the creatures are like in their natural state. They grow no bigger than this in their world and they eat mostly rodents. Yet their bite can still be deadly."

"Why not keep a cat then, instead of that foul looking thing?" Sheminal asked with much distaste.

Gonslen smiled at the question. "Because my dear these creatures are very loyal to their families, and there are rodents in this place that would kill even the largest of cats."

"So what caused the creatures to grow so large then?" William asked slightly intrigued.

"Ah . . . that would be the previous master of this castle and the one who did this to me." Gonslen then looked to Angion, and when he spoke again there was a hint of fear and remorse in his voice. "If that creature is breading, that will mean the end for us all."

"What do you mean by that?" Keriana ask perplexed.

"Let me explain. I am sure all of you have heard the tale of when Slanoth and Randor stormed this castle killed the two monstrous creatures and killed the evil wizard." When everyone nodded Gonslen went on. "Well what the tales do not tell is that moments before they killed the wizard he cast a spell upon one of the hatchlings and something entered it. Something of great evil, and the spell was left unfinished so you see that creature is able to absorb the strengths and abilities of anything it kills, or any spells cast against it."

Cestator stood up quickly and a fire burned behind his eyes. "So are you saying this thing cannot be stopped?"

"Unfortunately yes, and if it is beginning to breed then the world is in grave danger."

Angion laughed at this. "I think not wizard, Cestator here killed both the female and the young one himself."

Gonslen's eyes opened wide with surprise. "Well now your whole group is full of surprises aren't you? I could count the number of men known to kill even one of these things, on one of my hands but two that is a feat of unimaginable skill."

Cestator glared darkly. This wizard knew something and Cestator was determined to learn what his game was. "I am a blade master just as Slanoth was, so what is it you are getting to Wizard."

"Ah yes a blade master, of course. Well if you wish me to be blunt, very well I have nothing to hide."

Get on with it wizard. You knew well the moment we arrived, William and myself are blade masters."

"Yes true and that intrigues me as well. Never in recorded history has there ever been more than one blade master, unless of course you count the unholy one's son."

"You are stalling again Wizard." Cestator said with venom in his voice.

Gonslen smiled and nodded to Cestator's pack. "You have it with you don't you? The Tome of Islangardious, after all these years it has returned home."

This was not what Cestator had expected, and it showed in the shocked expression on his face. "How did you know about that, and what do you mean it has returned home?"

Gonslen smiled and motioned for Cestator to sit. "Sit down and I will tell you." Cestator reluctantly sat down, and Gonslen looked at each of the companions, and made sure all were listening.

"The word Islangardious is from an ancient tongue no longer even remembered by the long lived dwarves. It means ages. You hold The Book of Ages. It was created here in this castle before the cataclysm, and like this castle it is one of the few remaining artifacts of that age."

"What are you talking about? What cataclysm?" Keriana asked slightly disturbed.

"Ah yes of course you do not know. You see before the second sun appeared in the sky and before the dwarves came about there was another race. They ruled this world and did many amazing things that we could only dream about, but their overconfidence and their greed was their downfall. There was a great war between two groups of them and they destroyed one another and threw the world into darkness. Nothing remained of their greatness save for a few artifacts."

"How do you know all of this?" William asked, unsure if he believed even half of what Gonslen had said.

"Ah my dear young paladin if you remember the tome was made here. The previous master of this castle possessed it for some time. It showed him all of its secrets, and drove him mad in the end. I looked upon its pages once myself, and what it showed me I will never forget. Nor do I wish to look in it again. That book contains magic's within it that no one should use, the kind of magic that caused the cataclysm all those ages ago."

"So it is evil." Angion said suspiciously.

Gonslen smiled at the comment. "The book in itself is not evil. It is more a matter of who uses the information held within, and how they chose to use it. Though what it showed Marlock drove him mad, it can do no real harm alone. Like many of the artifacts from that age however it does in a sense have a will of its own, but it is not evil."

"Wait, do you mean to tell me that that book has a mind of its own?" William asked skeptically.

"In a way yes it does."

"Think about it William it makes sense." Cestator piped in. "The damned thing only shows what it wants, and for some reason it brought us here."

"Blast me you may have something there Cestator." Angion said as he moved away from the pack between them.

"Yes Well I am truly sorry to all of you, I do hate to be an ungracious host, but healing the boy has drained me. I must get some rest for the eve. The boy will not be ready to travel until tomorrow so I have had rooms prepared for you all, and there are tubs in each so you may take a hot bath if you would like. Gareth will show you to your rooms when you are ready. I will see all of you on the morn so until then I bid you good night." With that Gonslen disappeared.

The companions remained in the dining hall for a time. They talked about the day's events, and what they had learned. For the first time since the journey began however they did not speak about Creashaw, or about their differences. When the hours began to wane on, they called for Gareth and he showed them to their rooms.

Chapter 26

Mother

Keriana was awoken from a deep sleep by a strange voice calling her. She lit the oil lamp beside her bed and looked down at Heroth, but he was sound asleep and she heard it again. *"Keriana come my child. Follow my voice. I have waited long for your arrival."*

Confused and unsure of what was happening or who was speaking to her, she got out of bed. She let out a small squeak when her bare feet touched the cold stone floor. She slipped her leather boots on and crept across the room and slipped out quietly.

"Come Keriana follow my voice." She heard again when she was out of the room.

Keriana could not figure out why but for some reason the voice seemed familiar like something out of a forgotten dream. Curious about who could have been waiting for her, she followed as the voice beckoned. She found herself traveling downward to the very bottom of the castle until she got to a strange door with a carving of a mighty dragon upon it.

Keriana pushed the door open, and found she was no longer within the castle. She was in an enormous cavern, and the light of her lantern she carried did little to illuminate the darkness around her. She could not see the opposite wall, or the bottom of the cavern. All that she could see was the small ledge she stood upon that seemed to lead down into the darkness below.

The air within the cavern was still, and it had the smell of something living within it. Somewhere in the distance she could hear the sound of a small spring trickling down the wall. Looking back behind her she could not find the door she had come through as though it had never been there. She became slightly alarmed at this, but she remembered what Gonslen had said about the castle and figured it for one of the tricks.

Deciding there was no other way to go Keriana began to follow the trail downwards, hoping it would lead to an exit, and not into trouble. As she moved down the trail she accidentally kicked a stone over the edge. Out of curiosity she listened for it to strike the bottom. After what seemed like an eternity she heard the faint echo of it striking the stone floor of the cavern.

Keriana swallowed hard and moved in a little closer to the wall now more fearful of falling. Just as she began to move again she heard a strange sound coming from below her. The sound was like that of claws from a very large creature scraping on stone. She swallowed again trying to disperse the knot that had built up there from her fear. She looked back up the way she came, and for a moment thought of going back to try finding the door again. She quickly dismissed that idea however, for lack of faith it would be there.

Suddenly she heard the sound of large wings beating the air, and she knew that turning back would certainly do no good. Whatever was below her knew she was there and it was coming up to her. She froze there against the wall waiting for the inevitable.

Moments later she heard the wings beat past her somewhere on the other side of the cavern. The wind thrown off from them pushed her back against the wall. For a fleeting moment she had thoughts of fleeing down the trail in hopes that she could escape before the creature returned, but she could hear it slow its wings and begin its decent likely looking for her.

When the creature came into view she stared in shock. It was a massive dragon with a wingspan of at least one hundred feet across. The dragon was a dark green and its scales shimmered in the light of her lantern. It was the most majestic and beautiful creature she had ever seen. Its four legs were tucked up against its body and each had five long claws. It had a long neck and its head was elongated and had two horns at the top. The creature's large mouth was filled with razor sharp teeth, and they were the length of a short sword.

When the dragon got to eye level with Keriana it stopped and stared at her beating its wings slowly to stay in place. After a few moments the dragon seemed to smile at her. Then in the same voice that had compelled her to come here it spoke. "Hello Keriana, I am Kallinserinthia, or as most call me, Mother. I knew you would come. I have waited many years for your arrival. Now come, climb onto my back the time is near."

Keriana stared at the majestic creature dumbfounded. She did not know what to think of what she had heard. She had heard tales of dragons, and knew they were highly intelligent creatures, but this one seemed to know who she was. "How . . . how," was all she managed to say.

Mother smiled at her, understanding her confusion. "Come please the time is near. I will explain all soon, but for now you must trust me."

Keriana not wanting to upset the massive creature did as she was bid, and climbed down the dragon's long neck. She found a small space just big enough for her to sit between the dragon's back spikes at the base of the neck. When Keriana was settled in, Mother began to descend in a slow spiral. Keriana marveled at the creature's grace of motion.

When they reached the bottom of the cavern the dragon landed gently then crouched down as far as she could so Keriana could slide off. Back with her feet on the ground Keriana looked around at her surroundings and was slightly surprised. There was a strange luminescence that filled the entire cavern, which seemed completely empty of anything.

Mother looked at Keriana and noticed her surprise. "What troubles you child?"

Keriana jumped slightly at the unexpected question. "I had heard that dragon's horde gold and artifacts, yet I see none."

Mother chuckled warmly. Strange as it may have seemed to her, Keriana was somehow comforted by this. "Dear child I have no use for such items, but I do have a treasure one far more precious than gold or jewels, and I have awaited your arrival for many years now."

"Wait, stop please." Keriana said in frustration. "You keep saying you have been expecting me, but how do you know who I am and how did you know I was coming?"

"Because you are the chosen one of course," Mother said matter-of-factly. "You are the last of your people so you are the only one who can take the responsibility. She is the first in five thousand years and without you she will be lost."

"What are you talking about? Yes the rest of my people were killed by a monster many years ago, but what has that got to do with anything now?"

"It has everything to do with her," Mother said as she moved aside to reveal what she had been concealing.

Keriana stared in shock. In a small depression she saw a single egg. It was the color of the purest emerald and it glimmered in the pale light. The surface was perfectly smooth and had no blemishes that she could see. "Is that . . . ?"

"A dragon egg, yes. It is the first in many years." A strange yet beautiful voice said from behind Keriana. The voice sounded almost like bells ringing.

Keriana turned quickly to see who was speaking. What she saw shocked her more than anything thus far. An elven woman of immeasurable beauty approached. She was dressed all in white with a long flowing gown. A soft glow of power surrounded her making it undeniable that she was a goddess. This however was not what had Keriana dumbfounded. What shocked her most was that not only was the goddess an elf, but she was of Keriana's people.

At the sound of the voice Mother looked back, and her face lit up. "Sepra, oh it has been a long time. I had so hoped you would come to witness this moment."

Sepra laughed softly. Kallinsernthia You should know well enough that I would not miss this moment for anything. She is the first in how many years has it been now?"

"Five thousand now and we are dwindling away one by one." Mother said sadly.

"Has it truly been so long? My how does the time pass so quickly?"

Now over her initial shock and slightly annoyed that she was being ignored, Keriana spoke up. "Will someone please tell me what is happening here? I know that this somehow involves me, but I cannot get an answer as to why I am here."

Mother looked down at Keriana, her smile undiminished. "As I said my dear you are the chosen one. As it has been in ages past one of your people must care for the hatchling."

"Wait just a moment. Are you trying to tell me that you want me to take care of a baby dragon?"

Sepra sighed softly. "Yes my dear our people have done so for millennia. Unfortunately you are the last so you have no guidance, but most should come to you naturally. I have tried to contact you at times in the past, but you refused to hear me."

Keriana shook her head vigorously and backed away. "I am sorry, I am truly honored but I cannot take care of a baby dragon. I would not know the first thing about how to care for it. Is there no other who can do it? Mother it is your hatchling can you not raise it?"

For the first time Mother's smile was replaced with a look of sadness, and it tore at Keriana's heart. "With all that I am I wish it were that I could. Unfortunately my time here is running short by a dragon's standards. I have grown far too old to care for and protect her properly. You see she will be the first female born in over five thousand years, and she is the last hope for my kind. You may of course refuse to the responsibility. No one here can force you to do anything against your will. All that we can do is ask, if you are willing to do this for me, for her, and for all of dragon kind."

"And if I refuse, then what will happen?"

"The egg will not hatch. She will await another which will likely never come considering you are the last. Then slowly the dragons will disappear.

Keriana shook her head angrily. "How is that giving me a choice? I could not possibly let the dragons die off. I could not have such a thing weighing upon me."

"No Keriana, as mother said it truly is your choice. It is only your own convictions that will not allow you to walk away. For perhaps the chance may be slim, but one day you may have a daughter and she could have the gift, and she will then be offered the same choice you have now, and with your guidance she may choose to accept the responsibility. Dragons live for many thousands of years it will be long before they disappear. If you chose not to accept then Mother will remain here to guard the egg, but eventually as all things do she will die and the egg will await the coming of the one."

"My convictions or no, you give me little choice. So if I choose to accept then what am I to do? As I have said, I know nothing of raising a dragon. You said Dragons live for many thousands of years, and she is the first in five. Where is the last born before her, or any other of the females?"

"I am the one before her, and sadly I am the last. I am too old to bear any more eggs. These mountains are where dragons spend our final years." Mother paused a moment seeming to reflect upon something, but when she spoke again her smile had returned. "Should you decide to accept there is help. Take her to The Dragon Spire Mountains. There are many who live there that would be overjoyed to see her. They will be more than willing to help you."

"The Dragon Spire Mountains, they are nearly three thousand leagues from here. It would take months to get there even if there were roads going there. Not only that the way there is treacherous. How will we ever make it there?"

Mother looked up towards the open space above them and after a moment of staring she nodded and looked back at Keriana. "You came with a group of companions. Their travels lead them there. They will be a fine escort for the two of you, but I must give you a warning. Beware the dark one he will betray you in the end."

Keriana shook her head vigorously. "No way, I will not travel a single league with that man. He is insufferable, and he will not listen to reason. If I were to travel any further with him I might kill him."

Sepra sighed sadly. "So do you refuse or do you accept? The choice is still yours, but let me say something. If you chose to take her into your care there could be no safer place for the two of you than with them. Two are blade masters and are sworn to Cargon to protect the likes of her, even if it means their own lives. You may dislike Cestator, but child he is meant for great things as your friend has foreseen. Change follows him and even I cannot see what may happen around him, but he has been chosen."

"No, you misunderstand. I do not dislike that man, I despise him even the mention of his name sends a cold shiver up my spine. He is a horrible man. I would rather travel with a pack of serpents than with him."

"Then alas, I fear that we must await the next." Mother said sadly, as she turned away.

Keriana's heart sank at the sound of Mother's voice, it seemed almost as though she had lost all hope, and was giving up the will to live. Even the spikes on her back did not seem to stand so straight and proudly as they had before. The mighty and majestic creature seemed to be slinking away in sorrow. Mother was just about to vanish into the shadows of the next chamber when Keriana had finally had enough. "Alright stop this, both of you. If you are trying to manipulate me it will not work."

Mother looked back at Keriana now somehow looking even more hurt, but this time Keriana ignored it. Pointing at mother she said, "I will not do this for you." She turned to Sepra who had been phasing out when Keriana shouted, but was now watching intently. "And I certainly will not do it for you." Keriana paused a moment to be sure she had both of their attentions. "I will only suffer that man and his rudeness for her." She said as she pointed at the egg. "So then now that it has been decided, I still have questions for you."

Mother instantly regained all of her majesty, and power as she turned back. "Yes of course child, ask as many as you like."

"Well then first we have been speaking of her, but still I do not know her name."

"That my child is for you to decide. It is your privilege as the chosen to name her."

"Yes," Sepra said softly. "It is the greatest honor to hold for one in your position. Think carefully about what it shall be for it should mean something to all concerned."

This took Keriana slightly by surprise. Taking care of the little one was one thing, but to name her, that was something entirely different. She knew that it would have to be something prestigious, but what she could not decide. She sat down on a large stone and thought it over for some time. It was not until she remembered what mother had said. That this hatchling was the first female in five thousand years, and that she was the last hope for her kind, that it came to her.

When Keriana finally stood, Mother and Sepra who had been watching and waiting patiently, smiled in excitement to hear the name. Keriana smiled and nodded to them. "I have decided on a name for her. I will call her Mieyatomia. It has always meant so much to me since that fate full so long ago. I have always waited for the time to come for something so great that it made me believe again."

Sepra nodded in agreement. "Yes that suits her perfectly. She is the miracle of tomorrow for all dragon kind."

"Yes Keriana that is a fine name for her. You have made me so very happy that you are willing to care for her. I knew that without your people there to teach you. You would find this overwhelming, but you have proven to be quite a savior. Thank you. Now go and touch her egg and she will emerge for you."

Keriana could feel, and hear the joy and relief in Mother's voice as she spoke, and she could not help but to cry. When mother was finished Keriana walked over to her and wrapped her arms around her neck as far as she could reach and hugged her tight. "I am the one to thank you Mother for this honor. I will care for her as though she were my own."

Mother did not say a word, but a tear ran down her nose. After a moment Keriana collected herself and walked over to the egg and touched it. Instantly a small hairline fracture appeared on the surface. It spread quickly, and a small squeaking sound came from within the egg. Then a small nose poked through the shell, and following it came out the rest of the small creature. She was pure green much like her egg. Her scales sparkled brightly, and she looked much like Mother only smaller in size.

The little one looked around, and turned to Keriana then cocked her head to the side. She seemed to know who Keriana was for she walked up and rubbed her snout on Keriana's leg. Keriana reached down and pat her on the head, and suddenly a rush of thoughts filled her mind. The two were instantly connected much like the connection she shared with Heroth only deeper.

Mieyatomia looked at Mother and screeched calling out to her. She ran over to Mother, and the two caressed each other lovingly. A tear ran down Mother's cheek as she pulled away. Mieyatomia screeched even louder, this time however there was not joy in her voice, there was only anguish.

Keriana's heart sank at the sound. It was as though someone was tearing something away from her. She could feel Mieyatomia's pain. She seemed to know that Mother was leaving.

Mother roared in anguish at the sound of her hatchling's pain. She hated to leave, but there was nothing to be done. It tore her up inside to see her child in pain. She dearly wanted to comfort her, but she knew if she did there would be no way that she could perform her duty. She looked down at Keriana with tears filling her eyes. "Please keep her safe and care for her as I would."

Keriana could not hold back the tears at this point. "I will, I promise." She said through her tears.

Mother nodded in thanks and spread her wings. "There is a portal to your left that will take you directly to your room. I wish that I could stay for a time, but unfortunately matters are pressing and the longer I delay the more damage is done." With that, mother launched herself high into the air and quickly flew out of sight.

Mieyatomia screeched again and tried to fly after her, but she was too young and her wings could not carry her yet. She screeched in frustration and ran over to Keriana and wrapped herself around her legs, crying out to Mother.

Keriana knelt down and tried to comfort the young dragon, but she could not quiet her. It pained Keriana dearly, for she could still remember how she had lost her family, and how it felt. When Mother vanished from sight Mieyatomia continued screeching for a few moments, but it slowly faded and died.

Keriana picked the little one up into her arms and kissed her forehead. "Shh . . . little one, everything will be fine. I am going to take care of you now, and we are going to find more of your kind so you will not be lonely."

Keriana's words calmed Mieyatomia down a bit more and she curled up in Keriana's arms. Then a voice came from behind Keriana that startled her slightly and she looked up.

"I am sorry to cut this so short there are many things I would love to talk with you about. Unfortunately however there is a very pressing matter that I must return to."

Having almost forgotten that Sepra was still there Keriana turned quickly, slightly surprised. "Yes well I have a great many questions for you, so for that reason I hope this will not be the last time I see you."

Sepra nodded smiling. "Yes I am sure you do. I cannot promise anything, but I will try to find enough time to answer all your questions at some point. For now however I must go." Sepra looked at Mieyatomia and her smile grew. "As for you little one I will send you with my blessing and reassure you that you are in good hands." Sepra kissed Mieyatomia on the forehead and stepped back, and she disappeared.

Keriana looked down in surprise at what she saw. In the center of her head where Sepra had kissed her Mieyatomia had a silver starburst. The bottom and longest point reached down to the tip of her nose. The mark glimmered brightly and seemed to accent her beauty.

Mieyatomia not noticing anything shook her head yawned, and curled up in Keriana's arms and fell fast asleep. Keriana chuckled at the irony of everything and she stood there a moment just staring at the little creature sleeping in her arms. After a few moments she collected her thoughts and stepped through the portal, and found herself back in her room, Heroth was still fast asleep. She made up a little bed for Mieyatomia then climbed under the covers herself.

Chapter 27
A Challenge Answered

Skreal awoke from his long nap, and he stretched tiredly. Looking around he saw the destruction that had occurred in his battle with the wizards and he admired it. Once again he roared out his challenge to any that dared to try and stop him. Much to his surprise this time he received an answer, a loud roar somewhere in the distance. He smiled wickedly overjoyed by his good fortune. He settled in to wait for his challenger.

A short time later Skreal heard a loud roar above him. He looked up just in time to jump out of the way as a large turret of searing flames struck the ground where he had been resting. He laughed in excitement, when he saw a green dragon pass overhead. "Ah at last, a worthy opponent, prepare to die Dragon."

"It is you who will not see the light of another day monster." Mother said with distaste. "You and your kind should have never been created." As she spoke mother called down a massive bolt of lightning that struck Skreal in the center of his back. Much to her surprise however it had no effect.

Skreal shook off the effects of the lightning quickly knowing he had little time, and he had to get the dragon on the ground. Quickly he shot a spray of venom at the dragon in hopes he would damage its wings.

Mother was caught by surprise by the attack. She had battled many of these creatures before and the lightning usually did much of the work for her. In most cases she only needed to burn the corpse to be sure that nothing tried to eat it, but this time it did not even stun the creature. The acidic spray was something entirely new to her as well, none of the others had been able to do so. Thinking quickly she breathed fire burning up the drops of acid before they could reach her. Then she dove trying to catch the beast in the flames.

Skreal roared in frustration when the dragon burned up his attack, and he jumped aside to avoid the flames. When the dragon reached the bottom of her dive, and as she turned up to avoid hitting the ground. Skreal jumped up and slashed her side with his front claws.

Mother roared in pain as the creature's claws tore through her scales. She swung her tail, and caught the beast on the side of its head knocking it to the ground and sent it tumbling. In his fall he tore through one of the few buildings that were still standing. When she was high enough to be out of range Mother healed herself and watched to see what the beast would do. It took the creature a few moments to emerge from the rubble, but when he did he seemed slightly dazed.

Skreal climbed out of the fallen building, and shook his head trying to clear the fog that filled it from the blow. When his head was clear he smiled. The dragon was just the kind of challenge he had been hoping for. He searched the skies for her and found her well out of reach. Skreal reached out with his mind and connected with her. "Do you fear me now Dragon?" He asked mockingly.

"I will never fear any of your kind. You are an abomination and you will never survive. Even if by some chance that you manage to defeat me others will find, and kill you."

Skreal laughed at her. "I am not like any other, Dragon. I am Skreal, and I cannot be killed."

"We will see about that. I will not allow you to continue this rampage." Mother said threateningly.

Skreal's laugh turned insidious. "You can try to stop me, but you will only die in failure."

As Skreal was speaking Mother noticed electricity jumping back and forth on his tail spikes. Unsure what was happening she put up a magical shield. She was not about to risk anything with this creature. He had already proven to be unlike any other.

A Challenge Answered

When he was finished speaking Skreal opened his mouth wide and a large bolt of lightning screamed towards Mother. The bolt hit her shield and exploded, blinding her for a moment and the concussion pushed her back a short distance.

Mother quickly regained control of her flight, and when her vision cleared she searched the ground for her opponent, but he was nowhere to be seen. "Do you fear me now Skreal? Have you decided to flee instead?" Mother said trying to coax him out. "Go wherever you wish, I will only find you and finish you then."

Mother held her position in the air searching all of the ground. She knew Skreal was still somewhere in the area. She could feel his presence, but she could not pinpoint where he was.

Suddenly she heard something rumbling behind her. She turned her head to see what was making the sound, and to her surprise a large green ball was headed right for her. After traveling through the air a short distance the ball burst into flames becoming a giant fireball.

Knowing that there was no way that she could stop the fire ball Mother folded her wings and she fell from the sky. The fire ball flew over her, but now the ground was coming up fast. Knowing she could not stop her decent without damaging her wings, she opened them partway to slow her decent enough to make it safe for her to land.

When she hit the ground everything shook, and a nearby building collapsed in on itself. The moment she gained her footing Mother launched herself back into the air, knowing that if she stayed on the ground she would be finished.

The moment the dragon hit the ground Skreal saw his opportunity, but he knew that he would not have much time to act. Instantly he was on the move with the intent to finish it quickly. The dragon was no fool however seeing him on the move she breathed fire at him, and Skreal had to act quickly to avoid the flames. Still he was not going to let the opportunity pass without an attempt. He moved around past the flames then leapt at her trying to get an attack in.

Mother was correct, but luckily she was expecting the attack. The moment she saw movement she breathed fire to at least slow Skreal down long enough that she could get into the air. It worked to a point, but the creature was faster than she had expected. He leapt at her, mouth open wide. Mother acted quickly and swung her tail around and caught him on the side of the head knocking him to the ground. She quickly leapt into the air and flew up to get away from the beast.

Skreal shook his head to clear the fog in his head from the blow. He smiled wickedly. This dragon was certainly a worthy opponent. However he was not going to let her win. When his head was clear he looked up and found her out of reach once again, but he had a plan.

Mother was amazed at the resilience of this creature, but she refused to allow him to continue his rampage. She knew there had to be something he feared, she had only to find it. She looked down at Skreal as she circled well out of his range. She knew that somewhere in her thousands of spells there had to be something that could kill this monster.

Suddenly Mother felt an unexpected attack, like a stiletto he pierced her mental defenses while she was preoccupied, and she found herself battling for control. She was amazed by his strength, it was almost overwhelming, but she had been around far too many years to be defeated so easily.

Using the link Skreal had created Mother sent her own attack. When her attack hit him Skreal reeled back and broke the link. For an instant he was stunned and Mother wasted no time, she folded her wings and went into a high velocity dive. When she was within range she sent a torrent of flames at him.

Skreal was dazed by the attack for a moment. This dragon was stronger than he had thought. When he again shook off the daze of her attack he saw flames roaring straight for him. He quickly jumped aside to avoid the fire. Before he could collect himself the dragon clipped him on the side of his head with the tip of her wing and as she passed struck him with her tail sending him tumbling.

Skreal jumped to his feet quickly, but Mother was just as quick. She pulled out of her dive and turned back to breath fire at him once again. Skreal moved away again, but this time she anticipated the move and caught him on his side. He roared in pain and spit a ball of venom at her. When she moved to avoid it he shifted colors to blend into his surroundings, and moved away.

A Challenge Answered

Mother avoided the ball of acid and Skreal disappeared again. She did not waste time pondering how he did this, and she did not want to be caught unaware so she flew up out of reach. She searched the ground trying to find any sign of Skreal, but she found nothing. "So do you fear me now? Is that why you hide from sight?"

"I fear nothing Dragon. You are a worthy opponent but as all others you shall fall, and I will take your power for my own."

"If you do not fear me then why do you hide? Would it be perhaps that I have wounded you and you are weakened?"

Mother suddenly heard an insidious laughter, and it chilled her to the core. It was laughter of shear confidence and pure insanity. It was the kind of insanity that could only be from someone purely evil to the core. For the first time in her life Mother felt fear. She had faced death many times in her long life, but this was something more.

"I told you dragon that I cannot be harmed. I am only allowing you time to regain your strength. I knew you would move away so I allowed it, but sadly soon I must end this game for there are many more places such as this that I must destroy."

Mother was appalled by his words, and a cold shiver ran down her spine at the matter of fact way he mentioned it. Even the most evil of rouge dragons did not wipe out an entire city for the sheer pleasure of it. In that moment as she looked for Skreal, Mother took in exactly what had happened here. Blood covered everything, and mangled bodies of people were scattered everywhere. Some looked like they had tried to fight, but more seemed to have been fleeing for their lives. Seeing this enraged Mother all the more, she had little use for humans herself but to kill them especially in such a manner, that he had was an abomination. Her rage gave her renewed strength.

Suddenly she caught a hint of movement. A cloud of dust rose from a pile of rubble not far from where he had disappeared. Mother wasted no time in reacting. She sent multiple bolts of lightning down on the area.

Her attempt paid off by revealing exactly where Skreal was. Yet again the lightning seemed to have little effect upon him, but now she could find him even with his camouflage. His ability to conceal himself was amazing, but it was not perfect. "I can find you now Skreal even if you try to hide yourself, it is no use to try."

"Perhaps, but I would guess you were not expecting this." Skreal said as he opened his mouth and released a massive bolt of lightning back at her. As he had expected the bolt struck an invisible shield before her and exploded. At that moment however he sent a mental attack to try and dominate her, but as before he met a solid defense.

"You will have to do better than that to overtake me Skreal. I cannot be defeated so easily. I have faced many more dangers than you. I have seen all the tricks that you may try."

Mother's words suddenly gave Skreal an insidious idea. "Dragon hold, I have a proposal for you. We can continue battling here until one of us is dead, or you could join with me, and together we could create a new race that would rule over all, and we could control them. Imagine the power that we would possess you and I. None could challenge us."

Mother was appalled by the suggestion she refused to think of something so horrible. "You are mad Skreal. I would never join with you. I would rather die than even consider it."

"So be it then die you shall. With your death I will find another that will join me, and if they refuse I will force them to join me."

"That is where you are wrong Skreal. I am the last female. Dragons are a dyeing race and if you kill me so dies your plan."

"You lie I can see it in your eyes Mother. There is one more. You may be able to stop my attacks, but I can still see your thoughts. Yes there is one more, your last offspring, and she hatched only a short time ago. Yes she will be easy to overtake and control. So think of it when I take your powers, they will be passed on to our offspring and with her I will create an unstoppable force under my command, and it will all be thanks to you. I will make it your legacy."

Skreal enraged Mother, she was not going to allow this thing to lay one finger on Mieyatomia. With all the strength that she possessed she called upon the most powerful magic that she knew. She called up every spell that she knew and combined them into one massive spell.

The sky grew dark as clouds filled it. The temperature dropped at an alarming rate freezing everything where it was. Then a giant whirlwind reached down out of the clouds and touched down

A Challenge Answered

where Skreal stood. It lifted him up high into the air along with tons of debris and rubble. It moved over the entire city destroying everything as it moved along. Giant hailstones pelted and smashed everything in sight. Hundreds of lightning bolts came down and hit the whirlwind turning it into a spinning cone of electricity, and all the rubble still within it broke apart with explosive force. Then the ground below it opened up and roaring flames engulfed the entire whirlwind. Everything left nearby burst into flames from the heat, then suddenly the funnel dissipated dropping everything within it including Skreal to the ground with earth shattering force.

Exhausted from the strain of casting the spell Mother landed unable to stay in the air any longer. Then for a final measure, she breathed fire on his remains with a fire so intense it melted the stone around him.

When she was certain Skreal was finished, she walked over to the charred remains that were still burning, and she sighed tiredly. "You will never have her, and now you will never terrorize anyone ever again." Mother turned away from the horror lying there, and she started to walk away. Before she could take more than two steps however she heard a sound that turned her spine to ice.

"I told you dragon that I cannot be killed and now you shall pay for your foolish mistake."

Mother turned quickly, and her blood ran cold. Skreal was getting up even as flames roared all around him. Mother knew in that moment what others meant by paralyzing fear. She knew in her condition there was no way that she could get away. All the strength she had remaining left her. She could see her death and it was coming straight for her.

"Now you die dragon." Skreal said as he loomed over Mother. Then like a viper he struck, biting her at the base of her neck and held her there.

She roared in pain as the venom rushed into her veins. She stumbled back trying to get away but Skreal's grip was too strong. Then shortly after the poison overtook her and she faded away into the eternal darkness.

When mother died Skreal tried to take her abilities, but for some odd reason she eluded him even in the end. He roared in frustration and cursed her swearing that he would find her offspring and take control of her.

When he finished Skreal suddenly heard someone clapping their hands behind him. He turned around and saw a tall man wearing a black cloak materializing out of thin air.

"A fine job killing that dragon I must say." Valclon said as he stepped forward.

Skreal sneered and roared in anger at being bothered, by a pitiful creature such as what had suddenly appeared. He wanted nothing to do with this man, except perhaps to kill him. He was however growing tired of these pitiful creatures trying to stop him. So he roared at the man to warn him to leave.

Keriana awoke to an ear piercing screeching sound. She jumped up to see what could be making such a sound and found it was Mieyatomia. She tried to reach the little one's mind to see what the problem was, but she could not reach her. She looked over at Heroth but he was trying to cover his ears with his paws.

Suddenly her door burst open and all of her companions were standing there weapons at the ready. "By the gods woman what is that insufferable noise." Cestator shouted over Mieyatomia's screeches.

"It is the baby there I have been deemed her protector and she was fine until just moments ago."

"Well shut her up or I will be forced to."

Cestator got a glare from the rest of the group for this, but Keriana only shook her head. "I would if I knew what was wrong, but I cannot even reach her to find out what is wrong."

Suddenly Keriana heard Heroth's voice. "She keeps repeating the same thing. She's gone, she's dead. Now please stop her."

At first Keriana did not understand what it meant, and then suddenly it hit her like a ton of bricks. Mother was dead, and with that realization she was washed over with Mieyatomia's agony and she fell to her knees and took the little one into her arms and began to cry.

CPSIA information can be obtained at www.ICGtesting.com
Printed in the USA
LVOW13*0223270114

371090LV00003B/13/P